DISCOVERY OF A QUEEN

The Resurrection of Queens, Book 1

ELIZABETH BROWN

Edited by Elemental Editing & Proofreading.

Chapter art by Jeanne Bradley.

Cover by the amazing Fantastical Ink. I want to send a huge thank you to Timea for creating such a stunning work of art on the cover of my book. I sure hope that the story lives up to the artwork!

✻ Created with Vellum

Acknowledgments

This book is for my son. My beautiful little boy. I took this leap because of him. I wanted to show him to always, always, reach for your dreams. He gave me the courage, and the sleepless nights, needed to finally get my butt into gear and start writing seriously with a goal.

This book is also for two of the most amazing women I've ever met, Kelly and Olivia, who star in this story. These ladies have gotten me through a lot of dark times, enabling me to write this and live my dreams. They are so powerful, insightful, loyal, loving, and all-around amazing human beings.

Finally, this book is for my husband. A man who puts up with a lot of shit. I'm pretty sure he's never going to read this, but hey, if you do, I love you!

∼

I want to take a moment to thank two people in particular, Laura, for being an amazing friend and critique partner. I love you to pieces, lady. Jeanne, for being an amazing artist, friend, sister, and human. Thank you for creating insanely awesome chapter art for me! Love you, boo!

Thank you to all of my beta readers, friends, and family who are supporting me throughout this whole process. I know a few of you have pre-ordered the book and most might not actually read it, but you bought it just to support me.

Dear family...This book has SEX in it. I'd rather you not stare at me awkwardly during family gatherings, so either skip those scenes or don't read if it'll make you uncomfortable.

Three Fates pure to keep the gate,
past, present, future.
Should one Fate fall the seals will break,
maiden, mother, crone.
Two Fates more shall fall, and Hell shall wake,
life, death, rebirth.
New queens will rise to fight for light,
female, queen, goddess.
A sacrifice will heal the breach,
shifter, witch, vampire.
Three new Fates will be the key.

Prologue

Thousands of years ago.

Wrath

As I sit here, wasting away in this realm that's not my own, this realm that functions as my prison, I dream of the beginning.

While our origins have been lost even to us, the time before the great imprisonment still lingers fresh and vivid in my mind—the screams, blood, anger.

They called us Sins, the complete opposite of their holy selves. We lived for chaos, bloodshed, war, and fun. They lived for rules and order. There were only seven of us, and yet we were still able to hold hundreds of them at bay for eons. We were powerful, rulers of the dimension we lived in, feared by those who bled gold, thinking that made them superior to those of us who bled black. If they were truly so superior, why did they tremble at the thought of us? Why were we able to light fire to their villages?

One day, the Óir vanished, and we had the realm to ourselves. Unfortunately, we weren't left on our own for long. No. The Óir soon decided they weren't content with creating their own realm and staying there. They wanted to try their hand at creating versions of themselves, the pompous assholes. They wanted to see if they could create beings that were similar to themselves.

We slaughtered every single attempt.

Until the guardians were created, led by fierce and powerful female dragons. Somehow, the Óir, the very cowards who failed to face us in the past, created beings that could actually hold us at bay. We could tell it was a struggle for them to do so, but they did it anyway.

And then those gold-blooded weaklings created this pit, our prison, sending one of their own here to keep watch. Sending their guardians to throw us into our cells and sacrificing one of their very first creations to seal us in.

My memories fuel my need for freedom, my need to seek out those who have imprisoned me and my siblings and rend them limb from bloody limb. I want to drink their golden blood, paint my face with it, rain it down on the earth. I want to drain every last one of those bastards dry.

I've been stuck in this fucking flaming garbage realm for millennia, able to watch but never touch my home dimension, trapped here because the assholes in charge decided we were too much of a threat to their little experiment. Humanity. And they were right. When we get free of this place, we will lay waste to the realm they now refer to as Earth before we rip open the gates to Heaven and slaughter the Óir in their golden cities.

My mind circles back to humanity. What bullshit. Why would the Óir create something so subpar and weak when perfection had already been created? Why send Morningstar, one of their own, to play babysitter for them? They're nothing more than annoying apes. We saw humanity for what it truly was, an affront to our very existence. It had been offensive when they sent him here as our jailor. I seethed at the very notion, flames licking through my veins at the thought of humans polluting *my* realm. Those disgusting, marginally sophisticated apes needed to be shown their place. The guardians needed to be reminded of their status as well. Neither being is fit to be anything but slaves to our every whim.

I can't get out of this trash heap on my own. Anyone stuck in the pit stays in the pit unless someone from the outside breaks the seals and opens the gate. What sort of stupid bullshit rule is that? Were the Óir really so weak that they felt the need to go to such extremes? My siblings and I are something to be feared, this is true, but if those idiots were truly superior beings, they would have been able to eradicate or contain us themselves without the need for this insult.

Though I suppose I'm lucky. Morningstar can't *ever* leave the pit. From what we've been able to glean during our time here, that was the agreement when this realm was made. The rest of us had been forced into this dimension, no questions, no discussions, with just a snap of some asshole's fingers, and we were caged in here like rabid animals.

If they want to see a rabid animal. I'll give them a fucking rabid animal.

I need someone to open the gate. Unfortunately, aside from the Óir, only the Fates could break the seals that keep the gate to this realm closed. Those blasted loyal lapdogs. They would need to be corrupt to break the seals, all three of them, or it wouldn't fucking work. I'll need to be patient if I want that to happen, but what's a few thousand years compared to eternity? My abilities are limited in the pit, and it takes a great deal of power to influence anything outside of this realm. But I'm determined.

It needs to be subtle. If Morningstar or the Óir get word of what I'm doing, they'll find other ways to safeguard their precious creations.

A dark grin spreads across my face. The Óir love to influence their creations through the use of oracles. Humans are much easier to corrupt than their guardians—the existence of demons is proof of that. And so, I search Earth for the perfect oracle to deliver my prophecy. The humans would never suspect that such a thing would come from one locked away by Morningstar, and the Óir are stuck too far up their own asses to look into the matter of a new prophecy. The guardians always love a good prophecy, and so do the demons.

Regardless of how long it takes, I will sow the seeds of my release from this blasphemous prison. If my siblings are too stupid to assist, they can rot here for all I care.

I'VE LOST track of how many years have passed since I started my search, but I've finally found the perfect human to deliver my prophecy. Just as I knew it would, it catches the attention of demons, supernaturals, and humans alike. Now I just need to wait for the opening. Archdemons, the souls of humans who have been corrupted by what limited influence my siblings and I have here in the pit, are always so eager for a shot at impressing Morningstar, not knowing it's the Sins they want to impress.

There's so much I want to do when I get out of here. I'm practically vibrating with the pent-up excitement of it all. And what's a few hundred years more? Patience pays off, and it gives me more time to plan.

I feel an archdemon take interest in my prophecy. No, two archdemons. Splendid! And so my work begins. First, we need to take out the guardians and their pesky queens. Only then can the real fun begin.

My laughter echoes in the dark around me.

Chapter One

Six months ago.

Bam! Bam! Bam!

THE SOUND of pounding fists on my door rouses me from sleep. I blink my gritty eyes open slowly, the fog crowding my mind preventing me from coherently comprehending what woke me up. I stare blankly at my alarm clock as it flashes bright red digits at me. What are the numbers? My clock is trying to tell me what time it is, but my brain can't decipher what it's saying. More pounding. It's two in the morning. I blink one last time in an effort to clear my head. I hate being woken up, but this isn't the first time it's happened, and I doubt it will be the last. Crawling out of bed as the knocking continues, increasing in volume and now sounding frantic, I scrub my hands over my face as I clear the last remnants of sleep from my mind. My dragon grumbles sleepily in my head, wanting whoever is banging on our door to go to hell.

"What the hell do you want?" I shout loud enough for even a human to hear.

"Attorney McInnes?" a female calls out.

"It's two in the bloody morning. What could you possibly want an attorney for?" I make my way down the hall of my one-story home to the front door. At least the pounding has stopped.

"We need to talk to you, it's urgent."

"Who the hell is 'we?'" I yank open the door to see two women standing in front of me. One is a witch with blonde hair, the other a shifter with brown hair. Color me interested. Any stubbornly clinging brain fog vanishes at the sight of the two before me. Normally, witches and shifters stay away from each other—unlike a couple of centuries ago when they all lived in communities together. Hell, even vampires lived with us at one point.

"Kelly Shaw." The blonde points to herself. "And this is Olivia Fontain." The brunette waves. "We're from the local coven and pack. We need to talk to you about something. It's pretty urgent," she repeats. There's a note of fear and desperation in her voice, so I gesture for them to come in.

I lead them down the hallway, past my bedroom, and into my kitchen, where I flick on the light and start making coffee. Turning to lean against the counter as they seat themselves at my kitchen table, I silently chuckle as they stare at me. They're lucky they came to see me in the middle of the night in winter. I'm currently in boy shorts and an oversized men's shirt with my hair tied in a messy braid. During the warmer months, I sleep naked.

"Talk." They look at each other before Olivia nods.

"I realize you've kept yourself fairly distant from the shifter and witch communities despite being...well...whatever you are. We can respect that. But shifter females are going missing." I arch my eyebrow at Olivia. "They're dominant too. I'm one of the last few left."

"Morgan, the local alpha, is blaming the witches for it," Kelly chimes in. Oh, I know who Morgan is alright. Douche canoe at its finest. I'd love to see that asshat taken down.

"And you're telling me they have nothing to do with the females' disappearances?"

Kelly and Olivia both nod. I take a moment to study them —not physically, but their auras. Olivia is strong enough to be a beta for the right alpha, hell, she's strong enough to be alpha. Kelly is also insanely powerful. I'm surprised she isn't the coven's high priestess. My eyes narrow slightly as I read her aura. Some of her powers are blocked, which is highly unusual. She must have a dangerous gift. But they aren't lying, their auras would have muted colors if they lied.

"I have one question." They tense. "Why me?"

"You're the only local supernatural attorney around. We figured if something illegal was happening it would be best to have you look into it before calling the Council." Kelly explains with a shrug. "Besides, you're outside of both communities, so no one will notice you looking into things."

She has a valid point; I don't really have ties to either community. Keeping to myself all these years does have its advantages. "Okay. I believe you." They look shocked.

"That's it? You don't want to see any evidence?" Olivia glances at Kelly, dumbstruck.

"I can tell if you're lying. Neither of you are." I shrug. "So why drag this out?" My coffee maker beeps. I turn to grab three mugs from the cabinet, filling each. "I don't have cream or sugar in the house, so you'll have to take it black." I place the mugs in front of them, watching as they silently stare into the steaming caffeinated liquid.

"Thank you." Kelly's voice is soft and filled with emotion.

"Now what sort of help do you need from me exactly?"

Kelly remains silent, so it's Olivia who answers. "We need you to find proof. I've been working with the local coven, even before Morgan started pointing fingers at them, so I know there was no way they were actually involved. The majority of our pack believes me, but Morgan is stronger than he should be, so we can't do anything about it."

That piques my interest. "What do you mean by that? How is he stronger than he should be?"

"He hasn't been alpha all that long," Olivia continues, and I nod, recalling the change of power that occurred about ten years ago, "and before that, he didn't really seem like he was going anywhere fast. Yes, he was a dominant wolf, but I wouldn't have pegged him as alpha material. The pack was actually pretty surprised when he won his challenge and then won subsequent challenges against him. He's only gotten stronger over the last ten years too. It's weird."

That is weird. Typically, shifters come into their full strength when they reach puberty. It gives both their human and animal bodies time to grow and develop. I've never heard of a shifter becoming more powerful as an adult. Despite this, I don't understand why they need *me* to investigate for them.

"And why can't the witches just look into this?"

"If we attempt to do anything, move in any way, and Morgan catches wind..." Kelly pauses, looking up from her coffee mug with fear shining in her eyes. "Morgan might declare an all-out war against us. We need someone on the outside, someone who doesn't have ties to the pack or the coven, to look into things quietly while we try to keep the peace for as long as possible." Now Kelly appears frustrated.

My dragon rustles restlessly inside me, something sparking to life in our core. For some strange reason, we both want to protect the two women sitting in front of us. I've acted as a private investigator before, but nothing has ever stirred this kind of primitive gut reaction in me. My dragon has never felt this amped up over a job or this connected to two virtual strangers either.

"Done."

～

Three months ago.

I FIND myself staring down the barrel of a gun, fighting the urge to roll my eyes. While a pistol will certainly hurt, that thing isn't going to kill me. *Stupid human, you have no business playing with the big boys.* It took a few weeks, but the guys I keep on retainer for information found my new best friend here, a pleasant local drug dealer named Ian.

Although local authorities have had a hard time tracking Ian down, it was fairly easy for me to do so. Why would the Alpha of the New England Pack be dabbling in human drugs? What does this have to do with the missing female shifters? There's no way a human could even keep a dominant female contained, let alone do anything to hurt her. This just doesn't make sense.

I need this guy to talk, and he won't with that gun in my face. I toss a little glamor at him, and he's putty in my hands. Like vampires, who can hold humans spellbound with their gaze, I can glamor a human with my magic and gain similar results.

"What do you know about the missing women in the area?"

"If you're looking into those dead hookers, those were Ricky's girls, not mine," he tells me, his Boston accent thick.

That's not the information I'm looking for. I shake my head. "Not the dead hookers." I let my magic nudge his mind a bit. "The shifter women."

Something dark slithers through his thoughts. It's oily, slick, and sticky. Sinister. Cold. He's been tainted by demons. Fuck.

~

MY CELLPHONE RECORDS the fight between a bear and a fox shifter. They both appear smudged when I look at them, but when I check my phone, they look normal. That's odd as fuck. The drug lord's dark, tainted mind led me here to an underground, and very illegal, shifter fighting ring. I had to dig around in that trash nugget's head for a while before finding the fights buried in his mind. The memories had been blocked off with a spell, so he wouldn't have been able to access them on his own. Which meant he was a pawn—a demonic pawn.

While I knew these fights existed, this particular fight isn't what I expected. It had taken me a month to pinpoint the exact location of this fighting ring from Ian's head. The memory he had was of a bout in Boston, but since fighting rings move around to avoid detection, it had been relocated by the time I was able to get to the site on the shorefront. This fight is taking place in Connecticut, near one of the popular casinos.

I inhale deeply, trying to take in as many scents as possible. *Douche canoe, I've found you.* Morgan is here. I search the crowd, but I can't see him. His scent is strong enough to suggest he was here recently, but I must have missed him. I drag my gaze back to the fight once again, feeling little red flags rise in my mind. I think I know why they appear smudged. At least, I'm supposed to know. I shake my head and curse, knowing the information is just beyond my reach.

I feel like we should know this. Why don't we know this? I mentally nudge my dragon.

I'm not sure. It feels so obvious. I glance between the fight and my phone again. Still nothing on my phone. Damn it. I close my eyes and allow my magic to ease out into the room, but I'm instantly blasted with cold, dark energy. It's not magic, it's demonic power. My eyes snap open, quickly scanning the space again, but I don't spot any demons. I can sense their energies, but they aren't physically here.

I see a female from the pack. I don't know her, and I've only seen her around Boston, but she's a member of the New England Pack. She's stumbling and leaning against a tall man. Making my way over to the pair, I notice the man has a death grip on her. I bump into them, putting my hands on the female's shoulders.

"Hey! I've been looking for you everywhere, girl!" I plaster a smile on my face. "Where did you run off to?"

"Back off!" The male's voice is gruff, and his body language screams hostility. Judging by his scent, he's a tiger.

"I came here with my friend. She doesn't look so good. I think we should head home now," I state in a firm, no-nonsense tone.

"I said back off." His body ripples as he struggles to suppress the shift. "She's been paid for. Now get lost."

Paid for? Now I'm the one struggling to suppress the shift. Oh, no. Absolutely not. Not on my watch. With a lightning-fast punch to the throat, I have the tiger on the floor gasping for air. For good measure, and to make me feel better as a female, I slam my foot down on his crotch. Given how drugged up the woman now leaning against me is, there's no way this is a consensual thing. I carefully drag the female away from the downed shifter. Thankfully, no one seems to be paying any attention to us with the fight that's still raging between the bear and the fox.

What the fuck is going on?

∾

One week ago.

"WHAT THE HELL are you doing here, bitch?" Morgan growls as I walk into his office. We've had a few run-ins in the past since I'm the only local attorney who deals exclusively with the supernatural communities. He's not my biggest fan. Morgan is the shiftiest motherfucker I've ever met, so the feeling is absolutely mutual. There have been several complaints against him from neighboring packs based on his aggressive behavior, and I've been the mediator at all of those meetings. I've ultimately ruled in favor of the other packs, thereby taking away any shot Morgan had at absorbing those packs into his own.

"Morgan, I'm just here to talk." I hold my hands up, palms out, as a gesture that I come in peace.

"You always come just to 'talk.' What the fuck is it this time?"

"I've heard about the missing females—"

"That's none of your business. You aren't pack."

"Not technically, no. But, Morgan—"

"I said this is none of your damn business, latent trash." Spit comes flying from his mouth at the force of his scream. Gross. I blink, my mind reeling with the confirmation that he knows what's actually going on. He wouldn't put up this kind of a fuss otherwise. His scent at the fight wasn't a coincidence.

I calm myself and try to read his aura. There's something off about him. He's not quite smudged like the fighters at the ring the other night, but he still doesn't feel right. I'm not sure what it is, and I can't get a good enough look at his aura right now to tell either. He's right in my face, and I refuse to close my eyes for a second. My protective instincts are screaming at me.

"Look, I'm just trying to make sure no one else gets hurt."

He comes flying at me, and I let him, I won't blow my cover. He wraps his hands around my neck.

"See here, you latent bitch, I don't need you asking questions." Oh, good, he's used both his favorite words for me in one sentence, how thoughtful.

"There's talk of going to war with the witches." I keep my statement calm even though he squeezes his hands tighter.

"That's right. I'm going to fucking wipe those witch bastards out." His eyes are wild and there's a hint of insanity creeping into his tone.

Shock sends icy tendrils through my veins. He just admitted he's going to cause an all-out war with the witches. Is he fucking crazy? Or brain damaged. Both? Both.

My dragon roars in protest. The witches have done nothing wrong and he wants to go to war with them? *We can't let this happen!* My dragon struggles to get free, wanting to rip Morgan limb from limb.

"Over my dead fucking body, you piece of flaming garbage," I hiss.

"Over your dead body, latent trash? Is that a challenge?" That smug look on his face is going to be the first thing I rip from his corpse.

"It's a promise, you twat." So much for being careful.

"I'm sorry... You did what?" Olivia's voice hits an interesting octave as she paces in my living room.

"I challenged Morgan."

"For alpha?"

"She didn't exactly challenge him to a chess game, Liv." Kelly is leaning against the wall with her arms crossed. "So it's reasonable to assume that Ayla challenged for alpha." There's a teasing lilt to her tone.

"But..." Olivia gestures to my entire body. "You're latent."

I simply arch an eyebrow in response.

"You are latent, aren't you?" Olivia steps closer to me, her nostrils flaring as she takes in my scent. "What the hell are you?"

"I'm about to be your damn alpha. Calm your tits."

"My tits are calm. The rest of me is freaking out. I can't even tell if you're dominant or not. Christ." Olivia runs her hand through her hair and starts pacing again.

"Look, I appreciate the concern. But I swear I've totally got this." I shrug and reach for my glass of wine. It's been sitting on my coffee table all by itself, poor thing. It needs me to be its friend.

"How are you this calm, Ayla?" Kelly comes over and grabs her glass off the table, taking a small sip. "You just challenged for alpha and you're sitting here drinking wine. Shouldn't you be, I don't know, training?" She glances over at Olivia for a second before looking back at me. "I thought you were a witch. Your aura suggests you have magic."

"Ladies, honestly, I've got this. All that matters is I've got this." Although, with the two of them bringing up what I might be, I'm second-guessing my decision to challenge for alpha. Do I just hand over power to someone when I win? And there's no question in my mind I will win. "Drink your wine. We've got a fun day tomorrow." Though now I'm cursing my rashness.

"Fun," Olivia mutters, shaking her head. "Are you listening to this insanity? Fun, she calls it." Olivia stalks over and grabs her wine, downing it in a single gulp. Impressive.

"Morgan needs to be dealt with. I'm going to bloody deal with him." What happens after that is a question I don't want to think about right now.

WHAT THE ACTUAL FUCK? Why do I always put myself in these situations? Am I really this stupid? Maybe I just really hate myself.

I'm staring down an insanely pissed off lion shifter. There's saliva everywhere, his eyes are bloodshot, and he's growling in that way cats do when they're not happy, all deep and guttural. I'm going to have to kill him, I know that. I knew it the moment I challenged him for alpha, but why the hell did I have to go and catch feelings for people? What the hell is wrong with me?

I toss a quick glance to my right and see the faces of the witches and shifters of the New England area. They're gathered around the center of the town the shifters use as their pack land. A small girl with gorgeous, brown, curly pigtails tugs on her mother's hand, smiling up at her. Right. That's what's wrong with me. I can't let any more shifters go missing, and I can't let the witches take the blame either, not when I know they aren't behind the disappearances.

Another growl from the lion shifter in front of me pulls my attention away from the girl and back to him. He looks strange again, and I still can't figure out why. It's almost like his entire body is vibrating with energy. Now that I have a minute to focus, he looks like the shifters from the fighting ring. His aura appears smudged, like someone who put pressure on ink that's not quite dry yet. Both of these make him appear, to me anyway, fuzzy, as though I need glasses to see him properly. I've never experienced this before I started this investigation, which concerns me just as much as the missing shifters. Thinking about the missing shifters fills me with rage. How could this, this thing, call himself alpha? How could he let any of his pack go missing? What sort of leader did that? While I had been able to save one shifter, a wolf named Sasha, the rest remain lost. And try as I might, I haven't been able to track them down.

I let the rage build, sending streams of hot lava through my veins. I know I can't let the shifters or witches see what I am, but there is no way I'm going to lose this fight. I can't shift, and I'll need to be creative to use my magic. I smirk as the heat of my rage warms my muscles. I could just rip him to shreds with my bare hands. That will be fun.

The lion charges me, his giant front paw swinging at my head. I wait until the last possible moment before stepping out of the way, aiming a roundhouse kick at his face. My foot connects with his eye socket with a satisfying crunch. Even in my human form, I'm much stronger than most shifters in their animal forms. This douche canoe has no idea what's coming for him. I may not be the protector I once was, but I've seen enough of this man's shit to know I need to protect these people. I quickly follow through with a superman punch to the same spot while he's dazed from my kick, and the resulting sound of bone grinding together is music to my ears.

I want to make this asshat pay. I want him to feel the fear those females must be feeling if they're even still alive. I want him to hurt because there's no way anyone can convince me they aren't hurting. I want him, in his last moments, to realize he's so weak and pathetic I can take him in my human form. I don't see him as a threat, me, a petite female. I have no fear of this creature, and I'm going to make damn sure no one fears him again.

I allow my magic to flood my body. I don't want to publicly use it and raise too many questions, so I'll let it give me an internal boost so I can ramp up the pain. I'm not typically a bloodthirsty person, but there's just something about Morgan that makes me want to bathe in his blood, my dragon egging me on.

He staggers to his feet, blood streaming down his face and congealing in his mane. He lets out a roar, which I'm sure was supposed to sound impressive but comes out shattered and pained. He starts to circle around me, looking for a weak spot. He won't find one unless I allow it. I close my eyes so I can follow his aura. He's smudged like this too. I wonder if he's working with demons. There's a similar feel to their auras and energy now that I think about it. Every muscle goes rigid, and the heat of my rage soars higher.

No.

My eyes snap open and I whirl on him, my magic trying to burst from my body to burn this fucker alive. He's selling females. Regardless of who is paying for them, he's allowing members of his pack to be sold as though they're just lumps of meat. And if demons are involved, there's a potential that some of those females are in their hands. Either way, it's a fate so much worse than death. I was going to toy with him, but now I can hardly hold myself back. And honestly, there's no reason why I should restrain myself.

So I don't. I let the rage consume me as I practically fly at Morgan. I wrap my arms around his neck and squeeze. His neck snaps like a toothpick.

Fuck you, asshole.

Chapter Two

Present.

I sit down at my desk with a sigh. It's been a long-ass week since I killed Morgan, and I'm not nearly finished. I look at my computer as it flashes the date. Fuck, it's only Tuesday.

How the hell is it only Tuesday?

Need I remind you that you're now the alpha and high priestess of New England? My dragon, who is normally quiet while I'm at work, turns on the sass. Just what I need.

No. I haven't forgotten. Have you forgotten that we're an attorney, and we have twenty cases we need to work on right now?

There's silence. Of course there's silence. I work exclusively on supernatural cases. It's been six long months since Kelly and Olivia pounded on my door in the middle of the damn night insisting on speaking with me about the missing shifter females. They both happen to be my betas now. Kelly is an extremely powerful witch and would be even more so if her powers weren't partially bound. I make a mental note to ask her about that. Olivia, a panther shifter, could be an alpha in her own right but decided she wanted to work with me after I made Morgan into a chew toy. Morgan was a worthless trash fire of a person, no one seems to be missing him.

I gently massage my temples as I think back to the challenge. I surprised the shit out of the New England Coven, and they all assumed I was an extremely powerful witch. Most of them are still confused. The coven elders have been arguing about what I am since the challenge, and I'm not in any mood to disclose such valuable information. I've kept my dragon a secret for the last four hundred years, moving constantly to keep myself hidden. Hell, I even got rid of my Irish accent in favor of a fairly neutral American one. I still sort of hate myself for that decision. The New England Coven, without actually meeting me, had simply assumed I was a high priestess. Their ranking system within the coven is based on a witch's aura, and considering mine is packed with powerful magic, it makes sense. The New England Pack, again without meeting me or discussing me with the local coven, assumed I was a latent shifter.

Nope.

I'm a dragon shifter. One of the last remaining female dragons on the planet, and to my knowledge, the only queen dragon remaining. Male dragons are rare, but females are almost unheard of anymore. Queens are, at least to the general shifter and witch population, a myth. We were extremely rare even when dragons were abundant. As a queen, I can harness and use magic as well as shift into a dragon. This makes me a pretty hot commodity to the male dragon populous.

Dragons are a matriarchal species, and as a queen, I'm at the top of the food chain. Being a queen's consort is something alpha male dragons would kill and die for. Only a queen can produce another queen. Unlike every other shifter, a queen can only mate and reproduce with an alpha male dragon. Which, I feel, is shitty because all other species of shifters can mate with whomever the hell they want. I, on the other hand, am stuck with a macho, chest-pounding caveman. Well, I would be if I had a mate, which I don't, thank the gods.

Unlike other dragons, who have heads roughly the size of a bus, a queen is smaller in stature. I'm only about eight feet in height when standing on my back legs. I saw *How to Train Your Dragon* once, and that Toothless dragon is pretty close to what I look like shifted. I'm lean and built for speed and stealth. And, as my fight with Morgan demonstrated, I'm stronger than I appear. I just happen to be faster than a male dragon, which isn't that hard, to be honest, because they're big and clunky. I can also harness my magic while in dragon form. Other dragons can only shoot fire. Pretty fire, but just normal, run-of-the-mill fire.

Queens have a unique ability. We can sense and kill archdemons. We were created for that task. My mother had been the last great battle queen, tucking her daughters, all queens, into hiding before she was slaughtered in battle by Malick, the oldest archdemon she had ever encountered, but she took Malick with her as her final act. My mother had put my two older sisters into a sleep-like stasis but ran out of time and couldn't do the same for me, so she helped me flee Ireland instead.

I'm the only one of my siblings awake that I know of, and I have no idea how to wake my two older sisters, or even where they are. Once it became apparent that they weren't going to awaken on their own, I started looking for them. I was attempting to research the spell my mother had used on them when I met Kelly and Olivia. There had been no way I could allow Morgan to continue selling females, so I stopped my research and kicked tainted alpha ass.

Which is how I am now both high priestess and alpha.

Rubbing my temples again, I try to fight the migraine that is steadily building behind my eyes. Morgan had to have been working with demons, though I hadn't sensed any in the area leading up to my challenge of him. I don't sense any now either. My challenge shattered my well-earned security, which is what I get for catching feelings and making friends. Gross. While I hadn't used my magic outright during the challenge, the witches had been able to sense it building in my body, which demonstrated to them that I outranked all of them. They had peacefully named me high priestess, against my wishes, directly following the alpha challenge. The shifters had stood in stunned silence after I killed Morgan, shocked that I had been able to remain human the entire time. But the dominant energy I had been giving off made the entire town fall flat on the ground, even the witches buckled to their knees.

And then there's the Council. I hadn't been thinking, not really, when I challenged Morgan. A part of me knew I would need to report the shift in power to the Council, but that part of me had been small and screaming from a distance so far away it was a mere buzz in the background. The more emotional part of me hadn't cared. In fact, that part of me had punted the rational, Council aware part of my brain to another planet. My instincts had screamed at me to protect the community. It appears my DNA finally kicked in after being dormant for centuries.

The Council is the united governing body of supernatural creatures dedicated to keeping the peace and holding back demons. They essentially took the place of queens after my mother died. The Council is currently run by an alpha male dragon, who is considered by shifters to be the Alpha of all alphas. The rest of the Council consists of highly powerful representatives of each species. I had been keeping my existence a secret from the Council before my challenge, fully aware of their nasty little habit of making rare species either vanish or assimilate.

The shrill screech of my cellphone startles me out of my thoughts. I stare at the screen for a minute—an unknown caller. Well, that's never good. I hit the button to answer and put the phone on speaker.

"Hello?"

"Ms. McInnes?" a female with a light British accent asks.

"This is Attorney McInnes."

"Please hold for Alpha Caleb O'Dwyer."

Fuck me sideways with a cactus. That didn't take long.

How did the Council know already? I hadn't even had time over the last week to report the change in power. Someone else must have done it.

"Alpha McInnes," a deep timbre rumbles through the speaker. He's got a Scottish lilt that makes me shiver and sounds as smooth as a glass of aged Scotch. "This is a courtesy call to inform you that myself and two other Council representatives will be traveling to visit your pack."

"Alpha, I—"

"McInnes, there is no room for discussion." The line goes dead.

Did he just...?

Hang up on us? Yep. He did. Typical alpha male. My dragon snorts, and I can practically feel her eyes rolling.

Great. A visit from the Alpha of all alphas and the Council. There was no way this could end well. I kind of want to just bang my head against my desk, but that would only make my migraine worse. Instead, I lean down and open the bottom drawer of my desk, pulling out a bottle of whiskey. I don't bother to grab a glass, choosing to pull the cork out and drink directly from the bottle.

I let the warm liquid soothe my insides. I need to let the others know. Dialing Kelly, I put the cork in the bottle and tuck it back in its drawer.

"Hey, Ayla." Kelly's greeting is chipper, which serves to just irritate me further.

"I'm glad you answered." My tone is clipped, and I wince at the sound of it.

"You sound ready to kill someone. What happened?" A hint of worry creeps into her question.

"The Council. The Council happened."

"What do you mean?"

"They're coming here. Sometime in the vaguely near future. He didn't really specify."

There's silence on the other end of the phone, confirming my apprehension. No one will be thrilled to have the Council pay a visit. Considering the unique nature of our current leadership here in New England, with both the coven and the pack being ruled by one person, things are going to get interesting very quickly. Not to mention the coven's own unique problems with them, and the shifters, ever loyal, taking up the grudge in solidarity.

"You said he? Who is he?"

"The Alpha."

"As in, Capital A, Alpha?" I can hear the wince in her voice.

"That would be the one, yes."

"Awesome. Well, that'll be a day." I grin and can practically taste the sarcasm coming through the phone.

"I'm not sure how long they'll be here, he didn't say that either. I'm assuming they'll arrive tomorrow or the day after." I pinch the bridge of my nose and close my eyes as I listen to Kelly curse in several languages.

"I'll let the coven elders know we need to keep a close eye on everyone for a while. I'm assuming you'll tell Olivia. But, Ayla, we need to talk about what happened during the alpha challenge."

"I know." I sound tired. "Why don't you come to the packhouse in an hour? I'd rather talk about this before the Alpha and the Council get here, and I only want to tell the story once."

"I'll bring some ice cream."

"Bless you, you beautifully stunning amazing unicorn of a woman."

Kelly chuckles softly before hanging up the phone. Pack land is a state forest in Vermont. We have members of the supernatural community in every form of government to ensure that our secret doesn't get out and that we have safe places to gather. The packhouse is a mansion. It was built with the understanding that people would be coming and going constantly, so the thing is massive.

I stand and look around my office, realizing it'll probably be a few days before I'll be able to step foot in here again. It's not exactly neat, there are files piled everywhere, but I know where everything is, which is all that really matters. The back wall of my office is a wall of floor to ceiling windows, giving me an amazing view of the harbor. One of my walls has a large bookshelf crammed with legal reference materials and other books. The opposite wall displays my degrees, all twenty of them, and various licenses, as well as awards I've won throughout my career. I'm proud of the work I do and the people I've helped.

Grabbing what I'll need to work remotely from the packhouse, I quickly type out an email to my office manager on my phone, explaining about the Council's visit, asking to reschedule my meetings, and telling her to also take the time off. I finish by informing her that, as always, I will be available by phone or email. I don't like to cancel on clients on such short notice, but many of them have my personal number anyway. I turn the lights off and lock my office door, walking down the hall to stand before a blank wall.

I quietly chant a spell under my breath and a soft light slowly appears on the wall, taking the shape of a doorway. I step through and walk directly into my bedroom in the pack-house. Placing my things on my bed, I dial Olivia's number.

"Ayla, what's wrong? I can feel your unease through the pack bond."

I keep forgetting about that damn bond. I need to shut it down.

It's there to ensure the safety of the pack. You know this. If you open up a bit more, you would be able to talk to Olivia like you talk to me.

Because I need another voice in my head. I gently nudge my dragon to the back of my mind.

While the pack bond can be a blessing, it's also annoying as all hell. As alpha, I'm connected with all members of the pack. I also have a blood bond with the witches that allows for the same kind of bond. The links allow me to know when a member of the community is in danger, and also lets the community know if there's something wrong. But if I'm not careful, my emotions can leak through the bonds and cause problems. I haven't been connected to a community in so long I keep forgetting the damn connection is even there. Unlike the instant bond that is formed when a shifter wins an alpha challenge, the bond with the witches requires actual effort from the coven. The coven gathers around their leader and pours a bit of their collective power into that person, linking everyone together in a way very similar to a pack bond.

"The Council is coming." I'm focusing on attempting to

shut down the bonds, so I'm not paying much attention to what Olivia says next.

"Please tell me this is a joke." Olivia's tone takes on a hard edge. While the Alpha is technically the alpha of all shifters, that doesn't mean the pack won't see his arrival here as a potential threat, especially to me.

Challenges for alpha are allowed within the pack, it's shifter nature and allows a pack to remain strong and healthy. It's not unusual for a younger shifter to challenge an older alpha. Fighting amongst other pack members is discouraged, but each pack member has a right to challenge for alpha any time they want. It's the same for the beta position. For most, it's extremely difficult to win an alpha or beta challenge. Not only do you need to be physically strong, but your animal has to be extremely dominant as well. Submissive shifters, while completely necessary for a healthy pack, don't last long in either position, if they can win the position at all. As a queen, I'm more dominant than even the Alpha. I'll need to be careful while around him so he doesn't notice.

"I'm assuming they'll be here tomorrow or the day after. Olivia, you need to meet me at the packhouse. I need to explain to you and Kelly what happened at the alpha challenge with Morgan. There's so much you don't know. I'm sorry I've kept secrets."

There's a pause on the other end. "Ayla, I know you're something we haven't seen before. I'm not sure what exactly, but I know you're powerful and that you have the best interest of this community at heart. So trust me, no matter what you are, the pack won't have an issue."

I'm worried that when the pack finds out what I am, they'll attempt to either kill me, turn me over to the Council, or let a demon know where I'm hiding. Being a queen isn't a bad thing, but the Council has made it clear that the rarer species are to be brought before them for "protection," which is a fancy way of saying they're mated off to a councilman to keep an eye on them and control them. Being a queen also paints a very large target on my back. If it gets out that the New England Pack is harboring a queen, demons and other packs will most likely attempt to attack to get their hands on me.

My status as a queen isn't the only secret I've kept from my community. While I'm not entirely sure my sisters are alive since they've been sleeping for the last four hundred years. I've been on a quest for the last century to find where my mother hid them. They had willingly allowed our mother to put them to sleep, the gods only know where. Once it became clear they hadn't woken, and it didn't appear that they would any time soon, I knew I needed to find out what happened to them. I don't plan on telling anyone about my sisters unless I absolutely need to.

"Ayla? I'm on my way. I assume Kelly is heading over too? What's she bringing?"

"Ice cream."

"Excellent. I'll bring some wine." The line goes dead.

I take a minute to bask in the silence. My bedroom is soundproof, all the bedrooms are because shifter hearing means you hear things you really don't want to at night. Starting to change, I slowly and carefully remove my Armani suit. Since I'm occasionally an extra bitch, it's a three-piece suit accompanied by my classic black Christian Louboutin pumps. I wave my hand over my suit to clean it and put it back in my closet. It's so nice not needing to pay for dry cleaning.

Turning to look at myself in the mirror, I trace my eyes along my body. I'm not all that tall, at least not compared to other shifter women, hitting just under five feet four inches. I believe the term for my body is "slim-thick," as I've seen the youths use on Instagram. I sound so old. I'm muscular, but not in a bodybuilder sort of way. My body still has soft curves with wide hips, a generous ass, and boobs that won't quit—thank the gods for shifter genetics because these bitches would be saggy as all hell otherwise. The right side of my head is shaved, while the rest of my silky, pin-straight black hair falls to my waist. My eyes are emerald green, both in my human form and my dragon form. My skin is a pale porcelain color. I would joke that I look like a ghost, but that's offensive to the ghosts.

I have tattoos covering both of my arms, my right side, between my breasts, and on my left thigh. I'm able to magic them away while I'm working, though I don't usually need to unless I'm dealing with one of the older coven members. My right sleeve is a nature scene, starting with wolves and trees and working up into a mountain scene with dragons flying overhead. My left arm is all about space. The cosmos is painted in bold colors across my skin, and I've added a touch of magic to make the stars shine. The tattoo on my side is a family tree and made out of Celtic knots. The tattoo between my breasts is of the waxing, full, and waning moons. And the tattoo on my thigh is my dragon's face. This tattoo I keep hidden all the time except when I'm alone. I don't want anyone getting curious about it.

By both witch and shifter standards, I look pretty human. Which is the look I've been trying to go for to help me fly under the radar for so long. I typically keep how dominant my dragon is on lockdown and don't let my magic show either. I don't want to cause any unnecessary attention to drift my way.

I strip out of my thong and bra as I walk toward the en-suite bathroom. Thanks to my enhanced shifter vision and the solid glass roof, I don't need to turn the light on, the light from the moon and stars is more than enough to see by. I start the shower and turn the temperature up all the way. I love my showers hot, melt the skin off your bones hot. Once it reaches its peak, skin melting temperature, I step under the spray and feel my body instantly relax. My dragon purrs inside me, happily soaking in the hot water. She'd lie in a nice volcanic pool all day if I let her.

I take my time scrubbing, exfoliating, shaving, moisturizing, and pampering myself. Tonight is going to be difficult, so self-care now is a must. I stand under the spray, staring off blankly with my hair piled on top of my head, letting the deep moisturizing conditioner do its work. I hardly notice the drops of water falling before my eyes.

It was raining the last time I saw my mother. I remember her being stunning, seeming to glow from the inside. My skin and hair color are an exact match to hers, though where I got my height from, I'll never know, both of my parents were tall. My father standing at almost seven feet and my mom at almost six. My sisters were also tall amazons, reaching almost the same height as my mother.

My mother had been so fierce, a warrior goddess in the flesh. She had always been cautious with the three of us growing up. By the time we'd been born, rare queen triplets, queens had been hunted to near extinction. Despite this, I remember growing up thinking that there was nothing that could stop a queen and her mate, my parents had seemed invincible.

It was on that rainy night, four hundred years ago, that my mother took my two older sisters out with her. She promised to come back for me. And she did. But she was wounded, the screams of battle and the flash of fire swirling around the small house we shared. She told me she had placed a sleeping spell on my sisters to keep them safe. She had been planning on doing the same with me, but we were under attack and out of time. She told me to run, hide, and never let anyone know what I was. She died to get me out of Ireland that night. I haven't looked back since.

I shake my head and turn the water off. It won't help me to think about the past right now. I wrap my hair and body in a towel and walk back out into my room. I need to figure out how to tell Kelly and Olivia what I am, who I am. I've put the pack and the coven in danger. They'll be a target if I stay. Which means I need to leave. I need to run again. Fuck. I'll get Kelly and Olivia set up as my successors and then I'll disappear.

What the fuck have I done?

Has it not occurred to you that we are safer and stronger with a community around us? Think for a minute! Yes, your mother put your sisters to sleep, but that was only because her own community had dwindled.

What? I don't remember it that way. Yes, we sacrificed, but surely not that much.

Take a minute to think. My dragon sounds annoyed. *What do you remember about the community around your mother?*

I sit on my bed, still in my towel, and recall. My mother's pack had been large when I was a child. I remember witches, vampires, and shifters living and fighting together.

And then? my dragon prompts, urging me to remember.

I close my eyes, trying to think back to right before I fled. I can feel the blood draining from my face as I realize what had once been a thriving community had dwindled to no more than a handful of shifters, the witches and vampires gone. But what happened? I can't remember. It's all blank.

She made us forget, but that isn't the point. With a larger community, we were better able to hold the demons at bay.

If that's right, we may have a fighting chance at taking out more demons and keeping the community safe. All shifters and witches know about demons, but I'm not entirely sure what they did about them now aside from seeking help from the Council. I had done my best to keep out of this world for so long, I'm going to need to catch up, and quickly, to ensure the safety of my community.

You are a queen, Ayla. Queens naturally attract communities. Your presence in the pack bond will help stabilize the entire community, the coven as well. This is what we were meant to do. You should also start attracting vampires.

I know that. But it's hard to shake the centuries of running that I've done. The belief that I need to remain hidden.

I think Mother put a spell on us to make us forget, to make us run, my dragon suggests solemnly.

But...why?

It makes sense. Why I'm suddenly able to push this point now, why we can't remember the community dissolving. Everything.

I drop my head into my hands, letting the towel that's wrapped around my hair slowly slide to the floor. Have I been living a lie? I know my mother wanted me to live, but everything she'd done to my sisters and me doesn't make sense. Why take away my memories? Why put my sisters to sleep? Why hadn't her community been able to stay together? None of it makes sense.

I can feel Olivia tugging on the pack bond, letting me know she's here in the packhouse. I can't dwell on all of this now. I have so many other things to worry about that thinking about my mother's motives needs to wait until after the Council's visit. I groan and run my fingers through my hair. Right. Focus on the Council.

I stand and go over to my dresser, grabbing a black sports bra, a neon orange tank top, a black thong, and black yoga shorts. I quickly tie my hair into a high ponytail and walk out the door. The first thing I notice when I step into the hall is the utter chaos going on around me. I'm thankful for the soundproof rooms, I wouldn't have been able to hear myself think otherwise. Clearly word about the Council's visit has gotten out. Witches and shifters are running around, cleaning, organizing, planning, and apparently just freaking out. There's one woman crying on a bench near the entryway to the house. Okay. So I'm going to need to address everyone once I talk to Kelly and Olivia, maybe give out a few hugs or shots. Maybe try to find some of these people a Xanax. I know this is a big deal, but my community doesn't know just how big a deal it really is, because if the Council finds out what I am, I'm essentially going to become a lab rat or worse...a housewife.

I eye the chaos for a few more seconds before heading into my study. Kelly and Olivia are already there. Kelly has natural honey gold hair that falls to her shoulders. It always seems to have a solid beach wave to it, which I'm mildly jealous of. She's taller than I am too, which is no surprise, coming in at five feet seven inches, so when she wears heels she may as well be a giant. Her eyes are a crystal-clear blue, and it's easy to see how intelligent she is when looking her in the eye. She always seems to be studying everyone and everything around her, absorbing it like a sponge. Where I'm curvy, Kelly is willowy, not supermodel skinny, but in an athletic but not obsessed about it way. She's also got a soft golden glow to her skin, which I'm also jealous of because I look like the walking dead whenever I'm next to her. She's essentially the girl next door.

Olivia is simply out of this world stunning. Her hair is a milk chocolate brown and falls to her waist. She usually wears it braided in a way that reminds me of Viking shieldmaidens, which is pretty badass. Her hair is fairly straight but has a gentle wave to it that gives it some decent volume. She's an amazon, coming in right under six feet, and has one hell of a rack and ass. She's all lean muscle with some serious lady bits to go with them. The woman has legs for days I seriously lust after and have a raging lady boner for.

But their physical appearances pale in comparison to their personalities. Fiercely loyal, stunningly kind and understanding, and so damn loving of their people, both witches and shifters. I am constantly humbled that they believe in me, are friends with me, and desire to help me lead this community. While we may not have been born of the same mother, our trials over the last few months have made us sisters. The tribulations that are heading our way will cement that bond for eternity. I am one lucky bitch.

They glance over with smiles when I walk in the door, each holding a glass of wine and a bowl of ice cream. Bless their hearts. I close and lock the door to my study behind me, taking one last deep breath before joining them around the fire, sitting at the spot saved for me with a glass of wine and bowl of ice cream. I can see their curiosity behind their smiles. They're attempting to reassure me that whatever I have to say, they're still my friends, but they'd also really like to know what I've been hiding. They must be dying to talk about the Council's visit as well, but there's no more to tell than what I've already talked to them about, so we're all left in the dark there.

I take a sip of my wine, looking between the two of them and trying to figure out where to start. Do I dive in? Do I ease into things? I feel like this should be a rip the Band-Aid off sort of situation. At least they aren't rushing me.

"I'm a queen."

Chapter Three

Just word vomit it out there, great strategy. But it's out. I know I'll need to explain further, but it's in the open now. I feel oddly relieved. Hiding that secret for so long has weighed on me, and I hadn't realized it until just now. It's also mildly horrifying. While I trust these two women with my life, giving them this information shifts our relationship slightly. Trusting them with my life is one thing, trusting them with my secret is entirely different.

But their response isn't quite what I thought it would be. They're just...well...staring at me blankly. It's making me fidgety and anxious as all hell. I want to scream at them to say something, anything! Are they shocked, scared, confused, what?

"A queen dragon?" I supply. They blink and glance at each other.

"Aren't queens a myth?" Olivia looks at me as though I've lost my damn mind.

"Not myth exactly," Kelly chimes in, "But I thought they had all been wiped out by the demons."

"We're certainly not a myth. And, if you'd like, I can prove

I'm a queen. I'm the last one left." I feel bad hiding the truth about my sisters, but I won't risk their safety, not when I'm not even sure they're still alive.

I let down the wall I have that blocks other shifters from sensing my dragon and witches from fully determining my power level. When mixed, it's a pretty heady combination. If I push it, I could have these two flat on their stomachs without even lifting a finger. I can tell the moment they feel my power. Shudders run through them, their pupils dilate, and they gasp in shock. They struggle to remain in their seats, sweat breaking out along their foreheads.

"Holy shit," Olivia whispers in awe when I rebuild my wall. "I can't believe you're real. Why have you been in hiding all this time? Why not let shifters and witches know you're alive?"

"It's not that easy. The Council would have snatched me up in a second. They still might if they find out what I am while they're here. Not only that, but drawing attention to myself also paints a red flag on any community I'm in. Archdemons wouldn't think twice about destroying an entire population to get to a queen."

"Why step out now?" Ah, there's the Kelly I love, her wheels always turning in her head.

"Because I couldn't stand by and let Morgan continue to sell off female shifters. Not after getting to know the two of you, knowing you both didn't want a war between witches and shifters, and especially not after my investigation."

"Your protective instincts were triggered, it makes sense." Olivia nods in agreement with Kelly's deduction.

"I suppose you're right. My dragon mentioned earlier that we are meant to live in communities like this. She reminded me that we're meant to protect those around us. I had almost forgotten about that." I go quiet and start to play with the ice cream that is melting in the bowl in front of me.

"There is no shame in survival," Olivia states, firm and unyielding. "Don't ever feel bad about surviving. For all you know, this is what was meant to happen. You were meant to survive until you found our community."

"Olivia is right, Ayla. You survived to help us. Your resurgence into our world may mean the turn of the tide in the war against the demons and the reconnection of our communities."

"I don't think I would go quite that far. But I do feel like I'm where I'm supposed to be, doing what I'm meant to be doing."

"But we can't let the Council know what you are." Kelly's tone is calculating, as though she's already formulating a plan. "We can't be sure that the Council won't just force you to mate with one of their members, or hide you away, or worse, use you as a weapon."

"So you hide your power level like you've been doing. And we stick with you being latent."

"But that won't explain my magic."

"But only the witches know about your magic," Kelly points out, grinning broadly. "And we aren't huge fans of the Council, not since they turned down my mother as a member. All I have to do is make mention of it to the elders and everyone in the coven will remain silent."

I look between the two of them. It can't be this easy, can it? It's not unheard of for a latent shifter to be an alpha of a pack. So long as you're strong and dominant, it doesn't really matter if you can shift. I just worry that the Council will dig deeper. Not every leader is able to pull a community of shifters and witches together as I have. A community like this hasn't been seen since the last of the queens. What if they question it?

"We'll need to work on it. There's so much that can go wrong here. Shifters and witches haven't lived together like this in centuries. They're going to ask questions about that. They'll want to know why, now, the two species have decided to band together again," I reason.

"That's not as easy to explain, but we can give them a partial truth." Olivia leans forward, a grin spreading across her face. "We admit that Kelly and I went to you for help. We explain what Morgan was doing, how the dominant shifter females were going missing and he was blaming the witches. We explain that after you challenged and killed Morgan, we realized that the best way to keep something like that from happening again was to put aside any differences we might have and learn to get along. What better way to do that than to agree that you are our community leader?"

"Since I'm technically the voice of the coven both normally and while the Council is in town, I can simply state that the witches acknowledged that while you're latent, you're extremely powerful. That, plus your willingness to help us when you could have easily sided with Morgan and his ilk, means that we've decided to allow for a shifter leader for the community, taking a page out of their book."

Olivia nods before stating, "We need to make this about the community. Stress that everyone has been integrating well. This isn't a matter of shifter or witches, it's a matter of our community. We don't see ourselves as two separate species working together, we see ourselves as a family. Ass kissing doesn't hurt either."

"That's a great point, Olivia." Kelly smiles. "Stating we're functioning as a family, instead of two separate entities who just happen to have a common interest, might just help sway them enough to get them to not dig too deep. They won't want to ruin what we've built here. It's one of their objectives, to see communities like this spring up around the world."

I lean back in my chair. This feels way too easy. There

has to be a catch. But we won't know what it is until the Council is here. We're going to need to be quick on our feet and able to improvise. Thankfully the majority of the community has been given a story along similar lines of what we've just discussed, so while there may be some differences, they won't be blaring enough to raise eyebrows, I think. I hope.

∾

KELLY AND OLIVIA set off to discuss specifics with the community, leaving me to swirl my red wine and stare into the fire. The plan, as it now stands, is to tell the community what I am. Kelly and Olivia believe the community will rally around the fact that I'm a queen and want to protect me from being taken by the Council. While I want to believe them, I also know that when fear or money are involved, people do things they wouldn't otherwise do. But I can't exactly lead this community if I don't trust them.

I'll be addressing the community in the morning, answering any questions they may have, and reassuring them that everything is going to be fine. I just need to make myself believe that. I sip my wine, letting the earthy notes burst on my tongue, swishing it around in my mouth a bit before finally swallowing. Shifters can't get drunk, not off normal alcohol. It needs to be made by witches. This is just normal wine, but it helps to settle my nerves. I have to believe that everything will play out the way it needs to. I've finally got a community and I'm starting to feel whole. It has to mean something. I don't believe the gods would be so cruel as to let me have this only to rip it away from me.

You need to rest. Even my dragon sounds exhausted. The emotional roller coaster I've been on since the alpha challenge seems to finally be catching up to me. I can feel all my limbs get heavy, almost numb. My thoughts are sluggish too. I finish my wine and head back to my room. I need to sleep.

THE NEXT MORNING dawns far too quickly for my liking. I lie in bed staring up at the ceiling. I still haven't figured out exactly what I'm going to say to the community, but I didn't get any frantic calls from Kelly or Olivia last night, so I'm assuming everything went well. I get out of bed and grab some clothes. Dress for the job you want, right? Since both the witches and shifters are fairly laid back, jeans and a tank top will do. I'm just tugging on my pants when I feel Olivia brush against the pack bond. I open up my end to see what she needs.

"Are you ready? We have everyone out in the town center."

"Yeah. I'm going to slip on some shoes and head down."

"Hey. Everyone is really excited. They're thrilled to have you as a leader. Some of the old-timers even remember other queens."

"That's reassuring. Thanks." I try not to sound sarcastic.

"See you in a minute." Her tone is cheerily optimistic.

We disconnect. It does feel better knowing that the community is excited about having me around. I'm not sure if it's because I'm a queen or because I killed Morgan, but I suppose it doesn't really matter. I slip on some flip-flops and head off for the town center. It's clear everyone in the community is there, since no one is running around the pack-house getting ready, and the houses along the main street leading to the center of town are all quiet. I can see the community gathered in the town center as I approach. There are almost fifteen hundred of us total, which is a low number considering we take up the entire New England area. Hopefully, now that Morgan is dead, more shifters and witches will come to the region.

Olivia and Kelly have everyone sitting around a wooden platform. Awesome. Because I want to stand on a literal soapbox. Great job, ladies. Rolling my eyes, I step up on top of the box and look out at the shifters and witches gathered around me. These are my people, my community. I now live to protect them. I feel a swell of pride as I gaze at them. I'm finally where I'm supposed to be.

"Good morning, everyone." I smile awkwardly. They return my greeting softly, and I can practically feel the curiosity oozing out of the crowd. Kelly steps up next to me and puts her hand on my arm.

"As you all know by now, Ayla is a queen dragon shifter. Olivia and I have already explained everything to the community. Ayla will answer any questions you have this morning, and she's going to give us some instructions for when the Council gets here. Okay?"

The silence that greets us is our answer. They're waiting on me. No pressure.

"Thanks, Kelly." She steps off the box and sits down. "I guess I'll open the floor for comments and questions and go from there."

A witch from the coven elders stands. She casts a quick glance around the crowd as other people stand, waiting to ask their questions. Her eyes turn to me and take me in. I know the witches can see a person's magical signature, that's how they gauge where a person sits within the coven. I didn't bother to mask anything about myself this morning, wanting to be completely open and honest with my family.

"It's been many, many years since I last saw a queen." Her voice is soft, hardly carrying across the crowd. Thank goodness for shifter hearing. "You feel the same as the last queen I knew, stronger, but your signatures are very similar. Yet how can we be sure? Can you shift for us?"

I knew someone was going to ask me to shift. It's been a

long time since I've shifted in front of other people. I'm nervous. Shifters don't have any hang-ups about nudity, we all have to get naked to shift or we run the risk of completely ruining our clothes, so that's not it. No, it's been centuries since someone else has seen my dragon. These people don't even know what to expect from a queen dragon, so will they even know what they're looking at? I look so different compared to a typical dragon.

"I can shift. But first, I want to explain what I look like. I don't look like a normal dragon." A confused murmur goes through the crowd. "You all have this image of a dragon in your heads. Big, blocky heads? Large, stocky bodies? Huge wings? Spits fire? I don't look like that at all." More confusion pulses through the community.

"So what do you look like then?" a small shifter boy shouts from his seat on his mother's lap. She goes to quiet him, but I shake my head, letting her know it's alright.

"That's a great question. I'm a lot smaller than that. My dragon is built for stealth and speed, not brute force." I see a few shifters nod. There are other animals that are also built for speed, so they understand the concept. "Instead of my head being the size of a bus, it's maybe about the size of my torso." I gesture to my midsection. "And I'm white. Actually, dragons come in all different colors, we aren't just green or anything like that."

"So, you're like a midget dragon?" a young teen witch asks, snickering.

"No." I narrow my gaze on the teen, letting him know he's not funny in the slightest. "Queens have an entirely different purpose, we also have an entirely different skillset, so we don't need all that extra bulk."

"What?" The teen looks perplexed.

"I can also use magic. I can harness all of the elements, not just fire, both in my human and dragon forms." Shocked silence blankets the crowd. "We are able to sense demons, specifically archdemons. Together with the other dragons, and our communities similar to this one, we fought off and killed legions of demons and their archdemon leaders." The teen's eyes go wide in surprise. "That's why I'm the only one left. Archdemons, instead of attacking humans, decided to use the humans to break our communities down and hunt queens. They didn't want anyone standing in their way, and we're damn good at killing demons."

The witch elder nods in agreement. "I remember the raids. My mother lived in a community led by a queen, but we fled when I was a child when it became clear that no one was safe anymore because of the humans." I see others nod in agreement.

"We can get into that more in a minute. You wanted me to prove that I'm a queen by shifting. So, okay." I step down from the box and quickly shed my clothes. But that's as far as I get before I hear a murmur go through the crowd. Shifters don't have an issue with nudity, since you want to take your clothes off or you're going to ruin them as you shift, and the witches have been around shifters long enough to not really let it faze them either. So they can't be up in arms about my nakedness. I look over to Olivia and Kelly, both are fixated on a point at the back of the crowd.

"I'll go see what it is." Olivia starts forward, easily making her way through the crowd. *"Uh...Ayla? You're going to want to see this."* She broadcasts this to Kelly as well. I quickly step back into my clothes and follow Olivia's trail through those gathered around her.

Smells like a lion. My dragon rumbles a warning growl. *He's not part of the community. How did he get here?* She's not happy that there's a trespasser, and frankly, neither am I.

"He's hurt." Kelly's soft declaration pulls my attention away from my dragon. She's crouched next to the shifter who isn't moving. There's blood all over him. Hell, he looks like he's literally been to hell and back. What happened to this guy? Shifters heal fast, so whatever did this to him was trying to kill him, and they damn near succeeded too by the looks of it. Almost every inch of his body looks as though it's been shredded. If I didn't know any better, I'd assume he'd gone through a meatgrinder.

"I don't want to do more damage to him." Kelly looks up at me. "I'm going to heal him a bit here, but we'll need to eventually move him to the infirmary. I'm worried whatever did this to him might not be too far behind."

"Do what you need to." I start scanning the area as Kelly begins healing the shifter. "Where the hell did this guy come from? Did anyone see?" Silence rings in my ears as the people gathered look at one another, hoping someone saw something useful. But it seems no one did. Weird.

Chapter Four

I usher all of the gathered shifters and witches home, not wanting anyone out when we have no idea where the hell this strange lion came from. Olivia takes several of our most talented trackers to the forest around town to search for any sign of how this guy got into our community without anyone noticing. I assign several witches to scour the area as well, trying to see if there is any magical residue. Kelly takes the shifter back to the infirmary for more healing.

I want answers. None of this sits right with me, and my dragon is practically burning me from the inside, trying to get out and maul the shit out of whoever dared threaten our community. It unsettles me that there isn't a trace of anything in the area. Shifters can't just pop in like—oh, fuck. I'm so *stupid*. So fucking stupid.

Witches, my dragon rumbles, a growl rising in my throat. *The only way he could have gotten into town was with the help of witches.*

Which doesn't make any bloody sense. I pull lightly on the ends of my hair, pacing up and down the street as I think. So witches helped this shifter get into our town. How? Why?

Especially in the condition he was in when he arrived. Something did that to him and someone wanted him alive, so they sent him to us. But why?

I close my eyes, inhaling deeply as I release the tight hold I have on my magic. My coven members haven't been able to detect anything, neither has Olivia. Both parties are keeping in contact through our shared bonds. I clearly need to bring out the big guns, no more playing around. If they can't get answers, I will. I let my magic flow out of me, allowing it a minute to rejoice in being free before giving it its task. *Go. Hunt down any trace you can find.* I relax my body, dropping my hands by my sides and allowing my head to fall back. I give myself over to the magic, permitting it free rein to find any scrap of information it can. Like a heat-seeking missile, my magic homes in on anything that isn't familiar, anything that isn't part of this community. I've gotten to know the community so well, even in the short time I've been alpha, that weeding through foreign magic is easier than I thought it would be.

It doesn't take long before a chill runs down my spine. My magic appears as a cascading kaleidoscope of colors shining brightly regardless of the lighting outside. It shimmers and moves with a fluidity that suggests it's always thrilled to be useful. What my magic finds, however, is black and feels like sludge when my power touches it, causing me to gag. I wrap my arms around myself. It feels as though I've been plunged into an ice bath, my head held beneath the surface. I know what this is.

~

KELLY'S HEAD snaps up as I burst through the door of the infirmary. She's a bit paler than she was an hour ago, so the shifter must be in worse shape than he appeared, which doesn't seem possible. She's used a lot of magic to try to get him through the worst of it then. But if I'm right, those wounds are going to take a long time, even for a shifter, to heal. Which is bad, so very, very bad.

"Demons."

Her eyes go wide. "Come again?" She looks around the room, her body tense as though she's waiting for an attack at any minute.

"Demons." I can't seem to make myself form a coherent sentence. Every instinct screams at me to shift, hunt, fight, and protect. I stalk over to the still unconscious lion shifter, a growl rumbling through my chest. Kelly eases away from him as I draw closer, not wanting to stand in my way. She knows that I'm protecting the community now, and if this shifter has any will to live, he's going to tell me everything he knows.

"He's led them straight to us." My accusation rings with fury. "I need answers. I have to find out how much time we have before they get here." Rage floods my system, sending fire surging through my veins and causing my heart to flutter wildly. My dragon screeches inside my head, grappling for control so we can take to the skies. *Fight, defend, hunt, protect.* The room goes out of focus as I train my eyes solely on the lion shifter in front of me. He may not be able to physically answer me, but he will still give me what I want. Making up my mind, knowing what I'm about to do is insane and danger-ous, I stride over to the shifter. My community will not be unprepared for a demon attack. Over my dead body.

"Ayla, wha—" Kelly stops speaking when I touch the shifter's head, placing my palms on his temples. Everything disappears as I dive into the shifter's mind.

Jonas. His name is Jonas. Good. I push deeper, sending my magic into his brain like little ants running through an anthill. Each tendril of magic has a specific purpose—seek out any information Jonas's mind has about demons. It's a complicated process, since memories are stored differently in each person, some by feeling, some by time, some by people, any way that makes sense to that individual. So finding the information I want can be exceedingly difficult. Under normal circumstances, I would never think to dive into someone else's mind. Not only is it an invasion of privacy, but I also run the risk of permanently damaging the mind I'm diving into. Neither of those things matters right now. All that matters is finding out how close the demons are so I can keep my people safe.

Holy. Shit.

～

KELLY HAS a glass of water thrust under my face when I finish with Jonas, but I can't make myself reach for it, my arms tingling as though they've fallen asleep. I'm weak, but the adrenaline that courses through my veins from what I've just learned is pushing aside the worst of the effects of the mind dive. I don't care about the consequences of the act, it's both illegal, according to the Council, and causes extreme physical pain because of how magic is tied to the soul. Diving into a person's mind quickly saps the diver's magic, draining their soul in the process. If you drain too much magic too quickly, you can easily shred a person's soul. But this was worth the risk. I needed to know if he led demons right to our doorstep. I stare numbly at Jonas, watching his chest rise and fall. I have no idea how to take what I found in his head. I can't even feel my dragon stir, she's too shocked as well.

We are so fucked.

No. No, I can't think like that. I won't think like that. I scrub my face with my hands, frantic to come up with some semblance of a plan. One that won't get everyone killed would be a huge bonus. It's times like now I seriously question my sanity when I challenged Morgan. Then again, they'd still be in this position, and having Morgan at the helm would have gotten every shifter in his pack slaughtered.

"Ayla," Kelly murmurs softly. She's trying not to startle me. I want to throw my head back and ugly cackle at the thought. After what I just learned, nothing will startle me again for quite some time.

Get your shit together. My dragon comes roaring back, flooding my system with magic and fire. *It's not just our community at risk.* She's right. At least for the moment. I have a decision to make. One that hopefully won't risk the safety of the entire community.

"Jonas" —I gesture to the shifter on the bed— "is part of the Council. Or employed by the Council, I think is a better way to put it." Kelly's eyes go wide as they bounce between Jonas and me. Olivia comes slamming into the room, her eyes glowing, ready to shift and fight. She's panting, clearly having just sprinted from the woods outside of town to the infirmary, which is in the heart of town, one of the most defensible spots aside from the packhouse.

"I felt..." She stops, looking at the three of us. "What's happened?"

"Ayla dove into Jonas's mind." Kelly's still staring at me, waiting for me to share what I learned or for me to pass out. Probably both.

"Who the fuck is Jonas?"

Kelly gestures to the unconscious shifter in response.

"What did you find out?" Olivia's focus turns to me.

The weight of both their gazes settles on me. Strangely, it doesn't rattle me. Instead, it soothes me, making me feel more confident about what needs to be done. Making me feel stronger.

This is what a community does, my dragon whispers.

"He's employed by the Council. He was sent here by

them." They're both staring at me, waiting for me to continue. "The Council is under attack."

"Demons," Kelly whispers. She instantly flies into motion, gathering medical supplies from around the room, quietly muttering to herself.

"How the hell do you know it's demons?" Olivia sounds alarmed as she starts pacing the room.

"*I* know it's demons. I felt their tainted aura with my magic. I thought..." I look down at Jonas then back at Olivia. "I thought Jonas had led them right to us. But he hasn't. He was sent here, both as a warning and to seek help."

I stand, Olivia stops pacing, and Kelly moves closer to my side, her arms filled with potions and bandages. I take a few deep breaths, a plan forming in the back of my head. It's stupid, so insanely stupid, but it's the only thing that's going to work against what I saw in Jonas's mind.

"The Council is being attacked by a legion led by an archdemon."

"I'm sorry," Olivia all but shouts, "but I could have sworn you just said a legion of demons led by an archdemon is currently attacking the Council. *The* Council."

My tone is grim when I reply, "That's right. They're in the Rocky Mountains. They were visiting another pack that was having trouble with missing members when they were ambushed. Jonas was sent to us. As far as he knows, things weren't looking good."

Shocked silence rings through the room, both of my betas are too stunned to say anything. I can't just sit here though. I need to act as quickly as possible. I may have come up with a dumb idea, but I was born for this, it's my very reason for existing. And if I can take out even one of those motherfuckers, it'll make my life that much better. I stride toward the door, Olivia and Kelly falling into step just behind me.

"What are we going to do?" Kelly asks.

"We're going to kill as many of those assholes as we can. And I'm going to kill myself an archdemon."

~

AT MY COMMAND, Olivia and Kelly have regathered the community, this time outside the packhouse, while I finalize my plan. I wanted to keep myself hidden from the Council, even after becoming alpha, but that's not possible now. So I may as well let those dicks on the Council know about me in the most spectacular fashion possible. I'm going to do their job for them. I'm going to take down one of the baddest motherfuckers around because I'm the bigger badass. I look out at the shifters and witches assembled around me. If I can't do this, they'll be next. I won't let that happen. My dragon roars her agreement. She's eager to head into battle, our instincts screaming at us to rain fire down on all those who would threaten our community. She wants to roar to the heavens so demons and supernaturals alike will know that a queen is in town and she isn't taking prisoners.

"Form groups. I need the strongest ward casters to stand to the right, the berserkers to the left. The healers need to form two units, those who can heal quickly and those who have a slower healing rate. I need my fighters front and center. Everyone else, you're to stay here at the packhouse, we're going to need you when we get back."

Murmurs break out, but everyone does as they're told. The adults who are staying behind herd the children into the packhouse, not wanting them involved. I glance over at Kelly. She's looking better than when I first came to see Jonas, which is good. She's strong, and I don't want to go into this shitshow without her. I nod as I look out at the community. We may just be able to pull this off, especially if the Council is still fighting. But we don't have much time, we need to get out of here fast.

"Kelly, take several of the strongest portal casters to the center of town." I hand her a piece of paper. "This is where we need to go, but don't open the portals until I say so. We don't want to let anything in." Kelly nods, taking a handful of individuals and moving off toward the center of town. I know she'll tell them what's going on, leaving me to explain to everyone else.

"The shifter we found is an employee of the Council." The murmurs all die at once. "The Council was checking on another pack when they were attacked by a legion of demons." This is the hard part. "And an archdemon." The murmurs start back up again, so I raise my hands to silence everyone. "All I need you to do is hold the legion off while I take out the archdemon. I can do it, I'm a queen."

As I watch, amazed and stunned, my shifters and witches all step forward, their hands over their hearts. They're ready to die if need be, but I don't want that to happen, and I'm going to do everything in my power to make sure that as many of these amazing people make it home as possible.

"Once Kelly and the others have established portals to our location, I want the witches who can ward to go through first along with the berserkers. Establish a perimeter around the portals." My gaze focuses on the witches, then the berserkers. "Don't let any demon through those portals." They rush off to join Kelly's crew.

"Those with slower healing powers, stay on this side of the portals. You'll need to coordinate with the remaining community members to ensure proper care for those who come back injured. As you know, demon wounds heal slower even with the help of magic, so make sure you're prioritizing correctly. Those with faster healing abilities are going to set up around the portals. I want you to triage, ensuring that everyone who goes through the portals will be able to make it to the other side alive. Don't focus your efforts on anyone who doesn't seem that wounded, send them straight through." They all nod and break away, heading to their respective areas.

"Now my fighters." They all stand a little straighter. "Half of you are going to stay here. We need you to protect the town. The other half is coming with us, following up behind the berserkers. Help them hold the line long enough for me to do what I need to. Once the archdemon is down, the legion should scatter." And like that, we're ready for war. The fighters divide themselves and rush off to their designated positions.

Olivia looks over at me, studying my face. I've shut down the bond, so I can't tell what she's thinking. I'm not sure I want to know. The expression on her face tells me she isn't happy. I haven't specifically given her orders and for a damn good reason. But she's going to be pissed.

"I need you to stay here," I whisper. "If I fail, I can't have both of my betas killed along with me. You have to stay here in case the worst happens. The others will look to you for direction."

She opens her mouth to argue, thinks better of it, then nods. "Fine. I'll stay. But if you get your ass killed, I'm going to find a way to bring you back and kill you myself."

"Fair enough. I can live with that."

"I'll make sure we're ready for the injured." She hugs me, squeezing so hard I can't inhale at all. "You better not fucking die."

"That's the plan." We break apart, and she goes into the packhouse to organize the remaining community members. I reach out to Kelly through the bond, letting her know to open the portals. I feel the surge of magic as the portals rip apart time and space. Kelly's bond shivers as she steps through with the ward casters to start securing the area around the portals. I lock down the rest of my bonds, closing off any potential distractions. Kelly and Olivia both have their bonds open and will be able to tell if someone is in danger. My sole focus is getting to that archdemon.

I take one more deep breath, and then I shift.

Chapter Five

My dragon surges to the surface, thrilled to be free and hunting her prey. When I'm in dragon form, my scales are an iridescent white, shining almost every color of the rainbow depending on the angle of the sun. I feel strong, free, and fierce. This is what I was made to do. This is my destiny. My dragon roars happily before heading toward the portals. The witches and berserkers have already gone through, and the healers and fighters are preparing to go next once they get the all clear from those on the other side. Kelly, it appears, stepped through with the first wave. A surge of pride and affection flares through me. She'll take care of our people.

I circle once before gaining speed, tucking my wings close to my body as I slam my way through the portal. While I had seen the fighting through Jonas's eyes, I'm still not prepared for the sight before me. Screams echo through the air. The scents of blood, magic, death, and demons assault my nose, causing me to shake my head. The mountain we've arrived at is littered with bodies, both councilmen and demons alike. It's difficult to tell who's winning at the moment since the battle is taking place mainly in the forested parts of the mountain. I pray it's the Council. It looks like the summit has been left untouched. Odd. That's the high ground, surely one party would want to claim it.

I instantly soar to a higher position in the sky, wanting to take everything in and find the archdemon as quickly as possible. A roar loud enough to shake the earth blasts through the sounds of battle. I turn my head to watch a massive, golden dragon take to the air, rising above the trees at lightning speed. Caleb, the alpha of all alphas. He's massive, I don't remember my father even being that large.

He roars again, fire streaming from his mouth, taking out a large group of demons. Impressive. Before I can stop her, my dragon releases a roar of her own. The battle below stills for a moment as everyone turns their gazes in my direction. While my roar lacks the physical depth needed to shake the earth, it's high-pitched and haunting enough to shake the soul. Given the position of the sun right now, I'm also literally a shining beacon. Surprise, everyone. Caleb turns his massive head in my direction, and I watch as he inhales deeply. He's trying to scent me. Surely he must know what I am...

The next roar he releases isn't a battle challenge, it's the sound of a turned on and very frustrated male. My dragon preens while I lose my shit. No. No, this can't be happening. No!

Mate! my dragon purrs, clearly forgetting why this is a *bad* thing.

Nope, we're taking a hard pass on that right now, possibly forever.

But he's here! We've been waiting for him!

I mentally slap my palm to my face. *I know that. But let's also remember where we are and who he is. Now is not the time.* My dragon mentally shakes herself, both of us fighting against the mating instinct that is surging through our body, causing lust to rage a scorching path through our veins. Caleb is heading right for us. Fantastic. This is just what I wanted to deal with today. I literally do not have time for this crap.

A blast of demonic energy flares from the summit, sending a shock wave rippling onto the battlefield below, and councilmen and demons are thrown off their feet. My crew remains standing thanks to the wards we've erected around the portals. The air grows thick, and my wings strain to keep me aloft. Archdemon. It's been such a long time since I've come up against one, I've forgotten their aura feels like tar—thick, sticky, and dangerous. That's where I need to—the gold dragon slams into me, sending us both careening out of the sky into a thick patch of trees. His limbs wrap protectively around my body, a low rumbling growl thrumming through his chest.

What the fuck is he doing? My dragon is just as confused. Great, so this doesn't appear to be typical idiotic male behavior then. I hear the sounds of battle starting up again as we make it to the tree line, I'm worried that the blast of demonic energy from the archdemon gave the demons a boost. I wriggle in Caleb's grasp, trying to get away from him to fight and save our people. He only holds me tighter.

We land in a tangled heap of dragon limbs, so I shift back to my human form and he follows suit moments later. He's on top of me and we're both naked, which, if he wasn't who he is and we weren't where we are, I'd totally be all about. But this is not acceptable. He buries his nose against my neck, inhaling deeply, a low rumble starting in his chest. Everything in me freezes, and before I can even think, I arch my neck to allow him better access.

The battle.

I slap my palms to his chest and push him back as much as I can. He has to be at least a foot taller than I am, and he probably has at least a hundred pounds of solid muscle on me too. While that normally wouldn't be an issue, the urge to mate drives through every cell of my body, making it feel as though I'm fighting to get my arms to push him away. He rears his head back, his eyes flashing to his dragon's before settling back to a normal green color. It's different than my own, his eyes have more brown hues to them than mine do. I kind of like it. No. No, I don't like it. I don't like it at all.

"You need to get off me." My demand comes out stronger than I thought it would. I'm mildly proud of myself.

"You're..." He takes another deep inhale, his eyes once again shifting to his dragon's. "You're a queen."

"You got that right, big guy. Now I need you to get the fuck off me." My tone is firm but patronizing as I slap on my best resting bitch face and just stare at him. But he doesn't budge. I need him to get off me because my body is starting to notice all the things he has pressed against me while we're both naked—one thing in particular, but I refuse to name it. If I name it then it's real. It's not real, therefore it has no name.

"Mine." His voice rumbles with the sound of his dragon. I can feel my eyes flash. We're both struggling, but we know now is not the time. Clearly, Caleb needs to be reminded of his status.

"Now is really not the time. In case it slipped your mind, your people are being slaughtered not too far from here." My tone takes on the tenor I use when I'm talking to people who are just willfully stupid. "What do you say we go kill the bad demons? Hmm?"

His hand comes up and grabs my breast. I have to fight every instinct in my body to ensure that I don't arch up into his touch. Instead, I drop one hand from his chest and push his hand away. He growls low in his throat, clearly not liking that his new toy doesn't want to play. *Trust me, pal, you couldn't handle me.*

"You don't want to make me force you off of me. Now, I suggest you get the fuck off." My dragon throws more force behind my words, adding extra oomph to my threat as well as a layer of dominance to really show him his place. Caleb blinks slowly, once, twice, before he shifts off of me. I stand in a flash, moving quickly away from him. My body aches to return to his, burning for his touch and missing his heat. I can't let him get under my skin. I have an archdemon to kill. He's also the alpha of all alphas, he *is* the Council. There is no way I will go with him no matter what my body wants. *Just remember, Ayla, you are the baddest bitch in the room, don't let this male make you his bitch.* His chest is heaving as he holds himself back, his hands clenched at his sides.

I will not look.

Nope.

Not going to do it.

I look. He's well over a foot taller than I am and muscular enough that it's clear he's a shifter. Like me, he has tattoos covering most of his body, and while I'd love to stare at them all day, I force my eyes to keep moving, and I avoid the lower half of his body. His shoulders are insanely broad. How the hell does he make it through doors with those things? His hair is shaved close on the sides of his head but is longer on top. It's a deep black color that shines with hints of blue in the sunlight.

"You must be Alpha McInnes." Now that he doesn't seem like a sex crazed idiot, his timbre is deep and raspy, sexy as sin, and has my mouth watering. That accent may just be the death of me. He's watching me warily, almost as though he expects me to just disappear into thin air. I wish.

"Correct." I shoot him a strained smile. "Now, Alpha, I suggest we get back to business. We have demons to kill." I stress the word "alpha" so he understands that he has no sway over me. I want him to understand I'll respect his authority as Alpha of all alphas for as long as it suits me to do so, but ultimately, I'm the more dominant badass here. And yet I couldn't push him away. I don't want to think about that.

He takes a step closer to me and I tense. "You're going to have a lot of explaining to do, McInnes." His eyes run down my body, leaving burning lust raging in their wake. "And I am not leaving your side."

I roll my eyes, pop my hip out, and plant my fisted hand on it. "I don't have time to tell you just how wrong you are on both counts because people are dying." Now I take a step toward him, my hand raised with a finger pointed at his chest. "You're being a shitty alpha by being here with me and not fighting for them. Get your shit together."

He reacts as if I just slapped him, and a tiny part of me wishes I had if only to cop a feel of that hella strong jawline. A guttural growl rolls out of his chest and his eyes flash to his dragon's again. He's got some control issues. Either that or I'm affecting him more than I realized. I'm surprised I can think straight. I've been told that the mating urge is really hard to resist.

It is, my dragon whispers to me. *But because there are demons nearby, those instincts override everything else. Once we're done here, it's going to be a lot harder.* Her voice takes on a wistful note.

Great. More problems. *Does that mean you're going to be a whiny bitch after this?* I toss back at her. She snorts and doesn't answer, which means that yes, she will, in fact, be a whiny bitch once this is all over.

"You're right." He doesn't sound happy about it. "We need to head out. I assume you're going to head for the archdemon." When I nod, his eyes narrow. "Not without me. And before you argue, you know you need an alpha dragon to help you take him out." I don't like to admit that he's right. My mother always went into battle with my father at her side, and she was stronger because of him.

"Fine, you can tag along. Don't get in my way. Don't get all macho on me. Don't think that I need saving. Remember what I am while we're up there with him."

"You're my mate." He sounds stubborn and gruff.

"I am a queen." My retort leaves no room for negotiation.

He moves so quickly I don't have time to react. One of his hands snakes around my head, cupping my neck, while the other grasps my hip, pulling me flush against him. His mouth closes on mine. My body stiffens as he plunders my mouth, my brain screaming at me to push him away. But I just stand there, dumbstruck, letting him thrust his tongue into my mouth like he owns it. The feel of him hardening against my stomach snaps me out of my stupor, and I push him back, causing him to stumble slightly.

"You do *not* get to put your hands on me without my permission." His eyes flash, and he snarls and takes a step toward me. I clap my hands together in front of me and pull them apart, an electric blue line of magic forming between them, sizzling and sparking. He stops moving. "You. Don't. Touch. Me." My dragon adds power to my command, hating to be manhandled just as much as I do.

I can see him fighting his dragon when he states, "You are mine."

"No." My response rings with power. "I am my own. If I want you to touch me, I will ask you to. Until that happens, you don't lay a finger on me, am I clear?" I allow my magic to grow. His eyes narrow into dangerous slits, and I can feel the dominance radiating off of him. It's too bad he isn't more dominant than I am. But he's close. Shockingly, disturbingly close.

"We have an archdemon to kill. Let's go. We'll deal with this once it's dead," I tell him. He shifts and takes to the air. I allow myself a second to breathe, reabsorbing the magic into my body before shifting and flying after him. I'll let him think that we'll deal with the mate issue once the archdemon is dead, but it'll be a really cold day in hell before I let that man make me his.

~

THE BATTLE below us is still in full swing, and it appears the demons are winning, even with the added help of my community. Thankfully our wards are holding, and I can see my people getting the injured through the portals. Now I just need to take the head off the snake. How I wish I could do it in true Longbottom fashion, pulling a magical sword out of a magical hat. Alas, it's not meant to be.

Caleb releases another earthshaking roar as he shoots for the summit. I silently follow in his wake. I need to figure out exactly how I want to attack the archdemon. I very much doubt he'll be alone; they never are. So having Caleb around will actually be useful for something. I can't let the archdemon get away. If he does, all of his little friends will know there's a queen in America. I'll be dead before I can blink. That means I need to stay in dragon form, since I'm a hell of a lot stronger and I can utilize my magic. Don't die. That's the plan.

The instant we fly over the summit, looking to land as close as possible, we hit a barrier. We're able to make it through, but I feel my dragon go suddenly dormant. I panic, struggling to hold my dragon form as I plummet out of the sky. A quick glance confirms that Caleb is having the same issue. Shit. Our little interlude in the forest gave the archdemon time to pull up a strong barrier. He's got a mage. That motherfucker.

Mages are witches who work with demons. In exchange, they get a power boost and typically get to live as long as the demon who owns their soul. They're pains in the ass to deal with, but nothing I haven't come across before. I have no idea why I didn't realize there would be at least one mage here.

I slam into the ground, my body creating a large crater, which only widens a minute later when Caleb crashes into the ground inches from me. I can't hold my dragon form anymore and am forced to shift back to human. I'm a bit battered, and from the looks of Caleb as he stands next to me, so is he. I take a moment to close my eyes, letting my magic flare around me. Thankfully, that's still working. I'm able to pinpoint the group of demons on the summit. Fifty plus the archdemon, but I don't sense a mage.

"How many?" Caleb rumbles.

"Fifty."

"Total?"

"Plus the archdemon."

"What about that damn mage?" Ah, so he is sufficiently intelligent when he isn't thinking with his dick.

"I don't sense him here on the summit, and the demons are starting to close in, so I don't have time to look for him."

"Ayla." My name on his lips causes me to snap my eyes open. "You need to stay with me."

"Caleb." His eyes heat when I say his name, but I ignore it. "I'm a queen. This is what I'm made for. I need you to help me take out the lower-level demons. That's the best way this will play out."

"Well, certainly not the best way, my dear." The voice has a familiar, strong British accent, but instead of bringing a sense of nostalgia with it, it sends ice racing through my veins. I know that voice.

Chapter Six

Malick. But he...My mother, she...My mind is reeling. Malick was the archdemon my mother fought the night she died. She killed him. I had been so sure she killed him. All the reports of the battle state that he fell. Confusion wars with rage as I take a moment to attempt to reconcile what I've known for hundreds of years with what I've just learned.

"I see my brothers failed in their mission to kill all the queens." Malick laughs, slowly clapping his hands as though he's been given a precious gift. I still can't see him, but I can sense him moving closer. My body starts to shake as I suppress the urge to find Malick and take him out. But I know better, I can feel the demons edging closer to our position, which means that Malick is coming to me. Caleb shifts to stand in front of me protectively. The demons begin materializing in front of us, slowly forming a loose circle around the crater we're standing in. We are so fucked.

The wall of demons in front of us parts, allowing a stunningly handsome man, almost as tall as Caleb, through. Archdemons, unlike lower-level demons, can change much like a shifter can, between human and demon forms. Lower-level demons can only ever appear demonic with pitch-black skin, shining red eyes, and horns of various lengths, sizes, colors, and shapes atop their heads. Archdemons have all that and wings in their demonic form. Malick has changed in the four hundred years I thought he was dead. While his human form is still stunning to look at, he's allowed his hair to grow out and he has it pulled back at the nape of his neck. He's also rocking a five o'clock shadow where he had a full-on beard before. But just as he was four hundred years ago, he's dressed to impress, clearly flaunting whatever wealth he's accumulated.

He shouldn't know who I am, just what. My mother made certain that my sisters and I were hidden, even as children, from the likes of him. I don't know why it was so important that the three of us remained concealed, but it was. Not even our community knew we existed. We had each been given a visual memory of Malick from our mother. I need to play this delicately. I place a hand gently on Caleb's back. He stiffens but lets me step up next to him.

"Stunning, isn't she?" Malick's tone is laced with heat as he runs his gaze over my body. I shiver and fight the urge to vomit. The demons around him jeer. Caleb plasters himself against the back of my body, wrapping his hands around to rest on my stomach, molding me to him. "And she has a pet! How charming." His cheery degrading tone has me bristling. Caleb's thumb gently strokes my stomach, stopping me from saying anything stupid.

"Now, if you would be so kind as to step away from my queen." Malick flicks his hand and Caleb is ripped from my body, causing me to stumble back. He's thrown into the throng of surrounding demons and they don't hesitate to start attacking. Caleb quickly disappears in the mass of demons. "That's much better." Malick materializes in front of me, his eyes still glowing with heat as he once again runs his gaze along my body. Little red flags are popping up in my mind, but I'm not sure what's wrong aside from the raging creeper vibes he's throwing out.

"You're going to regret that," I singsong.

"Am I, little queen?" A grin slowly spreads across Malick's face, reminding me of the Cheshire cat from *Alice in Wonderland*. I've always hated that damn movie. Not to mention that creepy-ass cat.

"You don't rip an alpha male from his mate." I tsk. "I thought even demons knew that much." I make sure that my voice is now cheerily degrading. If he wants to play the *who's the biggest bitch in the room* game, I'm going to win, hands down. I'm a damn attorney, and when I need to, I can absolutely make anything I want sound like I'm a condescending bitch—in the politest way possible of course.

"Ah, but he isn't actually your mate, now is he?" Malick's tone has changed from amused to threatening. His eyes start to darken with fury. Why the hell does he care? It's creepy as fuck.

"He is my mate." In a flash, Malick has both of my hands in one of his above my head, and I'm pinned to a tree on the edge of the crater. His other hand tightly grips my face as he leans his head in close. I can feel his breath fan across my face, and I wrinkle my nose at the feeling. I don't fight his hold on me, choosing to wait this out as long as possible while Caleb fights off the group of demons he was thrown into. He's an alpha male dragon, there's no way he won't thin the herd as quickly as possible. If Malick honestly thought that throwing him to those lower-level demons would kill him, he's a bit rusty in dealing with dragons. His hand tightens on my face slightly and my gaze focuses on his.

"That's where you're wrong, little queen. You don't have your mate mark, and you don't carry his scent." He runs his nose along my neck and breathes deeply. "You're ripe for the picking."

I feel as though I've been dumped in ice water. Every cell in my body is screaming for me to break away from him and fight, but I need to give Caleb time to thin Malick's herd, and I have every confidence that's exactly what he's doing. I can't have Malick calling in for backup. I struggle against his hold and realize it won't be as easy as I thought to break free when I need to. Shit.

"Regardless" —I try for haughty— "I am far from *your* queen." I spit the words out in disgust, letting him know just how rancid the thought truly is. Malick throws his head back and laughs, allowing himself to shift from his human form to his demon form. He's almost ten feet tall in his demon form and doesn't need to lift his arms to continue holding mine above my head. It looks as though pieces of armor have melded to his skin at his shoulders, pecs, forearms, and hands. He's wearing skintight leather pants and armored boots. His hair is now free, tumbling down to his hips. Blood-red horns start at his temples and curl up and around the side of his head twice, with sharp points ending close to his ears.

"Little queen, do you even know the reason your kind was hunted to extinction?" He crouches down to bring his face closer to mine again. "Because I can promise you whatever excuse you've been given is a lie."

Now it's my turn to laugh. "That's nice. I'm sure you tell all the queens that." I use my best sarcastic tone, rolling my eyes for effect. My eyes then flick beyond him, straining to see how Caleb is fairing against the other demons, but I can't see him yet, so now isn't the time to strike. I keep trying to reach for my dragon, but she's been pushed so far inside of me I can't even catch a faint whisper of her. I'm not sure when the barrier's magic will subside. I'm grateful I can still feel my magic coursing through my veins. Technically my magic and my dragon are two entirely separate entities, making situations like this more manageable. Malick runs a finger down my face, a claw gently scraping against my skin. I bite back my anger and disgust to stare him dead in the eye.

"My brothers killed your sister queens because they didn't want me to get my hands on one. And you've just delivered yourself on a silver platter! How delightful." He sounds like a kid in a candy store. His eyes sparkle with a sick glee that leaves a bitter taste in my mouth. His brothers killed all the queens off because of *him*? That goes against everything I've been taught, everything the supernatural community has been led to believe for centuries. Queens were picked off because of their abilities to sense demons and destroy archdemons. They hadn't liked that the planet was no longer theirs to do with as they pleased, so like the petulant children they are, archdemons sought revenge. Right? There's no way it could have been solely because of Malick. No, I can't believe that. But doubt starts to creep into me with vicious teeth that gnaw at my mind. There's more to all of this.

"Why the hell do you want a queen?" While I need to keep him talking, I also need to get more information out of him. If he is truly the reason the other archdemons killed off queens, I need to know why. Knowing that they would go to such lengths because one of their own wanted to get his hands on a queen makes Malick far more dangerous than I'd ever thought possible. Why hadn't they just turned on him? I realize queens were throwing off their groove, but to specifically seek out and kill all living queens because of one archdemon seems, well, excessive. There has to be more going on, and since I'm the only queen currently not in a magically induced coma or dead, I need to figure out what's happening. Quickly.

"Tut, tut, little queen. I can't be spoiling all the fun, now can I?" He is enjoying this far too much. It's exceptionally annoying. My eyes flick back to the demons behind Malick. I can finally see Caleb has made a fairly large dent in their numbers. I'm up. My hands have been plastered against the rough bark of the tree while Malick talked at me, absorbing as much of the natural energy around me as possible.

Unlike Malick, I don't need to move any part of my body to use magic. Sometimes it's better to help me shape the magic into something useful, but I don't need to do that to get the job done. So I merely smile up at Malick while I rip open the ground beneath him and create vines to grow at my feet and wrap tightly around his wings, pushing him into the pit. He lets go of me as he falls, a grin spreading across his face a moment before he stops falling, his wings snapping the vines. I quickly move back along the edge of the crater as he stalks my every move. He's fast, but so am I.

"Clever little queen." He sounds amused. "I like it when they fight back. A little spunk is so exciting."

He sounds so rapey. Why do they have to sound rapey? Can't villains ever threaten a woman and not sound like they're a rapist? I should teach a class: How Not to be a Rapey Villain 101.

I slap my hands together, pulling them apart as I did with Caleb, and form an electric blue whip that crackles with energy. Malick raises an eyebrow as he stalks closer to me. I plant my feet firmly into the ground before lashing out with my whip. It wraps around his neck and he stops, his body stiff, eyes flashing with pain. I allow my magic to flow freely through the whip into Malick, watching as his body jerks with each wave of power that flows through him.

He grits his teeth, grasps onto my whip, and gives it a strong tug, causing me to stagger forward. Quickly regaining my footing, I tug back, sending additional shock waves through the whip. I open up my magic further, sending rocks pummeling into him. He snatches one out of the air and reshapes it into a spear. Awesome. In an instant, I've reshaped my whip into a sword. I risk a glance to see how Caleb is fairing, and it appears he's finishing up with the last of the demons.

Malick is standing right in front of me when my eyes turn back in his direction. My body stiffens in shock before I once again go on the offensive, the years of sword combat training paying off as I hack at him. Fire rings my sword as my magic flows out of me. Malick is able to get a few well-placed jabs past my defenses, and I'm quickly covered in blood and dust.

The sound of Caleb's pained grunt echoing across the summit has me instantly whirling in his direction. Big mistake. The spear slices through my side with amazing ease, the force sending me jerking forward. My knees collapse under me, slamming into the ground with a sickening and bone-rattling thud, and my sword disappears as my hands smash against the dirt and rocks next.

Fuck me, that hurts. It's been a long time since I've been stabbed in the torso. My vision goes hazy and my hearing fades out a bit as I battle the shock that's trying to take control of my system. Caleb's outraged roar is the only thing I register before I'm dragged up against a hard, searingly hot body.

"I want you to watch him die, little queen," Malick whispers against my ear. His breath is abnormally hot against my skin, yet another sign he's a demon. My eyes can't focus. All my brain is registering is the alarming rate that I'm losing blood. I'm not healing as fast as I should be. What the fuck did he do to that bloody rock?

~

IT MUST BE moments later when my vision clears and I'm able to focus enough through the shock to understand what's happening. While Caleb had the upper hand when I risked a glance at him earlier, he's now being held back by two demons. He's covered in demon blood, his own blood mixed in from multiple injuries. There's a dagger sticking out of his ribs and his breathing is labored. I instantly start to struggle against Malick, my need to get to him almost blinding. But pain from the spear lodged in my body quickly slows any effort I make to get free.

"So you do have a connection to your little pet. How endearing." Malick's voice slithers through my head, making me want to vomit. "Now that you're awake, we can get on with the show."

Show? My head is still a little fuzzy. But I know this can't be good. My eyes connect with Caleb's and hold. With sick fascination, I watch as the two demons remove the dagger from Caleb's side. He hisses as they slowly stab him in the abdomen. My body jerks as Malick does the same to me. Caleb starts struggling against the demons, but he's lost too much blood. So have I.

"I'm going to punish you for telling me this worthless garbage is your mate." Malick's fury licks along my skin as he slices between my breasts. I refuse to cry out, instead, keeping my eyes locked on Caleb's.

I'm frantically trying to think of a way out of this when my dragon comes flooding back, my wounds instantly healing. I can tell Caleb feels this as well as his own wounds start to close.

What happened?

The mage. He's either dead or ran off. The barrier is gone, my dragon informs me.

About damn fucking time. Let's show this asshat who he's dealing with.

With pleasure.

My shift to my dragon form floods my system. Malick is

ripped from behind me, roaring with fury as I take to the sky.
He tries to come after me, but Caleb snaps his mouth around
him before he can reach me. My dragon releases a furious
roar, turning in the air as our magic gathers in our core. But
he's gone.

Malick is gone.

Where the hell did he go?

My dragon screams her rage to the sky, Caleb's dragon
following suit. I quickly land and shift back to my human
form, Caleb landing next to me. All the demons, even the
dead ones, are gone.

"Where the hell did that bastard go?" Caleb's question is
laced with the threat of violence as he moves closer to me,
inspecting my body for any lasting harm.

"That explains a lot," I mutter as I look around the
summit. Caleb gently grabs my face with his hands, tilting my
head toward his.

"What are you talking about?" His tone is a low rumble.
His eyes search mine for answers, but I'm still reeling from
even the small amount of information I've just learned.

"Malick. How he's still alive." I'm so lost in my thoughts I
don't realize that Caleb has no idea about my background
with the demon. "Must be nice to just pop in and out like
that."

A thunderous growl rolls through Caleb's chest. "You
know him?"

"Not personally, no." I remove my head from his grasp,
causing a snarl to rip from Caleb. His hands take hold of my
hips and he drags me to him, his face burying in my neck as
he inhales my scent. As shaken as I am, I take a small
moment to inhale his scent as well, ensuring that he's fine and
will heal. Once my dragon is appeased, I shift myself away
from him slightly. My eyes meet his again and hold.

"He's the demon who killed my mother."

Chapter Seven

Caleb and I stay in the Rockies until all of our people, as well as those from the Rocky Mountain Pack, are safely on my pack's land. It's devastating to see an entire pack almost wiped out and needing to relocate. Devastating and infuriating. I want to hunt Malick down and fuck his day up. My dragon roars in agreement. We're both still riding high on our protective instincts right now, and it's difficult to fight the urge to shift, take to the skies, and hunt. But it was made abundantly clear that I need to get my shit together before I engage Malick again. What happened on the summit of that mountain was embarrassing.

We're used to hiding, not fighting. My dragon gently brushes against my mind, attempting to soothe me.

Yeah, well, it was pathetic. I realize I sound like a petulant child, but after the ass-kicking I just received, I could use a good sulk.

We will train, practice, and get stronger. She sounds as though she thinks I'm brain damaged. I huff and push her aside for the moment.

Now that we're back on my territory, my eyes find their

way to Caleb, who is still bloody naked. Now that the demons are gone, lust surges through my veins, and it takes every ounce of strength I possess to keep myself from clinging to him as if I'm a damn spider monkey. Also pathetic. My dragon chuckles softly, a whole lot less upset about this turn of events than I am.

He is a worthy mate.

He thinks with his penis.

It's a nice penis.

I...Well...I can't argue with that. It is a nice penis.

I shake my head. *That's not the point. He's the damn Council. We are not cozying up to the Council.*

My internal debate with my dragon is interrupted when Olivia walks up, giving Caleb the stink eye. Bless. She studies the dragon shifter for a moment, her eyes slowly bouncing between the two of us.

"Alpha." She nods her head in Caleb's direction before turning to me, effectively telling Caleb she's my badass bitch, not his. It's childish of me, but I want to stick my tongue out at him in victory. "Ayla, we've been able to get everyone settled either in houses around town or in the infirmary. Thankfully the healers were able to do a lot on scene, so we aren't overrun."

"Great. How many are seriously injured?"

"Around a thousand." Not as bad as I thought, but also not a number to laugh at.

"Do we have any idea how many made it through the portal? There were a lot of dead." I feel like I've failed them. I didn't kill Malick. I was weak. I am weak.

"Not yet. There was a lot of chaos once the demons vanished. But..." Her eyes go to Caleb again. "It looks like the alpha of the Rocky Mountain Pack is dead. We haven't been able to find him."

Caleb's face is grim when he responds, "We can send a

wolf back to the Rockies. I can provide them with a scent pattern to see if they can find the body."

"Yes, Alpha." Olivia's eyes slide back to mine. "The beta is asking if they'll be absorbed into the New England Pack. They would feel safer under the eye of a queen." Caleb looks like he wants to argue, but I hold up my hand to stop him.

"I think it's best we give it some time before we make any sort of decision. Right now, everyone is in shock. We still need to go back to identify and bury the dead. I don't want to entertain discussions about a merger until we've been able to heal everyone and respect our dead." A low growl rumbles out of Caleb and I roll my eyes.

"What Alpha McInnes meant—" Caleb starts, and I whirl, glaring daggers at him.

"Did I stutter? No? Okay then. I was pretty damn clear, Alpha. I don't want to get into this with my beta here because it's between you and me, but know this..." I walk up to him and jab him in the chest with my index finger. "Those shifters have every right to determine how they want to move forward. Just because you have a god complex doesn't mean you get to tell them how they are supposed to feel safe."

"I am the Alpha of the Council, that's exactly what it means."

"Wrong. That completely invalidates their feelings and puts you in the position of dictator, not alpha. You can give them options, but you have no right to tell them how they're supposed to feel. If any of them want to join my pack after we've settled things a bit more, you're not going to stop them."

He raises his eyebrow. "I'm not?"

"Fuck no."

"You realize I have the authority to remove you as Alpha of the New England Pack and bring you back to the U.K. with the Council, right?"

I throw my head back and laugh. I'm clutching my side as my laughter subsides when I state, "Oh, you were serious?" I blatantly roll my eyes at him before turning and walking away. Olivia walks next to me.

"He's just gaping at you like you have about a thousand heads," Olivia whispers, laughter dancing in her voice.

"Good. I don't take orders from him. I'll work with him because it's in our best interest, but I'm a queen. I outrank him." Olivia nods thoughtfully, a smirk slowly spreading across her face.

I MAKE rounds to everyone who's been injured and ensure that the witches who are healing everyone have everything they need, including a schedule to rest, eat, and get water. They won't be able to help anyone if they collapse. They're instructed to rotate to keep everything running as needed. For the most part, there aren't any extremely serious healings that need to happen, since we were able to have our faster healers tackle those injuries on the field. Still, there were too many deaths. Those are my next priority.

It feels like weeks have passed since I got the initial call from Caleb that the Council was coming to visit. But it was only last night. What time is it? I'm not sure I even know what day it is anymore. Was it only last night I got the call? Has more time gone by? I'm honestly not certain. So many things that need to get done are rattling around in my brain, I can't concentrate on menial things like time.

"*Olivia,*" I call.

"*Ayla, what can I help with?*" At least she doesn't sound as exhausted as I'm sure she feels.

"*I need to talk to the beta of the Rocky Mountain Pack. We need to coordinate going back for the dead.*"

"On it. When do you want to do this?"

"Right away." There's a long pause, and I think she's gone to talk to Caleb and the Rocky Mountain beta. *"When was the last time you ate? Or had water?"*

"I—"

"I'm on it, Olivia. Get everyone in Ayla's sitting room. I'll have food and water brought up," Kelly says through our bond. There are too many voices in my head. I massage my temples and try to think.

Shut down the pack and coven links. Only allow Olivia and Kelly in. It will help. My dragon tries to soothe me, but hearing her only serves to frustrate me more. I have so much to do, there isn't time to sit down and eat. I need to be walking and talking. We need to ensure a respectful send-off for the dead, discuss the Rocky Mountain Pack's plans, figure out what to do with everyone while they're here, ensure deliberations go well with the Council, and I need to get my ass together so I can go hunt that fucker, Malick, down. What happened on that battlefield was a disaster. I could have gotten both myself and Caleb killed. If the barrier hadn't come down, we'd both be dead.

Calm. My dragon's firm demand rings in my head, causing me to wince. *You need to remain calm. Just like the witches, you're no good to anyone running on empty. Right now, just tackle meeting with Caleb and the Rocky Mountain beta. That's all that needs to be settled right at this moment. And eat. We can't get weak.* She has me there.

Fine. I head for my sitting room. It's a small room that's directly across the hall from my bedroom. I flick my hand at the fireplace and fire roars to life. While it's the middle of the summer, my dragon and I both need the heat, it'll help me settle.

"That's handy." Caleb's comment drifts from the corner of the room and I jump.

"It is," I reply blandly, trying to cover up my startle and subsequent flash of lust over his close proximity.

"Look, Ayla." He steps out of the corner and comes over to me. I back away, but he simply corners me against the closed door, bringing both of his arms to either side of my body. "We're going to need to talk about things."

I carefully smooth out my expression before replying, "I'm not sure what you mean."

His chest is pressed up against mine when he growls, and I can feel the vibrations down to my toes. It causes pleasure to fly through my body, heat pooling between my legs. He takes a deep breath, his eyes flickering to his dragon's.

"Don't play stupid." His dragon's voice rumbles with his, causing me to shudder as I attempt to avoid rolling my hips against his. "We both feel the heat."

"No." I state firmly. "We don't."

A dark chuckle leaves him as he leans in to sniff my neck. "Liar." I hate that he's right. My dragon purrs low in my throat, catching me off guard. "At least your dragon isn't trying to ignore what's going on." He's got a smug smile on his face, and I can't decide if I want to smack or kiss it off.

"Just because I find you physically appealing—"

"We. Are. Mates." There's a threat in his tone, daring me to deny what we are to each other. But that's what I have every intention of doing. I won't belong to the Alpha of all alphas, and over my dead body will I go with the Council.

"We aren't anything."

There's a soft knock on the door, but Caleb doesn't move. I glare up at him. If this is a dominance struggle, I'm happy to sit here all damn day.

"I can smell how I affect you, Ayla."

"That doesn't mean we're mates."

A low rumble rolls through his chest, vibrating my chest and causing more liquid heat to flash through my veins. He leans in to smell my neck again, staying there. "Your scent lies, queen." He lightly rolls his hips across mine, letting me feel how hard he is.

A part of me preens. My dragon is also thrilled that we've aroused our mate. *No. Keep it in your damn pants.*

But his nice penis...

Doesn't play into this. Shut. Up. An image of his nice penis flashes through my head and my hips involuntarily arch against his. Damn it. *Bad body. Stop it.*

"Uh, guys?" a male calls through the door, and Caleb lets out a threatening snarl, which causes me to roll my eyes. "Sorry to interrupt, but we're all waiting to sit down and talk."

My eyebrow shoots up at Caleb. He looks as though he's struggling not to punch whoever is outside the door. Ah, blue balls.

"We are not done here."

"Yeah," I scoff, "okay." He glares at me but moves back to his corner. I take a seat as far away from him as possible. He shoots me a satisfied smirk. *Dick.* My dragon perks up.

Dick? Are we getting dick?

For the love of—No!

But...Why?

Seriously? Fucking seriously? I can sense my dragon pouting, and I want to strangle her.

Kelly, Olivia, and three men enter the room. I study all three intently. Two are shifters, and the third is a witch. Interesting. One of the shifters, while tall, is not nearly as tall as Caleb and the other shifter that approaches him, they're small mountains. The shorter male smells of leopard, which is rare. He has short, light brown hair and brown eyes. There's nothing especially remarkable about him aside from his shifter, which means he's lethal.

"He's the beta of the Rocky Mountain Pack. Patrick," Olivia provides. Damn, clearly I hadn't shut down the pack link.

"Who are the other two?" I broadcast this to both Olivia and Kelly.

It's Kelly who answers, *"Connor and Malcolm, they're with the Council. Connor is the blond and Malcolm is the brunette."* I raise my eyebrows. Connor, the blond, is dressed in a three-piece suit and what smells like handmade leather shoes. While his hair is on the longer side, it's pulled back in a stylish manbun that draws the eye to his ice-blue eyes. His face is freshly shaven, which is rare for a shifter male, especially a wolf. But—I inhale deeply— he's a dire wolf? Also rare. Malcolm, on the other hand, has hair down to his shoulders and is dressed like a stereotypical hipster, complete with large-rimmed glasses over his dark brown eyes. His beard is trimmed close to his face. I would have figured the wolf to be the disheveled hipster, not the witch. Rock on.

"They insisted on sitting in." Olivia sounds annoyed, which has me fighting a smile.

"Why don't we all sit, gentlemen?" I gesture to the sofas opposite the chair I'm sitting in. Kelly, who placed a large tray of food on the coffee table in front of me, is sitting on the loveseat next to me with Olivia. Patrick, Connor, and Malcolm all sit, but Caleb remains standing in his corner, eyes fixed on me. I'm painfully aware of his gaze despite studiously avoiding looking in his direction. Patrick eagerly leans forward, placing his elbows on his knees.

"My pack, those of us who are healthy enough anyway, have all decided we would like to join your pack, my queen." Caleb grunts at that. "It was miraculous seeing you over the battlefield, my lady." He stops when I hold up a hand.

"Please, there's no need to call me 'queen' or 'my lady,' just Ayla is fine."

"B-But," he stammers, "you're not just anything! You are a

queen, a powerful alpha." Way to make this hella awkward, dude.

"I understand, Patrick." He beams when I say his name. "But I would much rather you call me by my name. All of my community does." I smile at him and he nods.

"Yes, my—Ayla."

"The Council doesn't think you should join with the New England Pack," Caleb calls gruffly from the corner he's occupying. I finally turn toward him.

"Please, Alpha, tell us why this is a Council matter to begin with." My tone has the tenor of someone talking to an internet troll.

"All pack matters are Council matters, Alpha." It's Connor who answers, and he has a genuine smile on his face, so I give him one of my own. "I understand that you might not be aware of Council policy, but we do make it a point to know and monitor when packs merge. We do the same for covens and nests." So shifters aren't the only ones being monitored by the Council, witches and vampires are watched too. While it makes sense, the queens had never tried to have this sort of hold over the different species. It doesn't sit well with me.

"I can certainly appreciate that," I respond, "However, wouldn't you agree that the wishes of the individual shifters should be honored? Unless you feel the New England Pack does not have sufficient space, resources, or anything else that would prevent the Rocky Mountain Pack from joining our community."

"You see," Malcolm begins, "with a legion of demons headed by an archdemon on the loose, especially one that has already attacked the Rocky Mountain Pack, it would be safer for the pack to join with the Council." Enter lawyer Ayla.

"I would argue the exact opposite. Based on Jonas's memories" —I don't miss the sharp look Connor and Malcolm share— "the legion didn't attack until after the

Council arrived on Rocky Mountain territory. Had they wanted to attack the pack, they would have done so before the Council arrived, it would have been far easier that way. No offense." I throw the last part out to Patrick, but he merely nods in agreement. "Therefore, it certainly wouldn't be safer with the Council, as they are the true targets of the legion. And let's address the elephant in the room, shall we? The pack is far safer here in an integrated community headed by a queen than they are with you." I make sure to use my best condescending tone.

"It remains to be seen if you will be staying here, Alpha." Caleb's timbre is low and dangerous, hinting at his dragon.

"How so?" The entire room stills. Everyone's eyes ping-pong between the two of us.

"You belong to me," his hisses. The flames in the fireplace flare, turning from red to blue as I struggle to control my anger. My dragon roars in my head. While she might agree with Caleb that we're mates, she does not like the word "belong." We don't "belong" to anyone. Period.

"Come again?" I ask sweetly. Kelly and Olivia tense next to me, well aware of the danger that tone indicates.

His voice is all dragon when he replies, "You. Belong. To. Me."

Chapter Eight

Y*ou. Belong. To. Me.*

CALEB'S WORDS echo loudly in my head as the fire continues to burn blue and the lights in the room start to flicker. Kelly looks to the other councilmen, while Olivia appears downright giddy. Patrick is flicking his gaze between Caleb and me, and the other councilmen are tense, ready to spring into action if needed.

"That's what I thought you said, but I needed to be sure you were stupid enough to actually say that out loud." Caleb takes a step toward me. "Patrick, your request has been granted." Connor and Malcolm look like they're about to argue, but I drop the hold I have on my dominance, flooding the room with power. Connor and Malcolm both instantly close their mouths, their eyes round. Caleb has to clutch the back of the couch to remain standing. Connor, Malcolm, and Patrick all slide to the floor.

"I'm pulling rank. If you have an issue with that, take it up with the twat behind you. Make sure you teach him about women too, I'm not convinced he knows where the clit is." I stand and march out of the room, Kelly and Olivia rushing out after me. A low roar reverberates through the hall from my sitting room, but I ignore it. Fuck fragile male egos.

"While that was amusing, I'm not sure that pissing off the Alpha of the Council is the best thing to do here," Kelly, always the voice of reason, remarks.

"It's not my intention to piss him off. But he doesn't get to make decisions he has no right making simply because he has a penis, and he thinks that makes him the boss." My blood is boiling. "But if it makes you feel any better, I'll talk to him tonight to make sure he understands why I just did what I did."

"You don't owe anyone an explanation. But smoothing over ruffled feathers might be a start toward making sure he doesn't just pick you up caveman-style and leave with you." Kelly has a point.

"He could try. But we all know he can't just up and take an alpha away from a pack. Unless I renounce my title or I'm overthrown, it would cause complete and utter chaos. He'd then need to fix that chaos. Not to mention the issues it would bring about in the coven. He's better off just leaving me here. He knows it, which is why he's acting like a petulant child."

"Do what you feel is right, we know you have the best interest of the community at heart, Ayla, especially after what just happened. But I personally think you should treat this a little more carefully. I don't want to see him lose it."

I sigh. "Point taken."

～

LATER THAT NIGHT, I make my way to the house that was given to Caleb and his fellow councilmen. My head is pounding, and I have no idea what to say to Caleb once I see him again. His caveman attitude is going to drive me insane.

The mating instinct isn't helping things. Remember, his brain is screaming that you're his mate and he wants to protect you, my dragon reminds me.

That's not how things work with queens. My dragon is taking his side? Seriously?

But it has actually been that way with queens. They needed their mates when they went into battle. Working as a team, a queen and her mate are far stronger together than any legion of demons.

That's the issue though, working as a team. He doesn't seem to be much of a team player.

And he won't, not until we fully bond with him. Annoyed, I shove her to the back of my head. While I can admit she's right, a mate would make me stronger, this particular mate would only cause far more issues than I want to deal with right now. Especially considering I've got to hunt down and kill Malick. We don't have time for childish games, we need to focus on the real issue here.

Sighing, I walk up the steps to the front door of the house and knock. I can sense Caleb is awake in the living room of the house. The fact that I am this aware of him already irritates me further. But I take several deep breaths while he makes his way to the door in an effort to calm myself. Going into this conversation in an adversarial way is only going to make him a dead man, a. And me the most wanted on the Council's hit list for murdering the Alpha of all alphas.

He doesn't look surprised to see me when he pulls open the door. Instead, he grunts and gestures for me to move to the lawn chairs in the front yard, following closely behind me. Awareness floods my system. I can feel his eyes burning their way down my body, leaving flames licking at my skin in their wake. Heat curls through my veins, leaving me wet and aching. Damn it. I hate that he can do this to me and I can't even see him. What the hell is wrong with me?

Mating heat.

Shut. Up.

We each take a seat and sit in awkward silence for a minute. I'm still struggling to find a way to explain why I need him to not be a caveman.

"I..." He stops and clears his throat. "I...apologize...for how I came across earlier." Well, that sounded like he'd just swallowed razor blades. I'm secretly happy this is difficult for both of us.

"I need to explain myself." Since we both seem so awkward about apologies, may as well throw my hat in.

"No. No, you don't. I shouldn't have used our mate bond like that." His voice is low, and he looks thoughtful.

"While I agree, you absolutely should not have used whatever is going on like that, I still need to explain." I take a deep breath before continuing. "I understand things are... difficult between us right now. But I need you to think about the packs merging from a more logical standpoint. It doesn't make sense to uproot all those people and move them to Council territory in a completely foreign country. While it'll be a big adjustment for them moving from one side of the continent to the other, at least it's the same country." I look over at him to see him staring at me, that thoughtful expression still on his face.

"Not only that, but the Council wouldn't have gotten involved had they petitioned us outside of current events. It would have just been paperwork for you. Yes, if you honestly thought that their pack was being pressured into joining ours you could step in, but aside from that, you wouldn't have. You only stepped in because you assumed I would be leaving the New England Pack to be with you. Therefore, the Rocky Mountain Pack should just go with the Council too."

He looks as though he's about to say something, but I raise my hand to stop him.

"Let me finish." I sigh and run my hand through my hair. "I need you to understand that I will not just up and leave this community. Especially not now that we've painted a large neon target on our backs. I am safer here with my community. I know I have a lot of work to catch up on in order to take Malick down, but that all needs to happen here, with my people. And frankly, I'm not willing to leave them even after all of this is over."

He's quiet for a moment before stating, "I see."

"Do you?" My question isn't meant to sound offensive. It comes out soft and uncertain.

"I do, actually, and I suppose if I were in your shoes, I'd feel exactly the same way. We do need to figure this out, Ayla. We're mates." He sounds contemplative, not argumentative, but there's enough stubbornness still in his tone to keep my feathers good and ruffled.

"We can't be if you're going to force me away from my people." And before he can answer, I'm up and striding back to the house. I'm fighting against every urge in my body to go back to him, curl up against his chest, and just let him make everything okay because it's *not* going to be okay. I also don't feel like arguing with him, and he needs to think about what this all means now that I've had my say.

It's almost dawn the next day when I finally get to head to my room for some rest. I'm exhausted, my heart is heavy, my limbs are tingling, and I can't feel my face. I sluggishly realize I haven't eaten, despite Kelly having brought all that food to the meeting earlier in the day. Fuck boys and their stupid heads. Yet another thing I can hold against Caleb. He food-blocked me and I'm hangry. I'm far too tired to get food for myself now. My eyes are heavy, and I just want to flop into my bed. I also refuse to make someone else bring me food.

The door to my room closes with a soft *snick* behind me, and I wave my hand to ensure it's magically locked to keep people away. Which typically isn't something I do unless my room is empty, but with the twat-waffle, food-blocker wandering around, I don't want to take any chances.

Look, I know you want him, but you have to agree he's an idiot, I tell my dragon.

He's struggling with the mating heat.

I know it sucks, but that's not an excuse to be a turd.

Would it really be so bad to mate with him?

You're kidding, right? Do you want to become a science experiment? Do you want to be locked away? We'd lose everything we've just gained.

You don't know that.

You're right, I concede. *But he hasn't given us any assurances that it won't happen either. Don't let the vag make the decisions here. We can just as easily take the edge off ourselves.* That actually doesn't sound too bad, but I'm too dead to actually do anything right now. I sleepily wave my hand over my body, magically stripping myself before collapsing into bed. My eyes are closed and I'm dead to the world before my head even hits the pillow.

I'M DREAMING, I know I have to be dreaming, but my dreams are strange, flashes of the past mixed with what I assume are my fears for the future. I hope they're my fears for the future. I'm not gifted with premonitions, unlike my oldest sister, but

I've learned never to assume anything. Still, the flashes all happen so fast it's hard keeping track of what I'm seeing.

My mother in battle, her silver scales flashing in the sunlight, flames spilling from her mouth.

Malick standing over my naked body, his eyes glowing with lust. My arms and legs are bound to a stone surface. I struggle, but he only gets closer.

Flames. Red. Blue. Orange.

My father's broken body covered in blood, his lifeless eyes staring up from a field of thistle.

My sisters, each encased in tombs of glass, as shadows dance around them in glee.

A set of glowing red eyes.

Darkness.

The sound of laughter echoing from all directions, sending a shiver down my spine.

Malick's voice ringing in my ear. "Do you know the real reason your kind was hunted to extinction, little queen?"

The lick of a whip against my back, the searing pain, and the explosion of the crack as the whip snaps against my skin.

Screams. My own. My mother's. Echoing screams.

The flashes fade. I'm surrounded by complete blackness. I strain my eyes in an attempt to see anything, but even with my enhanced shifter sight, I can't make out anything but darkness. I turn, trying to look in another direction, but nothing. Spinning to look behind me, I notice a pair of gleaming red eyes. I remain calm, fighting to keep my heart from racing.

"Ah! Little queen! I was so hoping you would join me tonight."

Malick? My dragon doesn't answer. I take a deep breath in an effort to remain calm.

"I can practically hear that wonderful brain of yours spinning, my dear." He sounds utterly delighted.

"Where the hell am I?"

"Why, you're in my mind, little queen." His mind? How the fuck did I end up here?

"You see, when I stabbed you with my little rock dagger earlier, I left a little piece of myself in you. I can't have you just disappearing on me again, now can I?" My heart sinks. How did I not notice anything demonic in my body?

"What the hell are you talking about?" I fight to keep the panic from edging into my voice.

"I can't spoil the surprise!" He claps his hands and light floods my vision, blinding me. "Now that we're both here, let's have a little chat and get to know one another, yes?" He's sitting on a large leather chair in his human form, dressed in a three-piece suit. He snaps his fingers, and another leather chair appears next to his.

I look down at myself and am relieved to see I'm dressed, though a full-length gown isn't what I was expecting to find. Malick holds his hand out to the chair, clearly indicating that I should take a seat. I remain standing.

"Now, now, my dear. You can't leave until I let you, so I insist you take a seat." A hard edge lines his tone, and I'm flung into the chair next to him. "Wonderful! Now that that's settled, let's chat. How on earth did you manage to slip by me all these years? You're fully grown!"

I keep my mouth shut. Displeased, Malick's eyes narrow into slits. He snaps his fingers again and vines shoot out of the chair, large thorns growing along them, digging into my skin. I grit my teeth. This is only a dream, he can't actually hurt my body, which is safely back in my bed.

"I asked you a question, little queen. I highly suggest you answer it."

He said that I couldn't leave this place unless he releases me. I find this hard to believe. There has to be a way to get out of this. Keeping him talking may just buy me enough time to figure out how. So I let my magic flow into my body, grateful that I haven't lost it like I've lost my dragon. I need to start searching for a hole in this illusion.

"I'm the only queen left. I blocked any sort of supernatural signature I gave off and lived as a human for most of my life."

"Now that doesn't seem right. You were born to rule! Why would you settle for something so pedestrian?" I raise my eyebrow at him, reaching further out with my magic.

"Really? Queens were being hunted. Why the hell wouldn't I hide?"

"We both know it's not in your makeup to hide."

"No. It went against every instinct I have. But I did it because the last thing I wanted was to end up surrounded by a legion of demons, dead."

He tsks.

"You were hiding from more than just me, little queen, weren't you?" He smirks and taps a finger to his temple. He can't possibly know what I'm currently thinking, or these thorns would have shredded me by now. So how does he know I was also hiding from the Council?

"I don't know what you mean." Playing dumb always works.

"Of course you do, my dear. Bringing attention to yourself would put you on a collision course with the Council." His smirk widens. "I see you still haven't finalized the bond with your supposed mate."

"There is no supposed about it. He's my mate." Even though it makes the thorns dig deeper into me, I straighten my back, my eyes narrowing. "Whether we've sealed the bond or not doesn't matter. We're fated to be together."

That wasn't what he wanted to hear. His rage is almost palpable, pulsing through the air like a living thing. The thorns dig even farther into my flesh, the vines tightening painfully around my body.

"I think it's time you learn not to make me angry." His tone is quiet and surprisingly calm.

Flames start licking along the vines. While most fire won't hurt me, this isn't ordinary fire, it's hellfire. And while I know my body won't physically be hurt, that doesn't mean my brain won't register the pain. The flames start to caress my skin and my muscles spasm as pain racks every nerve inside me. I viciously bite my lip to keep from screaming. Oh God, the flames are edging along the thorns as well, allowing the hellfire to burrow into my flesh.

My eyes roll into the back of my head, and my body starts convulsing uncontrollably. Try as I might to keep myself from screaming, I fail.

Chapter Nine

I gasp for breath, my eyes flying open and my body aching from the force of my shudders. I can still feel the phantom hellfire licking along the inside of my body. It takes a moment for my vision to focus, but when it does, I notice Caleb is leaning over me with one hand resting on my cheek. How the hell did he get in here? My mind is still fuzzy and sluggish, the pain taking forever to recede. I'm having a hard time concentrating on any one thought.

Didn't I lock the door before I passed out? I try to remember, but my brain just isn't functioning properly. The damn thing is still repeating the torture we'd just been through. Slowly, incrementally, I register that I'm not in danger anymore.

"I could hear you screaming." Caleb's voice, mixed with that of his dragon's, blasts into my mind, and I wince at the volume, but it's at least taken my mind off of Malick and his damn hellfire.

How? That's a mate thing. I shouldn't be able to hear Caleb in my mind until we've started forming a bond. While I'm a bit fuzzy on the specifics, I know that shouldn't happen unless both mates accept what's going on. I absolutely have *not* accepted even the slightest possibility of us being mates. Nope. Not even a little.

"*We* are *mates. Our dragons can talk to each other, and we can speak to each other through them, even if we haven't sealed the bond. Didn't you know that?*" He sounds concerned and confused, having clearly heard my thoughts. Should I have known that the bond would start without us actively trying? Is that a normal mate thing? I might have slept through the birds and the bees talk my mother gave me, far more interested in swords than boys, but I'm pretty sure I would have remembered that little nugget of information.

The bond has already started, Ayla, my dragon informs me. *Fate can't be cheated. Our magic has already started to tie me to his dragon. The bond will be complete once you and Caleb officially mate, connecting your human halves.* I feel like snarling. Of course, my dragon had to go and start the bonding process without my knowledge. Not for the first time, I curse being a queen.

Over my dead body, I snarl, mentally snapping my teeth at my dragon. I do not want a mate, much less this one. Mates complicate things, especially the fine piece of man meat sitting on the bed next to me. He is the definition of the word complicated.

"*Why are you so opposed to us?*" It's Caleb's dragon who asks. I slam my mental walls down, even cutting off my dragon. I need a minute without so many other damn voices in my head since I'm still rattled by what just happened with Malick. I knew once mates had solidified the bond they were able to hear each other's thoughts, but I wasn't aware this would happen so soon, especially since the bond hasn't been accepted.

Ayla. My dragon gives me a mental poke. *I've erected a wall between us and them. Talk to me.*

Were you going to tell me that we've started to bond with him?

Do you even care that our lives will be over? What about all that shit you spilled about protecting this community? How can we possibly protect them if we're completely under the thumb of the Council? He is the Council, there is no getting around that. Didn't you notice that both Connor and Malcolm have very rare and powerful gifts? Dire wolves were rumored to have all died out. Malcolm has power that rivals Kelly's, and I'm not sure what his specific gift is yet.* I'm not interested in sharing what I just went through in my dream with her right now. While I'm sure she can sense some of what happened, I don't want to talk about it, I feel betrayed over this bond business.

I should have warned you about the bond when it started forming. A queen's magic will automatically start the bonding process between the dragon spirits. It's meant to provide us with strength and even greater magical power to fight off demons. This isn't a bad thing, Ayla, and I'm sure we can figure out a solution for the Council issue.

That's not how it works, and you know it, I scoff. *You don't* solve *the Council. You get* absorbed *into the Council. Connor and Malcolm are prime examples. Do you honestly think he will willingly give up that sort of power? Especially since he's used to just absorbing any rare or powerful supernatural into his community? I will* not *leave this community vulnerable. Period.*

Can't we at least talk about this with him? I'm not sure why this discussion boils my blood, but it does. I understand that the bond has already started to form, but I have no intention of letting it continue to grow. My dragon's insistence grates on my already frayed nerves. I know I'm not reacting rationally right now, but I can't seem to stop myself.

No, I snap at my dragon, my tone angrier than I intended.

Caleb is watching me intently, and his emotions are seeping through the fragile bond forming between us. He's genuinely confused about why I'm rejecting him despite our earlier conversation, or maybe because of it. He's also worried. Apparently my screaming freaked him out, and since

I can feel his confusion and concern, it's possible he felt my pain. Too bad for him, that's not my issue. I didn't ask him to burst in here...which...he still hasn't told me how he got in here in the first place.

I let him in. My dragon sounds sheepish. *I couldn't wake you.*

Why you sneaky little— I cut myself off, not wanting to snap at her again. After all, she was just trying to make sure I was okay.

"Look, Caleb, I appreciate—" I don't get more out before his lips are on mine. His lust, fueled by the urge to mate, blares through the bond, even though I've still got my wall up. At first, I'm confused, and then I realize I'm still naked. Without a blanket to cover me. In my bed. The mating instinct screams through my body, causing liquid desire to pool between my legs. It's far worse than it was on the battle-field, or even earlier today, and I'm struggling to remind myself that Caleb isn't the mate I want...I think...right? His lips push all thoughts of Malick from my mind, and I'm only able to focus on him. His lips. How they are surprisingly soft yet unyielding.

His hand touches my hip, his thumb rubbing gentle circles along my skin before he slides his palm up to just under my breast, tracing his fingers lightly along the delicate curve there. My brain short-circuits, and instead of lying here inactive, I spring into motion, wrapping my arms around Caleb's neck and burying my hands in his hair. My back arches ever so slightly, trying to guide his hand to my aching nipple, which is already pebbled. I need this. I need to feel, to know I'm not still in that room with Malick with his hellfire scorching along my body. I need to erase the fear and pain I experienced tonight. I'm thankful that the only heat I feel now is lust, and I bask in it, letting it soothe the sting from my body.

A low rumble starts in Caleb's chest, and an answering

purr vibrates through mine, a clear indication of our dragons' approval. I rub my thighs together, trying to ease some of the tension building in my core, but it just serves to frustrate me further, drawing attention to just how empty I feel. I snarl into the kiss, nipping at his lip before lashing my tongue out to invade his mouth. He needs to touch me, damn it.

That thought alone sends my brain skidding to a halt, my body going stiff. I told him he couldn't touch me unless I asked him to, and I haven't asked him to. He lifts his head with a curse, his heated eyes drilling into me, his chest heaving and hair mussed from my hands. My grip goes limp and my arms drop to my bed. Do I dare? It's a line we won't be able to uncross. I'm not sure he will be able to stop himself from fully claiming me if I let this continue. As much as my body may crave his touch, my head still refuses to acknowledge him as my mate.

"Say it." His voice is harsh, his eyes narrowed and focused on my face. I nervously lick my lips, and his eyes hungrily track the movement. His fingers lightly brush against the underside of my breast again, and my breath hitches.

"Say what?" I hate that my response is breathy, needy.

"Say you want me."

My mouth opens to respond that I don't want him, but nothing comes out. My mouth snaps shut. I run my eyes over him. He's sitting on the edge of my bed in a gray t-shirt and black silk boxers. Huh...I took him for more of a briefs kind of guy. He looks good enough to eat and my mouth is water- ing, though I'd prefer it if he wasn't wearing the shirt. Okay, or the boxers.

"Say it, Ayla. I can feel your desire thrumming through the bond, but I need to hear you say it." His voice is low and dangerous, sinking slowly into my body and causing tingles of pleasure to shoot along my spine. My dragon is suspiciously quiet, although I know where she wants this to go, the traitor.

"Promise me you won't complete the bond." His eyes flicker to his dragon's and narrow, a quiet snarl leaving him. "I mean it, Caleb. Promise me you won't complete the bond, or this ends now."

"We don't need to complete the bond tonight." His tone is strained, his eyes closing for a long minute before opening to reveal they've gone back to normal human eyes.

"Then touch me. Now."

That's all the permission Caleb needs. He leans down, crushing his mouth to mine, nipping at my lips before his tongue soothes the sting away. His fingers glide up to gently pinch my nipple. My back arches again, and my hands fly into his hair, securing his lips against mine. I kiss him as aggressively as he kisses me, refusing to hold anything back now that I know this won't end with me as a prisoner or a lab rat.

I have enough forethought to snap my fingers, instantly removing Caleb's clothes before my brain goes entirely to mush. The man can kiss. I won't be surprised if I find my brain on the floor after this. He smiles against my lips once he feels his clothes vanish, an appreciative hum sounding in the back of his throat. He moves his large body to hover over my smaller frame, and for the first time in my life, I feel fragile. It's an odd sensation. The hand not occupied toying with my nipple grabs my left leg and wraps it around his hip as he rests his lower body against mine.

Did I say nice penis? There's nothing nice about this penis. It means business.

I arch against him, trying to ease the ache between my legs. I know how wet I am, and I'm pretty sure I'll need to burn this mattress once we're done. I've never felt this turned on before. Not sure where to focus first, my hands move from his hair to glide down his back, dragging my nails along his skin. My dragon roars with power when he shivers, and I roar along with her. We still haven't broken our kiss, each of us taking frantic breaths through our noses to keep our lips sealed together, our teeth and tongues merged.

My heel digs into Caleb's ass, trying to encourage him to rub against me. He simply bites my lower lip, ignoring my plea. Instead, his hand slides along the inside of my thigh, brushing lightly over my core. Once. Twice. I moan into his mouth, frustrated yet pleased he's finally touching me. But I need more. So much more. And I need it now. Right fucking now.

His chuckle seems to come from everywhere as he pulls his lips from mine, his eyes darkened with desire and a smirk playing across his face.

"Right now?" Ah, fuck. I forgot he can hear me if I don't keep my walls up. "Don't you dare put them back up. I want to feel you everywhere when I finally get to fuck you senseless."

"By all means. But I'm not sure what you're waiting for." I scrape my nails down his arms now, making sure to add additional pressure to emphasize that he needs to fucking move! He chuckles again before nipping my collarbone, instantly licking away the sting. I arch my neck to allow him better access, but he moves my leg off his hip and starts sliding down my body.

"You had better be a pussy eating champ." I make sure to directly aim that thought at him, and I can feel him smirk against my sternum. *"I'm serious. If you're gonna go down on a girl, eat that pussy for days, worship the pussy."*

"You don't need to worry about me worshipping your pussy, babe. You want to be eaten out for days? Fine. Cancel all your plans for the rest of the week." My core clenches, bringing my attention to

how empty I am, and I let out a frustrated groan, which is quickly replaced with a moan when Caleb's mouth latches onto the nipple he had been neglecting.

He suckles, causing me to lift my breast further against his face, his fingers pinching my other nipple. I widen my legs, thrusting my hips up in an attempt to rub against anything I can. Caleb lightly bites down on my nipple before releasing it with an audible pop. He switches to the other nipple and I moan again, weaving my hands into his hair as I try to push him down my body. Eager to experience his pussy eating skills.

When he finishes with my nipples, he moves slowly down my stomach, licking a teasing circle around my belly button before moving down to the apex of my thighs. Finally. But he doesn't dive right in. No. He starts kissing and nibbling on my inner thighs instead, making me want to scream. Fuck this. My hand moves to brush my fingers against my clit, but a warning growl from the male between my legs makes me freeze.

"If you touch this pretty little pussy, I won't eat you out. Choose."

"Eat me out already, you bastard!"

"You may outrank me outside of this bedroom, but in here, I'm the boss." I snort. Yeah, okay. He lifts his head and rests his chin right above my achingly empty core. Smiling, he cocks an eyebrow at me.

"Would you like to debate the issue?"

"No. I don't want to fucking debate anything. I want you to go to town eating me out like I'm your favorite damn meal."

He tsks. "You'll need to ask nicer than that."

My mouth falls open. "Eat. The. Pussy. Now."

"Or what?"

I growl. I didn't want to have to do this. In a lightning-fast move, I have him on his back with my pussy directly over his face. I'm lowering myself down when his hands grip my hips, halting my progress.

"You still haven't asked nicely."

"I will literally smother you with my vagina if you don't eat me out right now." I pause. "Please."

His laughter causes my core to clench again, and I grit my teeth in frustration, but I sigh when his hands tighten around my hips and he holds me firmly against his mouth. About damn time. His tongue does one long sweep over my clit—thank the gods he knows where the clit is—and my hips buck against his face, my head falling back.

"You taste as delicious as you smell." Oh, gods.

That's the only warning I get before he's eating me out with zealous enthusiasm and insane skill. Gods, is his tongue in two places at once? My hands go to my breasts to play with my nipples. Caleb pushes my hips more firmly against his mouth as I ride his face. My orgasm hits me suddenly, and I find myself on my back with Caleb's head still buried between my legs. Only now, two of his fingers are easing into my core, stroking my inner walls as his tongue continues to attack my clit. My orgasm is still going, my pussy desperately clenching around Caleb's fingers as he pumps them in and out of me.

"Again." He growls low, causing his tongue to vibrate and my hips to lift off the bed. Fuck it feels so good. I've barely come down from my first orgasm as my second one begins to build. I pinch my nipples, eager to catapult myself over the edge again. His fingers stroke my pussy faster, harder, deeper. My moans echo around us.

Caleb gently rakes his teeth along my clit. I'm gone. My eyes slide shut as I scream out my second release. I've never been able to come a second time this fast before, and it feels as though I've had several glasses of witch wine. My limbs tingle, my toes curl, and all I can focus on is how tightly I'm clenching around Caleb's fingers, fingers that are now stroking my G-spot, causing this orgasm to stretch out longer than the first.

I want more. So much more.

Chapter Ten

Caleb lifts his head and removes his fingers from my core, slowly licking each one while staring intently at me. I shiver at the sight. His eyes darken before his hand falls from his mouth to grip the base of his cock. A lopsided smirk spreads across his face as he pumps his fist twice, causing my eyes to narrow. I lick my lips, wanting to get that monster in my mouth so badly I'm salivating at the thought.

With a little less grace than I'd like, I move until my face is even with Caleb's cock. My gaze flicks up to his face to find him staring down at me with his dragon's eyes. His hand is still wrapped around the base, so I don't reach out to grab him, I simply lick the head. Humming in pleasure at his taste, I flick my tongue out again, this time dragging slowly over the tip before wrapping my mouth around him.

Caleb curses softly as I begin to suck on the head of his cock, his other hand tangling in my hair to guide me down his shaft. He doesn't know I don't have a gag reflex, so he keeps his hand at the base to ensure that I don't choke on his dick. My hand comes up to wrap around his wrist, pulling his hold away. I release him with an audible pop, moving my eyes back up his body, ensuring I make direct eye contact as I once again take him into my mouth. Hollowing out my cheeks, I glide further along his shaft, watching his face as I do. His eyes are rapidly flicking from dragon to human, an indication he's struggling to maintain control. I take all of him down my throat before swallowing around his cock. His eyes roll into the back of his head, his hand fisting tightly in my hair as he holds me there. I swallow again.

He rips my mouth from his cock, flipping me so I'm on my hands and knees in front of him. One hand is on my hip, and the other is between my shoulder blades. He pushes my chest onto the bed as he positions himself behind me.

"Tell me you want me to fuck you," Caleb growls. He starts to slowly rub the tip of his cock along my slit, causing me to buck against him. A soft snarl echoes through the air as he tightens his grip on my hip, keeping me in place. "If you want this dick, you need to tell me that you want me to fuck you, Ayla."

I groan. I know I told the man he needed my approval to touch me, but I already gave him that earlier. Why drag this out and torture us both? With the way I'm positioned, I can't reach behind me to touch myself or him. I'm left entirely at his mercy. I'm not sure if I love it or hate it.

Caleb once again starts to swirl the tip of his cock along my slit, grazing my clit with each pass. He seems perfectly content to toy with me. My hands dig into my sheets and a soft ripping sound tells me that I'll need to get new ones when we're finished here. If we ever finish.

"Just think about how good your little pussy will feel wrapped around my cock as I slam it in and out of you. You want it fast and rough right now, don't you?" I groan. "The mating instinct is hitting you just as badly as it's hitting me. I want to fuck you so hard you'll be screaming my name." The sheets rip a little more. "Just say it. Say you want me to fuck you."

My lips part, but the words don't come out. I close my mouth, swallow, and try again. "I want you to fuck me." I make sure to say it loud enough that I won't need to say it twice.

Caleb slaps my ass, causing me to moan, right before he slides the head of his cock inside me. Fuck. He's huge.

"I know you'll take all of me." Ah shit, the bond again. But I'm feeling too much pleasure to care what he hears. He puts a bit of pressure between my shoulder blades to tell me not to move before gripping my other hip. Caleb smoothly glides in until he's balls deep inside me. My eyes roll into the back of my head, and a moan slips from my lips. I feel so full.

"Fuck, babe. You're so damn tight." He pulls out until only the tip is inside before slamming home, my hands instantly flying in front of me to brace for the next thrust. Caleb doesn't pause this time, setting a fast, brutal pace that has me seeing stars in seconds. The bed creaks as he continues to pound into me, both of us moaning each time he bottoms out. I clench my pussy tightly around him each time he pulls out, causing him to curse every few strokes. Just when I begin to feel my third orgasm of the night building, he stops with his cock buried deep inside me.

"Move, damn it." My voice is breathy and strained with need. Instead of moving, his hand dips between my legs and starts to flick my clit. He starts grinding his cock deep inside me, not bothering to pull out. Oh, fuck.

My scream as I come a third time turns hoarse, my pussy pulsing rapidly around his cock. Caleb doesn't come and simply continues to grind his cock deep inside me while flicking my clit, dragging out my orgasm. Before I know what's happening, I find myself straddling him, his hands on my hips and his legs braced behind me.

"Play with those pretty pink nipples while you ride me." His timbre is a low growl, his heated eyes racing over my curves.

He lifts my hips, dragging every nerve ending in my pussy along his cock, causing my head to fall back as my fingers pluck at my nipples. Caleb grunts as he slides me down. Before he can lift me again, I start to swivel my hips against his, rubbing my clit against him as often as possible. His grip on my hips tightens and his hips surge up against mine. I grind down harder, faster, my fingers pinching my nipples frantically.

I'm going to come again. I can feel the orgasm building at a blindingly fast rate. I want him to come with me, so I reach behind myself with one hand and start to gently play with his balls. Caleb curses, his hips moving more desperately against mine. His head lurches up and his lips suckle the nipple I abandoned.

I shatter. I can't scream anymore, my mouth falling open silently. I continue to ride the wave, wanting to milk it for everything I can. Caleb shudders beneath me, and I feel his release as his cock pulses deep within my pussy. I'm clenching around him, not willing to let a drop escape. We're both still moving, neither of us willing to stop the pleasure that's flooding our systems.

I collapse against his chest, panting and sweaty. My entire body is limp, and I don't think I can get up even if I wanted to. Caleb's arms come around me, and he holds me close, a low rumbling purr starting up in his chest. I can feel his contentment through our bond and his pride at having made me come multiple times. I'll give it to the guy, he's earned a solid high five and a "good game." He chuckles, apparently picking up on my thoughts again.

"We're going to need to figure things out, Ayla. I'm not

going to wait forever to fully claim you. Especially now that I've tasted you."

Ah, shit.

～

IT's morning when I wake. I feel warmer than usual, and there's a heavy weight wrapped around my waist. My mind is fuzzy, and all I can think about is how badly I need to pee. I blink, dazed, trying to wake myself up enough to stumble to my bathroom without killing myself. I go to roll out of bed when I'm dragged against a very solid, very warm, very naked male body. Alarmed, I look over to see Caleb, who's still asleep.

Ah, fuck.

I had sex with Caleb last night. Mind-blowing, multi-orgasm, best sex of my life sex, but shit...still sex. We've absolutely crossed a line that we can't uncross. But I don't have the mental bandwidth to really think about any of this right now, especially not with my bladder screaming a countdown at me. Prying his arm from around my waist, I roll out of bed and scurry to the bathroom, closing and locking the door. While I may have just had sex with the guy, we're not at an open-door peeing relationship level just yet.

My mind is whirling so fast I can't focus. It's slightly dizzying. I finish in the bathroom and open the door to my room, studying Caleb, who is still passed out, sprawled in my bed. A strange warmth starts to fill my chest as I look at him. No. Panic starts to set in. I refuse to catch feelings for him. Nope. Hard pass.

I'm not going to point out how useless that train of thought is. My dragon sounds smug. Bitch. *I think you should talk to him about logistics. He's our mate, we need to work this out.*

Have you forgotten about the archdemon who killed our mother?

The one that's supposed to be dead? The one we just saw very much alive and leading a giant legion of lesser demons? We should be focused on that, not on the monster dick that can give us orgasms for days.

She goes silent. Neither of us has forgotten, the shock and rage are still fresh in my mind. What we need to be focusing on is how to find and kill that fucker, not how to tie ourselves to the leader of the Council. I press my fingers to my eyelids as I try to remember the last time I saw my mother. How was Malick able to hide himself away for so long? Had I simply been willfully blind?

"You know, thinking that hard before coffee is a sin." Caleb's morning voice sends a bolt of lust straight to my clit, making my core tingle. That damn accent sounds even better when he's just woken up, not fair. "It's recommended to have at least one orgasm and a cup of coffee before thinking that hard in the morning."

"Is that so?" I open my eyes to look at him, amusement lacing my tone. He flashes me a lopsided grin that sends pulses of pleasure shooting throughout my body, and my heart trips over itself.

"Aye." He purposely thickens his brogue, causing me to shiver. "'Tis the way of things, lass."

I roll my eyes and climb back into bed beside him, curling up against his side. I'm not so sure that fooling around this morning is wise, all things considered, but a bit of cuddling couldn't hurt. His arm wraps tightly around me, and he drags me flush against his chest. We fit together nicely, despite the difference in height. That warm feeling is back in my chest, causing me to scowl.

"What's wrong?" he questions softly, his concern evident.

"Malick." That's the safer topic. I don't want to analyze my feelings for him right now. "I don't understand how he's still alive. I thought my mother killed him before she died."

"That is absolutely a problem we won't be able to solve

without coffee." He leans down to nibble on my neck, causing me to shiver again. I gently swat his arm.

"None of that. Kelly and Olivia will be waiting for me this morning. We still have a lot to do."

"Aye." He thickens his accent again, his eyes gleaming playfully.

"I swear." I roll my eyes. "Do you use that accent of yours to your advantage often?"

"Why? Does it provide me an advantage with you?"

"That has yet to be seen." My lips twitch as I fight to suppress a grin.

Caleb lets out a robust belly laugh, leaning down to press a quick kiss to my lips before getting out of bed. He holds his hand out to me.

"Come on then. Let's go take a shower and meet with the others. I'll be needing that coffee before tackling the world's problems today." I take his hand, smiling as we head into the bathroom.

"I'm going to need a boatload of coffee too. Don't worry, we always have a lot stocked here. I'm not too sure about cream and sugar. I take my coffee black." Caleb raises an eyebrow as he looks me up and down.

"A wee thing like you?" I shouldn't have mentioned the accent. He's going to play it up now.

I allow the Irish in me to come flooding back when I reply, "Aye, a wee thing like me indeed."

AN HOUR AND A HALF LATER, Caleb and I are walking into the large dining room of the packhouse, our hair still damp from our shower. While I maintained not having sex, that didn't stop all the touching and tasting. I close my eyes briefly as heat floods through my veins just thinking about last night and this morning. I want him again, my body craving him like a drug.

"I can feel how wet you are," he growls.

"Oh, shut up," I snap.

"Do you want me to pin you to the wall in front of everyone? Have them watch as you scream my name to the heavens? Know that it's your tight little pussy I'm pounding into?"

I shudder, biting my lip to keep me from moaning. *"I said shut up. Don't make me close this bond down."* I feel as though I'm chastising a child.

Caleb simply chuckles and sits down to the left of the head of the table, leaving that spot for me. Kelly is to my right, with Connor beside her. Olivia is next to Caleb, alongside Malcolm and then Patrick.

"So, are Connor and Malcolm the only other actual councilmen here?" My eyes bounce between the two men.

"Yes. The others we brought with us are envoys that will be staying with various packs, covens, and nests. We also brought along warriors in case we ran into some rouges or demons," Connor states as he starts to scoop up some eggs that have been placed in the middle of the table.

"It's pretty standard," Malcolm continues, also helping himself to the breakfast spread. "Our envoys often find mates within the communities that we send them to, so we like to switch them out to allow them to be with their mates and start a family." Interesting.

"Ayla, about yesterday," Olivia chimes in, a guilty look on her face. "You're still sure you are okay with the Rocky Mountain Pack joining ours?"

"Of course!" I smile at Patrick, who nods his thanks.

"We've talked about it. I shouldn't have pushed things the way I did," Caleb says, glancing at Olivia who has a stunned look on her face. "The Rocky Mountain Pack had every right to seek asylum with the New England Pack, and had it not been for the demons, the Council wouldn't have even thought twice about the two packs merging. While we shouldn't negate the demon attack, it doesn't have any influence on the merging of your communities."

Stunned silence blankets the table. Clearly, Caleb doesn't admit he's wrong very often. Connor and Malcolm are both staring at Caleb as though he's grown a second head. I can practically hear them mentally talking.

"Well," Connor grumbles awkwardly, coughing to cover up his astonishment. "Now that that's settled, we should discuss the demons. What happened at the summit of that mountain? We need all the information both of you can give us. Then we need to send out teams to deal with the dead that were left behind. We'll also need to dispatch our best spies and trackers to hunt that legion down. We can't allow them to destroy any more communities. They were after something; we need to figure out what it was before they attack again."

"Before we give our account of what happened on the summit, I want to know what happened leading up to the battle, and during, from your side of things. It might help me better understand what Malick was after." I look between the four males at the table. The silence stretches for longer than usual, which means that the three councilmen are having another mental conversation. I start in on my breakfast while I wait for them to figure out how they want to share what occurred. Patrick appears to want to wait for them to begin before adding events from his point of view, which is fine.

My gut is telling me that Malick is the demon behind the missing shifter females. I don't have proof, but it's just too strange that dominant females start going missing because of an alpha with ties to demons, only to have another pack get attacked by a legion of demons led by an archdemon. I studied Patrick's aura before agreeing to take his pack into mine, but what if his alpha was doing the same as Morgan? Or someone else in his pack? Shit. I'm going to need to meet and interview everyone from the Rocky Mountain Pack to be sure no one coming into my community has ties with demons.

My eyes flick to Caleb's. I have more to tell him, and I can only hope I can trust him with everything.

Chapter Eleven

"**B**efore we do that," Connor interjects, "I'd like to know what happened to the messenger we sent— Jonas. I attempted to track him down yesterday, but with all the chaos, it was hard to figure out exactly where he was."

"I've moved him to a room here in the house. It's been warded to keep people away since he still has a long way to go before he's fully recovered." Kelly smiles over at Connor. "I can take all of you to see him after breakfast if you'd like."

"What do you mean 'fully recovered?' He was perfectly fine when we sent him off." Malcolm and Connor share a concerned look. Caleb merely narrows his eyes on me.

He's already assuming I did something!

Well... We technically did *do something*, my dragon points out.

But he *doesn't know that. Why does he have to assume it was me? Fucking rude.*

"We aren't sure what happened to him before he showed up in town," I inform them. "But he was pretty close to death when he got to us. I could feel the demonic aura once everyone in town had been tucked away. I initially thought he was working with the demons." When all three councilmen go to speak, I glare and hold my hand up. "We had no way of knowing he was with you. There wasn't anything on his person to suggest he was with the Council, and he was dead to the world. I needed to make the safety of my community my first priority."

"How did you know where we were and that we needed help?" Caleb remarks, his eyes still glued to me.

"I, uh..." I flick my gaze over at Olivia and Kelly, mentally nudging them to be on guard because the three males in front of us might freak out. "I might have done a little digging in his head."

I can feel the shocked rage that flies through Caleb thanks to our bond. Connor and Malcolm, judging by the expressions on their faces, are feeling similarly. Witches can dive into a person's mind, but it takes someone with a great deal of power to do so. It is also frowned upon by the Council because not only can it permanently damage an individual's mind, but it is also extremely excruciating physically because of the drain on the diver's magic.

"Look," I start in self-defense, "I honestly thought he was working with demons and he had led them right to us. The instant I realized who he was and why he had been sent here, I pulled out of his mind. He was also unconscious, so the damage to his mind should be minimal because he wasn't able to fight back."

"He doesn't appear to be brain damaged," Olivia chimes in cheerfully, a pleased grin stretched across her face. I fight the urge to facepalm. "I brought him some dinner last night. I had to have a community member bring him food this morning because of our meeting, but he's awake at least. And he's not drooling or anything, seems to have all of his motor functions. Not sure how bright he was before the mind dive, but he doesn't seem to be dumber than a rock or anything like that. Hell, if he was before, maybe Ayla actually helped him."

I groan internally.

"He will be fine, physically, in a few days. As I'm sure you all know, demonic wounds take a bit longer to heal, and his wounds were extensive. Based on my preliminary analysis, he'll fully recover mentally as well." Kelly glances between the three angry males with a kind smile.

"You had no right," Caleb grits out between his teeth.

"What would you have done? An unknown shifter suddenly appears out of thin air, nothing around him to suggest he was sent by friendlies, and he can't speak because he's barely clinging to life. When you're finally able to sense something, you realize there's demonic energy everywhere around where this mysterious shifter showed up. You can't question the shifter because he's still out cold. If there was a potential threat to your community would you just wait for it to come at you, or would you attempt to figure out when and how it's coming?" My eyes drill into Caleb, and I allow my own rage to blast through the bond.

"Look" —Connor holds his hands up, drawing everyone's attention— "right or wrong, it's been done. We can check in on Jonas after the meeting. While we certainly don't condone delving into someone's mind, given the circumstances, I think we need to move on here."

Connor's right, there's no point in arguing about this now. If Caleb wants to plant the damn flag here, that's on him. I know that, while not optimal, diving into Jonas's mind was the best decision at the time. We both know that Caleb, if he had the ability to do so, would have absolutely done the same thing.

"Patrick," Olivia calls, "why don't you recount what happened before the Council arrived? Then the councilmen

can give us their account. We'll fill in the blanks from there."
Patrick nods and takes a deep breath.

"We've had females going missing for about five years
now." My body stiffens. Five years? "My alpha had been investi-
gating, but every time he seemed to get close, evidence would
vanish. Most of the females would show up dead a few months
after they went missing, typically dumped in the surrounding
human towns and cities. I was concerned and kept telling
Sean, our alpha, that we needed to reach out to the Council,
but he was confident he had the situation handled."

I suppress the urge to snort. I just bet he had the situation "handled," but not reporting any of this for five years?
Was Patrick in on all of this?

"Admittedly, I hadn't been beta very long, and I'm sure
Sean didn't like hearing his orders questioned. His old beta
died, I'm still not sure how, and I won the challenges for the
position about a year ago. Everyone in the pack knew about
the missing females, but we all assumed Sean really did have
it handled. It wasn't until I became beta that I started to
notice some weird things going on. A lot of the females who
went missing dated Sean's friends. Now, I won't say that Sean
had any hand in what happened, but I couldn't just sit quietly
any longer. So I called the Council in to investigate."

"When Patrick told us what was happening, we realized
we needed to come see everything and talk to Sean
ourselves," Connor continues. "We should have been
informed of the missing females well beforehand, and it
concerned us that we hadn't heard even a rumor of any
missing females or their deaths."

"We made our way out to the pack with the intention of
putting the heat on Sean, especially since he should have
come to us about this," Malcolm explains. "We did a bit of
digging into the pack's paperwork, and we found some

random deposits into Sean's personal bank account. When we were able to determine who they were from, it confused us. A local drug lord, a human drug lord, had been wiring money to Sean. The times didn't line up with the missing females, but it was odd enough for us to ask him about it. Sean merely admitted to helping test drugs for shifters."

Drugs for shifters? Most shifters wouldn't ever put drugs in their bodies. We're raised to cherish our bodies and what they can do. Besides, adding magic to drugs is a tricky business and can go horribly wrong. Thank the gods alcohol isn't that risky, we need some way to let loose.

"Before we got a chance to dig any deeper, the demons launched their attack. Took us completely by surprise. I have no idea how they knew we were even in the Rocky Mountains. They weren't on our itinerary, we had been on a tour to change our representatives in Canadian, American, and Mexican communities when we got the call about Patrick's pack." Caleb sounds frustrated and rakes a hand through his hair. "Which tells me one of the pack members called them in."

All eyes go to Patrick, who is pale and looks horrified. I would be too if someone had lobbed that at me. But he really shouldn't be all that surprised, and he should have realized it himself. Though I ought to go a little easier on him since yesterday had been a complete shitshow. If Sean had been colluding with demons, it's possible more members of the pack were in on it. I close my eyes to read his aura—nothing demonic. I'll need to see Sean's body to determine if he was tainted, and I'll need to go through every member of Patrick's pack to make sure that no one else is working with the demons. The last thing we need is for the legion to attack us here.

"Alpha, I..." Patrick swallows, and his eyes frantically meet mine. "I have no idea how the demons found us. I swear."

"He's telling the truth." My voice doesn't allow room for arguments. "His aura is clean. He wasn't working with the demons." Surprisingly, Caleb nods and doesn't comment. Patrick slumps in relief. "Olivia, Kelly, I need you both to take Connor and Malcolm to see Jonas and round up the Rocky Mountain Pack with Patrick. I need to fill the Alpha in on things here. We'll keep the bonds open so everyone can stay in the loop." They nod and get up to leave, Patrick shakily scrambling to do the same. Connor and Malcolm, however, don't budge.

Caleb nods his head, and only then do they follow the others out of the room. If I wanted to push the matter, I could demonstrate that they have to obey me over Caleb, but it's not worth my time. If they want to act like children, that's on them. Caleb and I have a lot to talk about.

AFTER I'M through telling Caleb about the last six months, we each refill our coffee and head out into the yard. I need some fresh air. My head is buzzing with all the information I've learned, and I'm trying to piece it all together. Why do the demons want female shifters? Why the hell do they want drugs for shifters? Why use the humans at all?

"There are a lot of similarities between what was happening with the Rocky Mountain Pack and what happened here." Caleb's words rip me out of my thoughts. "You said that Morgan was tainted. Would you be able to tell if Sean was tainted, even though he's dead?"

"Yeah. It's not as easy, but if he spent the last five years having dealings with demons, the taint should be pretty strong. My concern is the rest of his pack. What if he wasn't the only one who was involved? I'm going to need to meet with each member of the pack to know for certain."

"Why don't we go back to the Rockies today and find Sean's body? We'll see if you feel anything else while we're there. We can tackle the pack tomorrow. I don't want you overdoing it. You're the only one here who can sense these fuckers before they come. We need you at the top of your game."

I bristle at the implication that merely searching for demonic energy will weaken me. But after my performance against Malick, I suppose I would question Caleb's strength and stamina if our positions were reversed.

"Fine. But we take a team with us to handle the dead. Then I want to train. I'm clearly a little rusty, and I need to degrease the wheels, as it were, before facing off against Malick again."

"You won't be facing him alone."

"That's not the point." I sigh, running my hand down my face. "I need to beef up if I'm going to take him out. And we need to learn how to work better as a team. You can't alpha-hulk-out every time there's a demon around me. I was made for this."

"I'll stop being so protective once the bond is fully formed." I wince at his words. "You know that's not just a dragon thing. All males are a bit more protective of their mate until the bond is whole."

The kicker is, he's right. Unless I fully bond with Caleb, he's going to be a hulking caveman who pounds his chest at any threat. That could be a demon or a rival male. Hell, someone could look at me the wrong way and it might set him off. He seems stable enough now, but I'm not sure how long that will last. Damn it, I knew I shouldn't have had sex with him. That makes this so much worse.

"I'm trying to stay out of your head, Ayla, but I can feel how hard you're thinking."

"I'm not ready for the bond. I told you last night that I

won't leave my community. And I doubt you're willing to give up being the head of the Council. So this isn't going to work."

He growls and steps in front of me, right in my space. I have to tilt my head back to look him in the eye.

"We are mates. You know this. The bond is already forming."

"That doesn't mean I have to let it finish forming."

He snarls at my words. "I'll give you time, but we are going to finish this bond." His brogue is thick and causes shivers to run down my spine. "You are mine. I am not letting you go. End of story."

I sigh and shake my head, deciding it's not worth my time or energy to fight with him. He didn't even mention leaving the Council, which tells me he won't, and he expects me to leave my community. There is no way I will do that. These people are etched into me now. I'm going to have to keep my distance from here on out. I can't let the bond progress any further than it already has. Maybe I can see if the witches know of a way to stop or sever the bond.

I won't let you sever the bond, my dragon roars.

I don't think you're in a position to do anything. This can't happen. She claws inside me, raging over the fact that I won't just accept Caleb.

A witch comes jogging up to us before we can continue our discussion.

"Alpha." He nods to Caleb. "High Priestess, there is an envoy of vampires here. They wish to talk to you."

Shock runs through me. I knew vampires might eventually find their way to me, but I didn't expect it to be so soon. Contrary to popular fiction, vampires don't burst into flames in the daylight. It does severely weaken them, and they need to feed more often if they're going to be day-walkers, but it's doable. Typically, only the older vampires choose to day-walk, since the older a vampire is, the more powerful they are, and they're less likely to be drained quickly.

"Bring them to my sitting room." The witch nods and races off. I turn to Caleb, who has his narrow eyes trained on my face. "No, you can't come. If they came to talk to me, this is my community's business, not Council business." He growls but doesn't argue. "Why don't you go see about getting a search party together so we can head off to the Rockies when I'm done?"

He growls one last time before walking away. I allow myself a moment to just breathe. Dealing with him on top of everything else is exhausting.

It wouldn't be if you just accepted the bond. If I could bitch slap a dragon, I would. I swear.

Now is not the time. I can't trust you when it comes to him, you think with your damn ovaries.

Do not. My dragon's tone is childish. I simply roll my eyes and head into the house.

WHEN I GET to my sitting room, the envoy of vampires is already seated and drinking wine glasses of blood. I didn't even know we had blood. There are three of them, all male. They stand as I enter the room, which makes me feel hella awkward.

"Please, don't get up on my account." I smile and take a seat near the fireplace. I flick my hand out and start the fire again. Being toasty is soothing. I close my eyes to scan their auras. After the last few months, I am not taking any chances anymore. All three are clean.

"Thank you for meeting with us," the man closest to me says. He's African American, insanely tall if his legs are anything to go by, with close cut hair, and stunning hazel eyes.

He's dressed in a three-piece suit and has on sneakers instead of dress shoes, which makes me smile. "We've come on behalf of our nest. We'd like to join your community. When word hit us that you had merged the shifters and witches together, we were all eager to become part of such a society. There are few of us who remember when such communities were common."

I arch my eyebrow at him. He seems a little too eager.

"I apologize for my progeny," the man sitting next to him interjects. He is Asian, and like his progeny, tall as all hell. Why am I the only short person around here? It's going to give me a damn complex. His hair is long and tied at the nape of his neck. He's also wearing a three-piece suit, but unlike his progeny, he's wearing dress shoes.

"I am Xin, my progeny is Dante, and this is Rafe." Xin gestures to the third man who has olive skin and blond highlights in his brown, shaggy hair. Rafe is dressed like he's a surfer ready to hit the beach. It's surprising because of how the other two are dressed.

"Why so eager to join our community?"

"I was part of such a community in China many centuries ago." Xin's admission is laced with ancient sadness. "It had been led by a queen. I had been sent to another queen to assist with some minor demons, while they weren't overly strong, they vastly outnumbered the other queen's community. Myself and some of our warriors were sent to aid as best as we could. When we returned, our community had been decimated. The seven of us have dedicated our lives to finding the demon who destroyed our community and ending its life." Xin studies me for a moment. "But I see now why this community has formed, and why we have felt such a pull. You are a queen."

Chapter Twelve

"I am." I'm not surprised he can sense what I am. If he had served another queen, he would know how to tell when one is in the room with him. "I'm sorry about your community, Xin. We recently merged our community with the Rocky Mountain Pack after they were attacked by demons. We're more than willing to accept your nest. But I have a condition." All three men tense. "I will need to meet each member of your nest. We have found a few shifters who have been in league with demons, I need to be sure none of your nest comes into this community tainted."

Xin relaxes and nods. Dante leans back in his seat with his arms crossed, but he doesn't appear to be upset by my condition. Neither does Rafe. Good. It doesn't appear like they know about anyone in their nest that's tainted, otherwise, they would have protested. Since Xin is here speaking on behalf of the nest, he's either their leader or their beta. Until I meet everyone from the nest, I can't be certain which, but to have someone higher ranking without knowledge of anyone having dealings with demons doesn't mean anything anymore. Patrick had no idea what Sean was really doing.

Patrick being a new beta is the most redeeming thing about the situation. If Xin is the leader of a nest that has dealings with demons and doesn't know it, that is cause for serious concern. Until I get to know him better, I'll have no idea how he handles his people. The way he presents himself in front of me today could all just be an act. But I'm willing to take the risk if they are. It's just as big of a gamble for the nest to uproot and move here as it is for us to take them in.

"How many are in your nest? We're not entirely sure how many members of Rocky Mountain Pack we've taken on, we need to do an official headcount soon, but the town has more than enough room for everyone. We were pretty low in numbers, even after the witches moved to town."

"We have two thousand members in our nest." This surprises me. Typically, vampire nests are a lot smaller. Vampires have the tendency to get pretty territorial over feeding grounds, rivaling shifters in their defense of their territories. But having such a large nest is actually a mark in their favor—a group of vampires who can all work together without bringing attention to themselves will be a valuable asset. "We hail from the Canadian border. Our nest took on nests from New England and New York, as well as more rural parts of Canada. The American nests were small and wanted more protection from the shifter and witch communities at the time. Now that leadership has changed hands in New England, we're comfortable coming down here."

"We'll certainly have room for everyone. And if anyone doesn't like the current homes available, we can always build whatever is needed." We've got plenty of land around town to expand as necessary. And thanks to the witches taking up residence, the wards around town are so thick most humans don't even know this much property even exists. Bless their tiny, simple brains.

"Excellent. I will leave Dante here and go with Rafe to

collect our nest. It will take us several days to return." Xin hands me a business card. "This is my cell number." I pull out my phone and type in his number, sending him a text so he has mine as well. "I will let you know when we are heading back."

"Perfect. We have a few things to sort out here to make your transition to the community a little smoother. So a few days is great. We need to take care of the Rocky Mountain Pack, do inventory and a headcount, and deal with the Council." Dante frowns when I mention the Council.

"What are those assholes doing here?" Dante asks in a low, accusatory growl, and he narrows his eyes on me. I glare at him in return. How dare he just assume we're cozied up to the Council? Does anyone actually like the Council? Now that I think about it, does the Council even like the Council? They're all a bunch of pretentious pricks.

"When I took over as alpha a week ago, they were informed of the power shift. This is a pretty standard proce-dure, unfortunately, everything else about what's happened the last few days is anything but normal." My tone is slightly defensive, and Xin gives his progeny a stern look as if to say "behave," before rising with Rafe.

"We will see you in a few days." Xin and Rafe speed out of the room. I can move fast, but damn, what I wouldn't give to be able to move like a vampire. I'm so jealous.

"Come on, why don't you come with me?" I stand, and Dante is instantly on his feet. We might as well put him to work while he's here. "You can help us with the Rocky Moun-tain Pack."

"Of course." Dante gives me a sheepish look. "I should have offered. I apologize."

"Just to set the record straight, we aren't BFFs with the Council or anything like that." Given his reaction to the news of their presence in town, I want it clear that as soon as they're able to leave, they'll be leaving. "We literally just saved their asses in the Rockies. I'm not sure how long they'll have to stay, but this isn't a permanent thing."

Dante nods stiffly. "I apologize for my reaction. We've had a few run-ins with the Council in the past. They aren't happy that Xin has been able to maintain such a large nest. They don't think it's right that so many of us live in one place. They assume we'll expose ourselves." That's food for thought.

"How do you all eat?" I'm curious now. How do they avoid exposure?

"We've invested in several blood banks in both Canada and the United States." Dante shrugs. "When there's a shortage of blood, we have arrangements with a few Canadian shifter packs. We don't like drinking from them because it gives us an unfair edge, but when food is scarce, we do what we must." Which makes sense. Vampires get a serious power boost if they drink from a shifter or a witch, but it's only temporary. I'm pretty impressed with the way their nest is run. Hella honorable vampires. I dig it.

We head out into the hall, making our way to the center of town to portal back to where the battle took place yesterday. We have the unpleasant task of sorting through the dead today. I shove back memories of the last battle I witnessed right before my mother died. I hadn't seen large numbers of corpses since, and the flashbacks were mildly annoying.

"How long have you been a vampire?" I need to take my mind off all of the death I'm about to be knee deep in. Learning more about my new community members is a good way to distract me.

"Only five hundred years. Xin is well over two thousand, Rafe is closing in on one thousand."

"Is Rafe also Xin's progeny?"

"No. Rafe was created by another. He doesn't speak much. And he never talks about his sire. The best we can guess is that his sire met a rather horrific end. Rafe is an excellent fighter. He and I are part of the elite guard of our nest, and I am next in line to become the head of the nest, once Xin decides to step down that is." Dante has a lot of faith in Xin to say that Xin will step down and not die. A spark of fondness for the vampire flickers to life in my chest.

"That's impressive. I'm glad to have you with us. It's nice to be part of a community again."

"Why was this community just recently formed? From what I know of queens, communities naturally develop around them. You should have had this community well established before now." Dante looks perplexed, and I can't help but smile.

"That, my friend, is a very long story. One that, should I divulge it, needs to be told at once to everyone. So I'm not going to spill my guts to you right now." He grumbles at my refusal. We'll need to talk about my history, especially considering what happened to the Rocky Mountain Pack, but not right now. Since he isn't the only one who needs to hear the tale, I'd rather tell everyone once than have to repeat myself.

BY THE TIME we make it to the town center, everyone who is coming with us is already assembled. The portals are being established, and Caleb is clearly seen standing at least a head above everyone else. Damn, that man is huge. I quickly make sure my mental walls are in place as we make our way through the crowd. When we come up to Caleb, he's talking with Connor, Olivia, and Kelly about how Connor and the other wolves plan to hunt down Sean's body for me while everyone else gets started on the other fallen fighters. They all nod before turning to Dante and me.

"Everyone, this is Dante. He's part of a Canadian nest. They'll be the newest addition to our little community here." Caleb seems to bristle at this, but Kelly and Olivia are smiling and radiating excitement through our bond. At least they know that the more members we have the safer we are. "Their leader, Xin, and another member of their nest, Rafe, have headed back to the nest to tell everyone about the merger and to get them all packed up and ready to move here. It'll take them a few days, so we can get things squared away here with the Rocky Mountain Pack before the nest moves in." I feel Caleb knocking on my walls, but I ignore him.

"This is great!" Kelly claps her hands together, smirking when Connor shoots her a glare. "We'll have a lot more fire-power against the demons now."

"Most of those in our nest are warriors, and we love nothing more than destroying demons. We will all be happy to assist in your fight, as it is now our own," Dante states. He sounds so formal. I roll my eyes slightly. He'll get used to how things are around here.

"Right. What's the game plan?" I look around the group, my eyes finally focusing and narrowing on Caleb.

"Connor already knows Sean's scent, so he's going to take point in tracking down the body. Everyone else that's assembled here will work to catalog and then cremate the dead. We're working in groups of three, a Rocky Mountain member, a New England member, and a councilman. Patrick will be working with us." Caleb gestures to Patrick who is stepping through one of the portals.

"Great. Dante can join our group." Caleb lets out a low growl, causing Dante to stiffen. My eyes narrow further. I am not in the mood for a dick measuring contest. "What the hell is your issue?"

Caleb grabs my arm and drags me off while gesturing for the others to make their way through the portals. My body instantly stiffens, and he has to force me to move. My dragon lets out a snarl. We don't like being manhandled. Finally, I tear my arm from his grasp, crossing my arms over my chest.

"What the fuck was that?" I don't bother to lower my voice. I don't give a damn who hears me rip him a new one, let this be a message to all—I will cut you.

"Are you seriously letting in a nest of vampires? Without screening them first?" he growls as he steps into my personal space. But I don't give an inch, instead, I tilt my head back to glare up at him. When will the tall people learn that short people aren't intimidated by them? If anything, stepping into our space like that makes us want to take them out at the knees. Slowly.

"The three who came here are clear. I expressly stated that I would be screening every member of their nest as soon as they arrived." I don't see what the big deal is, or why he sounds so butthurt. Even as Alpha, Caleb doesn't have the right to make calls for our community. If I want to let a bunch of demons into the community, that's my call, not his. The Council and the alpha are really only supposed to get involved if there's a dispute between packs or species, or if there are issues with demons. The day-to-day mechanics of running a community is left to the leaders of that community.

"You told them what's been going on?" He sounds outraged. I bristle at his tone. Seems to me like someone wants a swift kick to the shins.

"You wouldn't have? Caleb, these are your people too. Just because they're joining my community doesn't mean they aren't still aligned with the Council. I'm not forming a new faction here. Even though I refuse to go with you once this is settled, that doesn't mean I don't want to be allies. We're all going to have to band together to continue fighting the demons." Clearly I need to be the adult here.

"Until I know who we can trust, we shouldn't be giving any of this information out!"

"That's where you're wrong." My voice is deadly calm, and I know I'm radiating the rage I feel building inside me. "We need to warn as many people as possible. If we don't, more will fall victim to the likes of Malick. I don't know how the Council does things, but if they would rather leave their people in the dark to fight alone rather than join them together so they have a fighting chance, maybe the Council is obsolete."

Caleb goes completely still. His eyes narrow into deadly slits. He takes several deep breaths, trying to contain his own fury. I don't care if his feelings are hurt. He can't call himself a leader, Alpha, if he's going to leave his own people to be slaughtered simply because he doesn't know who's in league with the demons. And frankly, telling the other supernatural communities may make those involved rethink what they're doing. Regardless, if we warn people now, the chances of more missing community members go down because everyone is more aware. No one is alone.

"We can debate this later, right now the most important thing is seeing to the dead." I spin and start marching off. "Come on."

∾

ONCE WE'RE on the other side of the portal, Patrick and Dante instantly come to our sides. Everyone else is off on their specific tasks.

"I want us to go to the village the pack was living in. I need to see what Sean left behind as evidence," Caleb says as he gestures for Patrick to lead the way.

Now that I'm not in dragon form, and I'm able to see the bodies up close, there seems to be more dead than I remembered. I realize my brain simply didn't want to process the extent of the damage done because I needed to make sure everyone was safe by eliminating the current threat. But this was a massacre. If my community hadn't shown up, if I hadn't faced Malick, everyone could have been slaughtered. And I had the balls to fail. Gods, I can't believe I wasn't able to kill Malick.

I'm so lost in my pity party that I trip over a tree root, but Caleb catches me before I hit the ground. He holds me tightly against him, and his scent soothes my frayed nerves, helping me to think more clearly, which is irritating because I'm still annoyed that he's a chest pounding caveman. Training starts today when we're finished here. The next time I face Malick, I'm going to end him.

Caleb tilts my chin up, interrupting my thoughts. He studies my face, and a flash of worry crosses his features before he leans in and kisses me hard. I want to be mad, but my brain turns off and I'm instantly lost in him. My arms snake around his neck, and his hands drop to my hips, pulling me flush against him. My tongue laps at his lips, begging for entry, and I moan when he finally touches his tongue to mine. My hands tangle in his hair as I try to pull myself closer. Heat flares to life, spiraling down to pool between my legs.

"Uh...Guys?" Dante's voice cuts through my lust-filled fog and has me quickly stepping away from Caleb. "As much as I'm sure we'd all enjoy the show, we have things to do."

Cheeky little bugger. He's not so serious after all. Both Caleb and I chuckle as we start forward again. I step ahead so I can walk beside Dante, and Caleb doesn't seem to mind.

"Because I can watch your ass while you walk." I feel my face heat, but I look dead ahead and don't comment.

"Just wait until I get you alone later. I'm going to bury my face

between those gorgeous thighs and feast like a king. And then, because you haven't played well at all today, I'm going to take you slowly. I'm going to build you up but stop before I let you fall until you're begging me to let you come."

I snort and roll my eyes. Dante gives me a sideways glance as I reply, *I don't beg. Ever. So good luck with that.*

"Challenge accepted, my little mate."

Chapter Thirteen

When we finally reach the village the Rocky Mountain Pack called home, I'm surprised to see that it's mostly untouched by the battle. Given the carnage on the battlefield, I assumed the town would be leveled, and we wouldn't have much luck finding anything. But this gives me hope. There are a few bodies littering the main street, and what appear to be claw and scorch marks on buildings, but aside from that, the buildings all seem to be largely intact. The village is quaint, and the main street is lined with small cottages that have seen better days. There aren't many stores, but there is a large neon sign for a pub, which doesn't surprise me. Shifters love to party. What does surprise me is that there aren't any cars parked by any of the cottages. A few have a bike or two, but no cars.

"Did you all have a self-sustaining thing going on here?" I'm curious. Most pack land is so far off the beaten path the pack is either self-sustaining or everyone has a car to get into the nearest town for supply runs. Now that my pack has the witch coven, it's a lot easier to get to and from anywhere we need to go, but the Rocky Mountain Pack doesn't have any witches.

"Sean, his old beta, and some of his enforcers had cars. They were always put out whenever someone asked for a supply run, so we learned how to be as self-sufficient as possible." Patrick shrugs. "When I became beta, Sean said I needed to earn the right to use the car, but it was easier for me to command an enforcer to go into town to get things we couldn't make ourselves."

"Wait." I hold my hands up and everyone stops walking. "Are you telling me they didn't want to go get supplies for the pack? And the pack hadn't already been self-sufficient prior to Sean taking power?"

"No. From what I understand, the old alpha actually had everyone on a rotation for going into town. Most of the pack had jobs in town too. Sean stopped all that shortly after becoming alpha." I exchange looks with Caleb and Dante. That is highly unusual, and it makes little alarm bells ring.

"How long was Sean the alpha?" I focus on keeping myself calm and expect to hear the worst.

"About fifty years," Patrick replies. Both Caleb and Dante curse under their breaths. "I realize I'm fairly young to be beta, but like I said, I wanted to try to make a difference."

"This isn't about you, Patrick. I'm not discrediting you in any way. This is about the shitshow Sean left for us to deal with. I can't believe how badly he let your pack down." While fifty years isn't a long time for a shifter, it's nothing to laugh at either. For the younger generations of shifters, this is all they would have known. I can't fathom younger shifters growing up in a pack that doesn't care about them, that has an alpha who doesn't want to see the pack flourish.

"This way. The alpha's manor is down here," Patrick states, trying to diffuse the tension that has taken over the group at our discussion. He leads us down a dead-end road that comes to an abrupt stop at a large house.

While the packhouse on our land is a mansion, this house seems to simply be over the top. It looks like a small villa rather than a house. Patrick said it was the alpha's manor, not the pack's manor. I'd never met an alpha who didn't live in a community centered home. This house is the only one on the street, and it's set back far enough from the main road that it was clearly built for privacy. This screams sketchy.

The front door looks a little worse for wear, but it's still locked when we reach it. Patrick mumbles that he doesn't have a key, so I step up and use my magic to unlock the door. Patrick sidles up next to me and pushes the door open. The house is dark, and someone flicks on the lights.

"He lived here alone?" I ask, as I take in everything before me.

This place shouts wealth. There are marble floors and a polished hardwood banister, and signed artwork lines the walls. Most packs are fairly well off, it helps that we live so long, but for the most part, any money a pack member makes goes into a joint account for the entire pack. We all look after one another. If an elderly member of the community can't work, the joint account helps fund that individual's needs. It sends kids to college and funds repairs on everything—medical bills, legal fees, you name it. Individuals can certainly keep whatever they want of their personal funds, but typically there's no need since the joint account provides all the money a pack member could ever need. But this looks like Sean was living the high life. I certainly hope the rest of his pack members' homes look this good too.

Caleb and Dante both growl at the opulence before us. I can feel through the bond that Caleb is thinking along the same lines I am, so it's safe to assume Dante is as well. All members of the supernatural community are the same. We work to build the community. Which, I feel, is something the humans could learn from us. Humans are so focused on instant gratification and individual fulfillment that they forget they're part of a larger whole, and if that whole suffers, so do they. I'm not entirely sure how they don't grasp the concept, but there it is nonetheless.

"Do the other pack homes look like this?" Caleb questions slowly, his voice a low hiss.

"No. The rest of the pack lives far more modestly than Sean did. Frankly, once I became beta and I started to look into things, I quickly realized that while Sean might have been getting extra funds, he was spending far more than he was making. I'm not entirely sure of the financial state of the pack though. I was just starting to look into it when the Council arrived."

This time, I join Caleb and Dante when they growl. What a leech. If Sean wasn't already dead, I'd challenge him myself. He wasn't fit to be alpha. How the hell are the demons able to corrupt so many alphas? Admittedly, this is only the second one I've come across, and nothing is official against Sean right now, but even one alpha is too many. Demons shouldn't be able to infiltrate a pack that deeply. To do it to two packs defies everything I've ever known about being part of a community.

"Take us to Sean's study."

Patrick nods at me and guides us to the second floor of the manor. The door in front of us is also locked. What was with this guy and keeping people out? I quickly unlock the door with magic and step into the study.

Like everything else in this trash heap, it's over the top and far too expensive. An ornately carved desk dominates the room. Instead of bookshelves, there are antique guns mounted on the walls. There is only one tiny window, and that has bars over it. What the hell was this guy doing in here?

Turning to look at the others, I order, "Patrick, take Caleb and Dante to other areas of the house. The basement and Sean's personal room specifically. If the doors are locked, break them down. We need answers, and it's best if we split up. Patrick, once you've done that, I want you to go collect any of the information you were working with before the attack." Surprisingly, no one argues, and they all move off.

I'm inspecting the guns on the wall when I hear a crash, followed seconds later by a second crash. Sean apparently has a lot to hide. Not a good sign. Thankfully, the guns appear to just be for show. While guns don't hurt shifters or vampires, they can hurt witches and humans. I make my way over to the desk, taking a moment to look out the small, barred window. It's just a view of the trees. What was he trying to protect himself from? If demons wanted to get in here so badly, bars on a window wouldn't stop them. So were they just for show?

I turn back to the desk. The top has been cleared off completely except for a laptop. I'm going to bring that back with me and have Kelly hack into it. There are three drawers on either side and the typical center drawer. All are locked. Fighting the urge to roll my eyes at the level of paranoia, I unlock all the drawers with a wave of my hand. I completely pull out the center drawer. It's filled with pens, sticky notes, highlighters, and paperclips. An obscene number of paperclips. Who needs this many paperclips? I flip the drawer over, looking for anything attached at the base or any sort of false bottom either inside or outside the drawer. Nothing.

I move on to the set of three drawers that go down the right-hand side of the desk. Starting from the bottom, I pull out the drawer completely. This looks a little more promising.

This drawer was meant for filing, and even though he was a paranoid little shit, Sean seems to have at least kept great records. I stack the files on top of the laptop to look through more thoroughly later. Again, I search for any false bottoms. I place both discarded drawers on the floor beside me. I repeat this process for each drawer until I come to the middle drawer on the left-hand side.

"*Very clever, little queen!*" Malick steps out of the shadows, slowly clapping his hands. Instantly on guard, I reach for my dragon only to find her missing. How can he keep doing this? I grasp for my magic instead and feel it swell inside me. Sending it cascading out around me, I realize Malick isn't really here. *Am I...In his mind again?*

"*We have a winner!*" Malick grins at me as he leans a hip against the desk. "*You're once again inside my mind, little queen.*"

"*How?*"

"*I can't give you all the answers! What would be the fun in that?*" He chuckles as he stares into my eyes. I fight the urge to punch him in the face, knowing it won't do me any good.

"*What the hell do you want?*"

"*Why, I should think that was obvious, no? You. And you had best prepare yourself, I am going to have you soon.*"

WITH A HEAVING BREATH, I realize I'm back to myself again. Taking a shaky, deep inhale, I sit down on the chair I pushed out of the way earlier to get to the desk. I hate that I'm this unsettled by Malick. Hate that he has the power to rattle me at all. I run my fingers through my hair and take another deep breath.

"*Are you okay?*" Caleb's voice soothes my rattled nerves and helps steady me.

"*Malick.*"

"I'm coming." And I'm weak enough not to tell him there's no point. Every fiber of my being is calling out for my mate.

It was like you were asleep again. My dragon brushes against my mind like a cat rubbing against its owner. *One minute you were going through the drawer and the next I couldn't reach you.* I can sense her fear, it mirrors my own. Caleb stalks into the room, quickly kneeling in front of me and taking my hands.

"What the bloody hell happened?" His voice is gruff, and his accent is thicker than normal.

"It was like last night."

"Last night? You never said anything about being with Malick last night." I wince. I didn't exactly have time to tell him.

"There's a lot to share. I want to do it once in front of everyone. Will you help me go through the rest of the drawers? We can tackle the basement together."

"No need." His tone is still gruff, but his accent is back to normal now. "The basement is filled with cells. They were empty, but the scents in most were recent. Hopefully whatever you find in here will shed some light on who he was keeping down there."

I give a shaky nod, and Caleb stands to go through the drawer I abandoned. He stills and slowly lifts something out of it. I blink and focus on the item in his hand. A shiver crawls down my spine, and I instantly feel as though I've been submerged in an ice bath. It's a demon talisman. From what I understand of them, they're used when the demon has made a deal with an individual. It acts as a two-way radio and a spyglass all rolled into one nasty little package. They are typically either an actual mirror or, in this case, a piece of obsidian.

"Put that on the desk. It's best not to touch a demon talisman for long." Caleb looks disgusted and quickly drops the talisman on the desk. There isn't anything else in that drawer, so he opens the last. It's another series of files, which he puts on my pile.

He spends a small amount of time taking apart the rest of the desk to ensure nothing else is hidden within it. While Caleb's tackling the desk, both Dante and Patrick return to the study. Patrick has a small pile of files and Dante has a portable safe, what appears to be some journals, and a large trash bag. We're going to have our work cut out for us when we get back to the packhouse.

"Ayla, we found the alpha," the wolf shifter from my pack who went with Connor announces. I let out a tired sigh and physically nod before realizing that the wolf can't see me.

"Thanks, Sasha. We'll be right there." I look at my companions and gesture to the front of the house.

"They found Sean. We need to gather all of this and head out. But first—" I look down at the talisman on the desk. "First we need to put that in something so we can neutralize it before going back through the portals."

Dante nods, gently places his items down, and speeds from the room, returning moments later with a small cloth pouch. He flips the bag inside out to grab the talisman and puts it in the bag. I take it from him and tie the strings of the bag to my shorts. I really wish women's clothes came with pockets. Once it's secure, we head toward Sean's body.

"You said you found cells in the basement," I start. Caleb nods and points to his front pocket. Why do guys get all the pockets? Rude.

"I got pictures on my phone."

"Oh, that's great!"

He grins at me. "I was thinking that they were probably used to house the shifters he was selling before he could get them off pack land. It's a risky move, but if the pack met somewhere else and they weren't allowed at his house, it's doable."

"We'd have pack meetings at the old town hall," Patrick informs us. His eyes flick between me and Caleb before he continues, "Sean never had people at his house, not even women, as far as I know. He would always go to the lady's house. Some of the females had made it a bit of a competition to see if they could get Sean to take 'em home. He never did."

"Dante, what's in the bag?" I point to the large, black trash bag he's carrying.

"Drugs. It's nothing commonly used by humans, at least from what I can tell. It doesn't smell like cocaine, meth, heroin, or anything like that. This is new. It smells enchanted."

"I wonder if that's how he sedated the females. But there are easier ways to sedate shifters, even strong, dominant female shifters. I know Malcolm said something about producing a new drug, but do you have any idea if it was just to get shifters high or if Sean planned on using it for something else, Caleb?" Caleb shakes his head. "Damn. Hopefully, we'll be able to put more pieces together once we get back home."

WE MAKE it to Sean's corpse fairly quickly. He was taken out right outside of town. The state of his body suggests the demons who killed him didn't want him recognized. If we thought Jonas was bad when he showed up in our town, Sean is at least ten times worse. His face looks as though it's melted off, his skin has been shredded, and he's been scalped.

It only takes me a quick glance to confirm that he's tainted, and it's as though I've been hit in the face with a baseball bat. Memories flood my mind, breaking through a dam and inundating my brain with images, smells, and impressions, all of it coming at once. It overloads my system. I collapse to my knees, clutching my head. It's too much. The world goes dark.

Chapter Fourteen

When I come to, it takes me a minute to realize I'm in my bedroom. The last thing I remember is standing over Sean's body. Everything else is a blur. Why the hell does my head hurt so much? I gently run my fingers over my head, trying to determine if I've sustained some sort of injury. My vision is a little blurry, and I'm having trouble focusing on anything in my room because of the pain.

More of our memory was unlocked, but it happened so fast that our brain couldn't handle it. It feels as though we're still adjusting. My dragon sounds as pained as I feel. I am all for getting my memories back, but couldn't they come back in a way that doesn't knock me out cold? What if this happens during a battle? There's a knock on my door seconds before it's opened and Kelly pokes her head in, breaking me out of my thoughts.

"Oh, good! You're awake!" She beams as she rushes into my room. She's carrying a mug of what I very much hope is coffee. "I magically blocked your bonds for you for a bit, so your head didn't explode. And I brought you some chamomile tea!"

She places the mug on my nightstand, and I stare at it like a child who was told their pizza was made out of cauliflower. Why wouldn't she bring me the nectar of the gods? My very lifeblood? My reason for being? Is this a declaration of war? Is she challenging me? Does she hate me?

"Cool your thoughts there, my friend. Based on your face alone, I can see you're having some sort of breakdown over the tea. But it'll help, Ayla, it really will. I've also put a potion in there that will ease the pain a bit so you can process whatever happened. What did happen? You freaked everyone out, especially Caleb." Kelly smirks. "He was a disaster as he carried you to the portals. There was a lot of yelling, cursing, and orders flung around like rice at a wedding. There was a moment there I thought he might have a stroke."

We both chuckle. I slowly, petulantly, reach my hand out for the mug of tea. If it's got something to help get rid of this pain, I'll choke it down. I'd probably sell my firstborn at this rate to alleviate the pain. As my hand wraps around the mug, I let the heat seep into my bones. I hadn't realized just how cold I was before now. I flick my hand at the fireplace and start a roaring fire before placing both hands around my mug with a sigh. Dragons aren't meant to be cold; it makes us cranky and sulky. I take a sip of the tea and shudder as it makes its way into my stomach, and then I down the rest as quickly as possible.

"That's one way to do it." Kelly chuckles and takes the mug back. "Now tell me what happened."

"It's a very long story, and I'm going to need to tell it to everyone from the beginning. Can you get Olivia, Dante, Patrick, Connor, Malcolm, and Caleb in here? I don't want to move, and I only want to tell this once." Kelly nods and goes still, communicating through the bond.

"Done! Everyone will be here soon." She places her hands on either side of my head, and I feel a gentle, comforting warmth start to spread out from my temples. My eyes droop as my muscles relax.

"Thank you. I feel so much better."

"You know I gotchu." Kelly winks and flicks her hand to open the door for everyone.

Caleb instantly moves to the side of my bed and sits down next to me, picking up my hand and pressing it to his lips.

"I was so worried."

"Hey, big guy, I'm fine. Nothing a little magic tea can't help with. I promise."

"You're not allowed to do that again."

"I literally do not have the emotional bandwidth to tell you just how wrong you are. But just know you're insanely wrong."

Everyone else stands around my bed, each of them with concerned expressions. Wow. I must have gone down hard. I feel bad for causing them distress like this, but there isn't much I can do about it now aside from being honest with them about what's going on.

"I thought my mother killed Malick," I start. "I've spent the last four hundred years assuming he was dead. There had been this massive battle the night I went into hiding. My mother and father were killed." I take a deep breath. "I'm jumbling everything up. Let me try again.

"Four hundred years ago, my mother erased some of my memories. I'm not sure how many or which ones specifically. She also spelled me to run. Malick attacked our community, but by that time the vampires and the witches were all gone, it was just a small number of shifters left. My father held him off while my mother did whatever she felt she had to do with me. Then she joined the battle to give me enough cover and time to get away. It took me a while, but I was able to piece together most of what happened that night. My parents fell, but, at least according to most of the information I gathered, so had Malick."

"Where did you get your information?" Caleb inquires.

"I wasn't so morally opposed to diving into minds back then. And I was starving for information about my family. I waited a week and then returned to the area." Caleb scoffs. "I know, foolish, stupid, and insanely rash. But I needed to know. Only a handful of shifters survived the battle. From their memories, my mother and Malick went down together and the demons vanished as soon as it happened. Both of my parents' bodies disappeared with the demons, but a few of the memories I had been able to dive into vividly saw their broken bodies and lifeless eyes." I pause as my own eyes fill with tears.

"Is it possible those memories, the ones of the shifters who had been part of the battle, were tampered with at all? We know Malick is still alive." Caleb's got a valid point, and I'm curious about that as well.

"Honestly, I'm not sure. None of the memories specifically saw him die, I had just assumed. It's possible that in my grief, I misunderstood the memories. He might have been wounded and then carted off by his lackeys. I'm not sure."

"Why would your mother tamper with your memories?" Olivia muses, bracing her hands on the foot of my bed. "What purpose does that serve?"

"I'm not sure. I first started getting memories back right after you two came to talk to me about the missing female shifters." I can feel the others' interest rise. "I'll get to that in a minute. I didn't realize what was happening at the time, but things felt...off, I guess. I knew something was missing or wrong, but I couldn't tell exactly why. And then the night Caleb had called to let me know that the Council was coming, more memories resurfaced, specifically about my mother's community."

I pause, pressing my fingers against my eyes. I feel as though I've missed so many clues. What else could have been locked away? Why the bloody hell had my mother done this to me? I'm so woefully ill-prepared to face everything that's happening now because of this. I run a frustrated hand through my hair before continuing.

"I realized that when I was young, my mother had vampires, witches, and shifters all living together in harmony. Lots of them. But from my memory of the night my mother died, the community had drastically dwindled. I've been trying to think of reasons why, but I'm coming up empty right now. Let me step back just a little." I pause. "Six months ago, Kelly and Olivia came to me because, as we came to find out, Morgan had been selling dominant shifter females. Morgan pointed the finger at the witches in the hopes of slaughtering them in an all-out race war, but Olivia, who had been working alongside the witches to help modernize their records, knew they couldn't have been responsible. So they came to me to have me investigate.

"I believed them right away. One of my gifts is to tell if someone is lying. They weren't. I did what I do best, became invisible. I watched Morgan for weeks, following him and his inner circle. They had close dealings with a human drug lord, so he and I had a little chat. He knew about an illegal shifter fighting ring, and I went to check it out. I caught Morgan's scent while I was there but couldn't find him. I did, however, find Sasha, the wolf who was helping you, Connor. She was drugged out of her mind and being led off by this guy. He said she had already been 'paid for.' I can show everyone my records but based on what I'd already witnessed and what happened that night, I knew Morgan was selling the females.

"I realized something while I was fighting Morgan. He appeared fuzzy, almost as though he was a smudged photograph of himself. The drug lord had been like that to a smaller extent, but so had the fighters at the ring. I hadn't realized exactly what it meant, but it's the way I see someone who's been tainted by an alliance with a demon. It's how all queens see someone who's been tainted. My mother had stripped that information from my mind four hundred years ago too, and I had done such a damn good job of avoiding people like the plague, I hadn't seen anyone with that smudge in the interim."

Stunned silence meets my next long inhale. Yeah, I know, right? This shit is fucked up.

"Ayla," Caleb murmurs. "What about two nights ago? You said you saw Malick."

Was it really two nights ago? Damn. I'd been out for quite a while.

"Right. Well, during the fight with Malick, he transformed an innocent-looking rock into a deadly weapon and stabbed me with it. As an aside," I explain, and slide my eyes to Caleb's, "we need to spar and train together because what happened on that summit was extremely embarrassing, and I refuse to go through that again." His lips quirk up. "Later that day, when I went to sleep, I had some strange dreams. And at one point I ended up in a room with Malick. He said I was inside his mind. I couldn't access my dragon again, but I could still control my magic. He said that he had left part of himself inside of me."

Five pairs of stunned eyes stare at me as the silence in the room screams in the space between us. Not awkward at all.

"So, uh, when we went into Sean's house earlier today, and we found that talisman, it happened again." More stunned silence rings in my ears. "He said he wants me, and I'd best prepare myself because he'll have me soon." Caleb's rage blasts through our still shaky and tentative bond, causing my eyes to snap to his.

He's seething. Behind all the fury is a desperate urge to protect. I grip his hand and squeeze it reassuringly. I have no intention of going with Malick, and I appreciate that Caleb would fight to keep me out of his grasp.

Of course he would, my dragon purrs, *he's our mate*. I want to groan and roll my eyes, but I stop myself since she only spoke to me.

"There is no way I'll let you go." Caleb's tone is guttural and strained, and it feels as if he's struggling not to shift.

"I know," I soothe. "I know you'll protect me. Which is why I want to train. It'll be easier if I'm in top fighting shape. As much as you'd like to just hide me away, you know that won't stop him. He'll just go through everyone else until he finds me. We have to rip the head off the snake, à la Neville Longbottom."

"Technically, he cut the head off the snake." Everything inside me stills. Caleb knows *Harry Potter*? My heart rate accelerates and excitement flares hot in my veins. Caleb knows *Harry Potter*! He's a nerd!

"Please tell me you didn't just watch the movies." Suspicion creeps into my voice.

"I've actually never seen the movies." That can be overlooked. The man has read *Harry Potter* and can keep up with any references I make. If he would just leave the Council, he would be perfect. That thought sobers me up.

"I hate to break up your fan-girling, Ayla," Olivia interjects. "But we need to make a game plan here. You're going to need security, both physically and psychically. We also need to create a training schedule for everyone, not just you. We all need to make sure that we can defend ourselves and our people when the demons come."

"Olivia is right," Dante chimes in, nodding his head. "I can assist with the training schedules. I can also help screen candidates for your physical security."

"I'll tackle the security for your dreams," Kelly adds.

"We'll help." Connor nudges Malcolm's side, and he nods his agreement.

"I want a Council security officer with her at all times when I can't be." Caleb's tone leaves no room for negotiation.

"Dante," I say before they can all leave to get things ready. "When is the rest of your nest getting here?"

"In about two days. I heard from Xin right before you woke up. The nest is very excited." Dante grins at me. "They'll be even more excited once they realize we're training to take down an old archdemon and his legion."

I snort. "I have no doubt about that. Olivia, before you go off and organize everything, can you make sure houses are ready for the nest when they get here? We have plenty of space, but I want to ensure the houses aren't all gross."

"I'm on it. The rest of you start planning and scheduling. Dante, come with me, I want to make sure the homes we select are appropriate." Olivia and Dante leave the room, talking about preferences and how many younger vampires they have that still need extra protection from the sun.

"Can someone bring me Patrick? I still need to weed through the Rocky Mountain Pack to determine if there are any more members involved with demons." Everyone just blinks at me. "What?"

"You aren't serious, are you?" Connor exclaims.

Kelly grins at Connor's question. Clearly, the man doesn't know who I am. "You've been out cold and have just regained some of your memories. That's not important right now."

"It *is* important right now. Do you think Malick is sitting back, sipping tea, and relaxing? No. He's getting ready to attack, and we can't allow a spy to tell him the best way to do it. Now get me Patrick." I loosen my hold on my dominance, and Connor, Malcolm, and Kelly all leave the room to do their specific tasks.

And once again, I'm alone with Caleb.

"You really shouldn't be bossing my men around."

"Well, if your men had any brain cells still operating, I wouldn't need to." Caleb chuckles and nods.

"Fair enough. They should know who they're dealing with. But you can't blame them for wanting to make sure that you don't push yourself too far." He pauses to look me over. "Do you need some time to adjust? If getting your memories back caused your body to go through that much strain, maybe you should take it easy for at least a few more hours."

"It was just the number of memories. My brain needed me to shut down for a bit in order to process. I've processed." Well, mostly. "It'll probably take me some time to sort through everything, but that shouldn't stop me from guaranteeing the safety of this community."

"Speaking of, I'm going to put in a call for reinforcements from the remaining councilmen and employees. We're going to need all the help we can get."

"As much as I hate to admit this, that's not a bad idea. We should still have enough room once the nest is settled." I sigh, feeling tired again, but I'm determined not to let it show.

"You're still planning to stay?" Caleb has a look of pure frustrated male written all over his face. We apparently don't like it when our new toy won't do as it's told. Oh, boo-hoo.

"Why would you expect me to give up my people if you're not willing to give up your own?"

Chapter Fifteen

After that little bomb goes off, Caleb stomps away, leaving a Council security guard in his place. I'd probably feel sorry for him, but he's got this archaic outlook on how this whole mate thing works. Which is hysterical because he's mated to a queen, and he's a dragon. We're matriarchal, for crying out loud! Why should a woman give everything up for a man? Especially if that man isn't willing to give everything up for her? It's an unfair ask. And he's been asking about it a lot. No. Not asking, expecting. He's been expecting me to just drop my life here to go be with him when all this is over. And that's what stings the most, the expectation that I'll just drop this community. It goes against everything I am both as an alpha and a queen. He should know that.

If I'm honest with myself, I don't know how I would react if he offered to leave the Council to be with me. Now that I've met him and Connor and Malcolm, they aren't this face-less threat now. While they may not seem like the boogeyman under my bed anymore, that doesn't mean I'm willing to give up everything I've fought for, especially if it means I won't have a community around me anymore. The Council may be a community, but they ultimately bow to Caleb, and they're a pretty broken system. As a queen, it's in the very foundation of my DNA to want to lead a community of supernaturals. I'm not sure I can do a hell of a lot better than Caleb and the Council, but the thought of losing my community now that I've finally gained one sickens me to the core. I can't do it. I won't do it.

And Caleb either can't or won't leave the Council. So it's been decided.

"Ma'am?" The guard at my door interrupts my thoughts, and I turn to look at him. "The Rocky Mountain Pack is ready. If it's alright with you, I'll let them in ten at a time."

"That's fine." It takes a moment for his words to register. Ten at a time? "Wait. How many are there? We didn't get a full headcount with all the injured."

"We're still not sure, ma'am, but I'll keep a tally as they come in, and then we can count those still in the infirmary."

"Look, if you want to keep your balls, you need to stop calling me ma'am."

"Yes, ma—Yes." He gulps and turns to let the first wave of ten in.

∾

SEVERAL HOURS LATER, I finally finish with the last of the healthy Rocky Mountain Pack members. They're all clean. Caleb came into my room a few hours ago and has been sitting in bed with me while I've looked at each person's aura. I hadn't realized how exhausting this would be, then again, I'm not exactly on my A-game right now. Stifling a yawn, I stretch before getting up to go to the bathroom. Caleb stands as if to follow me.

"Caleb, we are so not at the point where you can watch

me pee. Stay here." I point firmly at my bed and only move toward the bathroom once he's seated again.

A girl needs to be able to pee by herself. Sometimes we want to be able to stare off blankly into space, sometimes we want to play on our phone, sometimes we just want to die internally—either way, we want to be alone while we do it. While I'm in the bathroom, I stare at myself in the mirror, not liking what I see. I have deep black circles around my eyes, making me look like I've gone ten rounds in the ring and lost. My hair doesn't have its usual sheen, and my skin looks paler than usual. Apparently getting memories back does not do the body good. I scrub my face, throw my hair up into a messy bun at the top of my head, brush my teeth, and make my way back into my bedroom.

Caleb is lounging on my bed like he's the damn king of the world, and in a way, I guess he is. He's also staring intently at me.

"Creep."

"But I'm your creep."

I roll my eyes. *"Don't try to be cute, it doesn't work for you."*

He puts a hand on his chest and looks offended. "Are you saying I'm not cute?"

"Of course you're not." I school my features to keep myself from smiling.

"Well, excuse the shit out of you, madam. I'll have you know I am very cute." I know what he's doing. He's trying to make me feel better, at least emotionally, and get my mind off the insane dumpster fire my life has become. And I hate that it's working.

"Who told you that? It's like calling an annoyingly recurring yeast infection cute." I start digging through my closet, turning my back to Caleb so I can better hide my amusement.

"At least I'm recurring in the vag." He is dead serious. I

groan loudly before I snort back a laugh. Seriously? Coughing slightly to cover up my slip, I pull out a sundress that's a riot of bright colors, looking almost like a kid's painting project. I pull out an equally bright bra and thong set, hot pink, just what I need for a pick-me-up. When all else fails, at least have stellar underwear. Finally, I pull out a pair of white wedge sandals. I'm going to dress in bright, happy colors, determined to look fabulous and not like I'm on the verge of death. I'm also going to do my hair and my makeup, because bitches slay like that. I refuse to let everything that's happened stop me from being a boss-ass bitch.

I get distracted from my excitement over my outfit by a low growl. Turning, I arch my eyebrow at the hungry look in Caleb's gaze.

"So you want to have some fun sneaky sex, huh?" He gestures to my dress as he wags his eyebrows. "Because I can think of a lot of rooms to flip that skirt up in." I force myself to roll my eyes as heat courses through my body. I know he can tell I'm horny as hell.

"If that's the best you've got, you better keep it in your pants, Alpha." I take my outfit into the bathroom and start the shower, quickly stripping out of my nasty old clothes. My mind begins to wander, and I don't hear the door open or register what it could mean before there's a warm, large, and very naked male body pressed against mine. Caleb wraps his arms around me and fits my back against his chest. I tilt my head back to lean against his shoulder.

"You need to rest," he growls.

"Is that an order?" I meet his eyes and smirk.

"Does it need to be?" He doesn't return my smirk. Oh, so we're being serious.

I turn in his embrace and wrap my arms around his neck. Keeping my eyes on his, I start to play with his hair. I know I need to tread carefully here because I don't want him to think that I don't appreciate his concern, but I also don't want him to assume he can just steamroll me whenever I so much as sneeze. "I swear. I'm fine. A little tired, but totally fine."

"Ayla." He's got that sexy rumble in his voice again, his brogue getting thicker. "You were clutching your head one moment, and the next you were almost lifeless on the ground. You just went through all the healthy members of the former Rocky Mountain Pack. You need to rest before tackling those who're still recovering."

"This is me resting. I'm relaxing in the shower, or I was before I was interrupted." I lightly poke his chest. "If I drop my walls more and you see for yourself that I'm fine, will you let me finish?"

He remains silent, merely lifting an eyebrow. I groan. It won't hurt to finish with the others tomorrow, and it would have the added bonus of giving me time to sort through the new memories. I'm afraid to admit I'm scared to close my eyes again and run into Malick, so sorting through my memories may need to take a back seat for a while.

Resting my head against Caleb's chest, I let the water pour over both of us. I'll have to face this sooner or later, not that there's much of a choice. The memories could provide an answer to all of this, or at least give me some insight. Sighing, I close my eyes as I try to organize my thoughts. I've never felt this scatterbrained before. I can only hope this is a side effect of regaining some of my memories.

"Come on back to me, Ayla," Caleb murmurs soothingly, nudging me gently to open my eyes.

I blink them open and tilt my head back to look at Caleb's face. He smiles, and my heart stutters in my chest. He's so damn handsome. I hate that I'm so conflicted about him. I hate that he won't offer to leave the Council for me. I hate that I want him to.

"Let me take care of you for a while." He leans down to brush his lips against mine, sending shivers down my spine. "What do you say?"

I'm still turned on from earlier. While I know he didn't mean he'd take care of me in that context, it wouldn't hurt to have an orgasm or five. Endorphins and all that...right?

"I've heard that orgasms help with headaches." I grin up at him when he chuckles.

"Is that so?"

"Yep! So I think a few might help me feel better. A lot better." I force myself to sound serious.

"Well, who am I to argue with that?" He nods grimly, equally as serious.

He backs me up until my spine is pressed against the shower wall then kneels in front of me. But because I'm so short, his head comes up to my sternum even when he's kneeling. He proves resourceful and lifts me up. My legs instantly rest on his shoulders. He inhales deeply and growls low in his throat.

"Good girl." He gently bites the inside of my thigh, causing my leg to shake. Since he's doing me a favor, I decide not to push him to move faster. But if he could move a bit faster that would be fantastic.

He chuckles and leans in, flicking his tongue lightly against my clit, causing my head to fall back against the wall. One of his fingers comes up and traces my opening. My hips buck against his mouth, which appears to be the signal he needs to start eating me out with the same enthusiasm as the other night.

"Touch your breasts." Sir, yes, sir. My hands come up to play with my nipples. His finger continues toying with my opening, and I just want him to sink it into me. He dips the tip of his finger in, ripping a moan from my throat when he removes it.

"Don't worry, I won't make you beg, just focus on the feeling."

And that's what I do. I concentrate on the waves of pleasure that crash through my body with each flick of his tongue, each dip of his finger in my pussy, each flick of my nipples. My legs start shaking. I'm trying to hold off my orgasm and let it build until it consumes me, but Caleb is having none of that. He slides two fingers into my pussy, expertly rubbing against my G-spot. My orgasm slams through my body, a scream leaving me as I happily welcome the pulsing pleasure that courses through my veins.

He isn't content with just one orgasm, and soon he's wringing another from me. I'm mindlessly panting his name by the time he stands, helping me wrap my legs around his waist. Not giving me time to come down from my current high, he slowly eases himself inside me. I become acutely aware of my pussy spasming around him as he sinks himself to the hilt, the aftershocks of my second orgasm still surging through me. My hands wrap around his shoulders, my nails digging into the back of his neck.

"Mark me." His voice is gruff as he bottoms out, making us both moan. "Scratch me up, show everyone whom I belong to."

A part of me balks at claiming him in any way, but my dragon rises to the surface. If I won't allow the bond to fully form, she needs at least this. Some way to make sure that every female here knows that this sex god is ours. My nails sink into the flesh of his shoulders. He hisses and sets a rough pace. The only sounds in the shower are our moans, the slapping of our bodies as he drives his cock in deep and hard, and the smacking of my body against the wall as my greedy little pussy takes all of him with each thrust. I lean in, avoiding his neck, and bite down on his collarbone, my dragon mostly in control now.

"You. Are. Mine," Caleb snarls, his dragon lacing his tone with power, and each word is punctuated with a firm thrust.

"Yes," I reply softly, barely audible, but he hears me.

"Look at me, Ayla." My eyes open, and I lean back to look him in the eye. "Watch me as I make you come again." A ragged moan leaves me when he pauses. "Watch your sweet little pussy take my cock. Watch me fill you up."

My eyes drop to where we're joined, and I observe as he slowly drags himself out of me before he slams back inside. My eyes roll into the back of my head as pleasure floods me, and I fight to return my gaze to our bodies.

"You're so wet and tight." He grunts as he starts to pick up his pace again. "Each time I pull out, your pussy clenches so tightly around me like it doesn't want to let me go."

I'm not sure I can form actual words at this point. I just want him to make me come again. I want us to come together. I need it. Picking up on my thoughts through the bond, Caleb growls softly. "Do you want me to come in this tight pussy?"

I can only moan my agreement.

"Look me in the eyes, Ayla." My gaze flies up to his. He leans down and brushes his lips against mine. Our gazes stay locked as my orgasm builds. My legs shake, my nails dig deeper into his shoulders, and my pussy starts to clench tightly around his cock. I'm so close.

"That's it. Come all over my cock, milk me. Make me come with you." My scream rings out again as I explode around him. His own roar as he comes has aftershocks rippling through my body. He stays locked inside me for a few moments, breathing heavily, his forehead resting against mine. He's waiting for me to recover, I realize, my shock dissipating some of the pleasurable lightning bolts zapping my nerves.

He gently nips my neck, causing me to freeze. We've

agreed we aren't going to finalize the bond. What the hell is he doing?

"When I mark you here, I want to be buried balls deep inside you, preferably somewhere that isn't soundproof. The entire fucking pack needs to hear you scream my name as you come on my cock with my teeth buried in your neck."

"You—" My brain stutters, causing me to pause. "You, uh, sound so sure of yourself."

He bites a bit harder but doesn't break the skin, snarling softly against me. "You are mine. It *will* happen." His attitude suddenly changes, and he lifts his head. "But we're not focusing on that right now. Right now, we're focusing on getting you rested." He eases out of me and slowly lowers me to the floor, keeping his hands on my hips to make sure I can stand.

"Right. Resting." I blindly reach out and grab my soap, lathering my hands before starting to scrub his chest.

"As much as I would love for you to wash me, if you do, there won't be much resting." He takes the soap from me and washes himself quickly before cleaning me. There's no teasing touches or kisses, he means business.

Okay then, I'm resting. Once my hair has been washed and is wrapped in a terry cloth towel, we move into my bedroom before snuggling up in bed together. My exhaustion quickly catches up with me, and I'm fighting to keep my eyes open.

THREE FATES PURE TO keep the gate.

Should one Fate fall the seals will break.

I hear these words chanted repeatedly in my dream. Thunder booms and lightning flashes. There are three women standing on the edge of a cliff while a storm rages. The ocean batters the cliff face violently. Despite the chaos all around them, at the core, the three women create an image of peace, such utter calm.

Darkness. And then voices.

"Nay! Nay, I won't accept this."

"Aine, ye know we don't have a choice. They were chosen."

"Nay! They are babes, Cillian, babes!"

"My love, we will do aught we can to protect them. But you know as well as I, once the Fates have chosen, there is no going back."

"I was to be chosen, Cillian. To spare them, I was to be the sacrifice."

Chapter Sixteen

The next morning dawns too soon. I'm confused by the images I saw in my dream last night and what I heard echoing through the stillness of my sleep. My mother's voice is still clear in my head. She was to be the sacrifice? Sacrifice for what? Why?

Does that make us a sacrifice? My dragon rumbles. I'm worried she has a point. Was my mother only talking about me or all three of us? My sisters and I are triplets, and the limited memories I've regained suggest that the three of us were meant to be some sort of sacrifice to the Fates. But mother bargained for us in exchange for her own life? Is that why we were to be put to sleep? How did that tie in with the archdemons?

I think our memories were taken because Mother didn't have time to put us to sleep. My dragon stills at my thought and something deep inside me tells me I'm right. That was the only other option my mother would have had.

The heat radiating from Caleb's body, which is molded against my own, turns my thoughts from Fates and sacrifices back to sleep. I bury my head into my pillow, determined to take a few extra minutes to not think about visions, memories, and demons, and just be. Knowing it's only June, six months after Kelly and Olivia first knocked on my door, feels off. So does knowing I've only been alpha here for a little over a week. It feels as though years have passed.

And we haven't even started the truly challenging tasks, my dragon, ever the optimist, reminds me. Which causes the last few days to come flooding back. I take a minute to try to inventory my new memories. It's strange because they don't feel new or as if they were ever missing in the first place.

Any individual, regardless of species, that has been tainted by a demon, will appear to a queen as being smudged or fuzzy. That's the clear indicator of demonic interference.

Our mother told us where she would be hiding all three of us. Sorcha is in France. Isobel is somewhere in Africa. I was to be hidden...I can't remember.

Mother found something out when we were young. It made her more paranoid than ever. She became obsessed with keeping the three of us safe.

Three women in hooded robes stand over my sisters and me, chanting in a language I don't understand. Lightning flashes, and I catch a glimpse of the face of a young woman with wildly curly red hair under one of the hoods.

My mother whispering the key to waking us all up. But I can't hear her words.

Caleb's arm, which has been draped limply around my waist, tightens. His hand reaches up to cup my breast as he nuzzles his face into my neck. I arch teasingly into him, feeling him harden against my ass. His fingers start playing with my nipples and heat pools between my legs. My arm comes up and loops behind his neck, my nails digging into it. He groans and nips my shoulder, then moves his hand to lift my leg before sliding smoothly into me.

He hooks my leg around his arm as he slowly drags his

cock out of me, forcing me to feel every delicious inch of him. My moan echoes in the silence around us and he groans in response. As he thrusts into me, I purposely clench down around him, causing a soft snarl to erupt from his lips.

"Touch your clit." His sleep roughened voice has me shivering and clenching around him again. I quickly do as he asks. But I lazily stroke myself, keeping pace with his easy, unhurried thrusts.

We're in no hurry to finish, simply taking this moment to be together and enjoy each other's body. He feels so damn good, and I can't focus on anything other than the sensation of his cock dragging slowly inside my pussy over and over again. His breathing rings in my ears, mixed with soft groans and growls. All I can feel is him, everywhere, surrounding every inch of me. Our minds are linked, bouncing our pleasure back and forth until we both shatter. I've never experienced anything so intimate, so beautiful in my life.

"Neither have I." While I would normally be irritated by Caleb picking up on my thoughts, I'm too drunk on pleasure to care.

He stays inside me for a few more moments before getting out of bed. I hear rummaging in the bathroom, the faucet turning on and off, and then I feel him move me to my back. My eyes crack open as he cleans me, which is far more intimate than what just happened. My heart does a little flip in my chest, and I do my best to push it aside. But damn it, I think I'm falling in love with him.

After breakfast, I pull Caleb and Kelly aside. I need more training under my belt. My magic needs more fine-tuning in an offensive capacity, and my fighting skills were clearly lacking during the battle with Malick. If I want any chance at all of killing him, I'm going to need to be on my A-game.

"Do you two mind doing some training with me? I know I still need to meet with the injured Rocky Mountain Pack members, but I figure giving them another day or so to rest isn't a bad thing."

"Of course! A day or two to heal won't cost us anything. Even if there is a tainted member among them, none of the injured are in any condition to leave," Kelly reasons. Caleb nods in agreement.

"I figured you could help with magic, and Caleb can assist me with the physical stuff." Kelly snickers a soft, "*I'm sure he'll help you with the physical,*" through the bond.

"*That's enough out of you.*" I giggle quietly.

"I have a few Council related things I need to take care of. Why don't you start with Kelly? I can step in later in the day," Caleb offers.

"Perfect! Thank you both so much!"

Caleb leaves to do Council business, and Kelly and I head off to the gym. The gym isn't set up like a normal gym. There are several levels, each for a very specific type of training. This ensures no one gets injured from something they shouldn't be around. Spells can often go a bit haywire, especially with young witches, so they're best performed on a warded level without anyone who can't magically defend themselves around. Similarly, some shifters have difficulty with their shifts, so it's safer for everyone if they aren't shifting around witches or vampires who could be accidentally hurt during an unpredictable shift. There are several levels that allow for cross training, which will come in handy while we prepare to take on the legion.

"Dante said the vampires should be here later today. They made better time than they initially thought." I glance over at Kelly and can practically see her rubbing her hands together in glee. "I haven't had the chance to train with a vampire. It'll be exciting! Dante said that most of the members of their nest are warriors. We'll need all the help we can get if we're going to take down Malick's legion."

She's not wrong. Far from it. We will need all the help we can get. And I hate to admit that I should have a talk with Caleb about bringing even more of the Council over here. I know he called for reinforcements recently, but the more forces he can muster, the better off we'll be. I have a bad feeling that we'll need more than we have here currently if we're going to stand a fighting chance. Maybe it's just my insecurity over my current fighting abilities talking. Gods, I sure hope so.

As we head to a level that's warded to contain spell work, I recall that Kelly has blocked my bonds after I passed out upon seeing Sean's body. Embarrassing. "Do you think you can unblock my bonds? My head is fine, and it feels weird not being connected to everyone."

"Sure." Kelly comes over and places her hands on the sides of my head. I feel a warm tingling start at my temples that slowly spreads out to encompass the rest of my head and down my neck. "All set."

Tentatively, I poke at the bonds, pleased when Olivia instantly responds. I hadn't realized how much I would miss the weight of the pack and coven in my mind. What I had once thought of as loud and annoying now seems comforting, a fortifying weight that steadies me and gives me purpose.

The room we're in has a single door, a wall of windows opposite the door, and LED lights overhead. It's large, taking up the entire floor of the building. The door is in the center of the room, leading to the staircase in the middle of the building. The room also has various objects that can be used during spell casting along the wall, such as knives to be thrown using only magic, various armor and weapons, blindfolds, healing balms for all sorts of injuries, and a stretcher just in case.

"Let's start with defensive magic," Kelly suggests. While I had mainly wanted to focus on offensive magic, testing my defensive capabilities is a good call. I admit I have a tendency to sit squarely in the mindset of a good defense is a good offense, which doesn't always work out well. Setting a stronger foundation for my defensive magic may help the next time Malick decides to stab me with a rock spear coated in his essence.

That sounds too rapey. My dragon has a point. *And leaving his essence behind is such an extreme violation. It's gross.*

I know. I'll make a note for my villain school. You can be a bad guy without taking it to that level. Let's all be civilized here.

KELLY and I practice defensive magic for a few hours before switching to offensive. Typically, I prefer fighting with an energy whip. It's fast, effective, and doesn't use up a lot of magic. It also has the added bonus of keeping unwanted douche canoes away. But my fight with Malick has made me realize that I can't only rely on my whip. I opened up the ground beneath him, but I need to be able to harness the other elements effectively for a better follow-through.

I take a moment to center myself, closing my eyes and inhaling deeply, knowing that I won't be able to do this on the battlefield. My eyes snap open at the same time my hands come up in front of me. Bright red flames dance around my right hand while water shimmers around my left. It's go time.

Taking another deep inhale, I slam my foot against the floor, flick my wrists, and then release my breath. Kelly throws up a shield, but it's not enough to defend her from the air, water, and fire that fly her way. The floor beneath her feet quakes, throwing her off balance. I follow up with my energy whip, lashing it out to wrap around her arm and drag her closer to me. I make sure it isn't harmful, merely intending to practice the moves.

Kelly is able to break my whip and lashes out with a blast of air, sending me skidding across the room. Neither of us pause. Kelly attacks with a stream of fire, while I surround myself with a sphere of water. Freezing several small droplets, I send them hurtling toward her like bullets, turning them to water at the last minute to avoid serious damage. She's able to block a few but most hit her.

I can feel my dragon surge inside of me as my magic floods my system. With a flick of my wrist, the water around me dissipates. Kelly pants lightly as she stares me down in an attempt to determine my next move. Feeling the need to test myself, I stay still for this next bit of magic. Technically a truly talented and powerful witch doesn't need body movements or spells to perform magic. It helps me focus my power and intent. Magic is always more formidable when the intent is clear. But I want to be able to perform powerful attacks without giving away what I'm doing. Panting slightly, I visualize what I want to do in my mind.

I release my magic with a palpable wave of energy. It instantly circles Kelly before binding tightly around her, forcing her arms snugly against her body. Her legs pin together, and she topples to the floor, a grin spreading across her face.

"How did you do that?" She sounds excited.

I chuckle. "I just visualized what I wanted to happen. I can still feel the energy that's around you. In theory, I would be able to cut off your air supply, maybe sever a limb."

"Awesome." I roll my eyes before releasing my hold on her. "I can typically cast like that too, but never with that much force." There's a glint in her eye I know all too well. Kelly loves a good challenge, and now she wants to do casting with that much force.

"I'll let you practice on me," I offer, knowing I'm a little more indestructible than many of the others in the community and that Kelly will take me up on the suggestion.

"You're such an awesome friend." She claps and bats her eyes at me. I laugh.

"Likewise." We grin at each other. "Now why don't we take a bit of a break? I'm starving, and we've been at this for hours. I'm sure there's lunch back at the house."

AFTER LUNCH, I track down Caleb. I want to get some hand-to-hand training in before the end of the day. I can't fixate on what happened with Malick and how he's been haunting my dreams despite the fact that my mind always circles back to him. Instead, I need to focus on getting stronger and becoming the queen my community deserves. I notice Dante across the street and raise my hand in greeting. He smiles and jogs over to me.

"Xin just arrived with our nest. They're getting settled in their new homes." He sounds excited which warms my heart.

"Oh, great!" I beam at him. "I was just about to track down Caleb to get some hand-to-hand combat training in, but that can wait if they need additional help." He shakes his head.

"They're all fine, we've got plenty of other community members assisting. I know how the threat of the legion is weighing on you, Ayla. I'm sure getting some training done will help ease some of that weight. Would you like for me to join you?" He's got an eager twinkle in his eyes, as though the thought of kicking my ass appeals to him. It probably does.

"If you think you can spare the time. You said you're part

of the elite warriors of your nest, right?" At his nod, I continue, "Maybe you can help me brush up on my fighting skills? I'm very rusty."

He mock bows before me, dramatically sweeping his arm out behind him and almost touching his head to the sidewalk. I struggle to suppress a grin as I shake my head when he straightens.

"It would be my pleasure, milady."

"You are the absolute worst. Don't do that again." I can't keep the laughter from my tone, which seems to encourage him as he starts to bow in different ways, causing a laugh to slip past my tight control.

"Who has you in such a good mood? I'll need to punch him in the face," Caleb booms through the bond, startling me out of my laughter.

"It's just Dante. Calm yourself down several notches, sir." I make sure to bleed as much sass through the bond as possible. *"He's going to be training with us, being some sort of super vampire warrior and all. Are you on your way to the gym?"*

"Yes. I needed to finish up the paperwork to make the merger of the Rocky Mountain Pack and the New England Pack official." Aw, how sweet. *"I'll be there in five minutes."*

"Roger that." I realize Dante is staring at me. Ah shit, I stopped laughing and then must have just stared blankly off into space like a bloody idiot while having my little touch base with Caleb. "Sorry about that, Dante. I was just speaking with Caleb."

He simply shrugs his shoulders and extends his arm, indicating that I am to lead the way. "It's a mate thing. You get this gooey look in your eyes when you talk to him." He rolls his eyes. "I seriously hope I'm not quite that pathetic when I find my mate." I can tell he's teasing me by the tone of his voice, so I stick my tongue out at him.

"You'll be worse. A lot worse." I grin and give him a gentle shove to the shoulder. "The males are always worse than the females. Always."

"You realize I'm going to kick your ass, right?" Dante states, changing the topic. While I'd love to tease him more, my competitive side kicks in. Oh, it's on alright.

Chapter Seventeen

Once we make it to the gym, I nudge Caleb through the bond again. He's not here yet, so I usher Dante into a mixed space that can be used for both spell-casting and shifting, along with regular gym activities and battle simulations. I then let Caleb know what level we're on. I don't want to waste any time, feeling oddly amped up. Float like a butterfly, sting like a bee!

Yeah, because we're totally some world-class boxer. My dragon rolls her eyes at me. *Settle down and let the man show you how to kick ass.* Wow. Okay. That's how she wants to be, huh? Fine. Mentally sticking my tongue out at her, I turn my attention to Dante.

"You have one huge advantage none of the rest of us have," Dante starts. "You're a queen. You can sense demons well before the rest of us. Not only that, you can harness magic and shift. Remember that. Hone each skill. I assume you are truly one with your dragon?" I nod. "Excellent. We won't need to focus on that. Instead, I want us to focus on breathing."

Breathing? I feel as though I'm a sulky, pouting child, but I thought this was going to be a lesson in physical combat.

"Concentrating your breathing will ensure that you have the stamina needed to ensure victory. It will help you manage pain, harness your magic, and focus your attacks for optimal damage." Okay, I like the sound of that. "Have you meditated before?"

"I meditate daily."

"Excellent. You're already halfway there. I want you to breathe like you're meditating. Calm your heart rate and center your mind. You'll need to do this quickly on the battle-field, but we can practice this to ensure you'll be able to do it at a moment's notice. For now, I want to make sure you're in the proper frame of mind."

I take several deep breaths, blanking out my mind, focusing on centering myself. I stay like this for several heart-beats, letting a sense of calm wash over me. "Good. Now close your eyes and focus on my aura. I want you to learn to read my moves from my aura alone. It will become second nature, and you won't need to focus to do it."

I do as Dante instructs, concentrating solely on his aura. Like all other vampires, his aura is a deep burgundy color. I'd never thought to use my ability to see auras to sense some-one's attacks, but it makes sense. An aura tells me a lot about a person—if they're lying, what species they are, if they've been tainted by a demon, if they're sick.

I'm so busy focusing on Dante's aura itself, I realize too late that he's moved. I can't defend myself fast enough, and my eyes snap open to see he's about to hit me. My hands fly up to protect my face, but he's not aiming there. My breath leaves me with a soft grunt as I fold at the waist. He hit my diaphragm. The bastard.

"Eyes closed, Alpha." Dante's voice is stern, cold. "Do not

focus so much on trying to read my aura for my feelings. Try to read my intent."

Well, how the fuck do I do that? I sigh in a manner that clearly indicates to Dante that I'm very put out by this whole experience. He chuckles softly as I close my eyes again. I inhale deeply, clearing my mind. Read his intent. What does that even mean? How am I supposed to do that using just his aura? My dragon is silent, apparently she's just as confused as I am. Awesome.

I shake out my limbs, bob my head, roll my shoulders, and crack my neck. Okay. Focus. Clearing my mind, I once again allow Dante's aura to light up my mind. Instead of fixating on it, I relax into it and allow it to wash over me.

Left! I throw my hand up and block a strike aimed for my head.

Jump! I dodge a sweep of his leg to knock me off my feet.

His aura flashes ever so slightly in the direction he's about to hit me. I can feel the strike coming and know just how much I need to turn to avoid getting hit. Feeling more confident, I decide to turn the tables. With my eyes still closed, I go on the attack. Since this training session is meant to be solely physical and not magical, I refrain from using my magic...outwardly. Instead, I use my magic on myself, just like I did when I fought Morgan. I use it to make me stronger, faster, and more accurate. Adding my magic to reading Dante's aura feels like I've dived into his mind without the repercussions. I'm easily able to dodge his attacks, countering in ways he isn't expecting.

Finally, I have Dante pinned to the floor. He lightly taps my leg to indicate that I've won. Slow clapping starts near the entrance to the training room. My eyes pop open, and I see Caleb leaning against the wall near the door. He's got that stupid grin on his idiotically handsome face that makes my stupid heart rollover. He claps again as he pushes away from the wall, his eyes gleaming as he stares at me with every step he takes.

"Well done, Ayla." Dante's voice jolts me out of whatever the hell spell Caleb had me under. I shake my head before grinning down at Dante. "You did well. Now you just need to work on getting into that same space as quickly as possible. Demons won't just sit around waiting for you to find that sweet spot in your mind."

I place my hands over my face and groan. "I know. I'll work on it. Now that I know what I'm looking for, it should be a lot easier."

"How far out can you sense a demon?" Caleb's deep Scottish brogue pulls my gaze over to him. "My mother had been able to scan all of Europe with a single thought. How far out can you go?"

"I—" I stop to think. The last time I let my spidey senses out to check for demons, I had only been looking for them in New England. "I'm not sure, to be honest. It's been a long time since I've had to stretch my senses out that far. I typically only check within a few hours' traveling distance, so I know I have an out."

"Why don't you give it a try?" Caleb comes over and lifts me off Dante. He places me gently on the floor so I'm lying on my back, then he sits cross-legged next to me. "My mother said it was like visualizing a map in her mind. She'd then let her magic flow over the map and see what bounced back."

This is the first time Caleb has opened up about his mother. Given how powerful he is, it's not surprising that she was a queen. My mother had covered most of Ireland, the U.K., and Western Europe, at least after my sisters and I had been born. She hadn't mentioned another queen in the area, and I can't recall feeling one either. Had she died before I was born? I make a mental note to ask Caleb about his mother as I close my eyes.

I'm going to go big, so I picture a map of the entire world. This way I can truly get a sense for the range of my power. I release the hold I have on my magic, allowing its shiny rainbow light to playfully leap away from my body, thrilled to be given a duty. *Go*, I whisper to it. *Search out the demons.* It jumps into action, soaring out of my body and into the world.

Think of it like sonar. My dragon gently nudges my mind as I wait. *We should get little blips whenever something demonic touches your magic.*

Makes sense. I feel something. It's too small to be Malick's legion, but it's gathered in the Southern U.S., near the Texas-Mexico border. There are more blips to the north near Chicago. A particularly strong blip bounces back from Washington, D.C.

Archdemon, my dragon growls. Of course there would be at least one archdemon in the Capitol. Surprisingly, most of the demons I'm able to pick up aren't associated with an archdemon. Typically, lower-level demons can't really function well on their own. They need the guidance and dominance an archdemon provides. Otherwise, they either waste away, think zombie here, or they go rogue and run the risk of exposing everything.

A massive blast, this time from Alaska, makes me grateful I'm already lying down. Malick's legion. I can't be sure, but my gut is telling me the enormous surge of energy, as well as the sheer number of lower-level demons, means that's where his little base camp is. At least for now.

My magic doesn't stop there, however, it continues to spread. I'm able to see demons...everywhere. Holy. Shit. And what the fuck is that in Antarctica? I shiver. I don't want to find out. Let's not poke that bear.

"Malick is in Alaska right now," I tell Caleb as my eyes

focus on his face. "He's got an even bigger legion than he had in the Rockies."

"Fuck." Caleb's eyes harden. "How far were you able to see?"

"The whole world." I'm such a terrible person for enjoying the shocked silence that follows.

"Everywhere?" Dante's voice is filled with awe. "I've never heard of a queen able to search the entire planet."

"Neither have I." Caleb's gaze searches my face, a frown tugging at his lips. "If you're more powerful than past queens, we're going to need to worry about more than just Malick. Every damn archdemon and lower-level demon is going to want a piece of you. Either to destroy you or use you."

"It's a good thing I'm beefing up then. Between the magic practice lessons and the physical training sessions, I'll be able to take down any demon that comes at me." I mock jab the air in his direction. His frown only deepens.

"Dante, can you give us a minute?" Caleb doesn't bother to look over at the vampire, who simply nods at me and leaves the room.

"What's going on?" I sit up and scooch until I'm sitting cross-legged in front of him, my knees touching his. "You look worried about all of this. It's a good thing I'm powerful. If we want to destroy Malick's legion and any other legion that comes knocking, I need to be at the top of my game."

"I'll need to move the Council's headquarters here," Caleb mumbles to himself.

"I'm sorry. What?" I make sure to use my best impression of a mother who is *not* amused. "Move the Council headquarters? Where? Why?"

"Here." Caleb's eyes meet mine and hold. "If you won't leave this community, the Council is going to have to come here. It's the only way to ensure you're properly protected."

"We don't take too kindly to the Council 'round these

parts." I muster up my best deep Southern accent. "It wouldn't end well if y'all were to settle here."

"I'm serious, Ayla."

"So am I." I sigh and stand up, pacing the room as I talk. "Look, it's a sweet gesture. But it simply won't work. Kelly's mom got passed up, and the Council still hasn't told us why, so the witches are salty as fuck. After everything the shifters in this area have been through, without any aid from the Council, they aren't keen to trust you. Plus, they're loyal to the witches now, so if one of us holds a grudge, we all do. Especially knowing the Council's little habit of collecting rare and powerful supernaturals."

"We don't collect anyone!" Caleb stands and crosses his arms over his chest as he glares at me. "We protect rare and powerful individuals who would otherwise have a very large target on their back. It's easier to fight off what's hunting you if you have the numbers than on your own."

"Literally every rare or powerful individual the Council has ever come across has either mated into the Council or has been 'recruited.' You collect them, Caleb. Hell, one of your closest men is someone you've collected. A dire wolf, Caleb? Are you trying to tell me that you didn't try to sell him on the Council or force him to join once you realized what he was?" By this point, I'm frantically talking with my hands. My arms are flying viciously through the air as I speak. "You say that you let your envoys mate into different packs and covens, but from what I've been able to gather, they usually end up leaving with the Council, not staying with their community. Especially if one or both of the mated pair have a rare power."

Caleb snarls and reaches for me, but I flinch back, not wanting him to touch me. "They all choose to come with us."

"Do they really though?" I press. I'm not convinced. The Council seems to have too much power. While the threat from the demons is real, it isn't large enough to warrant this kind of mass collection of rare and powerful supernaturals. "The Council is this juggernaut that just plows over anyone and everything in its way. You might think that you're giving people the choice to join, but there is no choice, Caleb. And you aren't going to move the Council here. I won't allow it. My community won't allow it."

"The Council coming here isn't up for debate. I'm having the headquarters moved here immediately, end of story. I don't understand the issue, Ayla."

"No one person is supposed to have the kind of power you do. The whole point of multiple queens was so this wouldn't happen. I understand that I'm the last one left, but the Council wasn't supposed to end up like this. All the former queens are rolling over in their graves. Yes, they each had territory, but they were always in communication with one another, and no one queen was to be above any other queen, regardless of the size of her community or her strength.

"I'll put it to a vote with my community, but I'm certain I know the answer. They won't want the Council coming here. If you try to force the issue, there will be a huge problem." My tone is quiet and deadly as I finish.

"Oh yeah?" Caleb sneers. "What sort of problem?"

"I'll bloody challenge you myself."

I TAKE my time walking back to the packhouse, having left Caleb stunned in the gym. I meant every word. I will challenge him if my community doesn't want him here and he insists on moving the Council to town. That is not a unilateral decision, and the fact that he thinks it is has me seeing red.

I acknowledge the issue the Council presents for the both of us. I don't want to be with him because he's the head of the Council, and our discussion today demonstrated for me that my unease and animosity toward the Council goes far deeper than I realized. The Council spits in the memories of all the past queens, and that doesn't sit right with me. Being the head of the Council has inflated Caleb's ego and made him think that he's the be-all, end-all. Not even I can boast that.

No. If I need to challenge him for his position as head of the Council to get my message across, I will. I'll appoint someone else or dismantle the whole damn thing if I need to. I'm so lost in my thoughts, I don't see Xin approaching me until I almost run the poor man over.

"Alpha." Xin bows. "I wanted to provide you with an update on the move."

"You don't have to bow, Xin. I like to think of this as a sort of democracy." I chuckle. "I'm not interested in being a dictator."

"Of course, Alpha." I shoot him a look and he grins broadly at me. Sassy bit of goods. "We've been lucky enough to find homes for all of our members." I gesture for him to walk beside me. "I plan to step down as head of the nest. I believe Dante will serve as a better beta for you."

I'm shocked. While I certainly like Dante, and we click, I assumed Xin would continue as my beta given his experience with queens. But I suppose I shouldn't be all that surprised. The bond between a queen and her community runs deep. It might feel like a betrayal for Xin to serve as my beta despite his former queen's death.

"If you're sure that's best. I trust your judgment, Xin." I glance over at him, and he appears relieved. "Though, I need to confess, I don't know the bonding process between a queen and a nest." I smile sheepishly.

"It is a simple process and only involves the individual who is going to be your beta. Once I have transferred power over to Dante, he will need to bite you and share his blood with you. Then you'll have the same bond with him and the nest that you have with the rest of your community." Blood sharing, while I don't judge, is not my thing. But I'm happy to do it to ensure the safety of the nest and the rest of my community.

"When do you plan to transfer power to Dante?"

"I want to give the nest a week or two to settle in. They're all aware of the change, but I also don't want to make things too difficult for Dante so early into his leadership." Xin places a hand on my arm, halting our forward progress. "Ayla, I know you need to interview the members of the nest. There are a few who are extremely traumatized from their dealings with demons. If you would allow me to pull those individuals aside for you to have a private screening, that would probably be best."

My heart aches for those individuals. "Of course. It's no problem at all. We can do the interviews on a separate day so they have time to prepare if needed. There's no way for them to hide anything from me, but they might want time to just brace themselves. I honestly just need to look at their aura. It's nothing invasive."

"Understood. Thank you, Ayla. We are excited to be part of such a caring and strong community."

Chapter Eighteen

A few days of intense magical and physical training later, neither of which involve Caleb, I'm sore, bruised, and exhausted. I'm heading down for breakfast, my stomach roaring almost as loud as my dragon. But I feel much better about my ability to defend the community when we go head-to-head with the demons again. After our conversation in the gym the other day about the Council collecting supernaturals, Caleb has been avoiding me. Being slapped in the face with the truth does that to people.

I firmly stand by what I said. The Council spits in the face of everything past queens stood for. I understand I'm the only one left, but even if I wasn't, what's going on is a horrible way to honor all the queens did for the supernatural community. I've made a decision over the last few days. It's time for me to step the fuck up, put my big girl panties on, and be a damn queen. I'm not running anymore, so I'm going to trample all over the damn patriarchy like the fabulous unicorn I am. Destroying the patriarchy with glitter and sass sounds so wonderful. I evil chuckle mentally.

I don't put the full blame for how the Council currently

operates solely on Caleb's shoulders. The representatives could very well have said something or prevented any of this from happening. But Caleb needs to be man enough to acknowledge his part.

He honestly thought he was doing what was right, my dragon points out.

Did he though? Let's be hella real here. The Alpha of all alphas comes to you and says, 'You should join the Council for your own protection.' He stands in front of them with that damn look of his, and what, people tell him no? Don't make me laugh. It was an impossible position to put people in. I can understand wanting to protect rare and powerful species or individuals, but they should be given an honest choice and should be coming to those they feel can help them. Not the other way around.

I try to shake my thoughts away as I walk into the dining room to find Kelly, Olivia, Connor, Malcolm, and Dante seated at the table. Dante has a wine glass of blood in front of him, and the others all have plates piled high with food. Good. They're taking care of themselves.

"Where's Patrick?" I ask as I grab a plate of my own and start scooping up eggs, bacon, and waffles.

"He just left. He wanted to check on his packmates that are still recovering. He was thrilled to learn that the healthy members of his pack weren't tainted." Kelly hands me a mug of coffee, that's how I know she loves me.

"Speaking of, how many did I see the other day? I forgot to ask with all the training we've been doing, and they're all sort of blurring together."

"You saw around fifteen hundred." I did what now? "It was really impressive. You just got into this zone and went through them like you were on speed." Kelly chuckles.

"And there are a thousand injured?"

"About two hundred of those injured are Rocky Mountain Pack members, the other eight hundred are Council. But the

Rocky Mountain Pack lost about two thousand members in the fight. From what I've been able to gather, only about three hundred of the Council group died."

Well, shit. This brings our total count to roughly five thousand, two hundred members. That's a really solid community. And I'm in charge of all of them. Fuck. No pressure.

"Have you been able to neutralize the demon talisman?" Caleb's voice knocks me out of my shock and mild panic. He strolls into the dining room, his eyes narrowing on me as he moves to get food. Oh, right, that's a thing.

A thing we would have seen to had we not had our head blown off from recovering memories before becoming preoccupied with training. You need to delegate more. My dragon is not being very helpful today.

Keep the snark to yourself.

If you'd listen every once in a while, I would. I want to stick my tongue out at her, but then I'd get weird looks from around the table.

"Yes! Thankfully, because we knew the demon's name, it wasn't difficult. But it's been buried and warded just to be safe." Kelly pulls out her phone to show me a video of the process she used.

"That's perfect. Thank you." My reply sounds sheepish. I should have been more on top of all this.

"No need for thanks! This is what betas are for! You needed to rest, and we needed to do something. The Rocky Mountain Pack is eager to take the blood oath." Despite it being called a blood oath, no blood is actually exchanged.

"We can do the oath tonight."

"Great! I'll let Patrick know." Kelly gets up and heads out to find Patrick, Olivia following her.

Well, this is awkward. I glance over at Caleb to find him glaring at me across the table. I want to stick my tongue out at him now. Stupid male. I go back to ignoring him, eating quickly before departing.

$$\sim$$

I MAKE my way to the infirmary. I have a moment alone, and I relish the silence. The last few days haven't been quiet, and I've missed the silence of my office. I groan internally, knowing I need to check my phone. I snap my fingers and my phone appears in my hand. I wince at the twenty missed calls and over five hundred emails. Attempting to make a mental list of things to do today, I almost run right into Patrick.

"Alpha!"

"Hi, Patrick. I'm on my way to see your injured pack mates. I'll do their screenings. I figured we could do the oath tonight for the healthy members. I don't want to put too much strain on the injured right now."

"Let me walk with you?" I nod and he falls into step beside me. "Thankfully those who were seriously injured are well on the mend now. I think they should be able to attend the oath tonight."

"It really isn't an issue if they can't. I don't want to cause any additional injury or stress." We enter the infirmary, and I'm pleased to see most of the people are sitting up in bed and chatting with each other. A few are sleeping soundly, but they look to be in good health.

"Kelly had us move the beds around. All of my pack are in this building, and the councilmen are in the building next door."

"She's fantastic like that." I grin and slowly make my way down the center aisle, my magic flaring out around me. So far, so good.

When we get to the final room, I stop about halfway down the aisle. There are two male shifters at the end of the left-hand row that are tainted. Thankfully, they don't seem to think anything is wrong with my being here.

"We have a situation at the infirmary," I blast to Kelly, Olivia, and Caleb. *"Two members of the Rocky Mountain Pack have been tainted. We'll need to bring them to the barracks."*

The barracks is the building we use to house our prison cells. We don't have any issue with crime here on pack land, but during times of war, they're often used to hold the enemy. During times of peace, they're used to house the drunks who celebrate a little too hard. I look over at Patrick, and he's noticed something is wrong. I flick my eyes to the two men at the end of the row. His eyes follow and widen, but not in surprise, it looks as though he's fitting puzzle pieces together. I'll need to ask him about it once we've secured these two.

"We're right outside. How are we going to play this?" Olivia's tone is edged with steel.

"We'll need to magically bind them, then we need to manhandle them over to the barracks." I start slowly making my way down the row again to avoid any suspicion. *"Have the door to this room blocked in case they try to run. I'm going to attempt to bind them at the same time, but they might catch on and bolt."*

Patrick follows next to me, keeping up some inane babble. The man is smarter than he lets on. We're closer to the two tainted shifters when one suddenly shifts into a giant grizzly bear. He crashes through the wall of the infirmary and makes a run for it, his friend a bit slower on the uptake. I don't need to relay that the grizzly has broken free. I kept the bond open, and both pack members and councilmen are on his tail.

My hands thrust out and stop the other shifter—fox, by his scent—binding his ability to shift. Patrick moves in quickly, smashing his fist into the guy's face. Not necessarily called for, but I'll let him have it. Patrick wrestles the shifter's arms behind his back before turning his head to look at me.

"Shane and Kevin, they were friends with Sean. Shane here is a bit of an idiot," Patrick sneers. Condemning words.

As all the commotion dies down, I inhale deeply to get Shane's scent better and I freeze. The shifters from the fighting ring. My dragon claws at my skin, wanting to get out and show this flaming piece of garbage what those females must have felt. If he was at that fighting ring, he at the very least knows about females getting sold. He'd be exceptionally stupid not to. But given the demonic taint the clings to him like a second skin, he knows more than that. I bet good ole Kevin knows more too.

"Let's take our new best friend Shane, here, to the barracks. I have a few questions for him." Shane goes pale at my words, and I don't bother to hide the bloodthirsty smile that spreads across my face. *Good little idiot, be afraid, be very afraid.*

"Ayla, we need to send trackers after that bear," Olivia announces as she steps through the hole in the wall, Caleb following her. "Kelly was able to put a quick tracking spell on him, but she doesn't think it'll last long, we need to get people out there now." I nod to Caleb, letting him know I'll let him handle this. He nods and strides off.

"Olivia, show Patrick where the barracks are. I need to go change my outfit." I gesture to the sundress I picked out the other day and never got to wear. "This isn't appropriate torture attire. I really don't want to get blood on this dress."

Olivia chuckles loudly when Shane let's out a low whimper before taking his arm to lead him and Patrick to the barracks. Slowly lifting my hands, I magically repair the infirmary wall. I'm glad the building is a ranch-style and only consists of one floor. I don't need to worry about any debris falling on someone. Why do the bad guys always have to make such a mess when they escape?

For once, I'd love a thoughtful villain who didn't feel the

need to ruin literally everything they touch. I'll add that to the course offerings in my villain school. How to be a Thoughtful Villain: Step one, use a damn door.

≈

ONCE I'VE CHANGED into something a little more appropriate, a pair of leather pants and a leather corset, complete with knee-high, leather platform boots—so I might have moonlit as a dominatrix a lifetime or two ago, who hasn't?—I head to the barracks to talk to Shane. I wasn't kidding when I said torture. While I don't want to hurt anyone unnecessarily, Shane's allegiance is with the demons. He forfeited any shot at leniency when he sold his soul.

I get the sense he's just a lackey and won't know much, but I plan to bleed every drop of information from him. Shane was at the fighting ring the night I saved Sasha, the night I realized that Morgan was selling females. My mind is whirling with the implications. Shane was a friend of Sean's, could he have also been an associate of Morgan's? An intermediary? There has to be some sort of link, it's too coincidental.

When I finally get to the barracks, I pause outside the building. While I might want to rip Shane to pieces for putting the community in jeopardy, physical torture isn't something I'm overly eager to engage in. Given that he's been tainted, I don't think physical torture will be the most effective method either. But diving into his mind will get me everything I need, every tiny detail, even things he wouldn't have thought to be important. I'll know it all. If he's left a vegetable at the end? Oh, well.

He shouldn't have climbed in bed with demons.

≈

MALCOLM AND CALEB are standing in front of Shane with their arms crossed when I enter the holding cell. Olivia is leaning against the wall as though she doesn't have a care in the world. If only Shane could feel what I can through the bond, I have no doubt the man would piss himself. Frankly, I'm surprised he's looking Malcolm in the eye. Smart of him to not tempt fate by meeting Caleb's gaze.

When Shane sees me walk in, looking as though I'm about to string him up by his dick, he goes deathly pale. Caleb turns to look at me, a vicious growl leaving him when he notices how I'm dressed. He comes over, grabs my arm, and leads me back out of the room.

"What the hell are you wearing?"

"Are you telling me you don't like this outfit?" I'm mildly amused by the shade of purple he turns as he struggles to answer.

"Why are you wearing that?"

"I just need to set the mood."

"The mood..." He repeats it as though I've spoken a foreign language, or I have brain damage, hard to tell.

"Yes. I want him to understand that his balls may be severed from his body." A surprised laugh leaves Caleb.

"Ball severing attire aside, why did you feel the need to wear this particular outfit?"

"Why are you so focused on my outfit?" I adjust the corset slightly so my boobs are pushed up a bit more. "Is it the boobs? Are you too distracted? I mean, I get it. They're kind of amazing."

Caleb snarls before closing his eyes and taking a deep breath.

"Don't worry your cute lil' penis, Alpha. I'll be able to get answers out of Shane dressed like this."

I'll make sure you get up close and personal with my penis later. It seems as though you've forgotten what he looks like already.

I roll my eyes at him. "Caleb." My tone turns serious. "I need you to trust me. I can get what we need."

"But dressed like that?" He sounds exasperated, which only makes me happy.

"For the love of the goddess. Yes! Dressed like this! Now are you going to keep being a damn problem, or can I go torture the bad fox in the other room?" I make sure to ask about torturing Shane loud enough that he'll be able to hear me through the door.

"Fine. But I swear—" I cut him off with a look.

"If you do anything, *anything*, to compromise what I'm doing in there to get answers because you're butthurt, I will personally make sure that you're truly butthurt for a very, *very* long time. Am I clear?" He snarls again, so I pat him on the chest. "Good Alpha."

I push past Caleb and back into Shane's cell. Caleb follows me as though he's my damn shadow. Shane has resumed his stare down with Malcolm while we were out of the room. My dragon releases a low, sinister growl, reminding Shane of who he should really be focused on. The fox shifter seems to shrink into himself, his eyes lowering to the floor. Good, I need him off-kilter. It'll be easier for me to dive into his mind if he's scared out of his pants. There's an extra chair by the door, so I drag it over next to Malcolm. Caleb stays by the door, his arms crossed and eyes narrowed. Gracefully lowering myself into the chair, I cross my legs and pick at an imaginary piece of lint on my pants, taking all the time in the world before deigning to speak to Shane.

"This is how it's going to go, Shane," I chirp, acting friendly, as though I'm about to share a fun little secret. "I'm going to go digging through your brain. If you just happen to turn into a vegetable after, I don't think anyone here is really going to care."

"Y-You c-can't d-do th-that." Stuttering already, Shane

looks to Malcolm for support. "T-The Council w-won't l-let you."

"Oh, honey, haven't you heard? I'm a *queen*. I don't have to listen to the Council." A slow, toothy, predatory grin spreads across my face. "If my pals Malcolm and Caleb here don't approve of me digging through your lil' noggin, they can certainly discuss it with the rest of the Council. But it's not going to stop me." I widen my eyes slightly, emphasizing the crazy. "Nothing can stop me, Shane."

"By all means, do what you must, my queen." Malcolm grins and gestures at Shane, while Caleb remains a silent guardian at the door. "Given the attack on the Council and the Rocky Mountain Pack, we're willing to allow for an unorthodox method of retrieving information."

"Wait!" Shane screams. "I'll tell you what you want to know, just ask me, I swear!"

"The problem with that, Shane, well..." I sigh. "I'm not going to fucking believe a word that comes out of your sorry tainted mouth. Are you, Malcolm?"

"Nope." Malcolm's lips pop on the "p." "Not a damn word."

"Caleb? Olivia? Chime in any time if you feel like Shane's going to be a good little trooper and be honest with us." Their silence screams throughout the cell, a damning answer. "Strap in, dickface, this is going to be one hell of a bumpy ride."

Chapter Nineteen

S hane is very much aware of what is happening to him. He's resistant and is actively trying to make this harder than it needs to be. Unlike when I dove into Jonas's mind just a few days earlier, I'm going to need to use far more magic to get what I want out of Shane. Frankly, I'm too pissed off to care about the backlash, and I have no problem watching Shane form puddles of drool everywhere for the rest of his miserable life. I don't hold back, aggressively pushing past any mental walls he tries to erect, letting my magic savagely invade his mind.

As I suspected, Shane is a brainless lackey. He wasn't privy to any real information, just bits and pieces he needed to accomplish whatever tasks he was assigned. He pushed drugs, fought in the underground rings, drugged females so they could be held in the cages we found in Sean's basement, and... fury rages through me as I catch a memory of him assaulting a few of those helpless women. While he hadn't had any direct dealings with any demon himself, his actions against the females of his own pack just earned him a one-way ticket to vegetable town. I keep searching for information, wrath now fueling my efforts and shredding his mind.

I pause at one memory of a fight from years ago, noting how many of the fighters appear smudged. This problem is so much larger than we realized and has been going on for far too long. These fights bring in shifters from not just the U.S., but around the world. I only saw Shane and Kevin a few months ago, but I also hadn't been looking for fighters, my eyes scanning for females. Just how bad was the infestation?

Shane was in a lot of illegal fights throughout the country, and each of them had numerous fighters who had dealings with demons. More worrying than that, however, is the amount of drugged up females I see leaving with not only shifter males, but mages too. Which further strengthens my belief that Malick is involved.

There's a dark memory. Seems like Shane was listening by an open window while shifted in the middle of the night. Voices float outside through the window.

"You said the drugs would keep the females sedated enough for transport! One almost broke out of her cell."

"Calm yourself, Sean. Remember who you're talking to." I freeze. Malick.

"If these females get out of their cages and go back into town, this is it. Our little arrangement is over." Sean doesn't sound scared of Malick. He sounds like a whiny, petulant child who isn't about to get his way.

"Yes, yes." Malick's tone is dismissive. *"You needn't worry, I have a new batch being prepared as we speak. It'll be strong enough to take down even a councilman."*

"It had better be."

The fox then scurries away from the window and into the woods beyond, what I now realize, is Sean's house.

This memory is recent. I search through more memories and gather that Shane hadn't been given more drugs to push before the attack. Excitement zips through me. The new drugs Malick promised could very well be the drugs that Dante found at Sean's. We might have the most recent and potent batch.

There's another memory from a few months ago that also looks promising. Just as I'm reaching out to touch it, everything goes black.

～

I'M YANKED out of Shane's mind when Caleb rips my hands away from his temples. Shane slumps low on his chair, only staying in place because he's been restrained. I'm instantly hit with the slowly building burn of pain as my limbs begin going numb.

"Wha—?" My voice is weaker than I'd like and laced with the agony that is currently savaging my body.

"You've been digging around in his brain for almost two hours." Malcolm's voice is quiet and sounds far away. Caleb looks too furious to speak for himself. "We couldn't let you continue. It could kill you."

"I'm. Fine," I grit out, trying to strengthen my voice enough to keep the discomfort from showing.

My body screams in pain, muscles spasm, bones crack, and ligaments stretch. My dragon roars in agony. We knew the consequences, accepted them, but that means nothing when I'm living through the consequences. My body goes limp as I'm unable to hold myself up through the searing and unending pain that floods my system. Strong arms catch me before I hit the floor, cradling me against a solid chest that smells like heaven.

I try to fight the torment as best I can, but it's a losing battle. I viciously bite my lower lip in an attempt to prevent myself from screaming. The sensations of being burned alive and electrocuted rapidly and simultaneously wash through all of my muscles, coupled with the feeling of having each of my teeth ripped out individually, my nails pulled off slowly, my tongue cut off, and my eyes gouged from their sockets.

I hadn't realized how hard Shane was fighting me. Most of my magical reserves have been stripped. For any being that possesses magic, it's intrinsically linked with their very life force and part of the very fiber of their being, their soul. And so, to have magic stripped in this manner is akin to ripping apart one's very soul.

"Let me in, Ayla. I can help carry some of the pain." While I'm sure Caleb is actually using a quiet and soothing tone, his voice blares through my head as if I'm standing next to the world's strongest speaker. A whimper escapes me as I feel blood trickle down my chin because of how hard I'm biting into my lip.

There's no way to share this pain, and even if there was, I wouldn't put my mate through this. I'm not that heartless. My back arches in Caleb's arms as a spasm locks all of my muscles in a tight hold. My muscles start to quiver from being seized in this position the longer the spasm lasts.

Caleb curses and rushes us out of Shane's cell, heading back across town to the packhouse. He goes straight for my bedroom, barking out orders I can't make out thanks to the screeching that starts in my head. I can't be sure if I'm physically screaming or if this is all in my mind.

My vision goes gray, my eyes are unable to focus, and the ringing in my head grows louder. Why won't they just kill me? Goddess. Please.

My dragon is screeching in my head. Cold is starting to creep along my body.

Blissfully, my world goes dark.

~

"HOW LONG WAS SHE UNDER?" The voice is female, familiar.

"Two bloody hours." A thick Scottish accent, male.

"Two hours?"

"Aye, two hours." The male sounds furious.

"She's dying, Caleb." The female is panicked.

"Like hell she is," the Scot growls.

"I'll do everything I can to make sure that doesn't happen, but Caleb, two hours even for a queen is deadly."

"Save her. If she dies—"

"You don't need to threaten me. She's my high priestess, I'm very well aware of what happens to us all if she dies," the female snaps angrily.

~

TWO FATES MORE SHALL FALL, and Hell shall wake.

~

"DAMN IT, AYLA, FIGHT!" The female voice is back. Bossy bit of goods, that one.

Suddenly, an image appears before me. It's a male. He's handsome, devastatingly so. Something roars inside of me. He's the reason I have to stay.

"New queens will rise." The triad of voices sounds from every direction, soothing the pain and washing over me like a healing balm, but it's not enough.

~

I CAN HEAR screams as my mind starts to clear. It's the first thing I register before the pain creeps back in. Are the screams mine? My head feels as though it's being torn to shreds, so I can't tell if the screaming is my own or someone else's. I struggle to open my eyes, and when I do, I'm blinded by even the slightest light filtering through. I slam my eyelids closed.

The screaming continues. As I try to make sense of what I'm hearing, I'm also able to pick up on the sounds of fighting all around me. But I can't be sure if that's a remnant from my dream or reality. Gods, I wish the pain would just go away! I try to lift my hands to claw at my skin, anything to relieve the agony, but my muscles are too weak, the throbbing too crippling.

"Do *not* let them close in on this room. Do I make myself clear?" The Scottish voice is back. He sounds angry.

I feel a twinge of panic from my dragon.

Danger! Her roar is quiet compared to the shouts echoing around me. *Demons!*

I once again attempt to open my eyes. My instincts urge me to get out of bed, to fight, to protect. My body struggles to obey. I'm only able to crack my eyes open slightly, the light still blinding, and I'm unable to make anything out. Mustering as much strength as I can, hoping that my instincts can fuel my efforts, I attempt to roll out of the bed I'm on—only to go crashing onto the floor.

A grunt flies from my lips. My eyes close again as I attempt to block a new flood of pain that rages through every nerve in my body. I take deep, calming breaths, trying desperately to find my center. Anything to block out the torment and help my community.

Protect. Fight. Save! Damn it, I'm trying!

Oh, shit. Oblivion claims me once again.

Chapter Twenty

My eyes fly open, my lungs frantically filling with air. Panic surges through me when I realize I'm tied down. Despite my eyes being open, my brain can't seem to process what I'm looking at. It's still focused on trying to figure out why I'm restrained, on the panic flooding my system, and the remnants of my heightened protective instincts. Jackknifing my body, I rip through the ties and fly upright. I mentally take stock of my body since my last memory is of being in excruciating pain. While I'm not completely healed, I'm good enough to be up and about.

Something isn't right. I'm torn from my thoughts as I blink a few times to get my eyes to clear. When I finally open my eyes again, I'm staring around a barren room. Confusion and alarm swamp me since I've never been in this room before. I inhale, attempting to learn where I am, assuming I'm still on pack land.

I don't scent my community.

Instead, I inhale again, and my blood runs cold and my eyes widen. Demons. Oh, this is so not good. Very, very not good. And to make this day complete, my dragon is gone...again.

The bitter taste of panic begins to rise in my throat. Malick. His fucking mage stripped me of my dragon while I was passed out. I really need to kill that asshat. Both of them, I need to kill both of them. This is the second time they've stripped me of my dragon. Don't they know how damn rude that is? They're making things far more difficult for themselves, really, because now I need to rip them apart with my bare hands. I could have just killed them quickly, but they're forcing me to draw this out. I bet it's a kink thing.

I study the room around me. I'm sitting on a single bed. It has a threadbare fitted sheet and nothing else. Thankfully, I'm still fully clothed. If they'd had the audacity to remove anything, I wouldn't need my dragon to light this mofo on fire. There's a door directly in front of me, no windows, and only a chair next to the bed. Which is mildly creepy.

Please don't tell me Malick has been watching me sleep. Because that's a hard fucking pass. We clearly need to talk about boundaries before I kill him. You cannot be tying people down and then watching them while they sleep, even as a villain.

I feel like that's just basic common sense, but villains clearly work off different rules. But why do they always have to be so damn creepy? I want to encounter a non-creepy villain. Just once. It's like I'm on a hunt for a magical, sparkly unicorn. But hell, I'm not supposed to exist either, so there has to be hope, right?

My legs move to swing off the bed when I suddenly find myself tied down again. Well, this isn't going to be pleasant.

"Why, you're awake, little queen!" I struggle against my bonds, grinding my teeth at the sound of Malick's voice as he strolls into the room. "I'm happy to see you survived your little stunt." He sounds so condescending, which makes me want to throat punch him.

He smiles down at me, and I have to fight the urge to spit in his face. How the hell did I end up here with him? I try to remember more, but the last thing I can clearly recall is diving into Shane's head, after that it's all pain. Did Malick attack while I was doing the mind dive? Panic for my community works its way up my spine, and I desperately try to reach for my dragon again. Nothing. The silence sends searing pain through every nerve ending.

"I'm sure you want to know how you came to be in my care. All in due time, little queen. All in due time." He leans down to stroke my cheek with the back of his fingers. I shudder. "Right now, I am merely here to make sure you're adjusting well."

"Adjusting?" The word bursts from my lips before I can stop it.

"Indeed! After your little brush with death, I need to make sure you're strong enough for what's in store. I can't exactly have you dying on me, now can I?" Malick chuckles as he watches me, his lust-filled eyes burning my skin. I try to call on my magic, but that doesn't come to me either. Malick tsks. "Little queen, you underestimate me. We've stripped both your dragon and your magic this time. Can't have you hurting yourself." How did he know I was trying to use my magic? Something is very, very wrong.

"I suppose I should give you some answers. You really should be aware of what's going to happen to you." He cups my cheeks with his hands and leans down to press his lips against mine. My body instantly goes rigid, and I turn my head, breaking the contact. "Soon, you'll be begging me to kiss you, little queen."

"Over my very dead body," I snarl.

"No, thankfully you won't need to die for this process to work." Everything inside me stills. Process?

Malick pulls out a needle that's filled with a black liquid. Just the sight of it sends me into a panicked fit against the bindings tying me to the bed. I have no idea what the hell is in that needle, but I don't want to find out.

"You see, I've found that injecting other species with my essence allows me to form a bond of sorts with them. It makes them part demon." My struggles increase. "Do you want to know what I hope to achieve by injecting you with as much of this as I can?" No, I really bloody don't.

"I'm going to bind you to me." He pauses, clearly for dramatic effect. "As my mate."

～

MY EYES SNAP open for a second time. Did I pass out? I test my bonds only to find that I'm securely attached to the bed. Damn it.

"Ayla." The whisper is barely there, but I cling to it. Caleb! The mating bond! It's still there! I try to pinpoint it in my mind, but it slips away. No!

"Caleb! Caleb, please tell me you can hear me!" I try to reach for my bonds with my community, but I can't find those either. Once again, I'm completely alone. I never thought I would resent the silence in my mind, but now it creates this chasm inside me that aches with every breath. My body starts to shake at the realization that I may not be getting out of this. Without my bonds, without any connection to my community, no one can track me. I'm still not sure how Malick captured me, but my community could be completely wiped out. Stabbing pain shoots through my chest at the thought. No. There's no way Kelly or Olivia would have allowed that to happen. I have complete and utter faith in them.

I need to come up with a plan to find the damn mage and take him out. I refuse to even think about binding with Malick as his mate. Every cell in my body rebels against the thought, so it's easier to focus on other things. And the only way to get out of here is to take out the mage, and get my dragon and my magic back. Reclaiming my magic should open up the bonds again.

Shit. The realization slams into me like a runaway train. I'm essentially human. That leaves a bitter taste in my mouth. I'm physically stronger than a human, but it won't be enough against Malick.

How the hell did he get this far? Trapping a queen and ripping away her dragon and magic is no easy feat. To keep the spell up, he had to be draining other sources of power. Was the mage syphoning off others?

The sound of the door opening halts my thinking. A stunning woman, well over six feet tall with long, blond hair and striking blue eyes, enters the room. Mage. Despite not having my dragon, I want to snarl at her. I don't need my magic to see the corruption pouring off of her. It's disgusting.

"I'm so glad to see you awake." Her accent isn't British. South African maybe? Possibly Australian. "Lord Malick told me that you had an adverse reaction to your second dose, so I decided to come see how you were fairing for myself."

Second dose? I frantically try to evaluate my body to see what's different, but I can't tell if anything has really changed. How many doses are they planning on giving me? And what the hell do these doses do?

"Anyway, you seem to be fine, but I'll need to do a full examination of you to be certain." I hadn't realized that the mage had continued talking while I was having my mini-internal freak-out.

"What exactly is this doing to me?" Play it cool, Ayla. Play it fucking cool. Don't seem too interested. Just interested enough. Yeah. You've got this.

"I believe Lord Malick already told you." The mage's voice takes on a condescending note, as though she thinks I'm too stupid to follow along. "You are being given Lord Malick's demonic essence. It will not turn you into a demon, but it will change certain aspects of your DNA to allow for a viable pregnancy."

Viable...pregnancy? I shake my head. But I physically can't mate with a creature that isn't an alpha male dragon. That's how the magic of it all works. When the goddesses created queens, this was the stipulation to keep our strength and magic strong. What the hell is Malick hoping to gain by—I internally gag—getting me pregnant?

I can feel the panic slowly working its way through my body, like ants crawling over every inch of my skin. I try to breathe deeply to avoid having a full-blown meltdown. I almost died only to wake up in the hands of an archdemon who apparently wants me to be his baby mama. There's still so much I don't understand. My vision starts to go fuzzy, as though I'm looking at static on an old TV. My entire body goes numb.

"Oh, good. So glad I can accommodate some little hell-spawn as it rips its way out of my vagina. Just what I've always wanted." Word vomit. Great. This is how I'm handling the situation. Word vomit. "What would we name them? Here little Timmy! Time to light the world on fire!" And it just won't stop. What the hell is wrong with me?

"Silence." The mage's voice is laced with power and my lips instantly stop flapping. Well, damn. That's not fair. She gets to use magic, but I can't. Rude. "Much better."

The mage makes her way over to me, drawing blood, pressing down on random body parts, and placing her hands over my head. I'd fidget a lot more if I wasn't tied down. I don't like her hands on me. Something about her makes my skin crawl, and I'm actually happy my hands can't reach my body, or I'd be itching all over. After several minutes the mage sighs and walks toward the door.

"Wait," I call. Thankfully whatever power she'd put into her voice didn't have long-lasting effects. "Who are you and why are you helping him?"

"My name is Katia. Why I work with Lord Malick isn't any of your concern. Luckily you're healthy and not suffering any ill-effects of the injections. We'll be able to give you the next dose in the morning. Food will be brought up, and a servant will come by so you can relieve yourself. I don't suggest you try anything, queen. Lord Malick wants you alive, but that's the minimum requirement." With that, Katia leaves.

Okay. So I need to take her out quickly.

"*AYLA?*" Caleb's voice drifts through my mind, but no matter how hard I try to find the bond, it isn't there. I know that when I try to call out to him, he won't hear me, and what I'm hearing is the first sign of insanity.

The next time I wake, Malick is sitting in a chair by my bed. What a creep. Thankfully he isn't staring at me. He's studying a file that's thick with old papers instead.

"I can't seem to find any indication of you anywhere in my records." He doesn't bother glancing up. "It's as though you never existed, yet here you are. Who was your mother, little queen?" He finally looks up at me, his eyes drilling into mine as though the answer is there, just beyond his reach.

"I'm not here to answer your questions." I put just enough snarl into my voice to sound threatening despite my predicament.

"Oh, but you'll find that you are." He waves his hand dismissively in front of his face. "No matter. That can all come later. Shall I tell you a story, little queen? I'm sure you're dying to know why your kind was really hunted to extinction."

I remain silent. I don't want to encourage or discourage him. But he's right, I am dying to know what really happened. Knowing why the queens were hunted will explain why my sisters and I had to be in hiding our entire lives. Why Mother had to die. Hopefully, it'll unlock the rest of my memories. Or at least help me make sense of them anyway.

"About a thousand years ago," he begins. "I first heard a prophecy." I want to roll my eyes. Of course there's a prophecy. When isn't there a prophecy? It's so cliché. "It said that the Fates would be reborn and that if one should fall, the gates of Hell would open." My blood runs cold. "As I'm sure you can imagine, the archdemon who opens the gates and allows Morningstar free once again will be lauded a hero and will be granted limitless power. And so, I set out in search of the Fates.

"The Fates had notoriously always been born of queens in the past, purity of the bloodlines and whatnot. It was safe to assume they would be born to queens once again. But try as I might, I couldn't find them. It's entirely possible that with the cleansing they were wiped out. But it's probable that there is another way to open the gates." He pauses, a grin spreading across his face. "A child. One born of queen and demon lineage." He shrugs. "You see, the Antichrist is a real person. Well, will be a real person. But queens cannot mate with anyone other than an alpha male dragon, or so we were all made to believe. No species can reproduce with demons. It's not possible. We're incompatible. Unless we ease the way first."

"The injections," I whisper, unable to stop myself.

"Indeed. My brother and I discovered that through a series of injections, other supernatural creatures were able to carry our young to term. Once the other archdemons found out, they realized what Valik and I intended to do." Malick sounds angry, his eyes far away. "Instead of helping us, they decided to kill the queens instead. You see, not all of the archdemons want Morningstar to rise again. Especially if they aren't going to be the ones to bring about his return. And so, it was decided that none of us would break the seals. Your sister queens were eradicated, my brother was imprisoned, and I was left to fake my death to avoid a similar fate. I've finally perfected the injections. You will be the mother of a legion. You will bring about the end of days and open the gates to Hell. You will rule alongside myself and Morningstar."

Chapter Twenty-One

Caleb

S he's gone.

THE RAGE that sweeps through my body is a welcome reprieve from the worry that constantly plagues me. I let them take her. I couldn't get to her in time to stop them. My fist slams into one of the walls in Ayla's bedroom. The room that is saturated with her scent. I inhale deeply, allowing her fragrance to fill every cell of my body, longing ripping through me with the action.

That fucking bear that got loose, Kevin, he's the reason Ayla is gone. We hadn't been successful in tracking that dick down, and he'd brought back an entire army of demons to take her. Fury floods my system as I recall the last few days.

While Ayla had been recovering from diving into Shane's mind, Kevin, along with a small army of demons and the fucking mage, attacked the town. I knew that the longer it took us to catch Kevin the more likely he'd come back swinging, but I hadn't expected him to launch an attack that quickly. Kevin had been missing for only two days before he returned to town with friends.

The fight had been brutal. We knew why they'd come, knew it wasn't for Shane, but for Ayla. We knew what would happen if we lost. But I'd still been able to access my dragon, so I didn't think the damn mage was nearby. Cursing, I slam my fist into the wall again. I should have known better. The mage had been able to slip in without any of us noticing, the battles raging around town creating the best distraction possible. And I'd been dumb enough to step out of Ayla's room to try and help keep the demons at bay.

Ayla has been gone for four days now. Four fucking days. We're no closer to finding her than we were that first day. All of our bonds have been severed somehow. Kelly has a theory that they're actually being blocked using a similar magic that hindered our dragons when we battled Malick. Without those bonds, we seem to be running around in circles. I've put the best trackers from the Council, as well as the New England Pack, to work on hunting her down. And everyone who can help is assisting to find any scrap of information that may point us in the right direction. Malcolm told me the reason they're so damn hard to track is because of that fucking mage. Whoever the hell he is did a damn fine job of making sure they just appeared to vanish into thin air.

I take another deep breath, another pull of Ayla's sweet scent into my system. Anything to keep her close. My dragon roars its outrage, wanting to rip the world apart to find his mate. I'm hardly able to stop myself from allowing him to do whatever the hell he wants. But that won't help us find her. That won't bring her back.

Goddess, just let her come back safely. I will willingly give up the Council. Hell, I'll disband the thing altogether if I get to have her again.

I shake off my thoughts and head into Ayla's study. It's where Kelly, Olivia, Connor, Malcolm, and I have been holding meetings and brainstorming. Malcolm and Olivia are already in the room. I'm surprised to see them cozied up so close together, but I also haven't been paying any attention to anything but finding my mate for days. I can't even remember the last time I ate.

"Alpha," Olivia greets. "We were just talking about a way to try to combine the tracking skills of a shifter with a witch's ability to track magic. It may help."

"Oh, good, all of you are already here." Kelly comes into the study with Connor fast on her heels. "I want to hear what you've come up with, Olivia. And I think I may have found a way to get one of us through to Ayla. It won't last long, and it'll be dangerous, but I think I have it." There's hope ringing through her tone, and at the sound of it, my own hope starts to rise.

"If we tackle both approaches at the same time, we may get lucky," Connor adds. He's watching me carefully. I'm sure I look like shit. I haven't slept since Ayla was taken, and I've only been eating when someone forces a meal into my hands. There's no time for any of that right now, not when I need to focus on finding her. *Mate*, my dragon rumbles angrily in my head.

Right, big guy. We're going to find her. I promise.

"Okay. Malcolm, Olivia, and Connor, I want you three to see what you can do about tracking Ayla. Kelly and I will work on reestablishing the bond. The mate bond, even new and not finalized, will be the strongest link to try to reach her." I have to do something, anything.

"Whoa there." Kelly reaches out to put her hand on my

arm. "Slow your roll, big buy. We need to firm up the plan first." A low growl works its way up my chest. "Oh, hush yourself. I want her back just as badly as you do. But we can't walk into anything half-assed. As Ron Swanson would say, 'Never half-ass two things. Whole ass one thing.' So this needs to be one cohesive plan." She nudges me into a seat. "Sit and eat. I have someone bringing us food."

AFTER SEVERAL HOURS OF BICKERING, we seem to have a plan in place. It's dodgy at best, but if it works, we'll be able to find Ayla and form a better attack plan from there. I'm standing in the shower, my hands braced against the wall as the water pelts my back, running through the plan over and over again in my mind. Kelly is going to put me into a magical slumber, one where I should be able to fully connect with my mate bond, even if Ayla's end is blocked by magic. In theory anyway. I could just go under and never wake up again. But it's worth the risk, she is worth the risk.

It's funny. My mother always told me that when I met my queen, she was going to knock me for a loop. I'd grown up with the understanding that my queen would be my leader—after all, that's what queens were. But when they all died, my hopes of ever finding my mate died with them. And so I took over, assuming the role of leader. I'd become too comfortable in that role it seems, unwilling to give it up when I'd found what I'd thought I would never have.

Ayla is only a single queen. We can't simply go back to the way things were, but we can't stay with our current system either. She has a right to take up the helm if she so chooses. And from what I've seen around here, she'll do one hell of a job. The vamps haven't even officially bonded with her, but they're doing all they can to find her. I'd forgotten what being around a queen was like. How they pull and tie people together, make our differences our strengths, and create bonds that never fade.

She's a miracle. And there's no way in hell I'm going to let that bastard have his way with her.

∼

I CLIMB into Ayla's bed, the very one she was taken from, the one where I first got to feel her skin against mine, where I first got to sink into her warmth. Our scents are mixed here, and Kelly thinks that will help me focus on the mate bond. Little does she know, there's little else I can focus on. There have been a few times when I thought Ayla's voice was ringing in my head, but whenever I tried to reach out, there was nothing there.

Kelly is standing at the foot of the bed, her hands wrapped around a glass that holds the sleeping potion. "You'll need to drink all of this. You're pretty large, so this is an extra-strong dose. Once you're under, I'll guide you to your mate bond, but from there you're on your own. You'll need to coax the bond back to life. It won't be easy since the two of you didn't get a chance to seal the deal before she was taken." While I know she doesn't mean to rub salt in the wound, the reminder of the incomplete bond still stings. "Are you ready?"

"Yeah. Let's do this." She hands me the glass, and I down it quickly. It tastes like ass. I rest my head against some pillows and stare up at the ceiling.

∼

"OKAY." Kelly's voice blares through my mind. I blink several times, but I realize I'm out cold and there's no use blinking.

That was fast. *"I need you to steady your breathing and empty your mind."*

I take several calming breaths, allowing my body to relax and my mind to go blank.

"Good. Keep that up." After several moments of just breathing, I feel a nudge at the back of my mind. *"Now I want you to focus on Ayla. Feel the bond flow through you. You're her mate, the bond should be close to the core of who you are."*

She's right. My mate bond makes up the core of who I am. But while I can feel the bond, I can't see it. I need to be able to see it for this to work. And so, I focus on Ayla, her smile, her laugh. How that damn woman is so sassy she's going to need me to take her over my knee. She's passionate, kind, loving, and selfless. She's stronger than she realizes. The woman has six feet of personality jammed into a tiny little frame. She drives me mad in the best way. And she's mine. I'm hers. She's more than I ever could have hoped for in a mate. All that I hadn't realized I needed. She is everything.

She's made me reevaluate what's truly important. And it sure as shit isn't power. It's rolling over in the middle of the night to feel her soft, warm body pressed against mine, seeing her standing naked in front of her closet with that cute look on her face as she decides what to wear for the day. It's having her stand up to me and demand equal measure. It's her, plain and simple. Only her.

That's when I see it, shimmering softly through the darkness that's surrounding me. It's gold and thin, but as I get closer, it appears solid and sturdy despite not being fully formed. It's pulsing in a reassuring manner. She's alive.

Slowly, carefully, I reach out and gently grasp the bond in both hands. I'm instantly flooded with visions, I realize, of what Ayla is currently experiencing. She's tied to a bed with Malick standing over her. She's scared but determined. That's my girl. There's something else too. Something about her has changed. I can't reach her dragon, and I can't sense her magic through the bond, which tells me that Kelly's theory is spot-on. The damn mage is interfering again. But that's not what's different. I can't put my finger on exactly what's changed, but something close to the core of her has shifted.

"Ayla!" I shout as loudly as possible, knowing she may not even be able to hear me. But to my surprise, I feel her jolt in recognition.

"Caleb!" Her voice is faint, but I cling to it anyway.

"Ayla, I need you to sink into the bond. It'll help us find you."

"Oh, Caleb. I wish you were really with me." I feel her sorrow. *"I'm so tired, Caleb. So tired of fighting. So tired of thinking that I hear you."*

She doesn't think this is real. Dread coils in the pit of my stomach. If I can't get her to sink into what's left of the bond on her end, I won't be able to find her. I'll only be able to see what she's experiencing. I may even lose what little ability to communicate with her I currently have.

"It's really me, Ayla. I'm here. I need you to focus on my voice."

She pulls away from me and the bond, and once again, I'm surrounded by darkness with only the soft pulsing of our bond in my mind.

WHEN I WAKE, it's to see relief flooding Kelly's features. I can't share in her relief, however. Ayla pulled away from me. She didn't believe I was really there. Small claws of panic start to hook themselves deep into my mind. I'm not going to be able to get to her in time. Whatever Malick is going to do, I'll be too late to stop it.

"What happened? Were you able to find out where she is?" Kelly's voice yanks me out of my spiraling thoughts.

"No. I was able to speak to her, but she didn't believe I

was really there. She wouldn't sink into the bond. She pulled away before I could get any information. All I was able to determine is that she's bound and with Malick." I don't mention the change I felt, because I have no way of answering any questions if asked.

"Damn." Kelly starts pacing and muttering to herself. I sit up in bed and nudge Connor and Malcolm through our bonds. They have had some luck, but not enough to get us a solid lead. I want to punch the damn wall again.

"What the hell do we do now?" My tone is gruff and laced with frustrated anger. "How the hell are we going to get Ayla back?"

Dante walks into the room, his hair disheveled and eyes wild. "Caleb," he says frantically, "do you remember when we were training Ayla that first day?" I nod. "She said she'd sensed a large demonic presence in Alaska. She couldn't be sure, but she felt like that was where Malick was hiding."

He's right.

My dragon roars inside me, eager to head out and find his mate.

"Then that's where we're going. If there's even the slightest chance he's taken her to Alaska, we need to search for her." I stand, but Kelly comes over and frowns at me.

"Even if we go there, we won't be able to sense her. We'll have the same problem."

"But we may be able to pick up a scent trail," Dante points out. "It's better than sitting here and doing nothing."

"I suppose." Kelly seems hesitant to head off, not that I blame her.

"Why don't I pick a small group to scout Alaska? You can stay here with the rest and start getting everyone ready for the battle ahead. He won't give Ayla up without a fight." Kelly nods. "Good. I'll get a task force together. Focus on healing as many as you can and getting everyone ready to fight. The additional councilmen I called in should be here tomorrow."

"Alpha," Dante calls, "I would like to be part of this task force."

"You don't even need to ask."

Chapter Twenty-Two

I'm not sure how long I've been here, how long Malick has been injecting me with whatever it is he hopes will turn my uterus compatible enough with his junk to get me pregnant with little demon gremlins. But it appears to be taking longer than it has with the others. I'm not sure if I want to be happy or upset about that.

While there's a set schedule to the way things progress each day, without my dragon and without magic, I can't get out of my restraints. If I do, I'm just dragged right back instantly. I'm only allowed up a few times each day to ensure that my muscles don't atrophy and to go to the bathroom. I'm impressed they've been able to block me this long. It's a massive power drain to do something like this long-term, and I'm sure several people have already died to meet the power requirement. I'd say it's a shame, but I'd be lying. At this point, even the maid deserves what's coming.

And that's what scares me. That's not me. I don't think like that. Right? I don't want to exact revenge on those who have not actively done anything wrong. I don't place the blame of one person on all of the people around them. And yet, I want to. Goddess, do I want to. I want to rip out of these bonds and bathe in the blood of every single being in this place. I want to shift into my dragon and rain fire down on this entire building before rolling in the ashes. I want to bask in their screams as they see me coming, knowing I'm their end.

What has Malick done to me?

Katia stalks into my room, needle in hand. Oh, goody, another dose of demon sludge. She's frowning as she comes over to the bed, so I'm in for some fun after she's stabbed me. Studying me closely for my reaction, she slams the needle into my arm. I don't even wince. I carefully keep my face blank, despite the rage that quickly blasts through my body. I want her to watch as I slowly remove her innards, maybe even make her eat them. I blink. *No, I can't think like that. Snap out of it, Ayla. Don't let this get to you*, I chide myself.

"This dose may very well kill you. I told Lord Malick that we needed to give you more time between doses so we can assess the changes. But he's impatient." She grins down at me. "I don't particularly care if you die, but you are the last queen." She sighs dramatically. "I suppose I'll need to make sure you don't die."

Bitch. I know she'll wait until the last possible moment to save me. I've learned a few things about Katia in the time I've been here. She loves to see the pain and panic on the faces of those she tortures. There's no question in my mind she gets off on everything she does. While I haven't been allowed to wander, and I've mostly been bound to my bed, I've heard at least one other woman screaming.

Katia checks my vitals before leaving. She never stays to chat, which is such a shame. I have so many wonderful choice words for her. And I'd love to just let her have a piece of my mind. Who knows, she might slip up and tell me how the hell they're able to block my dragon and magic so well. Either way, it would be cathartic.

My heart starts racing and my breathing heaves in short, rapid bursts. My vision narrows and goes staticky. It feels as though my limbs will float away if the restraints are removed. Goddess, it feels like my heart is going to burst from my chest. It's all I can hear, and my vision is pulsing with each furious beat.

Ah, fuck. That's the last coherent thought I have before my world goes black...again.

$\sim$

WHEN I FINALLY COME TO, I'm not strapped to a bed anymore. I'm outside. How am I outside? The last thing I remember is Katia injecting me with more of that nasty black demon crap. So how the hell did I end up out here? Where is here?

I'm standing beside a giant weeping willow that is flanked by an old oak tree and a magnolia tree. I feel oddly at peace looking at the strange trio, as though I've come home. My heart feels lighter than it has in centuries. My worries about how I came to be here slowly fade the longer I look at the trees. After all, it doesn't matter how I came to be here. What matters is that I'm here, finally. I can rest. And so I do.

I make my way under the weeping willow, sighing as the shade provides shelter from the sun. I curl up next to the trunk, content to relax against the tree in silence. My eyes feel heavy, but I fight to keep them open, wanting to bask in the beauty of the tree.

Just as my eyes are about to slide shut, my determination to keep them open fading, light footfalls sound from nearby, perking me up. My gaze sharpens as I focus on the direction where the footsteps are coming from. More than one person is approaching the trio of trees, though I can't tell exactly how many. My head is pleasantly light. While I know I should care that I'm being approached by an unknown number of strangers, the feeling of peace that settled over me on first waking has firmly taken root. I'm not worried or scared, merely intrigued. How could there be evil in this place?

A triad of hooded figures emerges from the other side of the weeping willow, stopping to stand before me. I can't see their faces, their hoods are drawn too far down, but given their small stature, I assume they're women. One by one, the figures lower their hoods. My assumption that they are all women is quickly confirmed.

Shock shoots through my system when I realize who I'm looking at. Three goddesses. Brigid, Isis, and Freja. I scramble to my feet, my eyes wide with shock. Brigid is pale with a light smattering of freckles across the bridge of her nose. Her flaming red hair is braided down her back with ribbons interwoven into her curly locks. Her eyes remind me of the grass by the Cliffs of Mohr, a sharp green mixed with yellow and brown. Her lips are a deep red, almost appearing as though she recently drank blood and it left a stain on her lips. Isis, by contrast, is a deep golden brown, similar to the color of coffee with just a touch of cream. Her eyes are a startling gold that offsets her jet-black hair. Her hair is plaited with gold and tumbles down her back. Freja is also pale, though not quite as pale as Brigid. Where Brigid appears soft and Isis regal, Freja is clearly a warrior. Her hair is braided in the style of a shieldmaiden, with beads woven throughout. Her gray eyes are hard as steel, and the war paint gracing her face is a stark contrast to her pallor.

"My ladies!" I bow my head, but all three instantly reach out in a gesture that tells me I needn't bow.

"Please, daughter, there is no need for such formality." Brigid's voice rings with the sensation of home. Ireland. It soothes my frayed nerves. "We have come to you due to dire circumstances."

"Indeed." Isis's tone has a husky quality that surprisingly stirs a hunger within me. "We healed your body and brought your mind to this place. We have much to ask of you, precious daughter."

"Wait. Healed my body? What are you talking about?" Despite the injections Malick had been giving me, I wasn't injured, at least as far as I knew.

"The last injection stopped your heart, young warrior." Freja's voice is surprisingly soft given her appearance. "You are too important to lose. You still have much to do."

I'm dead. Not exactly how I thought I would go, being experimented on in an attempt for some psycho to impregnate me. My calm slowly gives way to anger the more I think about it. How could I have just sat back and allowed Malick to do this to me? Brigid comes over and gently places her hand on my cheek. Her eyes are soft, and a pale white light surrounds us.

"My daughter, there is so much I wish to tell you, but we do not have time. My sisters and I have healed your body, but the darkness still lingers. Do not let it snuff out your light." She rests her forehead against mine. "Remember who you are, dear one. Remember the power you once wielded and can wield again." With that, she steps away, only to be replaced by Isis.

"Daughter, there is still so much for you to learn. What Brigid says is true, there is still darkness that lingers within you. But there can be no light without dark, no life without death. Do not let the darkness snuff out your light, but do not be afraid to use that darkness to allow your light to shine brighter. You leave here with our blessings." Isis also rests her forehead against me. "Maiden of the past, you are but one piece of the puzzle. Find your sisters." She steps away and Freja takes her place.

"Warrior queen, we will aid you in your quest. Your sisters, not by blood but by bond, will take up the mantle of queen, thereby starting a new generation of warriors for light. Each of the three new queens will awaken when the moment is right, and you will guide them, strengthen them. The time of the old ways has passed. You, my warrior, will lead this new generation of queens." Freja searches my eyes for a moment before continuing, "But be warned, Malick is not your true adversary, and the darkest times are still to come. Embrace the bonds you have created, not just with your sisters, but with your man as well. For he will ground you during the trials ahead." She leans, then whispers, "You are a Fate reborn, young warrior queen. Do not fight it, embrace it with everything you are. Do not falter." She also steps back.

The three goddesses in front of me smile, crossing their arms over their chests. Freja and Isis slowly fade from view, leaving me alone with Brigid.

"One last word before I part," Brigid says, her voice soft. "Find the prophecy and know that we never deceived your mother. The darkness has always been determined to kill the light, and we did what we could. I will leave you with this." She hands me a small orb made of what appears to be jade. "This will show you the truth of your mother's final moments. Blessed be, daughter." She leans in to kiss my cheek before she, too, is gone.

I stand there staring at the orb for countless moments, trying to process what just happened. The orb starts to heat in my hands, and it clears, showing me the fields just beyond my childhood home.

～

I'M STANDING on the rise of a hill overlooking a battlefield. My mother's final stand, I realize, startled. A roar shakes the ground and fire lights up the sky. My father, a stunning obsidian dragon, shoots through the storm, cutting through the legion gathered on the fields below.

"Aine, my love!" My father's voice blares crystal clear through my mind. *"Ye've got to get the girls away. We won't last long, love."*

"Sorcha and Isobel are already safe. I'm heading home to collect Ayla." The sound of my mother's voice almost breaks me. I've missed them both so much. The love in their voices for us, for each other, is obvious.

Suddenly, a wave of terror washes over me. The night appears to get darker, the rain heavier, and the hope leaches out of every cell in my body. Malick steps onto the field near my house. No! I want to shift, fight, and save my parents, but I can't. I'm rooted to the spot, a mere spectator to the events of four hundred years ago.

Moments later, my mother steps out of our tiny cottage, head held high, power lighting her from within. My father shoots off another stream of fire before landing beside her. They make such a magnificent sight, especially once my mother shifts. Her dragon is silver and sparkles through the rain. Together, they attack.

It's like watching a dance, attack then defend, over and over again. But in a flash, both of my parents are back in their human forms on all fours. A new wave of power washes over the battlefield and the demons still, a hushed whisper spreading through the legion. Malick approaches my parents, his wings outstretched, a brilliant smile covering his face.

"I'm going to give you one last chance, Aine. Come with me." He kneels, pinching my mother's chin in one hand and slamming his other into my father's face, sending him flying. "You're the last queen. You will be the mother of darkness!

You will give birth to the Fates. You will help me break the seals and rule by my side."

My mother spits in his face, a snarl on her lips. "No."

"I'm going to kill your mate." Malick leans down to press a light kiss to my mother's mouth. "But first, I want you to see who has stripped you of your dragon, your power."

The sea of demons parts and a lone hooded figure strides toward my mother. My father, having been flung into a crowd of demons, is being held back, but he is given a clear line of sight to my mother and Malick. Once the hooded figure makes it to Malick's side, Malick stands, still gripping my mother, and rips the hood back. My mother cries out in shocked pain. It's Katia. I…I don't understand.

My mother's voice is a broken whisper when she finally speaks. "You! How could you? Katia, you were my beta! I thought you were dead! I mourned you!" As she talks, my mother's voice gets louder until she ends on a scream.

"I didn't want to just be a beta, Aine. I wanted more. So much more." Katia places her hand on Malick's arm. "Lord Malick has given me power beyond my wildest dreams. Would you like to see?" She cocks her head, a sick grin slowly forming on her face.

My stomach drops. Ice slowly invades every part of me. Oh, goddess. My eyes flick to my father. I know what's coming. I always thought Malick killed my father. It was Katia. One of my mother's betas. I fight not to get sick and force myself to keep watching.

"Katia, please!" my mother cries. "You don't need to do this."

"No." Katia's voice is dark. "But I want to."

With a flick of her wrist, my father's heart instantly appears in her hands. My father's body slumps out of the demons' clutches, his eyes open and staring vacantly toward the sky. I feel the bile rising in my throat, and tears sting the back of my eyes. *Daddy*. My mother's anguished scream rings through the fields as lightning flashes in the sky and the rain pours harder than ever.

"I'm going to give you some time to think about my offer." Malick pulls my mother flush against him. "You will give me what I want, warrior queen. One way or another."

∼

THE SCENE CHANGES. I'm now standing in a dank, freezing cell. My mother is huddled, naked, in a corner. How long has she been like this? Shock floods my system with the realization that she was alive when she left the battlefield. Although I'm sure she wished she died along with my father. While it's hard to tell exactly how much time has passed, I'm at least able to see that it's been a while. My mother's hair is matted, and she's thinner than she was in the last memory.

Footsteps have both of us jerking our heads to see who's approaching. At first, I think it's Malick, but as I look closer, I realize that while this new archdemon looks almost exactly like Malick, there's something darker and more sinister about him. I quickly glance back at my mother, fear trickling its way down my spine. My mother stands, her head held high and eyes defiant as she faces the newcomer. She crosses her arms over her chest, her body tense, though whether to attempt to flee or fight, I can't be sure.

"Valik." Dread mixes with the fear. "I was told you'd been imprisoned."

Valik tsks. "Now, Aine, do you really believe everything you hear?"

"You might want to let your brother know you're free." My mother's eyes narrow on Valik and she takes a small step away from him as he moves slightly closer. "I'm sure you two have a lot to catch up on."

"Now, now, my dear. I can't have my little brother ruining everything for me, now can I?" Valik continues to advance on my mother until he's inches away from her. "I'm going to give you what you want. I'm going to reunite you with your dearly departed mate."

Valik strokes my mother's cheek. My mother's eyes widen in shock. She lashes out and grips Valik's wrist, yanking it away from her face in disgust. Valik leans in, his lips sliding along my mother's neck before gently caressing her ear.

"Does my dear brother know about your daughters?" He doesn't give my mother any time to process his words before he rips her head from her body.

I let out a scream as I collapse to my knees, once again by the weeping willow. Tears stream down my face, sobs racking my body. The truth is so much worse than I ever could have imagined. My mother was alive. Malick had kept her like some kind of animal. And his brother...fury heats my blood thinking about how he slaughtered her. Valik is going to have to run very, very far and hide in the deepest, darkest hole he can find, but even then I will catch him.

The rage builds, mixing with my sorrow, and something in me snaps.

Chapter Twenty-Three

My eyes fly open, magic blasting out of my body and disintegrating my restraints. My dragon comes hurtling back to me, and with her, my bonds with my community, even the vampires. My mate bond with Caleb fully snaps into place, flaring a bright and pleasant heat inside me. I feel powerful, I feel complete. I feel ready to fuck a bitch's day straight to hell.

"Ayla!" a chorus of voices scream in my head. I wince slightly at the volume, but warmth spreads through me at the connection.

"Ayla," Caleb rumbles. He's shocked, scared, pissed, and... in love? My heart stops for a moment. He loves me? Damn straight he loves me. What the hell is there not to love about me? And, I guess, I sort of love him too. The turd. *"You better answer me, woman."*

"I'm here." I send this to all of them before answering just Caleb. *"Don't you sass me. I have been through an ordeal, sir. You are to shower me with love and snuggles when this is all over. I expect pampering. Lots of pampering."*

"I will do whatever the hell you want. Just tell me where you

are." That's a good question. I have no idea. But my magic doesn't need to know where I am. It spreads through our bond like a beacon, calling him to me. *"I'm on my way."*

I can sense Caleb and my community mobilizing. It feels so right. But now, I need to focus on my favorite mage. The darkness surges inside me at the thought of Katia. As Isis instructed, I don't try to run from it. Instead, I use it to fuel me. She's part of the evil that wants to spread across this world like a plague. I'm not going to let that happen.

Can I eat her? my dragon growls. I mentally hug her, thrilled beyond measure to feel her once again.

Sure. I head toward the door but stop, pausing when I feel a pulsing light within this festering den of darkness. *The goddesses said three sisters by bond, but I only have two.*

For now, my dragon murmurs. *Can't you feel her? Our final missing piece?* And I can. The pulsing light flares brighter when my magic touches it. A new, fragile bond is taking root inside me. *A new sister.*

We need to free her. Agreeing with my dragon, I change tactics. Walking out of my room, I head toward the light first, deciding to free my newfound sister. Death and destruction can wait. I'm surprised to find that no one is patrolling the halls. Odd. Then again, Malick and Katia both assumed I wouldn't be able to get out of my restraints. Clearly, they think the same of my new sister.

When I'm finally standing in front of the room containing the pulsing light of my sister, I pause for a moment. The new bond flairs brighter as hope filters to me from the female on the other side of the door. She knows I'm out here, knows I'm here to rescue her, and she knows about the bond. With a wave of my hand, the door shatters into dust. What I see before me causes my heart to stutter.

A female vampire stands in the center of the room, and a collar with a chain attached to the ceiling keeps her in place, while her arms are shackled behind her and her feet are bolted to the floor. Her skin is a gorgeous ebony, and her hair is natural, long, and curly and could use some detangler. Her eyes are locked on me. They're completely black. The darkness within me answers, and I feel my eyes shift. But they don't change into my dragon's eyes. I can only assume they flood with black as well. It clicks.

Malick gave us both part of his essence. There's a small part of each of us that's demonic.

Surprisingly, I'm not shocked by the revelation. I feel my eyes shift back to normal, and I step into the room. The vampire cocks her head, her eyes studying every detail.

"They said you'd come." Her voice is hoarse, as though she hasn't used it in some time. "I didn't believe them at first. But Brigid assured me you would come. And so I held on." The goddesses visited her too? Fate. Okay, I'm willing to hand out a little faith here.

"Well, sister, sorry it took so long. Had a few hurdles to overcome. Got stuck in traffic, you know how it goes." I glance at her restraints and they vanish. She stumbles, but I quickly reach out to steady her.

"Nothing worse than traffic." She grins at me. Her eyes slowly fade back, revealing stunning golden irises. "Please tell me we get to kill the fuckers who did this to us?"

"Do you honestly think I'd just walk out of here and tell them to reschedule?" I lift a brow. "I call dibs on Katia. I owe that bitch a heavy, heavy ass kicking. I'll totes let you get a few hits in though, I'm not a complete hoarder."

"I can live with that." She straightens. "I'm Darcy."

"Ayla." We head out the door. I let my magic flair out again, pinpointing Katia in seconds. I can't sense Malick, but there are a few other lower-level demons in the building. It doesn't matter to me if we run into them on our way, I could use the fun.

"We're outside. Kelly is taking down the ward around the building as we speak. We may have set off some sort of alarm, so just be ready." Olivia's voice provides a welcome flood of warmth through my system.

"Oh, good, it should call Malick home." I make sure to sound excited. *"You guys saved me the hassle of hunting him down. You're always so thoughtful."*

"Hey, anything we can do to make your life easier." Goddess, I love her.

"I'm not sure if you heard that or not, I know our bond is still fresh." I look at Darcy. "My community is right outside. Get ready for a fight. I'm sure Malick has this place watched or bugged to warn him if anyone breaches the wards."

Darcy excitedly rubs her hands together. "I get to kill all the demons." She sounds like a kid who's been given permission to have free rein in a toy store. "I know you're new to the whole part demon thing, but when used appropriately, it can be hella fun. I've given them a run for their money, which is why I was in a room that was heavily spelled."

I hadn't even noticed. Damn. "I want to take out Katia before she's tipped off. I don't want her stripping my people of their magic or ability to shift."

"She's such a damn party pooper." Darcy rolls her eyes as we keep moving toward Katia's location.

I can feel Caleb's impatience blasting through the mate bond. That man needs to cool his jets. While I appreciate that he wants to make sure I'm okay and go all caveman on the demons here, Mama's got this. He is mated to a *queen*. I don't need no man. But damn it all if I don't just want the crap out of him, so I'll let him destroy some demons in my honor. It's sweet really. Who doesn't want a man who's willing to take on a legion of demons for you?

"Let me take care of the mage before you come busting in here." He growls at that. I merely smirk.

"You've got ten minutes. That's how long Kelly thinks it'll take for her to get in. She said it's a pretty powerful ward, but, and I quote, 'I'm a boss-ass bitch who can ruin this damn thing.'" Fuck yeah, she is. That's my girl.

"You show that ward who's boss," I tell Kelly, sending along a wave of love.

~

WHEN WE FINALLY MAKE IT to the room Katia is in, somehow having avoided any confrontations with the lower-level demons lurking around, I feel Kelly's power surging through the bond. She's going to have that ward down well before my ten-minute deadline. I'm so proud. But that also means I need to get my ass in gear. Bitches to slay and all that.

"Why don't you go in first, warm her up for me?" I suggest to Darcy. "I'll make sure no lower-level demons try to crash the party. Just tap me in when you're ready."

Darcy cracks her knuckles, a dark smile spreading across her face. "You're so nice! We're gonna be best friends!" And with that, she struts in to confront Katia.

Chuckling, I stand outside the closed door. I'll give Darcy a few minutes of fun, but I want to make sure Katia can't block any of my community. If Malick is going to be joining us with reinforcements, I don't want any of my people hurt because of that raging pile of flaming garbage.

I feel Caleb's dragon mentally nudge mine, and I can't help the smile that breaks out across my face. My dragon eagerly nudges back, assuring him that we're fine. They're both thrilled that the mating bond is finally secure. Caleb and I still have a lot of things to figure out, but I'm pretty damn happy about this as well. The mate bond grounds me. I'm not afraid of the demonic parts of me because I know Caleb won't let me go fully dark. I'll fight to stay with him, and that means not letting that darkness consume me. Why the hell had I been so stubborn about this?

All of my memories are back too. The goddesses charged me with finding the prophecy. I didn't know what they meant at the time, but I think I do now. It's what caused my mother to hide us away. I don't know what it says, only having heard bits and pieces, and I'm not sure where to start looking for it, but I think finding my sisters may be the key. Which means I need to tell everyone about Sorcha and Isobel.

They're alive. My heart lifts. The goddesses confirmed my sisters are alive. After witnessing the horrific deaths of our parents, the knowledge that my sisters are alive provides a balm to my soul. I don't know their exact locations, but I have starting points, and that's good enough. And with help from my community, I know I'll be able to find them, save them.

A mental nudge from Darcy signals that it's my turn to play with Katia. As Darcy steps out of the room, a handful of lower-level demons come rushing down the hall.

"Don't worry." Darcy looks surprisingly unruffled after her bout with the mage. "I'll take care of these guys. Go take care of Katia."

KATIA HAS A BLOODY LIP, a black eye, and her hair is a disaster. The room around her is trashed, which brings me a surprising amount of joy. Katia stiffens when she sees me, her eyes darting to the door behind me. Her magic starts to swirl around her. I tsk, narrowing my eyes on her, sending her flying into the wall, my magic pinning her in place as I approach.

"Do you want to know what a little birdy told me?" My

voice is deadly calm. "Somebody betrayed their queen." I tsk again. "Can you imagine such a thing?" I stop, standing inches from her.

"Aine got what she deserved," Katia snarls. "The queens should never have been allowed to have all that power. There are more species than just dragons. Why should they get to rule?"

"See, I agree with you. Dragons shouldn't have all the power. The goddesses agree with you too." I smile at her. "But you need to earn the power, Katia. Taking it without earning it doesn't make that power yours. And it's time to pay up."

Katia's magic pushes her off the wall, her hands curling into claws aimed straight for my face. I sidestep just in time. She lashes out with magic again, sending me skidding across the room.

"You're not going to be able to block my magic or my dragon again." I allow my magic to pool in my hands.

Instead of a sword or whip, my magic forms a ball-headed war club in one hand and a small khopesh in the other. They aren't made of energy either, they're real and solid. Sweet. They're also exceptionally light, an indication that they're made of magic. I've never fought with either, but I'm sure going to have fun learning.

A pair of sai appear in Katia's hands as she takes a fighting stance. She doesn't rush me, choosing to stand her ground and have me come to her. She's not as stupid as I thought.

"Do you want to know how I kept you without magic and your dragon for so long?" She's trying to distract me, but I need to know how she got that much power. I don't answer her. As I slowly circle around her, she turns to keep facing me, grinning tauntingly. "I use conduits. Other supernaturals paid the price for keeping you on lockdown. I've had to drain fifty supes just to keep you sedated enough to continue with the injections. It's a shame they didn't last as long as the dominant female shifters. But I couldn't risk them when I have such grand plans for them."

I try not to let her words get to me, but fury starts to build in my stomach. She sounds so damn pleased that she's murdered fifty innocent supernaturals. I want to drain her just as dry. She also said her grand plans. She's Malick's underling, isn't she? She's too clever for a slip of the tongue.

"Where are the shifter females?" My voice rumbles with the presence of my dragon.

"You don't honestly think we'd store them here, do you?" Katia laughs. "The vampire was here because she needed close monitoring. But we don't keep all of our eggs in one basket."

"Where are they?" I don't want to ask again.

"That's one secret I'll take to my grave." Rage floods my system at her refusal to tell me where the female shifters are. While she's confirmed that Malick is the one taking the females, I have no way of finding them.

"You said 'your' grand plans," I taunt, "but Malick is the mastermind here, Katia. We both know it."

Rage spreads across her face. "I have had to ensure Lord Malick's continued dedication. I came to him and told him about Aine. I made sure that he attacked that night. I wasn't happy that he took her after the battle, so I had to make sure that he forgot about her until I could free Valik."

This isn't right. It can't be. She's the one in control here? No. I need more information, but she stops talking and I'm running out of time. The thought of torturing the information out of her sends a bolt of bloodlust through my veins. My eyes start to bleed black. I need to stay focused. I can't let my demonic side overwhelm me. How the hell did Darcy get away without a scratch?

"I used my vampire speed and hit her over the head before she

could turn around and see me. Then I punched her in the face, got her lab notes, and trashed the place. I didn't want to make this too easy for you." Darcy laughs through the bond. She's still out in the hall fighting the lower-level demons, where more joined the fight while I've been busy with the mage.

"Lazy bitch," I retort before returning my focus to Katia.

I take a deep breath before launching myself at her. I know she won't fight fair, but neither will I. The demonic energy inside me leaps at the chance to destroy something. A blast of black power shoots from my body, slamming into Katia moments before my weapons do. She struggles to shake off the inky mass that attaches itself to her, slowing her movements, allowing me to get more hits in.

We trade furious blows, each of us lashing out with magic whenever we see an opening. Soon, the coppery taste of blood floods my mouth, and the stale stench of sweat permeates the air around us, along with the acrid scent of burning flesh and hair. The sound of my breathing overpowers the crash of our weapons slamming together, the echoes of blows landing on flesh ringing louder throughout the room.

Katia starts to slow, the inky black mass I originally shot at her still weighing her down, gradually draining her magic and her stamina. I see an opening and I go for it.

"This is for my mother." My war club imbeds itself in her skull.

Time seems to stand still as we stare at each other. Katia's eyes are wide with shock. I can feel the black recede from my eyes as I watch the life slowly drain out of her body. My war club and khopesh instantly vanish, and Katia's body slides limply to the floor. I don't feel the way I thought I would. I'm not happy. Instead, I feel...I don't know...vaguely content? Maybe I'm still numb to everything. I have had a day.

"Uh, Ayla." Kelly's voice cuts through my thoughts. *"The ward has been down for a few minutes now. You may want to get out*

front. Malick is back with his legion, but that's not what I want you to see."

She's just going to leave it like that? Tease. Shaking myself off, I take a quick inventory of my injuries and send as much healing magic to the worst of them as I can, and then I head out the door. Darcy is sitting on a small pile of lower-level demons, inspecting her nails. She slowly looks up as I enter the hallway.

"What took you so long?" Her eyes slowly travel over my body. "Oh. Never mind. You look like shit."

"Oh, thanks." I roll my eyes at her. She hops off her little throne and joins me as I head outside. I'm extremely confused by the sight that greets me.

MY COMMUNITY IS SQUARING off against Malick's demon legion. The sounds of the battle ring through the air, accompanied by the scent of blood. But that's not what holds my attention.

Olivia is covered head to toe in...demon guts? That's nasty. She's got a horrified look plastered on her face, and she's staring at her hands as though she thinks they'll blow her up at any second. The bulk of my community has closed ranks around her, while my core group is standing near Olivia warily. Color me interested.

"Guys..." Olivia's voice is shaky. "I just blew up a demon! All I did was look at him!" She glances up at the group around her, and everyone leans back nervously. She quickly slams her eyes shut. "He just turned inside out!"

My experience with the goddesses rushes back. Freja had said my sisters by bond would take up the mantle of queen.

The mantle of queen!

Holy. Shit.

Olivia is a queen! I glance at Kelly and Darcy, expecting them to suddenly make a demon explode too. But then I remember what else Freja told me. They will each come into their power when the time is right. I fight the urge to facepalm. They didn't tell the ladies about this little change, did they? Well, I guess it's up to me then.

"I realize there's a battle raging around us, so I'm not going to share the memory with you right now, but I have news!" I know I sound oddly cheery given what's happening around us. *"Thanks to a couple of goddesses, Olivia is now a queen!"*

"I'm sorry." Olivia turns and pins her gaze on me, her eyes narrowed. *"But I could have sworn you just said I've been turned into a queen."*

"Brigid, Isis, and Freja made you into a queen." I beam over at her. *"I'll fill you in later, promise. But for now, you've got some epic new demon-killing skills. Go forth and slaughter!"* I make little shooing motions with my hands.

"I'm not sure if that's insanely cool or insanely horrible," she mutters.

"Both." I laugh.

I can feel the shock from the others through the bond. I'd purposely made sure to broadcast that out to everyone. I know there are a lot of questions, but we really don't have the time right now. So I urge them all to wait and make note of their questions for later. I'm not sure I can answer them all, but I'll try. And I'll need to warn Kelly and Darcy about the changes they're going to be facing as well. Being a queen is no joke.

I grab Darcy's hand and drag her over to my group. I'll need to explain Darcy as well. I have so much to explain but now isn't the time, damn it. I start mentally making a list of priorities—kill psycho archdemon, explain to everyone about new queens and Darcy, bang the shit out of Caleb, explain about my sisters, bang Caleb, form a plan on how to wake them up, bang Caleb. I should probably add eating and sleeping in there somewhere too. It's a work in progress.

"*Right then. Here's the plan,*" I broadcast. "*Make sure we communicate like this, I don't want Malick overhearing anything. Caleb and I are going to go head-to-head with Malick. Olivia, your powers are so new I don't want to risk overworking you right now, so focus on the lower-level demons. You'll be able to save a lot of lives that way. I want the main goal to be capturing one of the lower-level demons. Malick has other facilities like this one, and we need to know where they are. Questions?*"

"*I have too many questions. They'll have to wait.*" Kelly's voice washes over me like a calm, gentle stream. "*I'm just glad to have you back.*" The others agree.

"*Did you mean it?*" Caleb nudges me mentally, blocking out the rest of our group. "*Together?*"

"*Heck yeah, I meant it! Let's exact some justice!*" I beam up at him. He grins in return and nods. The others all take a moment to look at me before leaping into action.

It's clear Olivia doesn't have full control over her queen powers yet. She's unable to consistently blow demons up or harness any other magic. Malcolm hovers near her to help as needed, and I'm glad someone has her back. Darcy and Dante move with amazing ease, as though they've been fighting together for centuries. Kelly and Connor start tag-teaming, Connor shifting into his dire wolf form. I stand still for another moment, watching Olivia to make sure she has everything as under control as possible. Now to turn my attention to fucking an archdemon's day up.

Chapter Twenty-Four

"Well, well, well..." I grit my teeth as Malick's voice rings out over the sounds of the battle raging around us. "I truly shouldn't be surprised you let yourself out, little queen. After all I've done to you, it's only fitting you'd escape." I'm going to rip the satisfied smile I know he has on his face from his lips through his asshole if it's the last thing I do.

His voice seems to be echoing from everywhere, so it's hard to pin down where he's approaching us from. I take a deep breath and close my eyes, focusing on finding his unique signature out of the battle around us. I spin to my left just as the fighting starts to part to let Malick through. Caleb's arm wraps protectively around my waist, a low snarl rumbling in his chest. I melt a little on the inside. Thanks to the fully formed mate bond, I can feel that he doesn't doubt my ability to take care of myself. No. He wants to rip Malick to shreds before charring his remains simply because he hurt me.

"Together. We'll do this together." I feel his pleasure at my statement. *"We're mates. You make me stronger. We're going to take him down as a team."*

"Goddess, I love you, woman."

"We will come back to that statement once this is finished. Don't think you can just drop the 'L' word like that at a time like this and I won't remember." He chuckles darkly, a wicked grin spreading across his face. *"And don't look at me like that either. This is not the time nor the place for 'fuck me' eyes."*

I turn my attention back to Malick. With a grin, I state, "You've pissed off some very powerful ladies." I force my tone to sound bored, evening out my expression. "They want us to clean house. You're obsolete, Malick."

Malick, in full archdemon form, approaches Caleb and me. Malick's eyes flick over to Caleb's arm, which is draped around my waist, and his eyes narrow. The way he's so solely focused on the two of us surprises me, it's as though the battle continuing around him doesn't exist.

"I see you've killed my mage, little queen." He studies me again, tilting his head as he does. "That wasn't very nice, you know. Now I'll need to find a new one." He sounds petulant, and he folds his arms across his chest as though he's about to start having a tantrum in the middle of the damn battlefield.

"Look, it's your fault for picking a lying sack of wasted witch flesh in the first place. Don't do that next time, and I might be able to avoid killing her. I don't know what to tell you." I salute him. "That bitch had it coming, and you know it."

"I suppose you're right, little queen." Malick sighs dramatically, appearing completely put out. His gaze once again lands on Caleb's arm around my waist. Caleb holds me tighter, and Malick's eyes narrow, a frown marring his face.

"While I'd love to catch up over a nice cup of coffee, I have things to do. Demons to kill. I'm sure you understand." I feel Caleb brace beside me as my body coils to attack.

"Together," Caleb, his voice mixed with that of his dragon, rumbles.

"Together." I allow my dragon's voice to mix with mine.

~

I LET my magic flood my system, both my normal queen magic and my demonic magic. The combination is heady. I form a large broadsword and hand it to Caleb as we square off against Malick. I choose to go with a larger form on my khopesh. I want to keep one hand free in case I need help focusing my magic.

Malick's laughter rings out over the battle around us, a spear suddenly appearing in his right hand. He approaches us with a smug smile spreading across his face. I know how lethal he can be up close. I mentally nudge Caleb, reminding him to keep his distance as much as possible.

"Don't forget, little queen," Malick taunts, "you've got my essence inside you. Do you really think you'll be able to fight the darkness that courses through your veins now?"

I feel Caleb stiffen beside me, but he remains silent. I send him soothing thoughts through the bond, promising to explain everything to him when this is done. He doesn't seem worried that I'll lose myself to the darkness. The feelings I get from him suggest he's more pissed that Malick injected any part of himself inside me. I fight not to roll my eyes.

"They used a needle. Settle down, killer." My attempt at reassurance fails as I feel his rage spike.

"Anything of him inside you is unacceptable. I'm the only male allowed inside you." I fight the urge to facepalm.

"Really? Are you for real right now? We are literally in front of an archdemon about to engage in battle, and this is where you go? Does your penis do all the thinking for you?" Men are the worst. Cavemen who think with their dicks, every single one of them. I swear.

"You are my mate." His rage shoots higher.

"Yes. We've established that. I need you to stop. We have bigger things to focus on other than you being butthurt." I can't believe I'm soothing him over the fact that I got injected and turned into some sort of demon hybrid. And they say women are the weaker sex. Right.

"I don't need to fight the darkness, Malick." I allow my eyes to bleed black as I push Caleb and his butthurt temper tantrum from my mind. "Light cannot exist without dark. Life cannot exist without death."

Caleb and I launch ourselves at him. Despite having our training cut short thanks to my kidnapping, we move completely in sync. We trade blow for blow with Malick, quickly, furiously, and with as much power as possible. I feel my bloodlust rise the longer we hack away at each other. The scent of demon blood is thick in the air and mixes with the fragrance of my community's blood. This only fuels the beast within me that wants to bathe in the blood of my enemies. My protective instincts flare to life as my dragon lets out a shrill battle cry.

The noises of the battle fade as I embrace the darkness within me, until only the sound of my pounding heart thrums in my ears, punctuated with the clash of our weapons. Sweat breaks out and drips down my back, but I'm not tiring. Quite the opposite. I'm just getting started. I feel as though I could do this forever.

"Ayla." Caleb's voice is soft and distant in my mind. *"Ayla, come on back a bit, love."*

The screams and cries of my community flood back at such a high volume I wince. I was allowing the darkness free rein. The goddesses said to use the darkness within, not let it use me. Steadying myself, I focus on keeping a balance within me as I continue to swing my khopesh at Malick.

But attacking him like this isn't working. I need to use my magic. I allow it to swirl out of me, letting the khopesh vanish from my hands. I thrust my arms out toward Malick, and shards of diamond-hard rock fly at him. He's too slow throwing up a shield, and the rocks slice at his body and wings. I don't give him time to recover, blasting him with a wave of fire next. Caleb is circling around behind him. Good, I'll keep him distracted.

I raise my hands toward the sky, and a bolt of lightning slams down on top of me. I gather it around my form, allowing it to crackle along my skin. With a sudden burst of released magic, I shoot it out. Malick has trouble dodging it, and a scream tears from his lips as the blast hits him. Caleb, who has finally made it behind the archdemon, shifts and starts spewing fire.

I rip the earth open below Malick and slam it shut, trapping him up to his knees. This is it. I can feel his energy draining. I'm going to fry this douche canoe off the face of the planet. And it's going to feel amazing.

Suddenly, the community members and demons around us start to collapse in waves. I can feel the pull of Malick's demonic energy as he drains them all, and my blood runs cold as I realize what he's getting ready to use—death magic. But I'm not given enough time to act before he lashes out and horror floods my body.

A spear of black death magic shoots out toward Caleb. My heart stops and my stomach drops. The world slows, and I can see everything we're meant to have flash before me. The years of love and laughter, the children, leading a community together, the fights, the makeup sex, the nights spent curled up in one another's arms, everything. It's all gone in an instant.

No! Malick has already taken so much from me. I refuse to let him take Caleb.

In the next blink, I'm in front of Caleb in dragon form, a screech ripping from me as the death magic slams into my chest. Caleb's furious roar is the only thing I hear as I plummet out of the sky. I crash in a heap, instantly shifting back to human. I'm weak. I need to end this now. Caleb's large dragon body lands over me protectively.

Thankfully, Malick is still contained in the earth. I cough, feeling liquid fly from my lips. I refuse to think about what that could mean. Instead, I allow light to fill me. It floods my cells, warming me until I feel like I'm about to combust. My heart is racing, and with each breath I exhale, more liquid splatters to the ground beneath me. My limbs start to go numb as cold begins to replace my dragon's heat. My vision tunnels and the only sound I can focus on is my labored breathing. Strangely, I don't pass out.

"Daughter. My beautiful little girl." The world around me seems to freeze when I hear her voice, my heart stopping along with it.

"Mom?" Tears instantly gather in my eyes as grief swells inside me.

"My strong, brave daughter. I do not have much time." Though I can't see her, I feel the touch of her hand on my cheek.

"Mama! I'm so sorry I couldn't save you or Da." Sorrow floods my voice as my tears start to stream down my face.

"My darling girl, we knew the sacrifice we would need to make, and we did so willingly. We would gladly do so again. You are everything we could have hoped for and more." I feel a gentle kiss brush my cheek. *"Your father and I have one last gift for you. We locked away not just your memories, but one of your powers as well. I unlock it now. Find your sisters. You'll find a clue to the prophecy and your powers with each of them."*

"Don't go! Please!" But it's too late. I don't sense her anymore.

When the world speeds up again, I feel power flood my body. This is different than anything I've ever felt before.

Life. My dragon sounds weak and so very far away. *It's life.*

And with that, I explode.

WHEN MALICK HIT me with his death magic, he was actually hitting me with the souls of my community. He'd stolen them, as well as the energy and life force of the lower-level demons around him—since demons don't have souls—to launch his attack. And so, when the souls of my community hit me, instead of dispersing as they should have, they clung to me as though charged with static electricity.

Every magic-user can harness the four elements—earth, air, fire, and water. Typically, they're stronger in one element than the others. As a queen, I can control all of them equally. But as I lie on the ground, my very cells ripping apart, I realize there's one more element—the soul. Not all queens can harness the souls of the dead as well as the living, it's a rare gift passed down genetically. My mother didn't have the gift, but my grandmother did. It's different from necromancy in that I can't control a dead body. Instead, I can control the soul and have it do my bidding. In a way, I'm like the ferryman from Greek mythology, assuming I don't abuse my gift anyway. Helping souls move on isn't the only thing I can do with them, however, I can create life.

Demons are the opposite of life, everything about them is somehow related to death. Lower-level demons are made up of the souls of evil mortals. The more evil they do, the higher in the ranks they rise. Eventually, they become archdemons. Only Lucifer and the Princes of Hell out rank archdemons and weren't ever human, while every other soul in hell is some evil twat who was once mortal.

Queens are life. They're filled with it, brimming around the edges with magic that creates instead of destroys. That's why we're the best defense possible. Our magic allows us to create new forms of magic using the very building blocks of life. Being able to harness and manipulate souls makes my life magic far more potent.

And so, as I lie under Caleb, bleeding out, I release the souls Malick stole. They come screaming out of me, panicked and in pain. I urge them to reunite with their bodies and heal, soothing them in any way I can. But that isn't the only thing I release. Every ounce of magic still swirling in my body goes along with them, causing a massive shock wave to blast through the area. My last thought before I go off like a nuke is that I don't want any of my people harmed. I know, deep inside me, that my magic will keep them all safe while annihilating the demons around us.

My magic is tied to my soul, it's what keeps me alive. And I just expelled it all from my body in a desperate attempt to save my mate and my community. I was dying anyway, might as well take out as many of the bastards as I can before I go, right?

But I don't die. By every right, I should be dead right now. But I'm still alive. My heart is still beating furiously in my chest, and my lungs still frantically try to draw in air to keep said heart pumping. At my core, the thing that is keeping me alive is a small, glowing, golden thread. My mate bond.

Caleb, my dragon purrs softly in my mind. I'm too physically and mentally exhausted right now to truly figure out how he's keeping us alive, but I'm hella grateful. He is so getting a blow job for this. Hell, sex for days if he keeps it up.

My eyes are closed since I lack the energy to keep them open, so I don't see him shift into his human form. I do, however, feel his very human hands as they run along my body, awe filling the bond as he realizes that I am, truly, still alive. A wave of love, relief, and gratitude washes over me from him, and tears burn in the back of my eyes. This alpha, the alpha of all alphas, has been rocked to his very core, and I've never been prouder to call him my mate.

"Ayla?" Caleb's mind gently nudges my own, tentatively assessing my mental state. *"Love? Can you hear me?"* He pushes more of his strength through the bond. I grab hold of that shimmering, golden thread and grip it for dear life. It's my anchor.

"We can hear you," my dragon answers. I'm still too shocked by what's happened to attempt to string words together in any coherent form. *"You saved us."*

I feel Caleb's confusion, mirroring my own, but we don't have answers for him right now. Goddess, I'm so tired. I can feel my grip over my thoughts weaken. But I need to know. I need to know if I killed Malick. Did I send that fucker to hell where he belongs?

"M-Malick?" Even my internal voice is weak.

"Don't worry about that now. You need to rest, love. Rest."

Don't worry about whether I killed Malick? That's what all of this was about. But if Caleb isn't concerned then that has to mean something. And goddess, I'm so damn tired. But I'm worried I won't come back if I fall asleep. I'm scared, so damn scared, that this is the end. Scared that Caleb saved us just to have us fade away moments later.

Sleep, my dragon murmurs. *We're healing. I promise you'll wake up. It's going to take a while to recover, but I promise, you'll wake up.*

And so I sleep.

Chapter Twenty-Five

As I battle my way out of the darkness that encompasses me, I hear people around me arguing. At first, I can't make out what they're talking about, but it seems to be pretty heated. I continue to combat the waves of unconsciousness, fighting my way closer to the surface. Finally, I rouse myself enough to understand what's being said. I can't open my eyes or indicate that I can hear them, but I can at least listen.

"Do we have any idea what the hell happened out there?" Caleb's tone is laced with frustrated fury. I can hear him pacing near me. "How the hell did he make it out of that attack?"

Are they talking about Malick? Panic flares through me, pushing me back under the surface. I battle to stay afloat, needing to hear more.

"We're not sure, Caleb." Dante this time. "We all saw the same thing, but we aren't sure how it happened in the first place. All we know is that right before the blast hit him, something just came and scooped him out of the damn ground."

No. No, no, no. That can't be right. If they're really talking about Malick, that means I'm dying for nothing. Darkness threatens, stronger than before, and it takes everything I have to cling to consciousness. They have to be wrong. There's a mistake. They aren't talking about Malick.

"Our best trackers are out there right now looking for him." Olivia. She sounds stronger, more confident. "If he's still alive, we'll find him. I'm about to join them. I'm still not completely sure how to use these new powers, but I can sense demons, so that has to be of some use."

Their voices start to fade again. I struggle to stay above the waves that threaten to pull me back into the darkness I've just emerged from, but they're too strong. I slowly sink into the abyss.

"She's fine. Caleb, I swear. She's okay," Kelly states. I'm once again struggling to the surface of my mind, trying desperately to open my eyes, to give those around me some indication that I'm here. "When she released that blast a month ago, it completely drained all of her magic. If we thought mind diving was rough, it's nothing compared to what she did on that battlefield. But she's pulling through." There's a note of surprised pleasure in her voice at the last part.

Wait a minute...a month? I've been like this for an entire month? But what about the battle? What about Malick? How many were wounded? Dead? Have they been able to find any more of Malick's compounds? I fight harder against the waves threatening to pull me under again. I want to scream when I can't open my eyes, but no sound escapes me. Panic and fury wind sinfully through my veins. I attempt to harness them, hoping they'll give me a boost of energy so I can even just flinch a finger. Something. Nothing. Damn it, nothing happens.

"Och. I know." *Mate*, my mind purrs as Caleb speaks. "She only wakes to eat, and even then it's not really her, it's her dragon. How are her magic levels?" He sounds worried and haggard, as though he hasn't been sleeping. I want to reach out to him through the bond. I can feel it anchoring me here, keeping me alive long enough for my magic to replenish itself, but I can't connect with him through it.

"Based on what I can feel, she's close to what she was before all of this started. But given what's happened to her, I'm not sure how much longer it'll take for her to regain all of her magic. She's far stronger now than she was when she was taken. I'm hopeful she'll wake up soon though." Kelly comes closer, and a cool, soft hand brushes my forehead. "We don't really know what happened to her, Caleb. Malick did something to her while he had her. She also said something about goddesses on the battlefield. I'm just not sure."

I grasp on to the mention of Malick, willing them with every fiber of my being to mention something, anything, that will tell me what transpired. Caleb lets out a frustrated sigh as he, too, comes closer to the bed I'm on. He sits on the edge, the mattress dipping beneath his weight. I wish my body would move so I can touch him, but I can't seem to wrench my eyes open, let alone curl my body around my mate.

"We still haven't found that asshole." Caleb's voice is low and filled with menace. "Kelly, the bastard just disappeared."

"We're trying to find him, Caleb. It's possible that even though he somehow vanished, he was still too injured to survive. Even if he is still alive, Ayla wiped the floor with him, so we don't need to worry about him attacking while she's weak like this." Kelly attempts to soothe Caleb by keeping her voice calm and low. She's used that tone on me countless times, it's always helped keep me levelheaded, I hope it works on him.

Malick got away? How? Confusion whirls inside me. I try reaching out to my dragon to see if she can explain, but I can't find her. It's possible she only surfaces when I'm out, and I can only surface when she's dormant due to the extent of my injuries and the fact that I drained all of my magic. That doesn't make this any less frustrating though.

I can feel the depths calling to me again. I fight as hard as I can, wanting to stay with Caleb and Kelly a little longer, but ultimately, I fall back into the black void.

WHEN I FINALLY, *finally,* come to, it appears to be early afternoon, judging by the light that's streaming in through my window. I'm tucked neatly in my bed at the packhouse. I blink several times as my eyes try to adjust to the light. I've been in the dark for so long that my eyes sting something fierce. Surprisingly, I'm alone. I'm thankful for it though, because I need a minute to settle into myself now that I'm finally awake. I'm not completely sure how much time has passed since the battle, but based on the fact that I was completely drained of magic, I can assume it's been quite a while. My memories during the time I was recovering are hazy at best.

I struggle to sit up in bed, my muscles weak, but thankfully they haven't atrophied. My dragon must have been moving my body for me while I was recuperating. Still, I've lost a lot of muscle mass, and I'm going to need to work my ass off to get back to where I was before. My fingers inch their way through my hair, which is blissfully knot-free, and I notice it feels longer than I remember. The shaved part of my head has more than just a little peach fuzz too. At least a month, then, if not longer.

That's when the memory of listening to Caleb and Kelly floods back. I'm not sure how long ago that was, but it had been a month after the battle. And they hadn't been able to find Malick. The fucker could still be alive. I feel a small part of my soul shatter. That recollection opens up memories from earlier. Dante and Olivia had been talking about tracking Malick down. I feel tears prick the back of my eyes. Damn it!

If he's still alive, we'll try again. We'll be stronger. My dragon's voice settles me. She's right. We'll get stronger, train Olivia, and prepare Kelly and Darcy. We may even have Isobel and Sorcha with us. I plan on telling my community about my sisters. They have a right to know. And if we can find them before Malick does, we'll stand an even greater chance of stopping whatever he has planned.

Still, I feel as though I've failed myself, my mate, my community, my mother, and, well, everyone. I slam my fist down on the bed and hear a loud *snap*. Startled, I look down as my bed creaks. Cautiously, I hold my hand above the bed, not wanting to touch it again in case it breaks. I hadn't realized it was broken.

It wasn't. My dragon's voice is filled with laughter. *You just broke it when you punched the mattress.* Shock races through me. I broke it? I gingerly lay my hand on the mattress, staring at my hand like it has a mind of its own. *I told you,* my dragon giggles, *we're stronger.*

The door eases open, and I turn my head to watch as Caleb walks into my room. His head is down, and he's running his fingers through his hair. He's thinner than he was when I was awake last. He's also sporting a bit of a hobo beard. I giggle. Caleb's head snaps up at the sound, his eyes going wide, and the emotion I see in them brings tears to my eyes. In a blink, he's by the bed staring down at me, a broad grin spreading across his face.

"Ayla!" His dragon also rumbles a greeting in my mind, brushing against my dragon affectionately. Caleb sits next to me on the bed.

It collapses to the floor, causing Caleb and me to land in a tangled heap. Every worry, every question I had on waking vanishes. I lose it. My laughter rings out, breaking the shocked silence around us. I start laughing so hard my sides hurt, so I wrap my arms around myself in an effort to ease the ache. Caleb begins laughing right along with me, a deep, belly laugh that's so insanely attractive, it sends raging lust flying through my body, heating me pleasantly before pooling between my legs. Suddenly, I want to climb this man like a damn tree and stay there for days.

Caleb can feel my mood shift through the bond and an answering searing hunger slams into me. He's just as anxious to get at me as I am to get at him. But his concern for me floats through next as a gentle whisper across my skin as he checks to make sure I'm truly okay. I let him conduct his inquiry without fuss, opening myself completely to the bond so he can see I'm fine. A pleased rumble vibrates from his chest when he finishes, happy that, while I've lost weight, I'm otherwise perfectly healthy.

I turn my head to look at him, feeling love and lust dance throughout my body. Caleb's eyes darken with desire when I meet his gaze. We don't need to say anything, everything that matters flows through the bond between us. But it still isn't fully complete, I realize with shock. Caleb senses where my thoughts have drifted, and his eyes narrow on my neck. While our mental bond seems to be complete, our overall mate bond isn't. We don't carry each other's scent, our heartbeats haven't synced. Those won't happen until we mark one another. Which had better be about to happen.

I launch myself at Caleb, not giving him even a second to think before sealing my lips over his. Now that I've decided to see this through, I don't want to wait any longer. If he wants to wait, well, I can be the most annoying bitch on the planet.

Thankfully, it seems that Caleb is just as eager to cement the bond as I am as he starts ripping at my clothes, not bothering to remove them properly. I start to do the same, it's faster this way, and easier to get access to his warm, velvety soft skin. Skin that hides rock-hard muscles and brute strength. Skin that's slightly paler than the last time we came together. He's been spending far too much time inside with me. I make a mental note to talk to him about this later, right now we have better things to focus on.

When we're both finally, blissfully naked, Caleb rips his mouth from mine as he moves on top of me. We're both panting, and I can't seem to take my eyes off his lips. I want them everywhere. Now. Right now. But I also don't want to wait to feel him moving inside me. Does this count as a first world problem?

"I want to take my time with you." His voice is deep and laced with heat. "But that's going to have to wait. I need to be inside you. Need to feel you squeezing me."

I barely have time to nod before he's thrusting deep, my pussy clamping down tightly around him. It's been too long, and my body needs time to adjust, so I wrap my legs around his hips to hold him still. Caleb buries his face against my neck with a soft groan, shaking slightly as he fights the urge to move.

"Hey, Caleb, we need to go over..." The door opens as Malcolm's voice reaches us. "Oh, sweet goddess! I need eye bleach!" It quickly slams shut again. Caleb growls so loudly, my entire body vibrates.

"I realize you want to rip the naughty witch to shreds, but

you need to start moving now or I'm going to rip it off and finish the damn job myself." My threat breaks Caleb out of his trance, his head snapping up so he can look me in the eye. His eyes flash to his dragon's for a moment before returning to normal.

And then he's moving. Thank goddess, he's moving. This isn't a soft, slow, peaceful lovemaking. This is hard, fast, and rough. This is a reconnection to ensure that the other is safe, alive, and whole. This is mates who have waited far too long before fully cementing their bond and committing to one another. This is everything I never knew I needed and more. So much more.

I gasp when he pulls out completely, spinning me around so I'm on my hands and knees before him. He quickly thrusts back in, causing me to whimper as he slams against my G-spot. And he doesn't let up. Each rough thrust continues to hit the same spot until I'm a panting, moaning, whimpering mess of lust, my body right on the edge of oblivion.

Caleb fists his hand in my hair as he sits back into a kneeling position, yanking me up until my back is flush with his chest, never once stopping his relentless attack on my G-spot. He holds my head against his chest as his other hand snakes down and starts to gently circle my clit.

Oh, fuck. Oh, yes.

My hands fly up to cup my breasts, my thumbs and fore-fingers roughly pinching my nipples. I'm so close to the edge, but I don't want to fall until he does. I can feel him getting closer through the bond, but he's not as close as I am. With one hand staying on my breast, the other glides down my body and past his hand. I make a V with my fore and middle fingers, placing them just outside the entrance to my pussy, and I gently squeeze, providing additional friction at the same time I purposely clamp my inner muscles around him.

Caleb snarls loudly, his thrusts growing rougher, wilder,

until I shatter, screaming his name to the heavens. As he continues to move inside me, he quickly spins me around so I'm facing him again. Instantly, he sinks his teeth into my neck, causing me to come all over again. I quickly bite the same spot on his neck, riding out the waves of pleasure. Caleb comes with a roar against my skin, his hips jerking roughly against mine.

Reluctantly, we both remove our mouths from the other's neck, both gently licking the wound. I can feel his heart racing against my chest, and it's pulsing in time with mine. Awe and pleasure race through me as I realize that our heartbeats have synced. We'll be able to easily tell when the other is injured, scared, aroused, anything, even if the mental bond has been closed off. I inhale deeply, our mixed scents swirling through me, creating a sense of peace and contentment I haven't felt since I was a child. I feel complete.

"Finally," Caleb whispers huskily in my ear. I chuckle quietly. "I can finally fucking feel you everywhere." He tightens his hold on me, molding my body to his, still semi-hard inside me. "I'm never letting you go, queen." I laugh, thrilled.

"As if I'd let you go now, Alpha." I move my head back so I can look him in the eye. "When I woke up alone in Malick's little love den, I instantly wanted to reach out to you. I can't tell you how much I regretted not completing the bond, how much I regretted being so damn stubborn about not being willing to talk to you about potential solutions. Some damn attorney I am."

"Hey." Caleb's voice hardens. "I didn't fight to find a middle ground. And you were right." He looks at me sheepishly. "There was a part of me that didn't want to give up the power I'd come into. I'm so used to running the show that the concept of giving up power didn't sit well with me, even though I knew you outranked me. I didn't mind that at all actually. I don't know."

I gently place my hands on his cheeks, leaning in to give him a soft kiss. "I understand. Things aren't the same as they once were. Even if we're getting a new generation of queens, we can't go back to the system we had with the old queens. But we can't stay with this current system either. We'll need to work together to figure out a way to keep all of the supernaturals safe." His arms loosen around me as he leans back to look me over, a smile gracing his insanely handsome face.

"Together."

I nod. "Together."

Chapter Twenty-Six

Caleb and I made love again and again, and a few more times after that, finally stopping to shower as dawn began breaking over the horizon. We're standing under the spray of the water, still wrapped in each other's arms, and I really don't want to return to reality. I want to stay here, soaking in the water and touching my mate, but I know I need to get out soon and tackle the aftermath of being unconscious for a little over a month. Caleb hasn't said anything about how long I was out, choosing instead to focus on the here and now. Which I'm grateful for, but we can't avoid this talk forever.

Sighing, I turn off the water, easing my body away from Caleb's. He's silent as he reaches for my hair towel, waiting patiently as I wrap my hair up, and then he grabs my body towel. He reaches for his own towel, quickly drying himself off and wrapping it around his waist. I just stand in the shower, dripping slightly, as I stare at him. There's so much to say, so much to discuss. I want to just curl back up on the broken bed with Caleb and forget the world outside my room exists. It sucks that I can't do that.

Caleb arches an eyebrow at me, and I shrug. I step out of the shower, quickly making sure I'm dry enough to throw on some yoga pants and a t-shirt. I then quickly braid my damp hair and look at myself in the mirror. I've been avoiding this too, but I need to see what I look like now.

The shaved patch on the side of my head desperately needs attention, my cheeks are sunken in a little, and I have black bags under my eyes. I'm a bit paler than usual, which surprises me because you really couldn't get much paler than I was without being dead. I'm thinner than I was too, which I'm not happy about. But the biggest difference is the slightly haunted look in my eyes. Knowing that I'm different now, changed in a way I'm still coming to terms with, fighting a darkness inside me that could easily consume me if I let it, has clearly left its mark, not just emotionally, but physically too.

"But we won't let it." Caleb moves to stand behind me, wrapping his arms around my waist and leaning his chin on my shoulder, breaking through my thoughts. "Remember, we're in this together. We won't let the darkness overtake you. We'll learn the best way to keep you balanced. Together." He places a light kiss on my shoulder where his chin had been and then meets my eyes in the mirror.

He's right. We're going to get through this together. I'm not alone anymore. I beam back at him and turn just enough to press a gentle kiss to his cheek.

"Now let's go. Breakfast should be ready, and we really need to refuel if I'm going to break the bed more," Caleb teases. I laugh as we move back into my room and eye the bed in question. "What the hell happened to it anyway?" He shoots me an inquisitive look.

"Apparently being part demon means I'm physically stronger than I was." I rub the back of my neck and let out a nervous giggle. "I sort of punched the bed. I heard it crack right before you came into the room." Caleb chuckles, wrapping his arm around my shoulders and hugging me to his side. "We'll have to make sure that the new bed is magically reinforced." He laughs louder and leads me out of the room.

SURPRISINGLY, despite the early hour, everyone is in the breakfast room waiting for us. Kelly and Olivia jump to their feet, rushing over to throw their arms around me. I hug them right back, letting their love and strength flow through our bonds. My eyes meet Darcy's across the room. She's nervous and isn't sure if she should join in on the group hug. Sighing dramatically, I gesture with my hand for her to get in on the lovin'. She thankfully doesn't hesitate and comes right over to hug me from behind.

And that's when the waterworks start.

ONCE THE FOUR of us are finished ugly sobbing against each other, we pull apart, wide smiles spreading across our faces. It feels so good to be back with my family and to know that they made it out of the battle with Malick. I notice that the men of our little group are all standing around the table awkwardly, clearly not knowing what to do with a huddle of sobbing females. I roll my eyes and grab my plate, starving and eager to stuff my face now that I've had a chance to reconnect with my sisters.

Everything I experienced with the goddesses floods back at the thought. My sisters by bond and my sisters by blood. I've got a lot of explaining to do. Looks like we might be in this room for the rest of the day. At least there will be plenty of food.

I settle in at the table, and thankfully everyone allows me time to stuff my face before peppering me with questions. Like this morning, however, I can't avoid this conversation forever. I'm going to need to have this discussion, bare my soul, and roll with whatever happens after.

"Before I start, I have to know..." I pause, taking a deep breath. "What happened to Malick?"

The silence that greets my question is deafening. Suddenly, Olivia's finger goes flying to the tip of her nose, followed quickly by Kelly and Darcy doing the same. Good to see we're still in high school. Dante looks confused. He's old, so he probably has no idea what the hell is going on. Connor and Malcolm stare at my ladies like they're examining a science experiment. And Caleb is pinching the bridge of his nose. Through the bond, I can hear him praying to every god and goddess out there to give him the patience to deal with all of them. I snort out a laugh, coughing quickly to cover it up.

Thanks to the bond, however, Caleb knows that I find all of this amusing and shoots me a playful glare across the table. Placing his hands on either side of his plate, he takes a deep breath before speaking. "I'll tell her." He sends annoyed glares to everyone else around the table. "She's my mate, it should come from me anyway."

More silence echoes through the room.

"He's gone." A small flicker of hope flares within me. I heard wrong while I was completely out of my damn mind. "Something grabbed him from the ground and ripped him away right before your attack could touch him." Everything inside me stops, my heart plummets into my stomach, and I have to fight to keep the bile down. "But you did kill his entire legion."

"It was pretty badass," Darcy comments, trying to give me a reassuring smile.

"Where is he?" My voice is shaking with rage. Not at Malick, but at myself. I failed. I fucking failed.

"We don't know," Olivia chimes in. "But we're hunting him down. We haven't stopped since the battle."

"But you've been our top priority, Ayla," Kelly interjects, leaning over to grab my hand. "You were unconscious for six weeks."

Six weeks? My dragon rubs soothingly against me in my mind. She did most of the work while my magic stores refilled, keeping us both alive.

"We are one," my dragon murmurs, and I smile.

"Hell yes, we are." My dragon's pleased hum is my only reply.

It takes me a few moments to process that I've been under for six weeks. I knew it had been at least a month but hearing a firm number on it makes everything that happened so much more real. And it was all for nothing, that bastard got away.

"Not for nothing, love," Caleb rumbles. *"You killed off his entire legion in a single blow. You kicked the ever-loving shite out of him too. Wherever he is, he's got a long road back to where he was that day. You saved almost the entire community."* Which reminds me that some of the community died, making me feel even shittier. *"Only ten died, Ayla. Seven of them were councilmen. Only three were ours. And they died saving others."*

Okay, so I feel a little, tiny, itty-bitty bit better about that. But Caleb is my mate, which means that the Council, by de facto, is part of my community. Kelly's grip on my hand tightens, drawing my attention to her.

"All those who died, died before your attack, Ayla. Those deaths were not your fault. Even if they died after your attack or after you had engaged Malick, they still would not have been your fault. They died while we were trying to break the ward." She shakes her head when I open my mouth. "There's no point in arguing about this."

Well. Fine then. Bossy bit of goods, that one.

I return my attention back to Caleb. "You said something grabbed him from the ground?"

"Yeah. Just this black mass. It came in and scooped the fucker up, and poof! They were gone." Everyone else around the table nods. "From what we've been able to gather, no one saw anything more descriptive from any other angle either. Which is really weird."

"It's possible it was another archdemon," Malcolm cuts in. "But we don't know any with that particular ability. That's not to say that there isn't one out there, but he or she would certainly be a bigger threat than Malick if that's the case."

"I think we can agree," Olivia states, "that whoever it was is a bigger threat than Malick, regardless of their species." Murmurs of agreement float around the table. "But why don't you start, Ayla? Maybe that can help us fill in some information and provide some kind of answer as to what happened."

I sigh, puffing out my cheeks as I do. "Alright. That's fair enough." I begin tugging on the end of my braid as I try to figure out where to start. There's so much I have to tell them it's a little overwhelming.

"I guess I should start at the beginning," I murmur. "I've... Well...I've been keeping something from all of you." I look around the table, and thankfully no one seems surprised or angry. "I've told you all that I'm the last queen. That's not true." I glance over at Olivia. "Even before Olivia was gifted queen powers by the goddesses—" I pause as old anxieties rise within me, trying to keep me silent, but I know now that the only way we're going to be able to move forward is if I'm honest about my sisters. If we can find them, wake them, we may have a fighting chance at whatever is coming. The evil the goddesses hinted at.

"I'm the youngest daughter my mother gave birth to." I can feel shock radiate through all of my bonds. "My mother gave birth to triplets. I have two older sisters. Sorcha is the eldest, and Isobel is the middle triplet." I'd almost forgotten that Kelly is still holding my hand. She squeezes it now, offering me her steady belief and strength. "My mother separated us on the day she was taken." I pause, they don't know about that. Shit. "Okay, a little side story. My mother didn't die on the battlefield like I thought, Malick actually kidnapped her. I'll get to that later. What's important is that she hid my sisters away, putting them in a magical slumber. It wasn't until recently that I knew where they were."

"When are we leaving?" Olivia leans across the table and puts her hand on top of mine and Kelly's. "We are going to go get them, right?"

I nod slowly. "I hoped that once we talked about everything we would be able to come up with a plan to get them, yes."

"Well, I'm in," Darcy says. Everyone else quickly affirms their desire to wake my sisters. Man, I love these guys.

A FEW HOURS LATER, we're all still sitting around the table. I've caught them up on what happened, and they've done the same, telling me everything from the time I was taken up until they felt the bonds flare to life again. Now we're just trying to mull everything over, see if there's anything anyone might have missed that could help us.

"I don't think we've got anything on who took Malick,"

Malcolm says, breaking the silence. Dante, Connor, and Darcy all nod their agreement. "But we've got some great insight into his motives."

"Yes," Connor agrees. "That prophecy you spoke about, that's his driving force behind all of this. He wants to open the gates to hell. What we don't really understand is why he thinks having a child with a queen is going to be the answer. Ayla, you said the goddesses didn't give you the whole prophecy, they just pointed you in the direction of where you'd be able to find it?"

I nod. "Yeah. I have to start back home in Ireland. I guess more information about the prophecy and my sisters is there." I shrug. "I'm not sure our cottage is even still standing. I haven't been home since I left that night."

"So that's where we need to go first then." This is the first time Caleb's spoken since I started talking. "We head to Ireland, find whatever it is the goddesses wanted you to find, and then move on to locating the sister that's closest. France, I think you said?"

"That's right, Sorcha. Paris. In the catacombs." We stare at each other for a moment, and Caleb's determination to help me see this through grounds me. "I hate to say it, but I think we need to focus on things one step at a time. I have a feeling that getting what we need in Ireland isn't going to be all that easy."

"Malick could be stalking us," Kelly warns. "If he's that obsessed with the prophecy and opening the gates to Hell, he's going to want to keep an eye on us. We aren't sure if he knows about Olivia or not yet, but it's really only a matter of time. Word is going to get out and spread like wildfire. We've done our best to keep the knowledge within this circle, but let's be hella real here, that's not going to last forever."

"You're right," I say to Kelly. "Which is why we also need

to focus on training Olivia. I'm going to need to train you and Darcy as well. Just because you aren't queens yet doesn't mean it isn't going to happen. The goddesses said when the time is right you'll come into your powers. You two need to be ready. Hell, Olivia came into her powers in the middle of a damn battle." I still want to facepalm every time I think about it.

"Kelly has been helping me control my magic. My panther is a lot more active, but we've been working on finding balance between the two of us again. I haven't tried shifting yet. My panther told me she's changed but hasn't exactly explained. I wanted to wait for you to wake up before trying." Olivia grins over at me. "It's all been a lot of hard work, but fun as hell too. I rather like being able to explode demons with my mind." We all laugh at that.

"We can all work together. It shouldn't matter where we are. We need to be able to adapt to different environments quickly and efficiently," Darcy reasons. "We won't be surprised when we come into our powers thanks to you, Ayla, but that's only part of the process." Her eyes bleed black, and I can feel mine do the same in response. "We're going to need to train hard and with as many different partners as possible. While we've destroyed Malick's legion, it won't take him long to start finding new followers. He can be very charming. And there's no telling how they'll fight. We also shouldn't stick to a solid routine. Surprise attacks are a must. We'll never know when they're going to attack, and we need to make sure that we're ready in the blink of an eye."

"You're right." I groan. "I hadn't realized just how much there is to do. And you and I need to learn to control our demonic sides."

"I've had more practice than you, but it's still good to keep up the effort. I can tell you what's worked for me, and we can go from there. But it does get easier, Ayla. I promise."

"We're going to get through this." Olivia's voice is strong, sure, and filled with determination. "We're going to wake up your sisters, kick demon ass, and make sure that the gates to Hell stay closed." She looks around the table and nods. "We've got one hell of a community now." Her eyes find mine and stick. "And we've got one hell of a leader."

Chapter Twenty-Seven

When I wake the next day, I'm too sore to move. After catching up with everyone, I decided the best thing to do was to throw myself right back at it and insisted that Caleb spar with me. We spent a few hours training, and now I'm regretting every life choice I've ever made. I wouldn't have guessed that my body was able to deteriorate so much in only six weeks. Then again, six weeks isn't exactly an insignificant amount of time.

I lie in bed, pinned under Caleb's weight, which only makes me hurt more, and try to think of a game plan. We hadn't settled on anything concrete yesterday, knowing that we have a lot to do and wanting to take stock of that first. But I can't just sit here and do nothing while my sisters are out there. I can't be sure that Malick doesn't know about them already. I keep replaying my time with him in my mind, and I'm fairly certain I didn't say anything about them. But they also drugged the shit out of me.

Groaning both from my train of thought and from my current attempt to run my fingers through my hair while my arm muscles scream in protest, I try to stop worrying about my sisters. I need to have faith that my mother's spells will protect them until I can find them and wake them. I need to focus on rebuilding my strength. Caleb and I didn't even spar that long yesterday, at least not based on what I was used to before I'd been taken. I'm embarrassed I'm this sore.

Caleb shifts beside me, sitting up and looking down at me. He smiles before heading into the bathroom. I hear the toilet flush and then the water starts. Is he drawing me a bath? Hopeful little love bubbles rise up my chest and pop in my throat in excitement. I sure hope he's drawing me a bath.

"I am absolutely drawing you a bath." Caleb chuckles through the bond. *"Your discomfort is actually what woke me. I should have had you soak in the tub last night. I'm sorry."* More of those little love bubbles explode in my chest. He comes into the bedroom, dressed only in boxers, and my mouth instantly waters at the sight.

"None of that now, ma'am." Caleb grins at me. "If we do anything like what you're thinking, you won't be able to move for another six weeks. Now come on, hold onto me and I'll put you in the tub." I do as he says and wrap my arms around his neck as he picks me up bridal style. Since I slept naked, it's easy for him to just smoothly slide me into the bath.

He even added a bath bomb. I become one giant love bubble and tears sting the back of my eyes. I'm one lucky lady.

"Thank you." My voice is quiet as I stare at the water in front of me. "I love you, you know." Caleb stills, caught midway between crouching and kneeling on the floor next to the tub. His eyes fly to my face, locking on mine.

"I could feel it," he murmurs, "through the bond. But I wasn't sure if you were ready to say the words yet." A breath-taking smile breaks out across his face, and my heart stutters in my chest. To cover it, I playfully splash some water at him, narrowing my eyes.

"I seem to recall you saying you loved me while I was dying." I splash at him again. "That is terrible timing!"

"Excuse you," he counters while looking offended and fully sinking to his knees next to the tub. "I said I love you before you started dying on me! I'll forgive you because shortly thereafter you did start to die." He chuckles. I roll my eyes and cross my arms over my chest with a huff.

"I suppose you might be right." A grin breaks out, ruining my attempt at pretending offense. "But I do. I love you, Caleb."

"Och. I love you, you batshit crazy woman. I've loved you since the moment I saw you, floating there in the sky, surrounded by a ray of sunshine, shimmering like a damn beacon of hope. I should have told you sooner. I should have known what you truly meant to me. You're not just my mate, Ayla." He pauses, his hands tightly gripping the edge of the tub. "You are bloody everything." He reaches out to trail his fingers lightly along my arm, his eyes following the movement closely.

"When I realized Malick had taken you. I..." His voice breaks, and he rests his forehead against the side of the tub. I take his hand, lacing our fingers together and squeezing gently. "I went out of my mind. Malcolm needed to knock me out for a while. My dragon went insane. I went insane." He lifts his head to look at me and the depth of emotion in his eyes leaves me breathless. "I'd realized, too late, that the Council didn't matter, being alpha didn't matter, none of it bloody mattered. Except you." He brings our joined hands to his lips and places a kiss on the back of my hand.

My throat closes as love, so bright and fierce, grips me. This isn't the sweet kind of love people write about in love stories. It's visceral, raw, overwhelming, and so damn deep. Without him really needing to explain how he felt, I knew. I knew because if he had been taken instead of me, I would have felt the very same way. I'd experienced something very similar when I woke up and realized what had happened. My reservations about the Council were bullshit. Pure bullshit that I used to keep myself safe. If I had all my memories when we met, maybe I wouldn't have pushed against this so hard. My heart aches thinking about all the time I wasted being a twat.

"Hush now, love," Caleb soothes, picking up on my inner turmoil. "We both made mistakes. What matters now is what we do moving forward." I nod, tears silently sliding down my cheeks. He wipes them away and leans in for a gentle kiss. "You're right, we need a new leadership structure, and I'm more than happy to give up any claims to fame." He leans back again, still clutching my hand in his.

"I don't have the faintest idea how to go about constructing anything like that from the ground up. Caleb, I've only been the leader of this community for a short time, I don't think I can be this shining beacon for all of supernatural kind."

"You don't have to do that alone. Once we find and wake your sisters, there will be six of you. You're not going to have to do any of this alone. You aren't in hiding anymore, Ayla. You aren't running."

He's right. I'm not running anymore, and I won't need to do all of this alone.

"So let's go sit down with my fellow queens and figure out what the hell we're going to do now."

OLIVIA, Kelly, Darcy, and I are all sitting on the floor by the fireplace in my study. Caleb and the rest of the guys have all gone off, doing rounds and checking in with the trackers who are trying to find Malick.

"We've got a lot on our plate. Why don't we at least list out things that need to be handled or started immediately?" Kelly has a notebook and pen in her hand. That woman is literally ready for anything, and I live for it.

"We need to discuss a new leadership structure. Caleb is going to be abolishing the Council, but we can't go back to the way things were before with the old queens," I point out. "That's how they were all so easy to take down. They were alone."

"I agree," Olivia states. "While coming up with a firm leadership structure isn't necessary right now, trying to establish a loose idea is best. We should plan for a gradual transfer of power. We don't want to take on too much before we're really ready. Especially since Kelly and Darcy haven't come into their queen powers yet, and Ayla's sisters are still M.I.A." Everyone nods.

"We also need to come up with a plan for Ireland. If we need to go there to get information about the prophecy and Ayla's sisters, we should make sure we're planning for anything that could happen." Darcy looks at each of us. "We can't assume it's going to be an easy journey."

"That leads to figuring out what to do with Sorcha and Isobel. Who do we go after first? How are we supposed to wake them?" Kelly sighs as she quickly scribbles everything down in her notebook. "While that's only three things, there are a lot of subcomponents, so why don't we tackle these things first and handle anything else as it arises?" We all murmur our agreement.

For the next several hours, I sit by the fire with my bond sisters and plan. Food and drinks come and go, and we only get up to use the bathroom, but we stay and hash out everything. Given that I just woke up yesterday, I'm exhausted by the time we decide to call it quits for the night. We haven't finished everything we need to, but we're well on our way to a solid strategy.

Caleb is waiting for me in bed, his laptop open on his lap. We got a new bed brought to the room this morning and had Kelly reinforce it with magic. Hopefully, I won't be able to break this one. He glances up when I walk into our bedroom. I pause. Our bedroom. Goddess, I love the sound of that. With a dopey grin spreading across my face, I make my way over to his side of the bed and lean down to press a kiss to his cheek. Knowing that he's here to talk things out with takes a lot of weight off my shoulders. It's certainly going to take some getting used to, but I think I like it.

I strip down and crawl into bed beside Caleb. He finishes on his laptop and puts it on his nightstand. He opens the drawer and pulls something out, keeping it hidden in his hand. When he turns to face me, he's got this nervous look on his face. My heart drops slightly. Something's happened.

"What's wrong?" I reach out and touch his arm, needing to reassure myself that he's safe and real.

"Nothing!" he says quickly. Too quickly. "Nothing is wrong. I'm hoping this is actually a good thing."

"Okay..." I drag out the word, thoroughly confused. "What the hell is happening right now?"

"Well, it's a tradition in my family." He clears his throat, rubbing the back of his neck nervously. "The males typically give their mate a gift once the bond is finalized." My heart rate picks up, and I stare at his closed hand in his lap. "I, uh, I have this for you."

This is the cutest damn thing I've ever seen him do. He's nervous about giving me a mating present? My insides go all gooey, and I'm pretty sure I have little animated hearts floating around my head.

"Here." He holds out his hand and slowly opens it.

The ring inside takes my breath away. Its band is platinum

and studded all the way around with tiny diamonds. But the real showstopper is the top of the ring. Arching up in intricate, yet exceptionally delicate Celtic knots, sits a spectacular morganite stone. It's a gorgeous salmon pink color and is cut in a square. It's surrounded by light-colored sapphires and rubies. I'm stunned, and I can't stop staring at it.

"It—" He swallows. "It was my mother's. My father gave it to her when they mated."

And with that, I start crying. I hold out my left hand so he can place the ring on my finger and find that my hand is shaking. As tears stream down my face, Caleb slides the ring on my ring finger where humans put their wedding bands. The meaning isn't lost on me, and I start crying harder. Caleb now looks more nervous than ever, his eyes flicking from my face and then around the room, unsure what to do with my weeping, snotty self.

"This is perfect. I love it." I hiccup in a very loud and squeaky manner that has me blushing and Caleb chuckling. "I will do my best to honor it and you."

"So long as you honor yourself. I am just so damn proud that you're my mate." He kisses me deeply.

Need sparks to life inside me at his kiss. Not just the need to feel him buried deep inside me, but a need to assure each other that we're both alive, that we're both here, real, in the flesh.

I don't hold myself back. I push the sheet to the floor, pleased to find him naked underneath. I climb on top of him but don't sink down on him. Instead, I pry myself from his kiss and start to lick and nibble my way down Caleb's body, paying particular attention to my mate mark, his nipples, and each of his carved abdominal muscles. His flavor bursts on my tongue, reminding me of a perfect summer's day right before it rains—and man. Hot, sweaty, sexy man.

Caleb's hands fist by his sides when my mouth stops just

above the head of his cock. I blow on it, watching as it bobs with the clench of Caleb's stomach. Lifting my eyes to his, I gently trail a finger up and down his length, watching his eyes darken as he stares intently down at me. Licking my lips, I start to place a series of gentle kisses around the base of his cock, his hips arching as though trying to direct my attention to where he wants it most. But I want to savor him, savor this.

Hands tangling in my hair, Caleb impatiently moves my head so my mouth is once again poised above the tip of his cock. "Let me feel that hot mouth sucking on my cock." His voice is hoarse, his eyes flashing to his dragon's. My own dragon pushes toward the surface, changing my eyes. "That's right, love," Caleb growls, his dragon evident, "open that mouth and suck my damn cock."

I chuckle, a grin spreading across my face. "I didn't hear the magic word anywhere in there, sir." I keep my tone light and teasing, averting my eyes from his so I don't laugh. I wrap one hand around his base, giving him a swift but solid pump. "Is this the cock you want in my mouth?"

"Don't play games, mate." There's more dragon in his voice now.

"Or what?" My eyes meet his again. "What will you do if I don't do this?" Quickly, I fasten my mouth around the tip of his cock, licking the slit with my tongue before releasing him in a flash. A deep groan escapes him, and his hands tighten in my hair. "All I want to hear is a lil' ole please." I bat my eyelashes, and he lets out a vicious snarl. Pft. As if that's scary.

I watch as he struggles with his pride and his need to be dominant, waiting for him to make his decision. Little does he know, I want his cock in my mouth just as badly as he does, but I'm interested in seeing what happens. He's always been the aggressor in bed, but I want to know that I can take the lead when I want to. Caleb blinks and his eyes return to normal.

"Will you please suck my cock, milady?" I choke down a cough at how formal he sounds. I don't dare laugh at him, not when he's asked so nicely, but the formality of it all makes me want to cackle.

Rather than answering, I glide my tongue up and down his length before once again sealing my mouth around the head of his cock. His arms tighten, ensuring that I stay where I am this time. I fight the urge to smile, choosing to focus on his taste and bringing him pleasure. I work my mouth over him, never quite taking him all the way down my throat. He growls, arching his hips the next time I slide my mouth down on him. I take the opportunity to deep throat him, swallowing around the head of his cock again and again before moving my mouth back up to swirl my tongue around the tip.

Suddenly, his hands grip my hips and he moves my body so my pussy is directly above his face, my mouth still wrapped around his cock. I moan around him and swallow him all the way down. He instantly dives in, sliding two fingers deep into my pussy while his mouth suctions my clit. His other hand keeps me firmly planted on his face as he relentlessly brings me closer and closer to the edge. Moments later, we jump off the cliff together, and Caleb comes down my throat while I scream my release around his cock.

I lift my head when he's finished, licking my lips and panting slightly. Caleb is still hard as a damn rock, and he's still going strong between my legs. I let out a small whimper when he pulls my hips away from his face, but he doesn't give me time to think. In a move that's a blur, he's standing and has my legs wrapped around his waist as he strides toward my bedroom door.

"Where are we going?" I really don't care as long as he gets the hell inside me right fucking now.

"I told you I was going to take you and mark you some-place where the entire community could hear you screaming my name. I was too caught up in having you back, so I'm going to rectify the issue now." A grin spreads across his face as he enters the hall and slams my back against the wall. "There are no sound wards out here. And I want everyone to hear you scream."

Chapter Twenty-Eight

Caleb and I are curled in bed together, basking in postcoital bliss, when I realize I haven't told him what the ladies and I decided on. It is mildly important that he knows the plan since he's the one about to give up power to a bunch of kickass women. Just a little while ago, I wouldn't have believed he would actually do it. But now... now I believe it with everything I am. He's just as invested in making a change as I am. I'm stunned, pleased, proud, and nervous. It's a heady mixture.

"The ladies and I made a few decisions." I settle my head on Caleb's shoulder, pressing my body against his.

"Oh?" His voice is sleepy and low. His arms wrap tightly around me.

"We discussed how we want to lead together as queens. It's going to be a baptism by fire sort of thing because we know that the way the old queens did things didn't work well, but we aren't necessarily thrilled with a Council-like setup either, no offense." He merely shrugs. "We're thinking an Arthur and the round table type of deal, sans an arrogant head. Everyone is equal. We're not sure where we'd set up, or if we'd divide territory or anything like that yet, but we know we want to be far more close-knit than past queens."

"That makes sense." Caleb nods. "And I think it'll help the supernatural community transition if you all show a united front. To many of the younger generations, queens are myths. The older generations only know queens as female dragon shifters. This new breed will take some getting used to." He pauses, frowning slightly in thought. "Do you think Kelly and Darcy will shift? From everything we know, queens are supposed to be a perfect blend of magic-user and shifter. And Darcy is a vampire."

I put my finger against his lips to stop his musings. "The goddesses didn't tell me. But I assume they'll be able to shift into something. As for Darcy being a vampire, they're part of the supernatural community, so it only makes sense for a queen to have a little bit of vampire in her as well." Caleb continues to frown thoughtfully, mulling over what I said.

"You're right. And I'm focusing on the wrong issues right now." He grins down at me, placing a quick kiss on my lips. "Now, what else was decided?"

"We're going to transition power slowly. We don't want to shake things up too quickly, not with Kelly and Darcy not having their powers yet and my sisters still sleeping. So you can be all Lord Alpha for a while yet," I joke. "We're also planning to split up for the trip to Ireland. We're going to keep Kelly and Darcy here. If we need them, Kelly can portal them across the pond in a blink. But I want people here I can trust." I sit up and run my fingers through my hair. "We can't assume that Malick won't attack here while we're gone. There's no telling what he's going to do. I want to be prepared either way. We'll all keep training, but we'll need to do it separately."

Caleb sits up and places his hand on my thigh. "You're doing what's right. I agree that we need to divide and conquer for now. What about when we need to head out to find your sisters?"

"That depends on what we find in Ireland. But I'm going to want to stick with Olivia for as long as possible since she's still learning to control her powers. Ideally, I'd like us all together when we go to hunt down my sisters. I was thinking about leaving Xin in charge."

Caleb leans back on his arms, staring at the ceiling as he thinks. "That's not a bad idea. Xin is old, powerful, and has a lot of leadership experience under his belt. Plus, he's pretty damn loyal to you already. He was able to mobilize the vampires in moments when we needed him."

"I think we should also have someone from the Council helping him." The thought just popped into my head as Caleb was talking, but it feels right. "Even though my community doesn't really trust the Council, they trust and believe in you. If you appoint someone, they'll listen. And it will help ease the burden on Xin."

"Might as well have someone else from the community too. Have a vampire, a shifter, and a witch keeping an eye on things."

"I could just kiss you sometimes!" I lean over to place a kiss on his chest since he's still leaning back and I can't reach his face. "That's excellent!"

I MAKE my way to Kelly's room, still mulling over my choices for who to leave in charge when we all leave to find my sisters. I realize it's still a while before I really need to worry about it, but I like to be prepared. Patrick has always been helpful, or Kelly's mother. It really depends on who Caleb chooses from the Council.

Speaking of the Council, they've taken over my little

town. Caleb hadn't been kidding when he said he called in reinforcements. The town is bursting at the seams. He's assured me that most of them will head on back to the U.K. once things are settled and the queens take over more securely. Which is good, I can feel the unease and discomfort of my community through my bonds. They'll work alongside the Council, but they aren't overly thrilled about it.

I knock on Kelly's door and walk in when she calls out. I blink several times, trying to take in the state of her room. Normally very well organized and tidy, Kelly's room looks as though a library has just been dumped everywhere. She has books on every available surface, including on top of the two lamps on her nightstands. Kelly is standing in the middle of it all with her hands out at her sides and her eyes closed. She's reading them all with magic. Awe fills me as I watch her.

Several moments pass before Kelly finally lets her hands fall and she opens her eyes. She smiles broadly at me, gesturing for me to come closer. "I've been doing a little research."

"A little?" I gesture around us. "I'd hate to see what some serious research looks like."

"Oh, shut it." She laughs. "I've been trying to figure out what kind of spell your mother might have used to put your sisters to sleep. I know we don't have a lot to go off of, and we won't until you and Olivia travel to Ireland, but I wanted to get a head start. Some of the counterspells require very specific timing or ingredients to work. Since we have no idea when Malick will show up again, I don't want us sitting around twiddling our thumbs while we wait for your sisters to wake up."

"That's actually a fantastic idea. Are there any that we can prep ahead of time so we can bring everything we need with us when we go to find them?" If we can wake them up where we locate them, that would be ideal. Carting back an apparently lifeless body isn't high on my to-do list.

"A few. We'll have to see where they're hidden. I'd hate to have to wake one of them up with a bunch of dead people around."

"Valid point. Very valid point." I groan. "It's been four hundred years since they were last awake. How are we going to handle that?" I run my hand through my hair and start to pace, making sure not to step on any books. "I didn't even think of that. I've been so focused on finding them so we can wake them up, I didn't even stop to think about how they're going to handle waking up in a completely new century. Things have changed a lot in the last four hundred years."

"You're right." Kelly, as always, is rational and calm. Sometimes I envy her ability to just snap into responsible adult mode. "But they aren't going to be waking up alone. You'll be here, and so will we. I can see if I can gather some of the community to put together a crash course on all the major things they missed, as well as how to 21st Century."

"Teaching them to use a smartphone is going to be like handing one to an exceptionally old human." I start laughing. "Am I horrible for admitting that I want to see that?" I start miming exaggerated texting with a single finger. "I'd have something to finally hold over them."

"I see we'll be getting right back into sibling rivalry." Kelly crosses her arms with a grin as she watches me. "Do they have a lot of embarrassing dirt on you from when you were little?"

"Kelly..." I stare her in the eye. "I am the youngest. Of course they have a ton of shit on me." We both laugh. It feels good to have a semi-normal conversation with her again. I've missed this so much it makes my heart ache.

Sensing the shift in my mood, Kelly comes over and wraps

her arms around me. I sink into the hug, basking in the touch of a much-loved friend.

"You're back and you're healthy," Kelly states quietly. "That's all that matters. Goddess, Ayla, I was so worried. I wasn't sure how the hell we were going to keep you alive. I tried everything, but it didn't feel like it was enough."

I pull back from our embrace a bit to study Kelly's face. "Hey. None of that. You are one badass witch, and you did everything you could. Between you and Caleb, I was able to survive. You've always got my back, and I've always got yours. I love you, you know."

"Sisters from different misters." We hug again. "It's good to have you back, Ayla."

LATER THAT NIGHT, we're all sitting around the dinner table, talking about our game plan. I take a moment out of the conversation to study my little family. Kelly and Connor are in a heated debate about the best way to wake a shifter from a magical sleeping spell. Malcolm is side-eyeing Olivia in a way that has me thinking the witch has the hots for my bestie. Dante is in a discussion with Caleb about training, and Darcy is watching the two as though she thinks they're amusing but slow.

I realize I never got the chance to really introduce Darcy to the rest of my family. Thankfully, she seems to have settled in with everyone just fine while I was recovering. As if sensing my gaze, Darcy turns her head to look at me.

"I filled everyone in a bit on Katia," Darcy starts, studying me as she speaks. "I know you learned quite a bit about her before you took out the trash. I'd like to talk about it more, but to do that I'm going to need to tell you who I am."

"How long were you with them?" I ask, having a feeling

I'm not going to like the answer. It's off-topic, but for some reason, I just need to know.

"Almost ninety years." Everyone goes silent, and all eyes turn to Darcy.

Damn. I'd only been with them a few weeks. I can't imagine having to be subjected to that every day for almost a century. A new respect for the woman in front of me starts to blossom in my chest. She isn't just physically strong, the woman has a fortress for a mind. My own mind starts to whirl as the length of time truly begins to sink in. Had Malick tried to have a child with her? Perhaps he couldn't get her pregnant. I shudder at the very thought. Had he forced himself on her? White-hot rage fills me just thinking about it. If he had, he's going to experience what it feels like to have his balls ripped off and fed to him.

"You're no ordinary vampire. Or you weren't even before Malick experimented on you," Dante remarks, drawing my attention away from my rage-filled thoughts. "I could sense it the moment we met."

"You're right." Darcy sighs, looking each of us in the eye before continuing, "I'm an original."

Shock sends little electric jolts through my system. An original vampire. One of the first of her species. I stare at her in wonder, taking her in all over again. Her shiny ebony skin that seems to absorb and reflect the light at the same time, her glowing golden eyes. She had her hair tightly woven while I was unconscious, interlacing several brightly colored red, blue, and purple strands throughout. The contrast against her dark skin is incredible. The woman has cheekbones for days, and I'm pretty sure I could cut myself just looking at them. She's not as curvy as I am, but she isn't slim like Kelly either, falling somewhere in the middle to make her look just feminine enough to draw you in without you realizing that she's a damn powerhouse.

"We thought the originals were all killed." Dante's tone is filled with the awe I feel. "There was a great cleanse a thousand years ago that wiped them all out."

"Just as you thought there had been a great cleanse to kill all the queens?" Darcy raises an eyebrow. "As far as I know, only a handful of us survived. We took on new aliases and decided to live as quiet a life as possible."

"What line?" I'm surprised at the strength in my voice considering I feel as though I'm standing in front of a famous movie star. Darcy smiles over at me, pleased that I've asked.

"My birth name was Lilith."

"As in the first wife of Adam, Lilith?" Connor inquires, staring intently at Darcy.

"I do believe the bible made a few things up there, but yes." My mouth drops open. She's not just any original, she's the original vampire.

"You're the matriarch," Dante whispers. "You're the very first vampire."

Chapter Twenty-Nine

"That's why you survived being experimented on by Malick." My statement slices through the silence that has settled over the table. "He told me that only someone extremely powerful could survive what was happening, all of the rest died."

"That was my assumption as well," Darcy confirms. "And don't make a big deal about my history. Like I said, the other surviving originals and I are trying to keep a very low profile. It didn't work as well as I'd have liked since I got picked up by Malick, but if I'm to also become a queen, I'd really like to keep who I am as hush-hush as possible. People might assume I have too much power."

She has a point. The original vampire is now part demon and a potential queen. We'd be up to our eyeballs in demons and power-hungry supernaturals. The origins of the vampires as a species is shrouded in various myths, but they all agree on one fact—Lilith was the first vampire. Some said she was cursed by a god, some claimed she contracted a deadly virus and mutated it with some innate yet latent magic, others assumed she had been a witch who had made a pact with the devil. While I'm insanely curious, I don't want to push her to reveal more than she's comfortable with.

"If I'm to fully become a part of this community," Darcy continues, "I wanted to be open and honest with you all about who I am."

Everyone around the table nods. They're all probably just as shocked as I am. Is it too tacky to ask her for her autograph? Yeah, absolutely way too tacky. *Play it cool, Ayla, play it cool. Conceal, don't feel, don't let them know...Oh*, goddess, I'm singing *Frozen* in my mind. Fighting the urge to slam my head against the table, I turn my attention back to Darcy.

"Katia had been the one creating the injections. From what I've been able to gather, Malick gave her his blood and she did some magic with it to get it to stay in our systems without being rejected." Darcy shrugs. "I'm not entirely sure. At first, I was in too much pain from the transition to really understand what was going on. After that, well, Ayla can tell you how she found me." A grin spreads across her face.

"She was essentially bound in a way that assured she couldn't move or get out of the room." I grin back at her. "How many did you kill before they did that?"

"Almost a thousand. Malick underestimated how strong I'd be with a little demonic boost." Darcy flicks her braids over her shoulder, and my lady crush digs a little deeper. "I'd been kept in that room alone for about five years before they brought you in, Ayla. Prior to that, I'd been in another location, somewhere in Russia, I think."

"Katia mentioned there were other facilities where they were keeping females." If Darcy had been kept in Russia at one point, where else is Malick hiding females and experimenting on them? "Where were we?" Now that I think about it, I don't know where I was during the time Malick had me.

"Mexico," Olivia answers. "Middle of the damn jungle and warded seven ways to Sunday."

"We originally thought you'd be in Alaska, since you mentioned noticing a large demonic population there. We went to try and track you down, but you reached out to us with your bonds before we were able to gain any traction," Dante notes.

"We should assume his other facilities are the same. Out of the way so no one will notice and warded to avoid detection from any supernaturals in the area," Malcolm adds. "Russia and Mexico." He taps his fingers against his chin. "Two places pretty out of the way, and in two countries that have a fairly low supernatural population."

"Mexico has a fairly large shifter population," Olivia points out. "My family is from Mexico, and we still have relatives down there. Most of them stick to the jungle in small familial packs. They prefer the old ways." She shrugs. "But aside from that, there aren't many witches or vampires. Not since the Spanish settled there anyway."

"Good point," Malcolm concedes. "Does anyone know about Russia?" Everyone shakes their heads. "Damn. I can do some research, see what I can find out. I'll dig further into Alaska too, there has to be evidence of his base there if it was a larger operation."

"If he's selecting places where the supernatural population isn't that dense, that leaves most of Central America, Northern Canada, and the poles," Connor mumbles, looking as though he's lost in thought. "That doesn't leave too many places to search. A large demon population, regardless of the other supernatural species in the area, is bound to draw attention. Havoc follows them." He stands quickly. "I need to look into something." With that, he rushes out of the room.

Okay...I look at Malcolm and Caleb to see what they make of what just happened with Connor.

"He gets like that sometimes. Pretty sure he forgot he was even at the table with us." Caleb sounds amused. *"Once he's onto a theory,*

the rest of the world just sort of fades away. He'll come back once he has something." Right. So normal then. Weird, but normal.

"Back to the discussion at hand." Darcy sounds just as amused as Caleb. "I was moved around five times during my tenure with Malick. From what I can remember, the moves didn't seem to be because we'd been found, but because Malick had discovered someone he wanted to collect in a different location, so we'd all pack up and go. He'd leave women behind with some of his legion, but I can't tell you what happened to them once we left."

"Katia seemed to suggest they were still experimented on." I feel the rage start to bubble up inside me again, and I have to fight to keep it from surfacing, but my eyes bleed black anyway. I clench my fists tightly under the table. "She said she was able to suppress my dragon and my magic by draining supernaturals." Curses fly around the room.

"So that's how they did it." Kelly frowns, massaging her temples. "I wondered how they did it. To hold a spell like that for that length of time takes an unbelievable amount of energy, especially if they're injecting you to make you stronger. Goddess. I'm not sure how she was able to transfer the backlash to them, but I'll damn well find out." A notebook and a pen appear before her on the table, and she starts frantically writing notes.

"I wonder if they did the same for me," Darcy muses. "It's just as difficult keeping an original vampire subdued. I thought it was the demon blood they'd been injecting me with—the shit burned through me like lava. But if she'd been doing some kind of spell work while I was out of it, I wouldn't have had a clue. I don't have an animal nature like you do that would tip me off if something wasn't right."

"It's possible that's what they used the shifters at the other locations for." Kelly's suggestion causes us all to freeze. "If they weren't taking to the injections, it's possible they kept the females around simply to use them as vessels for that spell."

My stomach clenches and I fight the urge to vomit. My fists are shaking, and I feel blood dribbling down the sides of my hands from my nails digging into my palms. Darcy's and Dante's nostrils flare, but they don't comment on it.

"Hey." Caleb's voice is soothing and calm. *"It's okay. You killed Katia, and we're going to find and kill Malick. Don't you worry."* I want to believe him. I want to believe we'll be able to put a stop to all of this. But all I can focus on right now is my own failure.

"Teach me." Olivia's request is quiet and deadly calm. "Teach me how to use my new powers. That's the best way to get back at them. Having the new generation of queens take out his entire operation is the biggest 'fuck you' there is."

She's right. I can feel my eyes start to fade back to normal, the rage within me receding to a simmer. Having something more tangible to focus on helps keep me in control. Training Olivia is going to benefit me as much as it benefits her. I take several deep breaths as I continue to focus on calming my racing heart.

"Showing him that the supernatural community isn't afraid of demons anymore is one hell of a way to show the world that new queens are in town. Give everybody some hope," Dante remarks, a broad smile on his face. "If it's even half the hope my nest felt when we learned about you, Ayla, we'll be turning people away because we won't have enough housing for everyone here."

"I don't want to think about that right now," I grumble. "Let's focus on getting everything ready for our trip to Ireland next month. I want at least four weeks to start Olivia's training and to get Kelly and Darcy prepared for whenever their powers come in."

"Well then, let's get started!" Olivia stands, excitement

vibrating through her in waves that are so palpable they seem to fuel my own eagerness. "Who wants to kick some demon ass?"

"Whoa there, killer." I hold out my hands. "You and I are going to need to go over what you've already worked on. I was out for a month and a half. I know you've been playing with your new powers."

"Of course I have!" Olivia beams at me. "I mean, come on! I was able to turn demons into jelly with just a thought, Ayla. A thought! It was so epic!" She fist pumps. "I haven't gotten too far otherwise though. We've been pretty busy trying to track down Malick. But I've tried things out here and there. Kelly and Malcolm have been helping me."

I glance around the room at the men still with us. "Sorry, guys, but the ladies need some girl time. You're on your own for the next few hours."

~

I TAKE the ladies to the gym, choosing one of the dual-purpose rooms since we'll need to do a little of everything now that Olivia is a queen. It's been so long since I've had to focus on the basics, and I'm excited to sit down and explore queen lore.

"Before we start," Kelly says, and we all turn toward her, "I want to give you each these." She holds up stunning pendants. "They're dragon's breath opals. I've spelled them for protection and to immediately warn the others if something is wrong, even if our bonds aren't working."

"You brilliant witch!" I take mine reverently, and the others do the same, fastening them around our necks. "Thank you."

"I don't want any of us to ever get cut off from the group again."

"What have you been working on?" I turn to Olivia.

"Mostly meditation to try to gain control. A few basics like clothing and stuff too." Olivia sighs and runs her fingers through her hair. "It's not easy. The magic feels like it's this giant thunderstorm inside me."

"Queen magic isn't something to laugh at." I look at Kelly and Darcy, making sure they understand this as well. "While it's similar to witch magic, it isn't the same. It is raw power collected from all of the elements. It's life magic in its purest form. It's not going to be easy to control."

"So how do you control it?" Olivia asks.

"When a queen is young, just a toddler, she learns how to calm her mind and become one with both her dragon and her magic. You need to accept your magic as a part of you now." Olivia cringes. Seems like that's going to be easier said than done. "Meditation is a good way to get there. It will help you understand the depths of your power."

"Ayla, I literally liquified demons on the battlefield. While that is completely awesome, I don't know how I did it, and I don't want to accidentally do it to someone on our side."

"That's a valid concern." Kelly and Darcy frown at my admission. Queen magic, especially for a young, and it seems new, queen can be unpredictable. I don't want to sugarcoat any of this. They all need to understand what is about to happen to them, the good, the bad, and the ugly. "But intent plays a pretty big part in all magic. I'm sure that's been explained to you."

"Well, yeah." Olivia doesn't look convinced.

"That's not all there is to it, but if you don't truly intend anyone harm, you should be good until we can get you a little steadier on your feet." I can't really tell if my attempt at reassurance works or not, since she's shut down the bond and her face isn't giving anything away. "Why don't we practice a bit? You'll need to let some of that energy out anyway."

"Okay." Olivia sounds leery. "What do you want me to do?"

"I want you to throw a fireball at the wall." Her eyes go wide, but she turns to face the wall like the damn champ I know she is.

"I know we haven't covered offensive magic yet," Kelly starts, "but visualize the fireball in your hand first. Don't just think about a fireball flying at the wall. You need to form it." Kelly shoots me a look, silently judging me for failing to mention this extremely important first step.

"It's been a while since I've had to teach anyone how to use magic," I state defensively through our bond, addressing only her.

"How long is a while?"

"Never."

"Oh, good." Kelly rolls her eyes and focuses back on Olivia.

Olivia takes several deep breaths and closes her eyes, her right hand extended in front of her. I can feel the shift in the air around us as she attempts to summon a fireball into her hand. At first, nothing happens, but soon she's got a tiny dancing flame hovering right above her palm. She opens her eyes in awe, staring at the small flicker of light. As she continues to stare, the flame gets bigger, until it's about the size of a basketball. A bit too large, but hey, if we're up against demons, that would work in a pinch, so I don't bother to comment. With another deep breath, she flicks her hand, sending the fireball shooting out of her palm.

Only for it to land about three feet from her on the floor where it sputters and dies.

"Again," Kelly and I demand at the same time.

∾

"I HAVEN'T SHIFTED at all since I found out about becoming a queen," Olivia admits. She looks around at Kelly and Darcy before settling her eyes on me. "My panther has changed. She still feels the same, but she's certainly gotten an upgrade."

"Well, don't just tease us!" I glance at Kelly and Darcy, who both appear just as eager to see the changes in her panther as I am. "Show us!"

Olivia looks at the three of us one more time before shifting. Since she didn't bother to take off her clothes beforehand, they shred as her body expands. Her panther is a lot bigger than it used to be.

Are those...wings? My dragon perks up in interest. I inhale deeply, taking in Olivia's scent now that she's shifted. She doesn't smell like a panther anymore. What the hell is she? Wait a minute...does she have horns?

"Holy shit," Darcy breathes. "She's a chimera."

Olivia's face is still that of a panther, but she now has the wings of what appears to be an eagle, talons where her back paws used to be, and ram's horns on her head. She's also at least double the size she had been before. Awe fills me as I look at her. She's stunning. And quite possibly the only one of her kind.

"Abuela said there were flying jaguars in certain Aztec legends. I think I'm something like that now." Olivia's voice rings clearly through our bond. She must be broadcasting to Kelly and Darcy too, because they're both nodding. *"Abuela's mother had just left for what's now America when the Spanish came to Mexico, taking Abuela with her. But she still has so many stories about what life was like back in Mexico before the Conquistadors came and fucked everything to hell."* I snort, that's a gentle way of putting things.

"You're certainly something, Olivia," I murmur as I move around her, trying to take her all in. "Extend your wings for me, I want to see how big they are." She does as bid with an elegant stretch that is pure feline. "Your wings are bigger than mine, girlfriend." Kelly nods in agreement. "They'd have to be, you look bulkier than I am too."

"Did you just call me fat?" Olivia asks with a sharp yet joking quality to her tone.

"I would never." I make my way to her head and grin at her. Standing on all fours, her head is level with mine. Goddess, she's huge. She's got to be larger than my dragon. "You're just bigger than me." I shrug. "Which means you can probably kick more ass than I can. Clearly, the goddesses wanted to give the new queens some serious upgrades."

"Any idea what will happen with us?" Darcy gestures to herself and Kelly. "We don't shift. At least not right now anyway."

"I'm not completely sure. The goddesses didn't say. But I can imagine that you'll be able to shift once you come into your powers, that's sort of part of the perks of being a queen." Olivia shifts back, completely comfortable in her birthday suit as she takes a seat on the floor. I go over to one of the built-in storage units and grab her a pair of sweatpants and a tank top.

"I'm going to have one hell of a learning curve. I haven't done magic since before I was turned." Darcy tugs on her braids.

"Hold up," Olivia comments. "What do you mean you haven't done magic since before you were turned?"

"I was a witch before I became a vampire. Do none of you know your own species' lore? I'm not just the original vampire." Darcy looks at all of us. "I'm also the original witch."

Chapter Thirty

"I've..." Kelly looks mildly confused. "I've never heard that Lilith was the original witch." I can practically hear the gears in her mind whirling. "None of my research has ever indicated that. I don't think my nan or my mom ever mentioned it either."

"I shouldn't be surprised." Darcy shrugs. "Witches are creations of the gods and goddesses. Vampires are Morningstar's attempt at emulating that."

Well, I've never heard that before. Olivia and Kelly are just as shocked as I am, their expressions clearly showing their emotions. While the origins of shifters are murky, from what we understand, we were the gods and goddesses' first attempt at what are now humans. They took the essence of the animals around them and tried to create a form that was more like their own, not realizing until later that they'd created a being that had two souls and two bodies. Then came witches. They didn't have the ability to shift, but the gods and goddesses decided to give a small amount of their powers to the original witches, wanting to see how they would evolve over time. I had no idea that vampires had been made by Lucifer Morningstar.

"Lucifer figured he'd try to improve on the witches, and so he found little ole me and just had himself a grand time. It's not something I want to relive. I then changed the originals," Darcy explains vaguely, and my attention snaps back to her. We all know there's far more to the story than she's letting on, but we don't want to push her into discussing things about her past she isn't ready for. I'd be one hell of a hypocrite if I tried to force her into talking.

"Don't you think it's weird that we know a lot about how witches and vampires started, but we don't have an 'original' shifter?" Olivia's question gets me thinking. We have an origin story of sorts, but she's right, we have no idea who the original shifters were. "You didn't happen to know them, did you?" She asks Darcy.

"No. Shifters had been around for quite a while before the gods and goddesses made me. Although I do find it interesting that your panther has changed so much. You're the first of your kind." Darcy looks over at me. "Dragons are rare, but I wonder if the goddesses plan to change that. If they can change Olivia's panther and make us all queens, it's possible they may try to create more shifters. The shifter population, as a whole, has been declining for a while, at least compared to witches and vampires, and you guys were the original guardians of this realm. It's possible the decline in shifters has tipped the scales a little too much, and the gods and goddesses are trying to fix that."

"That does make sense," Kelly responds. "But why now? And why not create new shifters all at once?"

None of us has the answer, except... "The prophecy." All three of them turn to look at me. "I don't know if it's something they created or not, but the prophecy is why now. That has to be it. If what's happening now is the triggering event, or what happened with the death of the old queens, that's why they're stepping in now. They probably hoped they wouldn't have to."

"That's a valid point." Kelly taps her chin as she thinks. "Creating more shifters in the blink of an eye would most likely cause humans to notice. We were meant to guard this realm and ultimately humans once they were created. The gods and goddesses clearly saw what happened the last time humans knew of our existence. They helped the demons mass murder queens. They wouldn't want that to happen again while they were trying to create a new generation of queens."

"We could spend countless hours on the what-ifs," Olivia interjects. "And we all know we won't get answers unless they want us to have them. Frankly, I'm not sure that's a key to this particular puzzle."

"At this point, I don't think we should rule anything out." Kelly, always the scholar, wouldn't want to give up on the pursuit of knowledge, especially information like this. "We do have bigger issues to worry about, but it wouldn't hurt for me to do a little research." Research, Kelly's favorite pastime. "All information is good information. The more we know, the better we can prepare for the fight ahead of us." She does have a valid argument.

KELLY AND DARCY leave to go check on the others, while Olivia and I stay in the gym. There's only so much work I can do with them since they haven't transitioned yet.

"Are you sure I should be coming with you to Ireland?" Olivia asks. "I don't have a lot of control over my magic. I could be a liability."

"I know getting the hang of this is hard, and I can't even imagine what it's like spending your whole life without magic to just suddenly get it without warning. But you need to trust yourself more. Your magic will start responding to you as you become more comfortable with it. And we need to work together as often as possible until you get there. Besides, I'm leaving the other two here. I need at least one bestie there for emotional support while I dig through the ruins of my old home." I keep my tone light, but there's a heavy truth to that last statement and we both know it.

"Okay," Olivia concedes. "But the second, the instant, I become a liability, you portal my ass back here. I am not negotiating on that." There's a hard glint to her eyes and a stubborn set to her jaw.

I love this selfless woman so much. But I also just want to shake her right now. She needs to stop thinking like that or her magic will always react in unpredictable ways. She's smarter and stronger than she gives herself credit for. I highly doubt there will be much of an issue while we're in Ireland. I think she knows, deep down, that when push comes to shove and shit hits the fan, I'm not sending her ass anywhere.

"I make no promises."

"Sometimes I want to throat punch you. If I'm a danger, I'll just make Malcolm send me home."

"How did you know he's coming with us? And what makes you think he's going to listen to you?"

"His bitch-ass had better listen to me." Oh? What development is this? The tone of her voice suggests there's something going on. "We've been talking while we're training, and he mentioned that he's coming with us."

"Uh-huh." A sly grin starts to spread across my face.

"Shut up!" She crosses her arms over her chest and glares at me.

"I didn't say anything." My grin grows as I raise my hands defensively. Something is definitely going on.

"You made a face very loudly," Olivia grumbles.

"Did I? What face was that?" I have to bite back a chuckle.

"You know damn well what face you made. There is nothing to discuss." Olivia huffs before getting up and walking out of the room. Oh yeah, definitely something there.

SINCE TRAINING, meetings, and planning are finished for the day, I'm soaking in a bubble bath with the lights off, softly flickering candles, and a glass of witch wine on the edge of the tub with the bottle on the floor. The glow from the moon and star streams through the skylights, adding to the calming illumination given off by the candles. The only thing that would make this bath better is a book. I haven't been able to pick up even so much as a solid smutty romance since I became alpha. *That's got to change*, I vow to myself. Self-care is important, and I haven't really done any of that lately.

Sighing, I grab my wine glass and take a big sip, letting the potent liquid swirl in my mouth for a minute before it warms its way down to my stomach. I hadn't really planned on getting drunk tonight, but if it happens, it happens. I'm not normally one to use alcohol as a coping mechanism, but damn, I've been through hell. The very least I deserve is to get properly white girl wasted.

The soft sound of bare feet padding on the bathroom tile causes me to open my eyes and tilt my head back. I don't need to see who it is, Caleb's scent hit me the moment he walked into my bedroom. I just like looking at him. He is a damn fine piece of man meat.

"Man meat, huh?" Caleb chuckles as he kneels down next to the tub. Oops. The wine must have lowered my barriers. Oh well. I'm his mate, I can objectify him once I've had a few drinks, can't I? "Sure you can, just as long as you know I'm probably going to do the same at some point. Fair is fair, after all." A wicked grin curves his lips.

I wanna bite those lips. Suck on 'em. Then have them do all sorts of dirty things to my body. I take another large sip of wine, starting to feel damn good and relaxed. And horny. Really, really horny. Which leads to me thinking about Caleb's dick.

I told you it's a nice penis. My dragon laughs.

I admitted you were right. It's a damn fine penis. I like his penis.

Caleb chuckles louder. "I'm damn glad you like my penis. It would be awkward as hell if you didn't." He gently tucks some of my hair behind my ear. "As for all those things you want my lips to do to you, I'm game once you're a little more sober."

"You're such a party pooper." I stick my tongue out at him, adjusting myself in the water so I can reach for the wine bottle near his knees. "Your pants are telling a different story, O'Dwyer."

"That thing has a mind of his own. Ignore him." I don't want to ignore him. In fact, I want him to come out and play. So once I've poured myself another glass of wine, I reach for Caleb's pants. "Whoa there. What are you doing?"

"Getting you naked." Why won't his damn pants come off? Oh! I can use magic! I snap my fingers and he's blissfully bare. "Get in this tub right now."

"I will get in this tub, but we are not doing the nasty while you're wasted." Caleb climbs in behind me and settles me against his chest, holding my hips to prevent me from doing anything untoward.

"Party pooper." I settle contentedly against him, sighing as the heat of his body causes me to relax even further.

"I know you've had a lot going on, and I know that us leaving in a few weeks stresses you the hell out, but it's going to be okay." Caleb brushes a kiss against the back of my head. "We'll work our asses off so we're ready the next time that bastard makes an appearance."

"He has help, Caleb. Powerful help." I place my wine glass back on the edge of the tub, suddenly no longer in the mood to drink. "And we have no idea who we're really up against. How can we really be prepared if we have no idea what the hell we're facing?"

"Ayla," Caleb murmurs, "you are the most powerful woman I've ever met. You are a formidable queen. The gods and goddesses made you to kick ass and take names. With everything you've been through over the last few months, I'm not surprised you feel a little beat down." He adjusts me so I'm facing him, my eyes glued to his. "But, love, you are the most unique creature on this damn planet. I have complete and utter faith that you will do what is right and you'll win every single time. You're incredible."

Tears sting the back of my eyes as he leans in to give me a light kiss. Goddess, I love this man.

~

Four Weeks Later.

I'M STARING at the portal that will bring me back to Ireland, fear and excitement warring for dominance inside me. I know this is what I need to do, but everything I've learned about my mother is still so fresh and raw that I'm not sure how I'm going to be able to see our cottage in ruins and not completely lose it. My memories from before my mother's death have been locked away and buried for so long, I'm terrified of having to face them again. Of having to relive those moments in front of people I love, my new family.

Caleb's arm wraps around my waist, hugging me to his

side. I lean my head against his shoulder, soaking in his strength. "You can do this, love." He gives me a gentle squeeze.

"You certainly can." Olivia steps up on my other side, placing a gentle hand on my shoulder. "And you won't be going through any of this on your own. I know we all keep saying it, but you've been alone for a long time, so you need to be reminded often that you aren't like that anymore." She gently squeezes my shoulder. "I've got your back no matter what. And even with the super cool new demon ass-kicking powers, you're still my alpha. Where you lead, I will always follow."

I take a deep breath, then another, before straightening away from Caleb's side. His hand falls away.

Let's do this, my dragon excitedly rumbles.

Okay. Let's do this. And we step through the portal.

Epilogue

Malick

I land in a heap with a jarring thud. It's dark and dank wherever the hell I am. Smells like a cave. Disgusting. I take inventory of my injuries, thankfully all minor. Had I been hit with Ayla's final attack, I would have been dust in the wind. Which merits the question, who the hell pulled me from that wretched pit in the ground at the last moment? I slowly get to my feet as I think back to the battle against the little queen and her community.

Watching Ayla come into her power mere feet from me was a stunningly beautiful sight. Such a shame it had to happen after I hit her with a blast of death magic. It's possible I underestimated the depth of the mate bond in conjunction with her new demonic powers. Demons don't mate, not in the same sense.

Despite any claims to the contrary, I hadn't had to force any of those females into the act of copulation. Once their demonic sides took hold, it was only a matter of time before they sought me out for relief. While demons couldn't produce offspring, it appears hybrids can, taking after whatever their other half is. Even vampires could produce progeny with a demon if the balance of demonic energy was right. Ayla hadn't acted in any way I could have predicted, much like her newfound friend, Darcy. How interesting.

A low, rumbling laugh breaks me out of my thoughts. It seems to come from all around me, echoing throughout the cave. I bristle at the sound, readying myself for an attack.

"No need to worry, friend." The voice surrounds me, reverberating in the same way the laugh did, layering on top of itself until it sounds as though multiple people are talking. "I'm the one who pulled you from the earth at the last minute."

"Not that I'm ungrateful, but who the fuck are you?" It's irritating that I needed help at all, let alone that I have no idea who actually assisted me.

"An interested party." I can't sense anyone else physically here in the cave with me, so where the hell is this fucker? "I've been following your progress for some time." My back stiffens.

"Is that so? Why the hell do you care?" If he's been following my progress, that means he's either an angel or another demon. Angels are too worried about sticking feathers up their own asses to care about what happens down here. Another demon seems more likely, but I've been damn careful. After my brother killed Aine, I made sure that no others, not even my legion, really knew what I was up to. So how could this asshat know what I'm planning?

"I have a horse in the race as it were." The voice chuckles. "You see, I'd like, very much, to get out of this pit."

"You're—" Whoever this is, is in Hell? He's got to be very powerful if he could reach through the veils separating the dimensions, pull me into this cave, and then strike up a conversation with me. "You're in Hell?"

"That's right, friend. Luce isn't the only one interested in getting out of the pit."

"Who the hell are you?" Rule one of life, never fucking trust anyone.

"You may call me Wrath." My blood runs cold as shock floods my system.

Contrary to popular belief, Lucifer and Satan are not the same person. Lucifer is the Morningstar, fallen angel of heaven. Satan is one of the Princes of hell. He is the personification of the sin of wrath, and he's the very last being I want to piss off. No one plots revenge the way he does.

"Oh, well, if it's just you, Satan," I say casually, my mind whirling, "I'm not surprised you'd like to get out of Hell, but I hadn't realized I'd made waves down in Hell."

"Only a small group knows what you're about. We're extremely interested in seeing that you succeed in your goal. We can't exactly help you from here, not often anyway. But I couldn't let that little bitch kill you. Not when you're so close." Having the interest of a Prince of Hell isn't exactly what I'd been aiming for when I started this little adventure. Admittedly, I'd been hoping they wouldn't notice my little coup. Having to take them all on for the right to lead Hell is going to be a hassle. If they're free in Hell, that's going to be a large problem.

"The queen has sisters, you know," Wrath whispers. "Two sisters. They're both still alive."

Shock races down my spine. She isn't the last queen? "Where?" I'm willing to jump into bed with Wrath for the time being if it means I can get my hands on another queen.

"France and Africa."

"Do you have any idea how large France and Africa are?" I snap.

"Why do all the work yourself when the little bitch who almost killed you is going to find them for you?" He does have a point. Following my little queen will allow me to find her sisters without doing any of the leg work. It will also give me the opportunity to bring her back to me and tweak my injections ever so slightly to get her on my side.

"Where is she heading now?"

Wrath

THIS IS ALMOST TOO EASY. Although, after the day's failure, I've struggled to keep my rage in check. This idiot had been so fucking close, and he couldn't take out the queen's mate? All we really need is one of the three sister queens to align herself with the darkness inherent in every soul, just one. It's not that difficult. I'm sure a fucking monkey could do it.

I take several deep breaths, remembering the moron has asked me a question.

"Ireland. The queen is going to Ireland." Back to where it all began. The last set of Fates chose to pass their powers to the triplets when their mother was still pregnant with them. It had been irritating. Fates were rare amongst queens, they held powers normal queens didn't, and they were also the living embodiment of the three Fates—past, present, and future. The idiots upstairs only ever saw fit to produce new Fates when they felt the balance was threatened.

I'm not surprised they have an inkling about my little escape attempt. What they don't realize is that I have a plan B if this gambit fails. I'd rather it didn't, I happen to like the form I'm currently in, but I can give it up if it means freedom. And once I'm free, I plan on making those assholes pay. How dare they lock me away in this realm?

Rage surges through me once again. My siblings and I were not meant to be locked away. We were meant to rule.

Well, I was meant to rule. The creatures created by the others are weak and yearn to be dominated. You can't just create something and then abandon it to govern itself. I seethe at the very thought. If they don't want to rule over their pathetic creatures, I'm more than happy to do it for them.

I sever my connection to Malick as another of my pawns attempts to make contact.

"What is it?" My voice comes out harsh and threatening.

"My lord," they respond, meek and scared, "there has been a development."

"Go on."

"They have made another queen."

My body stiffens and my muscles start to shake from strain as I attempt to once again rein in my rage. Created another queen? "Explain."

"T-The beta of the original queen. She's somehow become a queen herself. I'm not sure how, but the community has been buzzing with the information since it was announced that the queen would be heading to Ireland."

"And you're just now telling me about this?" It's been almost two months since I pulled Malick from the battle. I haven't felt the need to inform him of that, he'll figure it out. He needed time to heal, and I had no desire to spend my energy healing him myself, so I kept him asleep until he was whole enough to not be annoying.

"M-My lord." I honestly hate everything about this particular underling, a sniveling, worthless, waste of space. "I didn't have confirmation until today. It was just a rumor floating around the community. Today I was able to hear them discussing it myself."

"I suppose you've been useful." The rage subsides and boredom takes its place. "Go back to your post and tell me the instant anything changes. If you don't, I will ensure you are terminated."

"Y-Yes, my lord."

Just what were those losers planning? Another queen was laughable, especially one who wasn't born into it. She would be useless as she trained, which had its benefits. I'm going to hold onto this little nugget of information, there's no need to tell Malick about her just yet, not when she isn't really a prize worth obtaining. She's not a Fate.

I chuckle darkly as I consider the implications of a new queen. It doesn't matter what they try to do, all I need is for one Fate to fall. They can create all the damn queens they want.

~

KEEP READING for a sneak peek at Vengeance of a Queen, book 2 in The Resurrection of Queens series, and Olivia's story!

Make sure to follow me on Instagram (@authorelizabeth-brown), Twitter (@authorelizabet3), Facebook group (Beth's Resurrected Queens), TikTok (RomanceAuthorBethBrown), and Goodreads! Also, remember to subscribe to my website (https//www.authorelizabethbrown.com) for bonus materials (like extra scenes from Caleb's POV)! Shoot me an email if you're so inclined (authorelizabethbrown@gmail.com).

I want to see where you're reading *The Resurrection of Queens* books! Snap a photo and tag me, you might get a really cool prize!!!

Other Books by this Author

Vengeance of a Queen (The Resurrection of Queens, book 2)—October 2021

Reign (Book 1 in the Reign of Blood series)—December 2021

About the Author

Beth is a loving wife and mother—both of the human and fur variety—best friend, enemy, *that* coworker, work wife, hero, and all around sarcastic badass. She advocates to get rid of the stigma around mental health—having CPTSD, anxiety, depression, and panic. She advocates for the understanding of ADHD in girls and women, having ADHD herself, and she wasn't diagnosed until she was thirty. When she isn't writing, she's playing with her young son, getting sassy with her husband, reading with the cats, roughhousing with the doggo, or sleeping for days. She loves to hear from fans and makes an effort to answer any messages sent her way and like any posts she's tagged in.

Chapter One

Ten Weeks Ago.

When the light from Ayla's attack fades, my heart hammers loudly in my chest as I pant slightly. Fuck me. She's killed all of the lower-level demons. That's badass. But something else catches my attention—Malick. Or the lack thereof. He's not in the ground anymore.

Where the hell did that fucker go? I glance around and notice everyone from our community is doing the same. Shit. No one seems to have any idea what the hell transpired.

"Those of you who saw what happened, I want to be debriefed as soon as we're safely back at the community, is that clear?" Caleb booms through our bonds. He must be using his mate bond with Ayla to talk to all of us. Immediately, the witches still able to do so begin creating portals back to our community land.

Strong hands grip the tops of my arms, spinning me around to face one of the most handsome men I've ever met.

Malcolm.

My panther purrs inside my head. She seems to like the witch just as much as I do. His scent, which reminds me of fresh rain in the desert, has been driving me insane since he showed up at our doorstep with the rest of the Council. Surprisingly, his hair is pulled back from his face today. He usually prefers to keep it loose and flowing around his shoulders.

I don't get the chance to think anymore. Malcolm's mouth lands on mine and my brain shuts down. My eyes slide closed, and stars instantly burst behind my eyelids. Time seems to slow as my entire being becomes solely focused on the sensation of his lips against mine. My panther releases a low, pleased growl.

Mate. Holy hell. Talk about life changing days.

~

Four Weeks Ago.

AFTER EVERYTHING AYLA'S been through, I'm surprised she hasn't taken it easier on herself. The woman has been like a damn machine since she woke up a few days ago. And the only reason we aren't heading to Ireland right now is because she wants to take some time out to train me.

I'm a damn queen. It's been six weeks, but awe still fills me every time I think about it.

My mind flashes back to the moment on the battlefield when I inadvertently exploded a demon by turning him inside out. My stomach still gets a bit queasy just thinking about it. I'd been feeling off all day, amped for the battle ahead in a way I'd never felt before. I love a good brawl, but this was completely different. I wouldn't go so far as to say bloodthirsty, but I was certainly eager to get into the thick of things and rip demons apart with my touch.

Accompanying those images is a memory I've tried my best to shove into a little box in my mind and forget. After Ayla released her life mojo on all the demons and the dust had settled enough for all of us to determine that we were all alive and going to stay that way, I felt Malcolm grab my arms. I stared up at him with excitement buzzing through my veins as he leaned in and kissed the ever-loving daylights out of me. It wasn't a sweet, gentle first kiss. It was a kiss to lay claim to my very soul. A kiss that curled my toes, blew my damn head off, and melted my knees.

And it hadn't happened again since.

My panther lets out a low rumble of annoyance at the thought. We finally found our mate, he planted the mother of all kisses on me, and then ignored me? Not all shifters are able to determine their mates by first scent, there isn't always that instant flash of heat the way Ayla describes what happened with her and Caleb. For some of us, it can take a while for us to realize what's directly in front of our damn faces. Especially if our mate isn't another shifter.

I'm not sure if becoming a queen made me realize that Malcolm is my mate sooner, or if I'd have known the instant his lips landed on mine anyway. That doesn't matter. What matters is that the man has been avoiding touching me ever since. He's been shooting me hungry looks but hasn't acted on them. I've been so busy trying to get my new magic under control that by the time I think about acting on the mating instinct, he's already scuttled away somewhere.

～

Present

As I STEP through the portal to Ireland with Malcolm beside me, I swear to all that is good in this world that if he doesn't touch me soon, I am going to rip his head off. You can't go around kissing people like that once and then never touch them again. Is he brain damaged?

He's a witch, Olivia. My panther gently brushes against my mind. *He doesn't feel the urge to mate the way we do.* Goddess, how can he not feel this heat? It's eating me alive. While I'm a dominant shifter female, I have no desire to go after a man who doesn't want me. Even if he is my mate. No. If he wants me, he needs to step right the fuck up and say so.

What if we nudge him along? My panther has no problem with the idea of us rubbing all over him. *We don't need to go at him like a cat in heat, but just enough of an indication that you're interested. We don't know how witches mate, what if it's not as instinctual?*

I suppose she has a point. I refuse to throw myself at a man, but there's no harm in subtly nudging said man, right?

I've been so caught up in my thoughts that I haven't taken notice of the stunning scenery around me. Now that it's claimed my attention, my breath catches and my eyes go wide. I've never been to Ireland before, but I've seen pictures. Pictures do not do the beauty of this land justice. The thrum of power, ancient and wise, pulses out of the very ground here.

Ayla said we'd be coming out of the portals at the Cliffs of Mohr, where her village used to be. The crashing of the sea against the cliffs only serves to amplify the power here. I can feel it singing through every nerve, every cell. I want to dance and cry out in joy. The energy is just so pure and light. I let it roll over me.

Ayla stands in front of me, slowly spinning with her arms out by her sides. She has an expression I'm sure is mirrored on my face. Wonder. Joy. Power. Her connection to this place is stronger than mine, so I can only imagine how she's feeling.

"I hate to break up the love fest," Caleb calls, startling

both Ayla and I out of our commune with nature, "but we need to find somewhere to stay. We can't be out in the open."

"I agree." Malcolm moves to stand next to me, gently placing a hand on the small of my back, causing my panther to purr.

"Our cottage was right on the cliffs." Ayla sounds wistful, her eyes unfocused. "Ma used to take us out flying at night over the water."

As she speaks, I feel a surge of magic drawing me closer to the cliff's edge. Following the pull of the magic, I inch closer to the drop off until I feel a large, warm hand close over my shoulder.

"What the hell are you doing, Liv?" Malcolm growls. "Get away from that damn cliff."

"Don't you feel it?" I can still feel the pull of the magic, so I let my own magic respond. It flares out around me, a beautiful amethyst mist shimmering in the light. It shines around a dome that appears to be empty, until it flashes and reveals a small cottage where nothing had been before.

Ayla gasps. "The cottage!" She doesn't make a move to get any closer, and Caleb comes up to wrap his arms around her.

"How did you know that was there?" Malcolm still has a firm grip on my arm.

"You didn't feel that?" I ask, looking at the others around us. Everyone shakes their heads, staring at me oddly. "There was this pull, I couldn't ignore it."

"She almost went off the damn cliff," Malcolm snarls. "The magic almost killed her. And listen to her! She sounds like a damn zombie!"

I bristle at his words. "Excuse the fuck out of you. I do not sound like a zombie. It's not my fault your 'wand' couldn't find magic even if magic hit it upside the head!" My rebuke ends on a shout. While I intended to be subtle about my approach to Malcolm, he just pissed me off, so I needed to, rightfully, call his manhood into question.

"Girl, you have so much explaining to do." Ayla's laughter echoes through our bond, and I grin in response. Malcolm starts to turn an interesting shade of purple, his mouth opening and closing as he struggles to respond. *"You just insulted a man's penis. That's savage. Something has absolutely gone down between the two of you and you will tell me."* Ayla proceeds to laugh out loud, causing Malcolm to turn and glower at her. Caleb has the good sense to hide his face by burying it in Ayla's hair, but there's no mistaking the shaking of his shoulders.

"My wand," Malcolm starts, pulling me flush against him, "can find magic perfectly fine."

"Prove it." The two worst words to ever be spoken between two individuals who have sexual tension so thick it would take a chainsaw to cut through it. Malcolm tenses against me, his eyes narrowing on my parted lips. I decide to push him just a bit more by slowly sliding my tongue along my bottom lip. His eyes narrow further, and a low growl forces its way out of his chest. It's impressive since he isn't a shifter.

And then his mouth is on mine, our lips fusing together as his hand tangles in my hair tightly, moving my head exactly where he wants it. I groan, and Malcolm uses that moment to plunge his tongue into my mouth. There is nothing gentle about this kiss. It's not the kiss of two mates discovering one another. It's the kind of kiss that tells you a man wants all of you, no holding back.

My mind stalls for a minute, unsure. Malcolm is my mate, and the urge to climb him like a tree is so damn strong. The fact that he hasn't touched me in weeks makes me feel insecure. But his kiss quickly wipes the feeling away. I'm only just starting to settle into the kiss when I hear a loud cough behind us.

"Guys?" Ayla is amused, and I can tell she's struggling not to laugh. "I appreciate the show. Malcolm, I need to give you a solid nine for hand placement, passion, and enthusiasm, but a one on timing." Caleb chuckles.

I pull away from Malcolm, blinking several times to try to get my brain to work properly again. Malcolm's grip in my hair tightens, not letting me pull too far away. He brings his lips close to my ear and whispers, "This isn't finished."

Damn it. I don't think I packed enough panties to be talked to like that. My panther purrs so aggressively it makes my chest vibrate. Malcolm's eyes go wide and drop to my chest as I continue to purr, a wicked grin spreading across his lips.

Caleb slaps his hand on Malcolm's back, breaking the moment. Malcolm throws me one last heated look before walking off with the alpha, going to make sure that the cottage is safe enough for us to investigate. Ayla is suddenly by my side, a shit-eating grin plastered on her face.

"You told me it was nothing. That you'd just been training with him." She waggles her eyebrows at me. "Is that what the kids are calling hot, nasty, sweaty sex?"

A surprised laugh bursts from my lips. "No, that's not what the kids are calling any form of sex." I shake my head. "He kissed me on the battlefield that day with Malick. Just laid the mother of all kisses on me and then nothing. Literally nothing. For weeks! And now he just swoops in with that?" I groan and tug slightly on my hair. "What the fuck was that? What am I supposed to even do with that?" I glance over at my friend to see her fighting back more laughter.

"Oh, honey." She sobers upon seeing the frustration on my face. "He's a dumb male, but learn from my experience with Caleb—don't hold back and go after what you want. I can feel the mate bond forming inside you, Olivia. I know what he is. Witches are different, they don't have the pull the same way we do. But his magic will draw him to you, even if he doesn't realize why. If you don't want to give it time, I can help with Operation Cave Explorer."

"I'm sorry" —I can't keep my laughter contained— "Operation Cave Explorer?" Ayla lifts one of her hands so it forms an O-shape and inserts the forefinger of her other hand, rather aggressively, in and out of the ring several times, winking lewdly at me. "Why the fuck am I even friends with you?"

"You love me, and you know it." She beams at me. "Now let's go see what those idiots are up to. We can form a solid plan to have your cave explored later."

I groan but allow her to lead me toward the cottage. The men have gone inside, so presumably it's safe for us to do so as well. I crack open the door and allow Ayla to go in ahead of me. It's her family home, after all. Despite her earlier reaction to seeing the cottage, she's more composed now, her eyes wide as though she's trying to take everything in all at once.

The cottage has been extremely well preserved. I wouldn't have assumed it had been sitting here empty for over four hundred years. As soon as I follow Ayla through the doorway, the door slams shut, the snick of the lock engaging causing all four of us to freeze. A gentle rumble shakes the cottage, slowly getting louder and more aggressive with the passing minutes. My hand just slaps onto the door before the cottage is plunged into darkness.